LEGEND OF THE FIVE RINGS

Rokugan – the Emerald Empire. For centuries, the samurai of the Great Clans have defended and served the Hantei dynasty. But now, danger besets Rokugan from all sides.

Emperor Hantei XXVI is dying, and the courts bristle with opportunity while rebellion stalks the land, and rumors of foul magic threaten to corrupt the Empire from within.

A forgotten evil is at work, and it hungers for power and blood.

With the Great Clans distracted and divided, seven heroes must take up the call and forge their own destiny or risk everything in the pursuit of glory.

The HEART
of IUCHIBAN

EVAN DICKEN

First published by Aconyte Books in 2022

ISBN 978 1 83908 184 2

Ebook ISBN 978 1 83908 185 9

Cover art by Larry Rostant

Rokugan map by Francesca Baerald

Distributed in North America by Simon & Schuster Inc, New York, USA

Printed in the United States of America

9 8 7 6 5 4 3 2 1

ACONYTE BOOKS

An imprint of Asmodee Entertainment Ltd

Mercury House, Shipstones Business Centre

North Gate, Nottingham NG7 7FN, UK

aconytebooks.com // twitter.com/aconytebooks

To Mom and Dad. The books I love best were the ones you read to me.

FIVE-DRAGON
GATE

Twilight Mountains

Crab
Lands

Rokugan

CHAPTER ONE

General Matsu Katamori already regretted visiting the tomb. It was a blocky, stolid thing, built to appease the spirits of the Imperial City's fallen. The field on which it stood had once been a cemetery for clanless samurai, at least until some ancient emperor had ordered their bodies disinterred and burnt, the ashes placed within the imposing funereal edifice before which Katamori now prostrated himself. No doubt there were those among the more self-important clans who would find his obeisance to dead rōnin humorous, but Katamori was a samurai of the Lion Clan, not some status-obsessed Crane courtier. He had resolved to begin his command by paying respect to those who had given their lives for the Empire, no matter their rank or standing.

That this tomb was the farthest away from the Crane mansion hardly figured into Katamori's calculations. Most of the other temple crypts were patronized by one clan or another; to visit them would show undue favor. At least that was what Katamori had said when Doji Hiroshige raised concerns about this shrine not being important enough to herald such momentous undertakings as a gathering of all seven clans.

It had seemed straightforward when Katamori swept aside Hiroshige's simpering complaints. Hantei XXVI might be old, infirm, and currently without an heir, but he was still emperor. He had named Katamori general of the combined clan expedition, not that preening Crane sycophant.

Despite divinations to the contrary, the day had dawned humid and overcast. The few tepid rays of sunlight that pierced the haze only served to accentuate the gloom, leaching color from Katamori's brightly lacquered parade armor and robbing his golden accents of luster. Although they threatened storm, the clouds had thus far been unwilling to part with anything more than swirling mist.

Yet it was neither the weather nor the temple crypt that soured Katamori's mood.

"I am sure the others will arrive presently." Bayushi Kogoro gave a noncommittal tilt of his head, causing his silken mask to flutter. Black, with crimson embroidery, it bore the crests of all seven clans, although Katamori could not help but notice they were arranged in the outline of a scorpion.

"It takes time to prepare such a noteworthy endeavor," the Scorpion continued.

"They have had three weeks." Katamori felt his hands begin to clench, and consciously willed himself to relax. As much as he disliked the Scorpion courtier's whispery insinuations, at least Kogoro had the decency to obey orders.

"I believe it was Akodo who said: 'Hawks and swine, oxen and hounds – all serve the same master.'" Asako Masatsuge spoke as if presiding over a religious rite, arms hidden in the folds of his voluminous sleeves. The wizened Phoenix Clan priest's orange and yellow ceremonial robes seemed somehow proof against the steady drizzle.

It galled Katamori to have a pacifist quote the Lion Clan founder. He studied Masatsuge's deeply lined face. Although the elemental priest's tone was measured, Katamori could not help but detect an air of detached amusement in Masatsuge's bearing.

"Even swine come at their master's call."

"Is that how you regard us?" Masatsuge raised a thin, white eyebrow.

Katamori was grateful his helmet hid the flush creeping up his neck. "I only mean we are all servants of the emperor."

"My point, exactly." The Phoenix priest nodded as if he had just handed Katamori a bit of purest jade. "We must work together."

"With the Lion in command," Kogoro added.

"The Lion control the largest army in Rokugan. We have defended the Empire since its inception." A thin runnel of water trickled between Katamori's shoulder blades, and he stiffened to avoid shivering. "It is only right we lead the expedition."

"The Lion have always been at the forefront of every battle," Kogoro replied. "Even those against imperial subjects."

"The rebels are no longer imperial subjects."

"Forgive me, general." Kogoro bobbed his head. "I misspoke."

Katamori waved a dismissive hand, irritated by the Scorpion's prodding. Master Chiaki had warned him that commanding a force composed of all seven clans would be no easy feat. Katamori had prepared himself for criticism and challenges, perhaps even a duel. Even so, he had expected his fellow commanders to comport themselves as samurai rather than petulant children.

He glanced back at the warriors arrayed upon the muster field. Hundreds of Lion samurai stood in close ranks, still as ancestor statues in the eddying mist. The sight calmed Katamori more than he cared to admit. If needs must, they could put down the rebellion alone.

As if conjured by his musings, the Crab contingent arrived.

They came like a funeral procession, perhaps two dozen samurai in battle plate, the slate grays and blues of their armor appearing almost black in the murky shadows.

"We march to cleanse their lands of rebels." Kogoro sniffed. "You would think the Crab could be convinced to part with more warriors."

Katamori's scowl felt etched in stone. Although the Crab had not requested the expedition, they had raised no objections. By all accounts, the rebels were a collection of miners and disgruntled laborers, the province in question part of a stretch of desolate foothills girding the Twilight Mountains. Were it not the location of Five-Dragon Gate, the revolt might have been allowed to fester indefinitely, but the rebels could not be allowed to seize so much precious jade.

Ignoring the other contingents, the Crab took up position on the far side of the field. Ranks shifted as the samurai formed a tight box as if anticipating attack.

"They act like you ordered us to marshal in the Shadowlands." Kogoro ran a hand through his long dark hair, casting a spray of water across the trampled grass with a casual flick of his wrist.

"A blade forever bared is bound to rust," Masatsuge said with a regretful tilt of his head.

Katamori ignored the banter. "You could both take lessons from the Crab. We march toward hostile lands, not a moon viewing. Attack could come from any quarter, at any time."

Katamori strode across the muddy field, his personal guard close behind. He was conceding some authority by visiting the

Crab rather than waiting for their commander to come to him, but it was a small price to pay to get away from Kogoro and Masatsuge's prattle.

The Crab commander was a small woman, seeming almost buried by the heavy plates of her battle armor. She did not remove her helm as Katamori approached, although her ironshod club did lower a fraction as he reached the outermost ranks of the Crab formation.

"You are General Katamori." It was not a question.

"Kuni Ikae, your reputation precedes you." Katamori waited, back straight.

The Crab commander studied him for a long moment, then gave a terse bow. Straightening, she removed her helmet to reveal a face that would have been unremarkable if not for the intricate web of warding trigrams tattooed over every inch of flesh.

Katamori acknowledged her with a nod. "I must confess to some surprise that your clan chose to send a witch hunter rather than a general."

"The clan elders felt your leadership ability adequate." A leafless compliment, but likely the best Katamori would receive from the Crab. More likely they wanted one of their priests around to ward Five-Dragon Gate from other clans, who might seek to recover the jade they had been required to commit all those years ago.

"I hope I am worthy of their confidence," Katamori replied.

"That remains to be seen."

Katamori made a show of regarding the Crab contingent. "Where are the rest of your warriors?"

"Protecting Five-Dragon Gate." Ikae lifted a hand to halt Katamori's next question. "The province straddles the Twilight

Legend of the Five Rings

Mountains. The rebels cannot move easily if they do not hold the pass."

"Good." Katamori ignored the Crab's insubordination. Although he had called all the clan contingents in full, it was foolish to expect the Crab to march hundreds of warriors toward the capital, only to turn around and trudge back. The emperor had bid the clans cooperate; a show of petulance would not endear Katamori to his comrades.

"I served a season on the Carpenter Wall." He hoped the admission might soften the witch hunter's cool regard, but Ikae's grim expression shifted not a hair. Truth be told, Katamori's tour on the wall had been relatively quiet apart from a skirmish with a band of feral peasants; that, and a single foray beyond in search of missing scouts. He remembered little of the Shadowlands apart from snarled snakegrass, dead trees, and fields of pale, crackling stone.

Discomfited by Ikae's unblinking stare, Katamori changed tack. "I have received no reports of malign influences among the rebels."

"You wouldn't."

He waited, but the witch hunter did not elaborate. After a long, slow breath, Katamori continued. "Because there aren't any?"

"That remains to be seen."

"I bid you welcome to our company, then." Katamori spread his arms in what he hoped was a friendly gesture. "May the ancestors look favorably upon our endeavors."

Ikae gave a respectful nod. "When do we depart?"

"Once all the contingents have arrived."

Ikae's gaze swept the field. Although she said nothing, the question was plain enough.

"The Unicorn, Crane, and Dragon Clans will be along presently, I'm sure." Katamori cursed inwardly. Barely an hour into his command he had been reduced to repeating Kogoro's vague assurances. He stiffened with an irritated grunt. "They will come. The emperor has ordered it."

"*You* ordered it," she replied flatly.

"And the emperor named me general." Katamori felt the familiar anger coiling in his stomach. "I command this expedition."

"That remains to be seen."

Sensing he would get no more answers from the witch hunter, he stalked back across the field. Muddy water seeped up through the wrappings of his sandals, squelching with every step. Katamori's imperial writ had been broadly worded, awarding him command without the authority to enforce it. In truth, the emperor's grip was weak, his health failing, his court divided. The position of Emerald Champion had been empty for over a year – yet another reason why the clans were being sent to quash a petty rebellion rather than the Imperial Legions.

Townsfolk from the Imperial City's outer districts had started to gather at the edge of the field despite the inclement weather. Katamori was beginning to regret spreading word of their departure.

A mutter went up from the crowd, the low hum of conversation punctuated by scattered cheers. Katamori turned toward the source of the noise and saw the townsfolk part before an oncoming procession.

Musicians led the way; the deep basso thrum of war drums ranged against the high skirl of flute and cymbal. Pale-blue banners bore the stylized image of a spread-winged crane, rows of samurai marching behind. Acrobats ranged along the edges, somehow surefooted in the roadside muck as they twisted and twirled. At its head rode Doji Hiroshige, accompanied by a dozen servants, their long-handled umbrellas raised to shield him from the rain. He wore parade robes of silver-trimmed blue, resplendent with embroidered cherry and wisteria blossoms in deference to the season.

The Crane noble was unarmed, his only concession to the martial nature of their mission a pale silk headband with a bit of polished steel on the front. His shock of white hair seemed almost luminous in the rain-slicked gloom. Behind him rode a well-attired valet bearing the Doji's ancestral sword, Higekiri.

Far too fine a blade for such a preening peacock.

Katamori watched the oncoming procession, jaw so tight he could feel the roots of his teeth.

The Crane were going the wrong way.

Doji Hiroshige rode onto the field like a conquering hero. Reining up a dozen yards from Katamori, he raised a hand and the parade ground to a halt, music tapering off with a few stray cymbal crashes.

Katamori could not help but glare as several servants scurried forward to unroll a bamboo mat upon the muddy grass. With a condescending nod, Hiroshige dismounted and dropped into a low bow.

"General Matsu, I beg your forgiveness." The Crane spoke with the musical lilt of high court speech. "We were unable to restrain the Unicorn and Dragon."

The rebuke died in Katamori's throat. "What do you mean restrain?"

"Late last night I received word that both Mirumoto Akemi

and Moto Börte planned to lead their contingents from the Imperial City ahead of the main army." Hiroshige remained bowed, as if he were addressing the ground. "I thought to reason with them, but they seemed convinced their forces were better employed ranging ahead."

Katamori shook his head, hand drifting to his sheathed blade as if it could cut the calamitous news from the air. He had granted neither commander such authority, but to publicly concede this would be tantamount to admitting Katamori had no control over his subordinates.

Fury made a fist in Katamori's stomach. He wanted to lash out, to whip his army into a forced march and hunt down the traitorous Unicorn and Dragon commanders. The emperor had named *him* general, not Hiroshige, not Kogoro, and *certainly* not Akemi or Börte.

With an effort of singular will, Katamori unclenched rage-stiffened fingers from the hilt of his blade. Master Chiaki had always admonished him to use his anger, lest it use him.

There would be a reckoning once he caught the wayward lords. For now, Katamori said the only thing he could, words ground through gritted teeth like the final confession of a condemned man.

"They follow my orders."

"Then all are in harmony." Hiroshige rose, brushing a stray bit of grass from the front of his robes.

"Indeed." Katamori turned to regard the shambles of his command. Five clan armies eyeing one another with the wary regard of duelists, another two skulking off like thieves in the night.

He was beginning to suspect rebels were the least of his concerns.

"Gather your warriors," he called loud enough for all to hear. By the ancestors, it felt good to shout. "We depart immediately."

Hiroshige gave a distressed mutter. As Katamori turned to regard him, the Crane courtier gestured at the road behind.

"As general, your place is at the head." Concern dripped from the Crane's words. "But I fear my procession is too large to maneuver."

Katamori glared at the bloated Crane contingent. Crowds hemmed the road, pressing in from all sides to get a better look at the performers and acrobats. It would take hours to clear room enough for the Lion to assume their proper place.

The fact this had clearly been Hiroshige's plan all along did nothing to dispel the exigencies of the moment. Either Katamori could allow the Crane to lead, or he could appear even more inept as he tried to bully the clans into some semblance of order.

He squeezed his eyes shut against the upswell of anger. "Turn your force around. You may march first."

"Truly you have taken the emperor's wishes to heart." Hiroshige clapped his hands. "Seven clans working as one, free of rivalries and pride. Together we shall present a shining example for all of Rokugan."

Not trusting himself to speak, Katamori could only nod. With another bow, the Crane noble mounted his horse, already waving to the crowd as he rejoined his procession.

"Hawks and swine," Kogoro muttered as he slipped up next to Katamori.

He ignored the Scorpion's jibe, turning to shout at his samurai to form ranks. Calls echoed across the field, the various clans preparing themselves to depart. Katamori's scowl felt almost a part of him as he mounted up behind the Crane procession.

There came an ominous rumble from the clouds overhead.

Finally, it began to rain.

CHAPTER TWO

"The rebels have felled trees across the main road." Moto Börte scratched the back of her neck, then turned to spit in the rocky dirt.

"We need your cavalry to range ahead."

"Three horses with broken legs, six lamed. I won't risk more." The broad-shouldered Unicorn commander shook her head like something clung to it. Börte always seemed to be in motion, checking weapons, armor straps, laughing, shouting.

"I've said it before – this land hates us." She glanced up at the rocky foothills beyond the pass.

"I have propitiated the local spirits." Asako Masatsuge spoke as if lecturing a particularly dull student. The Phoenix priest somehow retained an air of detached amusement despite a week of long, hard marching. "They shall support our endeavors."

"It is not the spirits we need fear," Kuni Ikae muttered.

As usual, the Crab did not elaborate.

Katamori swallowed the urge to sigh. He was growing weary of the witch hunter's cryptic pronouncements. He waved the commanders to a rough semblance of order.

"We must focus on the enemy at hand."

"My scouts roam the hills. The rebels seek to split our forces and ambush from cover once we leave the pass." Mirumoto Akemi spoke as if discussing the price of tea, his voice airy and disinterested. In contrast to his Unicorn colleague, the Dragon commander seemed only to move when absolutely necessary, his gaze distant, as if perpetually distracted by weightier concerns.

During the long march through the Crab hinterlands, Katamori had dreamed of relegating the wayward Unicorn and Dragon commanders to lesser roles, only to discover he desperately needed both. For all their local familiarity, the rebels could not hope to outpace the Unicorn cavalry, who ranged like ghosts through the broken valleys. With their knowledge of mountaineering, the Dragon scouts had been invaluable in rougher terrain, warning Katamori of ambushes and deadfalls long before his soldiers could stumble into them.

As much as it galled him to acknowledge the fact, the Dragon and Unicorn had been *right* to march ahead of the main force. It had been primarily their preparing the way that allowed the expedition to reach Five-Dragon Pass so quickly.

The gate that gave the pass its name was not a barrier in the physical sense. Even so, Katamori had expected at least *some* fortification. Instead, he found a wide gorge studded with rocks and debris, the "gate" itself a broad seal of purest jade set into the stone. According to legend, there had been an invasion; some manner of wicked demon from the Shadowlands, or perhaps it had been a foreign army – the details had grown hazy over the intervening centuries. All that mattered was the emperor had required each of the great clans to commit several hundredweights of irreplaceable jade to the gate's construction, after which it had sat, undisturbed and ignored, for centuries.

A poor use of imperial resources. Had it been Katamori's decision, they would be prying the jade from the ground even now – he was sure the Crab could find a better use for it than warding some remote mountain pass. But it was not Katamori's decision. The emperor had ordered him to crush the rebellion, and that is what he would do.

"General Matsu?" Doji Hiroshige's question held just the slightest hint of reproach.

With a start, Katamori realized the other commanders were waiting.

He leaned forward in his camp chair to study the makeshift map. Settlements dotted the low hills, a double handful of grain scattered across the wooded slopes. Although every village they had passed through professed loyalty to the Empire, the townsfolk seemed happy to relay information to the enemy, not to mention food and weapons. Katamori had hanged collaborators by the dozen, but that only seemed to inflame the resistance – scores of peasants disappearing in the night as entire villages emptied into rebel camps.

"We have not the forces to garrison every hamlet and farm in this miserable land," Hiroshige said.

Katamori favored him with a patronizing nod. The Crane courtier had a marked propensity for stating the obvious.

"What of the rebel leader?" Bayushi Kogoro asked. "This 'Bent-Winged Shrike,' might we find his location and strike?"

"Even the most venomous serpent is helpless without a head." Asako Masatsuge offered up yet another banality masquerading as wisdom. The Phoenix priest stroked his thin, white beard, nodding to himself. "We must work to limit violence in all things."

"The Shrike has thus far eluded all attempts to winnow him out." Kuni Ikae gave an irritated grunt. Shifting her iron-shod staff to the other shoulder, the witch hunter shook her head. "Unless our Scorpion comrade has assets we are not aware of."

Kogoro gave a helpless tilt of his head. "Alas, my talents lie elsewhere."

"And where is that?" Börte squinted as if the Scorpion courtier were a disagreeable insect. The Unicorn commander gestured at him, armor rattling. "Thus far, all I have seen you do is write reports."

"An army is composed of more than blades and bows. Not all who march are warriors." It was Masatsuge who replied. The Phoenix priest offered Kogoro a grandfatherly nod. "Our Scorpion friend has been vital to the continued flow of supplies."

Irritated by the bickering, Katamori held up a hand for silence. "If we are to win this war, it will be with blades and bows, not clever turns of phrase."

"If I may respectfully disagree, general. Perhaps clever turns of phrase are exactly what we need." Hiroshige bowed to soften his opposition. "Have we given any thought to discovering *why* the peasants revolted?"

"Something about a mine collapse." It was all Katamori could do not to slap the smile from the courtier's smug face. He dearly wished Hiroshige would give him a reason to strip him of command, but the Crane seemed frustratingly adept at stopping just sort of insult.

"One of the larger shafts. Several hundred workers died, I'm told." Kogoro gave an airy wave. "The miners demanded better conditions, the local lord refused. So, they revolted."

Hiroshige nodded as if the Scorpion had agreed with him. "Perhaps a few promises might accomplish more than an army."

"It is a wise general who can claim victory without a sword being drawn," Masatsuge said.

"The mines beyond Five-Dragon Gate provide iron for our weapons, coal for our forges," Kuni Ikae replied coolly. "Unlike other clans I might name, we do not coddle our peasantry."

"The emperor ordered us to punish the rebels, not placate them," Börte added, slapping her thigh for emphasis.

Katamori was happy to agree.

"Our mission is clear." He swallowed the urge to grin. Hiroshige had been sniping at him since the Imperial City, and it felt good to finally best the self-important Crane. "Your word may carry much weight in the capital, but out here, only blades matter."

Hiroshige clasped his hands as if in prayer. "What good will it do to reclaim these lands for the Empire if no one remains alive to work them?"

"There are always more peasants," Katamori replied.

Hiroshige conceded the point with a dip of his head, assuming the blank-eyed stare that passed for disapproval among the courts.

Even so, the matter remained: how was Katamori to defeat an enemy who refused to give battle and whose fighters were indistinguishable from loyal villagers? Not for the first time, he wished for Master Chiaki's guidance. The old warrior had seen much, she would surely have some lesson to impart. But Master Chiaki was back in the Lion lands, days away even by swift horse. It would look weak for him to go running back to his teacher at the first signs of trouble.

This was Katamori's command. Ultimately, he needed to stand on his own.

"What do you propose, general?" Börte asked. And once again, all eyes were on Katamori.

Truth be told, he had little idea. Although he led some of the most skilled samurai and priests in the Empire, the enemy was like smoke. Every day he delayed was more time for Hiroshige to undermine his command.

Fortunately, the rebels saved him.

Hooves thundered on packed earth. Katamori's blade was halfway from its scabbard before the Unicorn rider galloped into camp. The man's horse was lathered, his armor spotted with blood.

"They are massing, lord." He reined up, almost leaping from the saddle. "An hour's march to the west of Five-Dragon Gate."

"How many?" Katamori stepped forward, choosing to overlook that the scout had addressed his message to Börte.

"Thousands." The man dropped to his knees, finally showing respect. "Some had horses; stolen, no doubt. But we slipped away."

"They surely plan to destroy Five-Dragon Gate and make off with the jade." Katamori raised a fist. "We must strike first."

"Why not protect the gate?" Kuni Ikae scratched at one of her inscribed cheeks. "Even without fortifications, we could hold this pass indefinitely."

"And cede the western half of the province to the rebels?" Katamori shook his head. Such defensive logic was typical of the Crab.

"And if this is a trap?" Ikae asked.

Katamori turned to Kogoro. "See that it isn't."

The Scorpion courtier looked nonplussed. "General, it appears you have mistaken me for–"

"Enough dissembling, Scorpion." Katamori cut him off. "Inquire of your agents. Ensure we do not march into an ambush."

Without waiting he turned to Akemi and Börte. "I'll need your best scouts ahead." It felt good to be giving orders rather than mincing words. "Masatsuge, Ikae, prepare your rituals. We shall crush the traitors before they march."

"And what shall the Crane do, general?" Hiroshige asked.

"You?" Katamori tried, and failed, to hide his grin. "You shall guard Five-Dragon Gate."

CHAPTER THREE

Jaw tight, Katamori swayed away from the peasant's reaping hook. Usually used for harvesting rice, the curved blade had been lashed to the end of a staff to better cut flesh and drag riders from mounts.

With a grunt, Katamori brought his blade down, a heavy, overhand swing like he was splitting bamboo. The katana's razored edge sheared through the rebel's leather helmet, and the man fell back in a welter of blood.

As if conjured from the corpse of their dying comrade, two more peasants sprang at Katamori. The first thrust at him with a spear of sharpened bamboo, the move wild and unpracticed.

Katamori turned his horse to spoil the charge and slapped the spear aside. Reaching across his body, he grabbed the length of bamboo, then kicked his horse forward to drag the man off balance. He stumbled into his companion, who flailed about with a heavy rice-pounding mallet. Before the two could untangle, Katamori's blade licked out – once, twice – and the rebels joined their companion in death.

He reined up his mount, letting a line of Lion spears push into the disorganized mob. Samurai and rebel struggled in the crimson mud, shouting and straining. Here and there a blade glittered in the fading daylight, sprays of blood rising from the press like startled birds.

The plan had been a simple one. Lion, Phoenix, Scorpion, and Crab would engage the bulk of the rebel forces while the Dragon and Unicorn contingents circled behind. The rebels had few cavalry, and Akemi was confident his Dragon scouts could lead the Unicorn riders through the rocky hills without incident.

Except the charge had yet to materialize.

The combined clan forces should have pushed back the rebels, except it seemed only the Lion were actually interested in winning. Ikae and her Crab had dug in atop a hill near the rear of the valley, Kogoro's Scorpion skirmishing along the wooded flanks. At least they fought the rebels – Masatsuge's Phoenix followers remained uncommitted, seemingly unwilling to strike at the enemy with blade or spirit.

With an angry grunt, Katamori kicked his horse toward the low rise where his fellow commanders watched the conflict, dismounting as the guards stepped aside.

"There is something unnatural at work here." Kuni Ikae shouldered through the ranks. The Crab witch hunter had lost her helm in the fighting, and a long gash bisected the swirling symbols inscribed upon her left cheek.

"Could the rebels be corrupted?" Katamori wasn't sure which answer he would prefer. It would not be the first time servants of the dark god Fu Leng had infiltrated the Empire.

Ikae's frown became something strange.

"I discovered no evidence of Shadowland corruption." Masatsuge favored the witch hunter with a thin-lipped smile. "Have you, friend Kuni?"

"No." Ikae conceded the point with a twitch of her head.

The Phoenix priest turned as if dismissing a subordinate. Despite refusing to unleash his deadlier rites, Masatsuge seemed even more at ease amidst the raging swirl of combat. Katamori would have dismissed the pacifist Phoenix long ago had his priests not been vital in assisting the wounded.

Panting, Katamori surveyed the chaos. The rebels might outnumber the imperial expedition, but they were peasants – little more than a howling mob. His advance should have scattered them, the survivors skulking into the hills for Akemi's scouts to round up.

Instead, the rebels fought as cornered beasts. Screaming like damned souls, they hurled themselves at the imperial line, seemingly undaunted by the piled bodies of their comrades. Katamori had never seen such fierceness outside the ranks of Matsu berserkers. It was almost as if the peasants sought death.

If he survived, Katamori resolved to learn more about the local lord. The man must have been truly awful to inspire such hatred in his subjects.

"Where is Börte?" Katamori hammered a fist into his thigh.

"Waiting in the trees, I'd imagine," Bayushi Kogoro replied.

"Why does she delay?" Katamori asked.

"Why not?" Kogoro shrugged. "The longer Börte waits, the more heroic her charge becomes."

Katamori bared his teeth. The Scorpion's logic made uncomfortable sense. If Börte acted on his orders, Katamori would receive the credit. If her charge rescued a beleaguered imperial force, she would be lauded as a hero.

"What are your orders, general?" Kogoro asked.

It might have been his fury, but Katamori swore he detected a mocking lilt in the Scorpion's question.

Slipping off his helmet, Katamori breathed deep of the afternoon air, trying to leash his temper. He was reminded of an exercise Master Chiaki used during Matsu training. She would line all the would-be berserkers up in front of a massive, gnarled camphor tree just north of the dōjō. Then she would bid them rip it from the ground.

One by one, in pairs, and finally all at once they would beat at the ancient tree, feet churning the dark soil, shoulders lowered as they raged and strained. Sunup to sundown they would batter themselves against the uncaring wood, only to have Chiaki march them back the next day, and the day after that.

Finally, even the strongest warriors flagged. They had prostrated themselves before Master Chiaki, begging her forgiveness. But she had only laughed, her scarred cheeks a tapestry of countless victories.

"Some things cannot be moved."

Katamori repeated the admonition to himself like a mantra, a ward against pride. What good was victory if it cost him everything?

"Prepare to withdraw." Lips drawn back from his teeth, he waved his blade toward the low hills behind them. "We regroup at Five-Dragon Gate."

Lion warriors glanced back as drums beat cowardly cadences. They had fought bravely, were even now holding the line against far superior numbers, but the advantage had been lost. Without the Unicorn and Dragon, they could not turn the tide.

Stubborn pride would reap nothing but a field of corpses.

Shouts and laughter pursued them back into the hills, the rebels capering like wild beasts. Some of the enemy sought to chase, but the Crab had crafted a solid defensive line, and quickly dispatched those foolish enough to follow.

It seemed impossible the rebels could rejoice when the battle had left thousands of them in the mud, and yet to look at them, one might think they celebrated a harvest holiday.

Every echoing taunt was like an arrow in Katamori's back. That failure lay neither in his plan nor in his sword arm made the barbs sting sharper. The rebels would not have time to enjoy their victory. Like a smith hammering a blade into shape, Katamori would beat the clans into order – with brute force if needs must. Then the rebels would see defeat, complete and utter.

Back in camp, Katamori stalked through the lengthening shadows. Crane pickets marked his movements with shouts. Although their words were respectful, their tone seemed almost contemptuous.

"How fared the battle?" Hiroshige stepped from the darkness of his pavilion. With disgust, Katamori noticed the Crane hadn't even bothered to put on armor.

"Börte and Akemi never arrived." Katamori tried to slip past the courtier, but Hiroshige followed.

"Perhaps they ran into difficulty."

"The only difficulty I see is an inability to follow simple commands," Katamori said.

"Do not take your failures out on me, Lion." Hiroshige stopped, hands on hips. "As far as I can see, my Crane were the only ones who succeeded in our task."

Katamori didn't feel himself turn, no more than he felt his fist connect with Hiroshige's jaw. The move was unconscious, almost instinctive. The ground seemed to shift beneath him, his surroundings a blur of murky clouds. Then he was standing over the bloodied Crane, a sharp pain in his hand.

Like waves filling a hole in the sand, time swept back into

focus. Hiroshige's guards were shouting, weapons drawn, only to be met by bared steel as Katamori's own warriors reacted. He fought to push words through lips gone hard and wooden, surprised by the feel of his katana's tightly wrapped hilt in his fists.

Katamori blinked, unsure of when he had drawn his blade.

"So, the beast finally shows itself." Hiroshige pushed to his feet, one hand pressed to his bloodied mouth. "I would strike you down in an instant, had not the emperor bid us keep the peace."

At last, Katamori mastered his traitor tongue. "Go."

"With pleasure, general." Hiroshige sketched a mocking bow. "But do not think for a moment that things are finished between us. There will be a reckoning when you return to the Imperial City."

Katamori's grin felt almost feral. "I look forward to it."

A gaggle of servants scuttled forward, ministering to Hiroshige even as the courtier hurried into his pavilion. With one last glare at Katamori, the Crane guards backed away, weapons still drawn.

Katamori sheathed his blade. He would have shouted after the Crane had not the thunder of hooves drawn his attention. Börte and her riders pelted through the camp like children kicking through autumn leaves, whooping and shouting. Behind loped a mass of Dragon scouts, long bows slung across their chests, expressions uniformly grim.

"Where were you?" Katamori shoved through the press to glare up at Börte.

"Where were *you*?" She thrust her chin at him. "We waited for your signal, only to see your warriors flutter away like marsh ducks."

Katamori blinked. "What signal?"

With a disgusted grunt, Börte drew a crumpled scrap of paper from her breastplate and tossed it at Katamori's feet.

He knelt to retrieve the mud-spattered missive.

Take up position behind the western approach. An arrow of flame shall signal the charge.

Katamori turned the forgery over in his hands, unbelieving. The script matched his exactly, the orders even sealed by his personal chop.

He shook his head, confusion hardening to sharp, hot anger. His fellow commanders were arrogant and quarrelsome, but even in his darkest thoughts Katamori had never considered any might turn traitor.

"On my word, I did not write this." He crumpled the paper in one fist.

Börte rocked back in her saddle, uttering a low whistle. Any reply she might have given was cut off as Ikae and Kogoro came hurrying up.

"The Crane are breaking camp," Ikae said.

"What did you say to Hiroshige?" Kogoro asked.

By way of response, Katamori flung the balled-up paper at the Scorpion's chest. Unfolding it, he read the false orders aloud.

"I did not dispatch these." Katamori waved a hand at the paper, addressing his remark to Akemi and Master Masatsuge, who had drifted over, apparently drawn by the commotion.

"They could have been sent by one of your subordinates," Akemi said, leaning on his long war bow.

"Why would I hamstring my own assault?"

"To win glory for yourself," Börte replied.

"I am general, not champion." Katamori fixed her with a level stare. "If there is any glory to be had it is in a successful campaign, not battlefield heroics."

The Unicorn commander lapsed into a thoughtful frown.

"We all know who wrote this. If not directly, then by proxy." Katamori spread his arms. "The man who has coveted my position since I was named general, the man who has worked constantly to undermine us, the man who delayed while brave samurai lost their lives."

He held their attention like a drawn bow, glad none of the other commanders remarked on the fact that Hiroshige had sat out the battle on Katamori's orders.

"He will not come peacefully," Ikae said.

"He will if we move as one." Katamori made a fist. "All of us, together."

"Except the Crane," Kogoro said.

Katamori ignored the Scorpion, turning to face each of his fellow commanders in turn.

Börte slapped her saddle horn. "I never trusted that snow-haired peacock."

"Nor I," added Akemi.

Ikae gave a slow nod. Only Kogoro and Master Masatsuge looked unconvinced.

"I will not see a clan noble harmed." Masatsuge crossed his arms. "It would fly in the face of our mission."

"I, too, would prefer to resolve this peacefully." Katamori grasped his blade. "Hiroshige has put our lives at risk. Struck from behind like a coward while we battled on behalf of the Empire."

"Save your bombast for the warriors, general," the Phoenix priest replied coolly. "I have no interest in blood."

"And what of the dead?" Katamori asked. "Hiroshige's betrayal left scores upon the battlefield."

"The Phoenix will play no part in your vendetta." Masatsuge walked away, head held high.

Katamori wanted to call the priest a coward but held his tongue lest he drive the arrogant Phoenix into Hiroshige's arms.

"Why take him here?" Kogoro ran a hand through his hair. "Why not let Hiroshige return to the capital then bring formal charges against him?"

"Let the serpent slither back to its nest?" Katamori snorted. "If Hiroshige escapes, we may return to find *we* are the ones facing censure."

"And the rebellion?" Kogoro asked.

"Cowardly peasants." Katamori made a dismissive gesture. "We would have bested them if not for Crane treachery."

Kogoro let out a low sigh. "Hiroshige did not do this."

"Are you admitting guilt, little man?" Börte edged forward, spear in hand.

Kogoro reddened. "You forget, Unicorn. *My* warriors actually fought in the battle."

She wrinkled her nose. "Fine cover for a Scorpion plot."

"Who is to say you did not forge the documents?" Kogoro glared at her, then nodded at Akemi. "Or you?"

"I will have your tongue for that." The Unicorn took a step forward.

"Enough!" Katamori moved between them. "Even now, Hiroshige seeks to turn us against one another. All know the Crane have designs on dictating the imperial succession. Fracturing the other clans only advances their gambit. We must move before they depart. Surround them so there is no escape. Then we shall have our answers."

He glanced back toward Kogoro, only to find the Scorpion had scuttled away into the night – a coward unable to even stand for his convictions. Katamori should have expected as much.

"Just the four of us, then." He met the gaze of each commander in turn. "You all know what must be done."

With grim nods, they turned to their subordinates, orders given in hushed tones. For the first time since he had taken command of the expedition, there were no questions, no challenges, only cold-eyed samurai preparing to bring a traitor to justice.

Katamori didn't know whether to laugh or weep. Unable to present a unified front to their true enemy, the clans had come together to devour one of their own.

Sharp-eyed Dragon scouts led the way, arrows nocked but not drawn, backed by Unicorn cavalry in loose formation, ready to react should Hiroshige attempt to slip from the pass. Katamori and Ikae moved at the head of a broad wedge of warriors.

The Crane were ready for them.

Warning shouts rent the evening air, armed samurai massing behind a makeshift barricade. Katamori caught flashes of Scorpion crimson among the pale-blue armor.

Kogoro must have warned them.

To Katamori's right, in the shadow of the high cliff, Masatsuge watched. Scores of Phoenix samurai flanked the old priest, craven as their master. At least he had not joined the Crane.

"Traitors." Katamori ground the word through gritted teeth.

"What is the meaning of this?" a long-faced Crane captain shouted from behind a hastily erected blockade.

"We have come for Hiroshige." Katamori pitched his voice to carry. "He stands accused of treachery and deceit."

"You have no right, Lion."

"I have *every* right!" Katamori almost screamed the words. He heard the creak of bows being drawn, the whisper of swords hissing from lacquered scabbards. The night was full of torchlight and smells of scorched wood, stars almost invisible overhead. Katamori looked up, feeling like he stood upon a precipice, as if with one step he might slip free of the earth and fall into the deep and smothering dark.

With a low rumble, he pushed down the smoldering anger. "You are surrounded. We outnumber you four-to-one. Lay down your arms and you have my word none will be harmed."

"And Lord Hiroshige?"

"No blood shall be spilt." It was Masatsuge who answered. "By either side."

The Phoenix priest's promise seemed to calm the Crane. "You have brought an army to hear my master's words?"

"Bring Hiroshige out," Katamori called.

"You come in, general," came the shouted reply. "You have my word no harm will come to you."

Katamori gritted his teeth. He could feel the anger swell within him, inescapable as a rising tide. Even now the Crane sought to twist the situation to their advantage.

"This discussion does nothing but buy Hiroshige time," Ikae said.

And yet, despite his fury, Katamori could not give the order to attack.

"The Crane are a Great Clan." He spoke slowly, as if to convince himself. "I shall go."

Ikae shook her head. "If Hiroshige is a traitor, you will be giving yourself as hostage."

"Killing me only proves his guilt. There has been enough

blood spilled this day." Katamori handed his blades to a nearby aide. Hands raised, he walked across the empty ground.

True to their word, the Crane fell in around Katamori, guiding him through the half-struck camp. Shadows wreathed Hiroshige's pavilion, the few remaining lanterns serving only to highlight the deepening gloom.

"I would speak with your lord alone," Katamori said.

The Crane captain gave him an appraising look.

"Hiroshige is armed." Katamori spread his hands. "I am not."

"We shall wait outside." The captain offered a terse nod.

The skin between Katamori's shoulders tickled as he brushed aside the heavy curtain.

Even partially disassembled, Hiroshige's tent had the look of a pavilion plucked from some palace garden. Scrolls and landscape paintings adorned the walls, woven bamboo mats laid across the bare earth. A small dais had been erected on the far wall. In the darkness, Katamori could just make out Hiroshige reclining upon the platform. The Crane courtier shifted with a scrape of sandal upon wood, one hand tapping weakly on the hollow dais.

"I always knew you were ambitious," Katamori said. "But this moves beyond even Crane arrogance."

Hiroshige gave a faint hum, somewhere between a laugh and moan.

"At a loss for words?" Scorn whetted Katamori's rebuke. "No clever evasions? No simpering barbs?"

And still, Hiroshige made no reply. The Crane's silence infuriated Katamori more than any response. He took a step forward, snatching up a nearby lamp.

"At least look me in the eyes, coward!"

The anger curdled in Katamori's throat.

Hiroshige lay upon the dais, his chest bisected by a single, brutal slash. Blood bubbled from the Crane courtier's lips as his hands clawed crimson smears upon the wood. His wide eyes sought Katamori's, pinioning him with their desperate gaze.

Slowly, painfully, the Crane lifted a trembling hand, one finger extended to point at the shadows behind Katamori.

CHAPTER FOUR

A blade licked from the darkness. The strike would have laid open Katamori's throat had he not been turning to follow Hiroshige's gesture. Instead, it cut a line of cold fire across his cheek, slipping down to chip flecks of tawny lacquer from his shoulder armor.

His response was pure reflex. The attacker gave a soft grunt as Katamori's fist hammered into his midsection. The man was unarmored, attired like a Crane body servant except for the short, straight blade.

Katamori lunged, trying to come to grips with his assailant, but the man stepped back, unbelievably quick, and Katamori stumbled forward. Again, came the blade, slashing down in a short overhand chop. Katamori shifted to take the blow on his back armor, pivoting to grab the man's wrist in a wrestler's toss.

Rather than attempt to break free, the assassin released his grip on the blade, moving with the throw. He hit the ground in a tight ball and rolled twice before springing back to his feet.

Planning to pursue the murderer, Katamori snatched up the short sword, only to be tackled from behind.

"Assassin!" one of Hiroshige's guards shouted as Crane samurai poured into the tent, faces paling as they beheld the scene of slaughter.

"He's getting away!" Katamori twisted in the Crane's grip. Thrusting out a hip, he tossed him to the bamboo mat. More samurai surrounded him, shouting, stabbing, slashing. It was all Katamori could do to keep his head, let alone give chase.

The back wall of the pavilion fluttered as the assassin slipped below the edge. Katamori gave a wordless shout, waving his blade toward the escaping man.

But the Crane already had their murderer.

They advanced upon him, cold-eyed stares promising a bloody death.

The sweep of Katamori's short blade cut a long gash into the tent. Without a moment's hesitation, he dove out into the night. He dodged through half-fallen tents, leaping piles of equipment as furious shouts filled the night.

"Stop!" Katamori waved his hands as he ran toward the other clans' position, gasping in great panting breaths as he shouted for them to stand down, to sheathe their weapons.

But the first arrows had already begun to fall.

Dimly, Katamori picked out shadowy forms amidst the rocks. Thinking them advancing samurai, he staggered forward, only to reel back as the first stepped into the eddying circle of lamplight.

She wore a peasant's blouse, the ripped fabric stained the ruddy brown of old blood. In her hand she carried a harvesting sickle, its curved edge catching the lamplight. A spear had been rammed through her back, tip protruding just above her navel, broken haft jutting from the small of her back. It seemed impossible she could walk, let alone fight, and still she advanced upon Katamori, milky eyes darting left and right, her face concealed behind a featureless porcelain mask.

He took a step back as other masked peasants slipped from the gloom. Some had been slashed and stabbed; others were missing hands, arms, even portions of their heads, but none appeared discomfited by the mortal wounds.

Shouts became screams. Somewhere a horse gave a high, pained whinny, cut off abruptly. The air hung thick with the reek of rotting things, threaded with a sharp, almost oily smell Katamori could not quite place.

Hand raised as if to push the walking corpses back, Katamori turned and ran. There was foul magic at work. He needed to find the other commanders.

A Lion samurai rose from the shadows ahead. Katamori's relieved cry withered in his throat as the woman turned to reveal a shattered breastplate, ribs like broken twigs amidst the red ruin of her chest.

She lunged at him with a broken sword.

Katamori parried the strike and shoved her back, following up with a heavy kick to her leg. Brittle bones snapped, and she toppled, still flailing at him with her jagged blade.

He sprinted past. Sick realization was a stone in his gut – they had left many dead upon the battlefield, peasant and samurai alike. If all the fallen had been corrupted, it meant–

A crack like breaking stone dragged Katamori's attention to the distant clearing.

Elemental flame lit the forest up like day, as, glowing bonfire bright, Master Asako Masatsuge stepped into the sky.

"Servants of the Empire, cease this foolish conflict." His voice boomed like thunder from a clear summer sky. He raised a brilliant hand to point at the limping, shuffling mob that shambled through the trees. "Our true enemy has revealed itself."

Flames scoured the dead, corpses twisting like wind-caught silk as they were burnt to ash. In the killing glow, Katamori saw the walls of the pass crawling with dead. Like spiders, they scuttled along the jagged cliffs, single-minded and uncaring of wound or pain.

Clan samurai ceased their struggle, Crane, Lion, Crab, turning from one another to face the new threat. Buoyed by the glow of Masatsuge's flames, they formed a ragged line, shoulder to shoulder against the approaching foe.

Then, Masatsuge's light sputtered.

It began as a flicker, the barest thread of shadow amidst the crackling inferno surrounding the Phoenix master. Masatsuge reacted as if he had been struck, raising one hand as if to shield his eyes. Darkness grew, bruise-purple and bilious green tongues of flame swirling up to surround the priest.

"Impossible!" Masatsuge shook his head, fingers flying through arcane permutations as he sought to slip free of the sickly flames. Like a rope, one lashed about his arm, another his leg, and the master's robes began to smoke and shrivel.

Masatsuge raised hands to the sky, the expression on his face almost pleading. But either the spirits did not heed his call, or they were powerless to help.

The purple-green flames closed about him, and the Phoenix burned.

Any semblance of order disintegrated as the priest fell from the sky, a swirling flood of tainted fire billowing out to scorch flesh and blacken armor. Katamori saw Bayushi Kogoro, backlit against the flame for a brilliant moment. The Scorpion was dragging a wounded Lion samurai toward safety. Then the crackling tide washed over them both.

Riders thundered past Katamori, almost buffeting him to the ground. Howling their fury to the starless night, the Unicorn struck deep into the mob, scattering corpses like the prow of a ship slicing through ocean waves. For a moment, it seemed as if they might turn the hideous tide. Then the dead began to drop from the cliffs.

Most hit the hard stone, the wet crunch of bone sharp against the night. But some struck the riders. Blind to injury, they tore samurai from mounts, dragging horses to the ground with the sheer weight of numbers.

Swirls of nauseous flame illuminated the struggle. Carried on eldritch winds, they slipped through armored joints, into shouting mouths. Wherever the flame touched, warriors died.

A riderless horse galloped through the trees, mane and tail aflame. With a sting of terrible recognition, Katamori realized it was Börte's.

"General, this way!"

Katamori spun, relief like a cool cloth across his neck as he recognized Mirumoto Akemi.

The Dragon commander had discarded his bow for a pair of swords, their steel so pale as to be almost opalescent in the gloom. One of his pauldrons had been torn free, his blood-slicked hair pulled loose from its chonmage.

"Ikae has pulled back to Five-Dragon Gate." Despite the head wound, Akemi seemed surefooted enough as he led Katamori through the twisting shadows.

A trickle of hope worked its way through the cracks in Katamori's burgeoning despair. Ikae and her warriors were witch hunters, and if any knew how to defeat this hideous menace, it would be the Kuni.

The remaining clan forces were hard pressed. The survivors

of other contingents fought side-by-side with Crab samurai, their ironshod clubs shattering ribs and crushing limbs. Katamori bulled a cackling woman from his path, Akemi stepping into the space to lop clutching hands from a pair of corpses. Together, they forced their way to the Crab ranks, almost earning a split skull for their troubles.

"You survived." Ikae offered them the barest of nods before turning her attention back to the scrolls spread across the great seal that was Five-Dragon Gate.

With concern, Katamori noted the jade was cracked, long fingers of shadow marring the carefully carved surface.

"The seal is broken?" Hands on knees, Katamori drew a few whooping breaths. "You said this land was free of corruption."

"It was." She bared her teeth. "Someone in our camp did this."

"Who? How?" Katamori glanced to the scrabbling horde.

Ikae said nothing, only shuffled through her scrolls with increasing urgency.

The dead moved like loose-stringed puppets, all lolling heads and thrashing limbs, their gait sharp and jerky. Behind, tall shadows danced in the torchlight. Rendered almost insectile in the flickering glow, they seemed to move before their makers, as if the walking corpses were echoes of something far darker.

Behind Katamori, a Crab samurai slipped, his leg caught by grasping, bodiless hands. The dead were on him in an instant, the breach spreading as more masked corpses poured through the line.

Katamori cut the head from one. Shoving its thrashing body into the two behind, he cut at the tangled mess with heavy, punishing blows as if he were hacking through thick undergrowth.

Something flashed in the corner of his eye, and Katamori found himself on the ground, struggling to draw breath. His lips buzzed, his sword arm numb from the shoulder down.

He tried to stand but couldn't seem to get his legs under him.

Strong hands grabbed Katamori's armor straps, hauling him back as two Lion samurai rushed forward to slash at the scrabbling press.

Wheezing, Akemi dragged him to the center of the shrinking circle. The Dragon scout collapsed against a half-fallen tent and reached a hand inside his breastplate. It came back red. Lips curling from bloody teeth, Akemi regarded the crimson stain spreading across his armor.

Seeming almost irritated, he shook his head, then lay still.

Blinking against pain-blurred vision, Katamori propped himself against a sack of discarded equipment. His sword arm was a mass of blood, fingers limp and cold. Must've been one of those damned reaping hooks.

"I did not think it possible." Ikae tossed aside her scrolls with a snarl. "Not after all these years."

"What are they?" Katamori asked between whistling gasps.

"Ancient blasphemies," she replied. "Blood magic of the cruelest sort, power drawn from realms beyond the sight of heaven."

"How can we defeat them?" No matter how quickly Katamori breathed, the air seemed too thin to fill his lungs.

"We cannot."

She reached inside her breastplate, withdrawing a necklace from which dangled a small bell of black iron. Jaw tight, she drew her dagger, muttering under her breath as she struck the tiny bell – once, twice, again.

The chime seemed to resonate in Katamori's chest, small but insistent. He realized he could not hear the battle anymore, those who struggled around him little more than shadows in his fading vision. The pain was gone, replaced by a frightening numbness that spread through Katamori like ice creeping across a winter pond.

"What are you doing?" His words sounded strange, distant, as if echoing from the back of a great hall.

"I cannot save us." Eyes squeezed shut, Ikae rang the bell again. "But I can see us avenged."

"Good." Katamori felt as if he were falling. He had failed, but his mistakes would serve as a warning. Not the glorious legacy Katamori had hoped to leave, but one that must suffice.

"Hawks and swine." He managed a breathless chuckle as his perception narrowed to a tiny pinprick. All that remained was Ikae's bell.

Soon enough, that faded as well.

CHAPTER FIVE

Kitsuki Naoki never intended to be late. No matter that she left warning notes, no matter she carried an hourglass, no matter she bid herself listen for the timekeeper's call; somehow, the minutes seemed to slip past her, insubstantial as clouds racing across a pale autumn sky.

It was letters, this time. Naoki had descended upon the local Dragon Clan courier's post in the mountain town of Ueyama to seize stacks of correspondence, searching for some incriminating stroke of the brush. She knew the killer was a writer, after all. Had he not scrawled poems upon the walls in his victims' blood? The mad ramblings of a corrupt mind.

The divine order,
like sagging willow branches.
I climb beyond it.

Barely competent verse, but chilling, nonetheless. Each poem heralded the ritualistic slaughter of some Dragon Clan official. And yet, despite the trappings of dark sorcery, no priests had found evidence of Shadowlands taint.

"Are you quite finished?"

Naoki glanced up to see Mirumoto Heisuke standing just inside the doorway of the cramped office. The Dragon Clan official watched her with disdain, every inch of his aged frame vibrating with barely contained outrage at the epistolary chaos.

By way of answer, Naoki inclined her head toward several piles of unsorted post.

"Irregular, very irregular." Heisuke's wrinkled hands fluttered near the hilt of his katana. As a samurai, he was permitted to carry blades, but the official had the soft-bodied look of one who had never found cause to draw them in anger.

"Master Horikata has given me broad latitude to investigate." Although Naoki's magisterial charter gave her the authority to compel Heisuke's obedience, it did not extend to common courtesy.

"It is one thing to delve into the affairs of merchants and commoners," he continued. "But to intercept letters from high-ranking samurai and temple monks... bold, even for an Emerald Magistrate." He flicked his hands as if to brush her away.

"Eight dead." She turned to fix him with what she hoped was a steady glare. "All Dragon Clan officials."

That last was a bit of exaggeration. Although the victims *had* held rank in the clan, none were of particular note, a handful of murders scattered across the vastness of the Dragon's mountainous domain, remarkable only for their gruesomeness.

Heisuke chewed his lower lip. "Still, I must protest."

"Noted." Naoki turned back to the letters. "Now, if you have nothing else to add..."

"Captain Tada sent me to remind you they interrogate the suspect at the Hour of the Dog, with or without you."

Naoki glanced at the hourglass on the tiny desk and winced. She had set it at the Hour of the Monkey, two hours before she was supposed to meet with Tada. Now the upper glass bulb was empty. As usual, Naoki had no idea when it had run out.

She favored Heisuke with a sheepish look. "And what time is it now?"

"Rooster." He all but grunted the name.

Naoki flipped the hourglass, relieved there was still time. She would have to keep an eye on it. Ueyama wasn't a large town, but the constable's office was a brisk ten-minute walk uphill.

Frowning, she reached for her brush and marked a thin line halfway down the hourglass's upper half. There, plenty of time.

With one last, long-suffering sigh, Heisuke ducked from the office, no doubt off to lodge yet another complaint. Naoki ignored him. If her search uncovered evidence of the murderer's identity, Heisuke's grievances would become as dust beneath her sandals.

The murderer was no commoner, Naoki felt that truth deep in the pit of her stomach, heavy as a meal of pounded rice cakes. It wasn't what he wrote, nor how he wrote, but the *way* he wrote, every stroke of his bloodied brush sharp with tightly coiled hunger, as if the characters might lunge from the page to pluck the eyes from any who dared look upon them.

Blood flows bright and true,
free of elemental lies.
Escape your worthless flesh.

The killer moved too quickly, too quietly. Naoki suspected he was someone of note, perhaps even possessed of allies and informers. He would need to communicate with them somehow, and letters seemed the obvious choice since the priests could find no hint of Shadowlands sorcery.

Master Horikata had called it a theory, and the Kitsuki method did not deal in theories, only evidence. It was a testament to the elder Emerald Magistrate's desperation that he indulged Naoki's epistolary eccentricities. It cost him little. She was but one of a score of junior magistrates Horikata had dispatched across the mountains.

Normally, such tedious work would have set Naoki's legs twitching, muscles threaded with the desire to dash from the courier post and run until her lungs gave out.

Still, the letters drew her in.

Certainly, the illicit thrill of peeking into others' lives played a part, as if Naoki were strolling down one of the winding streets of Ueyama and suddenly found herself able to peer through walls. It was the feeling of being at the center of a thousand threads, a thousand partial tales.

Naoki had always liked puzzles, even though she wasn't very good at them. It was what had driven her to become an Emerald Magistrate, to gamble on Master Horikata's largesse in the hopes of distinguishing herself.

Naoki waded into the epistolary flood, sifting through torrents of crackling paper for flecks of gold. Ueyama sat at the conflux of several trade roads, not to mention one of the few navigable rivers that passed through Dragon lands. Despite its unprepossessing atmosphere, a surprising amount of post flowed through the small town.

Which was exactly why Naoki had come.

She found herself deep in an esoteric letter to a Phoenix Clan priest. Although the prose was near impenetrable, Naoki was enraptured by the glimmer of hatred peeking through the clouds of arcane formulations and elaborate conjecture. The writer had not signed a name, which was suspicious.

It was not the letter's content that caught Naoki's attention, but the brushstrokes. They were wild, almost frenzied, as if the writer had been in a hurry to scatter ink upon the page. Even so, the calligraphy was precise, almost reminiscent of the sweeping curves of classical script. Many scholars spent time copying ancient text, but few wrote in such archaic hand.

Throat tight as coiled rope, she withdrew the copies she had made of the murderer's poems and held them next to the letter. The characters did not match, not exactly, but the handwriting was close enough to raise suspicions.

The rattle of the door caused Naoki to look up.

"Oh, you're still here." Heisuke frowned down at her.

Naoki waved the letter at him. "Who dispatched this?"

He took it from her, pointedly looking away from the text as he turned the paper over to examine the courier markings.

"No name listed, only a recipient, Master Asako Masatsuge." Heisuke clucked his tongue. "I should reprimand Shinsaburo for accepting a letter like this." With a sigh, he shuffled over to one of the many cabinets that lined the tiny courier's office. After much opening of drawers and shuffling of paper, Heisuke produced a much-abused logbook.

"Sent by an itinerant monk." He frowned down at the lines of crabbed handwriting. "That explains the lack of name."

"I don't understand."

Heisuke sucked air through his teeth, lips curled like a teacher lecturing a troublesome pupil.

"Some holy orders require adherents to give up their name while on pilgrimage – to distance themselves from worldly matters. They receive a new one upon returning to the temple." He tucked the tag back into the drawer, turning back to glare down at Naoki. "Now, if you are quite finished…"

"When did the monk send this letter?" Naoki leaned forward, excitement prickling along her neck at the thought he might still be in the vicinity.

"A day ago." Heisuke held up a hand. "And before you ask, I wasn't on duty. Shinsaburo is running letters to Kitaguchi and won't be back until tomorrow afternoon."

Naoki took the letter back, arranging it next to the murderer's poetry.

"Don't you have somewhere to be, magistrate?" Heisuke could not quite hide his delight as he nodded at the hourglass.

Empty. Again.

With a muttered curse, Naoki snatched up the letter and stuffed the small bundle into the front of her robes.

Heisuke sputtered. "That is a bonded letter."

"It is evidence," Naoki replied coolly. Heisuke's truculence had begun to test her patience. "Now, if you will excuse me." She pushed past the courier official, who gave a muffled squawk of outrage.

"It will take me hours to set things right!" he shouted after her.

But Naoki was not listening. Already she had slipped her jitte into her sash. A symbol of her rank as junior magistrate, the twin weapons resembled unsharpened short swords. With thick blades and long hooked guards, they were made to trap enemy weapons and cripple joints, allowing criminals to be taken alive.

Naoki hurried up Ueyama's narrow streets. The cobbled roads often turned at a sharp angle, threading between rows of houses and a sheer cliff. With no rail or buttress, it made for a route that was both circuitous and harrowing.

Red-faced, Naoki arrived at the squat stone building that housed Ueyama's small constabulary.

Captain Tada was waiting for her. He was a broad-shouldered

man, dark-haired and strong, with a wide, round face that resembled nothing so much as a statue of some beneficent fortune. Unfortunately, the captain's jovial countenance belied his disposition. If Heisuke had been resistant to Naoki prying into local affairs, Tada was positively hostile.

He bent over a bowl of bloody water, lips pursed as he wrapped a strip of fabric around skinned knuckles. Although Naoki's sudden entrance brought strangled cries from several of the other guards, Tada spared her little more than a contemptuous glance.

"We finished the interrogation some time ago."

"And?" Naoki clenched her jaw against the sick tickle of distress that wormed its way up her throat. Although the Kitsuki investigation method gave little weight to testimony, she had hoped the bandit might provide some information. He had, after all, been apprehended attempting to sell the most recent victim's personal effects.

"He confessed to everything."

"Of course he did." Naoki's interest soured. Judging by the state of Tada's knuckles and the soft moans coming from the shadowed cells at the back of the office, the questioning had been rough. Such practices were regrettably common across Rokugan. Naoki had hoped to mitigate some of the more extreme methods, but she had arrived too late.

Again.

Frustration burned in Naoki's cheeks, all the more infuriating for its familiarity.

"You should be pleased, magistrate." Tada favored her with a sharp grin. "We found your murderer, didn't we?" He turned to the half-dozen guards milling about the office, who returned a halfhearted cheer.

"Your master should have come to me first." Tada stood, flexing his injured hand, then glanced at her from under lowered brows. "Don't worry, I am happy to share the credit."

"That man cannot be the murderer." Naoki thrust her chin at the crumpled shadow in the rear cell. After Tada's questioning, she would be lucky if he could talk, let alone provide useful information.

"And why not?" Tada asked.

"For one, he's illiterate." Naoki wrinkled her nose. "Unless your crude ministrations unlocked some secret store of poetic prowess?"

Tada gave an irritated twitch of his head, as if Naoki were a bothersome insect. "Could've had an accomplice write for him."

"That might also explain why he was seen by dozens of witnesses on the night of the murder," she replied. "Three villages over, gambling in a sake den, the *entire* night." Naoki ticked off the points on her fingers, trying, and failing, to hide her exasperation.

Tada reddened, jaw clenching and unclenching. "And I suppose you found a confession within the local post?"

"As a matter of fact." She drew the letter from her robe, unfolding it so the captain could see. Naoki knew she shouldn't let Tada's prodding get to her, but she was tired of rustic samurai.

The captain frowned down at the writing. "Looks like a temple inscription."

Naoki drew in a quick breath. She had asked Heisuke if the monk sent any more letters, but pilgrims often stopped at local shrines, writing prayers, poems, and luck charms in exchange for small donations.

"Is there a temple nearby?" she asked.

He shrugged. "Ishinakaji. Perhaps a mile upslope, near Red Cuckoo Ridge–"

Naoki was out the door before he could finish. She remembered the temple from her journey into town – a small affair, typical of mountain shrines, but well-appointed despite the remote location. No doubt the monks excised donatives from the many travelers who crossed the high pass.

"Wait!" Tada called after her.

When Naoki didn't reply, he shouted something back to the guards, then huffed after her.

"I know the temple monks. None of them are killers."

"Not them," Naoki replied, already puffing from the sharp incline. "A pilgrim. He passed through a day ago. Might still be there."

"I should gather the watch."

Naoki's lip curled. "You might as well announce us with war drums. This is a man who has slipped past dozens of guards."

To his credit, the captain didn't argue, only steadied the blades at his side.

"I should lead." He raised a conciliatory hand. "I know the path. One missed step and we'll be scraping you off the rocks."

Naoki nodded, stepping aside to let the captain pass. Although annoyed that the captain seemed bent on inserting himself into her investigation, she was happy to let him lead, if only because it would keep Tada from seeing how sweaty the climb had made her.

High lanterns lit Ishinakaji's red-painted eaves. A monk stood guard outside the gate, but after a few hushed words with Tada, he quickly ushered them inside.

Naoki picked at the hems of her robes while they waited for the abbess to be summoned. Perhaps she should have waited for the watch. She peered into the shadows as if she could peel back the darkness through sheer force of will.

After an interminable wait, a small, white-haired woman was brought forward. Seeming bent almost double under the weight of her prayer beads, the abbess informed them that yes, several pilgrims had come through in the past day, but alas, all had moved on.

Naoki's request to see any charms they had written was met with frowning scrutiny. Her writ might compel local officials, but temples remained outside the purview of secular authorities.

Only when Tada offered to purchase several charms were the poems brought forward.

It irritated Naoki to be in the captain's debt, although perhaps she was merely annoyed she had not thought to bargain with the monks.

Amongst the vague blessings and koans, she found it, handwriting unmistakable:

> *The gods rule above,*
> *souls bound to a broken wheel.*
> *What stands above them?*

"He was here." The words slipped through lips gone prickly.

"But where is he now?" Tada asked.

"Left at sunset. Strange to travel at night, but he insisted," the abbess replied. "Headed south. Pleasant enough fellow, fond of philosophy."

"What did he look like?" Naoki asked.

The abbess squinted at her. "A blur. Just like you."

"Surely someone must have seen him," Tada said.

"We receive many visitors, and his stay was brief." Frowning, the abbess waved forward one of her attendants, a broad-shouldered woman in roughspun robes.

"He was old, magistrate. Perhaps seventy winters, although still quite fit." The attendant glanced away, as if searching her memory. "He had a kind smile."

The letter seemed to burn next to Naoki's breast. A man of that age could not have traveled far, no matter his fitness. She was on her feet in a moment, thoughts scattering in all directions.

"We must follow."

Tada's heavy hand gripped her shoulder. "He is hours ahead of us – in the mountains, at night. If we leave now, the only thing we will find is a broken neck."

He might as well have punched Naoki in the gut. She rocked back, the world seeming to swim around her.

"Don't worry, magistrate," Tada said. "I bet my blades he doesn't know the passes like we do. Come sunup I'll be after him with a dozen scouts."

Naoki squeezed her eyes shut. To come so close. It was more than any other magistrate had achieved, and yet close meant nothing – especially if the man claimed another victim.

"Get some rest." Tada said, his rural sensibilities obviously excited by the prospect of a hunt. "We'll need you fresh at first light."

Naoki could only nod as they picked their way back down the rocky path. She had rooms at the Jade Pidgeon but knew sleep would be impossible. She left Tada at the guard post, drifting down the street like wind-tossed refuse.

Naoki was almost to the inn when she realized her satchel and hourglass were gone. In her haste to reach the constabulary, she must have left them at the courier post. Cursing herself for an absentminded fool, Naoki retraced her steps.

She expected to have to rouse Heisuke and prepared herself for the official's waspish temper. But the courier post was unlocked, the heavy wooden door slightly ajar. She frowned, suspicious, drawing her jitte to nudge the door aside.

Naoki smelled the blood before she saw it – sharp and coppery in the earlier summer heat.

The office was in shambles, crimson-soaked papers scattered across the floor. The cabinets had been torn from the walls, and Heisuke's desk shattered as if someone had been thrown atop it. But Naoki's eyes were drawn to the far wall.

She didn't recognize Heisuke, not at first. What remained of the postal official hardly even looked human.

Naoki pressed a trembling hand to her mouth, disgust warring with validation.

She had been right.

Her gaze flicked around the small office, searching for what she *knew* must be there. The poem was written on the far wall, hungry words seeming almost to reach for her.

> We grope in darkness,
> Not blind, but blinded, deceived.
> The truth in our veins.

Swallowing, Naoki bent to dip her finger in the nearest pool of blood – cool but still tacky, the edges rust brown.

The killer had been here recently.

Her shout brought a guard running down the street outside. Tada arrived a handful of minutes later.

"By the ancestors." The sight of Heisuke's mangled body set even the bullish captain back a step, knuckles white on his drawn blade.

"Now, you understand." Naoki swallowed. The skin of her face felt hot and tight, as if she stood too close to a fire.

"I'll send word to every post and watchfort south of the mountains." Tada paced back and forth, a tiger caged by helpless fury.

Naoki sighed. "You won't find him."

"How can you know?"

"Because whatever this is" – she nodded at the grisly scene – "it is more than just a man. There is something else, something powerful at work. Can't you feel it?"

Tada made a warding sign, jaw tight. "Shall I call a priest?"

Naoki nodded, although she did not hold out much hope. Despite the terrible slaughter, despite the feeling of something truly foul at work, the spirits could tell her nothing.

"Post guards around the office. I would search it." Naoki knew she would find nothing. Just like the other eight victims – a poem and blood. Still, she had to try. Just as she had tried to follow the killer.

Just as he may have followed her, waiting until her departure to strike at Heisuke. Truly, Naoki could not tell if she had interrupted his plans, or if the killer was merely toying with her. So little was certain.

"Where will this demon strike next?" Tada asked.

"I do not know." Naoki reached inside her robes, fingers brushing the folded paper within.

"But I know of someone who may."

CHAPTER SIX

The iron bell had been ringing in Kuni Tetsuo's dreams a week before he reached the ruined monastery. Tucked away amidst the Twilight Mountains, it was several days from the nearest Crab watchfort, the surrounding lands a heartless constellation of broken peaks and meandering river valleys. It was a haunt for outlaws, unquiet spirits, and worse. A scattering of hardscrabble settlements dredged the most meager of existences from the rocky earth and ice-cold streams, the villagers half-bandits themselves, their deference to the Empire little more than polite fiction.

Although nominally situated in Crab lands, no tax collectors came, no officials were sent to mark and measure. The region had languished for the better part of two decades. In truth, it was simply not worth the trouble to govern, and the Crab, being a practical people, were happy to focus their attentions elsewhere.

In keeping with local sensibilities, the monastery was a solid, blocky affair, all thick walls and sharp corners. Like everything the Crab Clan laid its hand to, the place was built to withstand assault, preferably for years. There had, indeed, been a time when the monastery served as a bastion against foul endeavors. Occasionally, a landslide or avalanche would unearth evidence of the myriad desperate battles that once raged across the cliffs – bones, blades, and bits of scattered armor churning amidst the ancient stone. Villagers would pick through the detritus, scraping gold filigree from ancient helms, snatching the steel from old blades.

The gate was black iron, wards of strength and perseverance etched amidst the names of forgotten heroes. It was closed when Kuni Tetsuo arrived, having sealed itself at the first chime of the iron bell – as had every other door and window in the monastery.

Had there been monks left to tend the ancient edifice, they might have welcomed Tetsuo, offering him the traditional millet cakes and dippers of cool, clear water drawn from the courtyard well. But there were no monks, the last having died years ago. Even then, the monastery had been a large, drafty place, hungry stone leaching the heat from even the largest hearth.

Tetsuo could hear the bell, its heavy chime seeming to echo within his very bones. He placed a hand upon the cold iron gate, vibrations tickling up his fingers, his heart almost beating in time with each ring.

There were mantras for Tetsuo to recite – less incantations than muttered oaths, ancient promises dredged from the smothering mists of history. Callused fingers moved across the inscribed symbols, his touch suddenly gentle as a fluttering moth. One by one the sevenfold locks clanged open. Heavy latch bars hissed back into sunken holes. Tetsuo moved through the ritual without hesitation, without thought, word and action circumscribed by the careful scrutiny of long-dead monks.

Even now he could feel them at his back. Eyes cold as the high peaks, their thin-lipped instruction frequently punctuated by a painful lesson. They had been old, even then – hairless and rawboned, but hard as the heavy teaching rods they carried. Their order was an oddity, even among the Kuni – a family known for all manner of esoteric interests. Created to battle an evil long dead, they clung, limpet-like, to the wind-battered rocks, unwilling or unable to abandon their vigil.

The monastery seemed strange without the monks' grim presence – a tomb without a body, a barren cenotaph, empty of name or deed. Tetsuo did not mourn their passing, no more than he mourned the setting of the sun. His old teachers would have been insulted by such sentiment.

At last, the iron gate ground open.

Two bandits came screaming from the shadow of the barbican. Wiry as mountain goats, they had the wide, red-eyed look of men pushed beyond breaking. One swung an iron-studded club at Tetsuo, his mouth open to reveal brown-spotted teeth, the hollow beyond yawning like an abandoned well.

Tetsuo took the club from him, then drove a knee into his midsection. The man sat back heavily, blinking like one shaken from heavy sleep.

"The chime harrows us!" The second bandit dove at Tetsuo, spear in hand, his whole body coiled behind the thrust.

Tetsuo slapped the spear aside. The man's head made a sound like a trodden egg as Tetsuo's club spattered fragments of it across the stone.

The other bandit made no move to rise, regarding Tetsuo with the slack-jawed awe of a child watching a shadow play. Tetsuo left him sitting on the cold stone. The man had never been a threat. If he wished to die, he need only follow.

Sucking his teeth, Tetsuo regarded the bloody club, then tossed it aside. There were those who said a warrior should never be without a weapon, but Tetsuo had always found it easier to take them from his foes.

There were more bandits inside, a score at least, half-starved and mostly mad from being trapped with the bell. They came at Tetsuo in ones and twos, their wild, erratic movements like insects struggling on the surface of a pond.

He killed those who wished to die. The rest he left alone.

They had made a lair of the monastery, blackening the walls with cookfires and piling refuse in the lower halls. Tetsuo stalked through the debris, unswerving, uncaring. It was as the monks had wished, after all.

The best way to protect something was not to hide it, but to make it not worth searching for.

Sound filled the inner temple. It was as if the air were water, every booming chime sending ripples through the empty nave. A dozen bandits surrounded the bell. They knelt like supplicants, hands outstretched, thin runnels of blood flowing from their ears. Some had tried to touch the bell, and sported broken hands, broken jaws. Each chime sent a shudder through the gathered folk, bodies twitching, mouths opening and closing like landed fish.

Hollow gazes followed Tetsuo across the cracked tile, but none rose to bar his path. He did not hear the bell so much as feel it within his spirit. It had sounded in his dreams these past long days, calling him home.

Head bowed, Tetsuo reached out a tentative hand.

The metal was warm, a stone baked beneath the noonday sun. It quieted at his touch. As one, the former bandits sucked in a gasping breath. Eyes rolled in bruised sockets, bodies convulsing as they collapsed to the cold stone. Tetsuo paid them no mind. They were empty vessels, spirits riven from uncaring flesh.

Tetsuo searched for meaning within the last echoing cadences. There were few who knew of the bell, even fewer capable of sounding it. Slowly, the message came clear:

He has returned.

Without preamble, Tetsuo turned upon his heel, slipping through the cloistered halls with the same unhurried stride with which he entered. The monastery stood silent now. Even the wind had faded to nothing, the cold, mountain air caught in the expectant lull before a gathering storm.

The gates closed behind Kuni Tetsuo, two giant hands gently ushering him into the evening chill.

He paused, head cocked.

It came on the night air, a leaf borne upon voiceless winds. The bell in the monastery might lie still, but that did not mean it was silent. At the moment, its call remained the barest tickle at the edges of Tetsuo's senses. He knew the chime would grow louder, much louder, as it led him to the source of corruption.

Kuni Tetsuo began his descent down the mountain without a glance back.

Just as the old masters would have wished.

CHAPTER SEVEN

This evening would be truly memorable. Doji Masahiro walked the length of the long hall, inspecting the seating arrangements. Servants swirled around him like summer midges. Every twitch of Masahiro's head set them fluttering this way and that, arms full of flowers, hanging scrolls, pillows, and serving trays. Everything needed to be perfect. Although Masahiro frequently hosted court luminaries, never had his manor been privy to such an august gathering.

To call it a conspiracy would have been impolite. Far better to think of Masahiro's coterie as a collection of concerned patriots, assembled by an unswerving dedication to the future of the Emerald Empire.

Masahiro allowed himself a small smile, setting aside that particular turn of phrase for the later festivities. It would no doubt tickle the prudish fancies of Otomo Yasunori and his gaggle of court officials. Although Masahiro and his Crane Clan allies had done all the hard work, it never hurt to remain in the good graces of high nobility. Let Yasunori claim the credit – all that mattered was young Tokihito was finally positioned to be the next emperor.

Almost by reflex, Masahiro bowed his head at the thought, causing a flurry of reciprocal obeisance amongst his flock of servants. It was a tragedy that the emperor's appointed heir had died – yet another victim of the crawling chills, an insolent little plague that had crept into the capital with the winter snows, striking folk down without regard for rank or title. The imperial pyre had not even cooled before the court began to swirl and foment, various factions aligning behind a gaggle of secondary heirs and distant cousins.

Masahiro surveyed the hall. All was in place, literally and figuratively. What did it matter if Tokihito was only eleven years of age? The Empire needed a firm hand, one skilled in the intricacies of court, able to navigate the vagaries of clan politics while carefully guiding the ship of state through the shoals of short-sighted ambition.

In short, it needed Masahiro.

Otomo Yasunori might have been the child emperor's guardian, but all knew it would be Masahiro and his brother Hiroshige who truly governed. Seeing to the final preparations, Masahiro restrained the urge to clap with delight. It had been a perilous, expensive road – cajoling, bribing, flattering, and bullying the other factions. They had suffered numerous setbacks, such as when that Matsu brute was chosen to lead the clan expeditionary force instead of Hiroshige. Such a triumph would have added much needed polish to their family's military record.

The Empire needed a new Emerald Champion, after all.

But all that lay behind them. At last, Masahiro stood poised to pluck fruits grown through years of careful cultivation.

He flicked his fingers, sending servants scuttling for their various corners. The air prickled with scents of cedar clippings and early summer flowers, tastefully arranged in viewing alcoves about the hall. If he concentrated, Masahiro could detect the barest hint of dragon's pearl rice and roasted sea bream from the kitchens – the first of a dozen courses to tickle the palates of his honored guests.

With a deep, satisfied breath, he turned to the wide screens that separated the hall from the inner garden. The night was silent but for the pleasant melodies of biwa and bamboo flute, songs carefully selected to appeal to the rarefied sensibilities of Masahiro's attendees. They were, after all, heroes of the Empire.

At least, they would be soon enough.

Masahiro took up position as the screens were drawn aside. It would have been crass for him to peer into the garden like an unlettered peasant. So Masahiro simply sat, head turned as if admiring the wall scroll – a wood block portraiture by the artist-ascetic Ryūkōsai, a sixth-generation disciple of Shinsei himself. After a respectful moment of reflection, Masahiro's guests would introduce themselves in order of rank.

And yet, the garden remained silent.

The back of Masahiro's neck prickled. No doubt Yasunori was behind the slight. The fact that the Otomo noble technically outranked Masahiro had given Yasunori pretentious airs as of late. To publicly acknowledge the emperor's guardian would play into Yasunori's petty concept of reputation. It was a small snub, but one that still rankled.

Masahiro considered letting the silence stretch, but ultimately decided against it. Tonight, of all nights, he could afford to be magnanimous. They celebrated a great victory.

Masahiro could not restrain a choked moan as he turned.

The garden stood empty.

Only Masahiro's sense of decorum kept him from leaping to his feet. His hurried gesture brought one of the outer servants scurrying forward. The man did not even raise his eyes, hugging the ground as if he were personally responsible for the debacle.

"Where are they?" Masahiro's question came as a low hiss.

"We set out lanterns, fresh mats, refreshments, and bamboo cuttings, lord."

It was not an answer, and they both knew it. Masahiro dismissed the man with an irritated flick. The servant could no more explain the movements of his betters than Masahiro could ascertain the will of the Fortunes.

His first thought was that Yasunori's petulant pride had boiled over into outright hostility. But no, Masahiro had spoken with the Otomo noble's attendants just this morning. Well bribed, they had reported nothing amiss. In fact, Yasunori was even said to be preparing some of his famously uninspired poetry to commemorate the occasion.

Granted, the celebration was a bit premature, but Masahiro had received credible reports that the imperial expedition had engaged the rebels. What hope could a gaggle of peasants have against the best warriors from all seven clans? Although Matsu Katamori might be a boorish ruffian, he was, by all accounts, a competent general. It seemed impossible the expedition could have achieved anything short of total victory. Undoubtedly, Hiroshige had already turned the others against the uncouth Lion. They would be singing his brother's praises by the time the expedition returned.

The flap of sandals drew Masahiro's attention to the garden shadows. Servants bowed as a small palanquin was borne along the crushed stone path. Daidoji samurai flanked the procession, spears at the ready. Masahiro's own guards moved to intercept, but, recognizing the personal crest on the palanquin, he waved them back.

Bamboo screens were lifted to reveal Lady Doji Otose, Hiroshige's wife. She had discarded her normally extravagant robes for traveling attire – a tasteful kimono belted at the waist, serviceable sandals with only the barest embellishments, and a single jade ring securing her long white hair.

Masahiro's confusion at his sister-in-law's attire only deepened as she dispensed with the formal greeting, waving him over as if he were some minor functionary. Had it been anyone other than Otose, Masahiro would have bridled at the insult, but she had been as much a part of their success as Hiroshige.

Again, Masahiro's guards moved to accompany him, and again, he waved them back. If Otose wished to speak to him in private, matters must truly have turned dire.

He dismissed the servants, sending his own guards to the garden periphery. They were the clan's samurai, not Masahiro's, and he couldn't trust them to put his interests over those of the Crane. Those warriors loyal to him marched with his brother in the imperial expedition, to better burnish Hiroshige's reputation in battle.

"Where is everyone?" Masahiro asked, unable to contain himself any longer.

"Preparing to flee the capital." Otose shook her head. This close, Masahiro could see the redness in her eyes, expertly concealed.

She had been crying, a realization that unsettled Masahiro more than he cared to admit. He almost could not bring himself to ask the question, but now was not the time for hesitation.

"Hiroshige is dead." Otose leaned forward to grasp his hand.

Her firm grip was the only thing that saved Masahiro from collapse. It was as if the ground had become water. His heart fluttered like a caged bird.

"Impossible." And it was. Hiroshige was a skilled politician surrounded by loyal warriors and bearing their ancestral blade. The other clans might be jealous fools, but none would be so brazen as to strike at a high-court official.

"They are all gone. Hiroshige, Katamori, all of them." Her gaze sought his.

"The rebels?" Masahiro shook his head. "How is this possible?"

"We do not know," she replied. "The reports are scattered. Apparently, there were no survivors."

Masahiro opened his mouth, but, for perhaps the first time in his life, could find no words.

"The other claimants are already moving." Otose's voice was low but insistent. "Otomo Yasunori fell from his horse this afternoon. They do not know if he will recover."

Like a paper castle in some children's play, Masahiro's ambitions crumpled under their own weight.

"We must gather the others." He glanced about, as if the shadows might hold some answer. "Plan for a counterstrike."

"There *are* no others." Otose shook him. "Don't you understand, Masa? They are coming for us. If we are not exiled, it will be poison or knives in the dark."

He blinked, licked lips suddenly dry. "But…"

"I am bound for my family's estate in the south." Her response was flat, almost workmanlike. "Do you have anywhere to hide?"

Masahiro waved a trembling hand at the manor. "Everything

we have is here. All our resources are invested in Tokihito's ascendancy."

"Then it is already gone." Otose glanced away. "I would shelter you, but I am already imposing upon my birth family."

"You would abandon me? After all we have accomplished?" Sorrow hardened to anger, a spike of ice in Masahiro's breast. "You are my sister!"

"Was." She released his hands. "I *was* your sister."

"Go on then." He stood on unsteady legs. "Scuttle back to your people. I will not forget this slight."

Her expression darkened, becoming something cold and strange. "I came to warn you. Did any of your other so-called allies display such loyalty?"

As quickly as it had come, Masahiro's fury fled, leaving him empty and bereft.

"Forgive me. I spoke from grief, not anger." He sank to his knees, hands bunched in the sleeves of his robe. "What am I to do?"

She drew in a slow breath. "Perhaps there is some official posting you might take, somewhere distant, somewhere safe?"

"One step short of exile?"

"And one step away from the pyre," she replied. "Our hopes are shattered, not gone. You have allies in court, even if they cannot safely identify themselves. Let our enemies believe they have beaten us; let them grow overconfident."

Otose was right, of course. As much as it burned Masahiro to admit the fact. With Hiroshige gone and Yasunori on his deathbed, Masahiro would be prey to all the squabbling factionalism of an imperial court without a strong emperor. He would be lucky to escape with his life.

"We shall rise from the ashes," Otose said.

"Would we were Phoenix, not Crane." Masahiro made a sound that was half-laugh, half-sob.

Otose laughed as well, tears glittering in her eyes. "Hiroshige, he would want me to–"

Masahiro raised a hand. "You have done more than enough."

"Would that I could help more." Her smile did not reach her eyes.

Masahiro ran a hand across his chin, considering. There were distant postings a plenty, far islands and forsaken villages in need of imperial oversight. His enemies at court would block those with any real power, leaving Masahiro a selection of disgraceful, disreputable, or outright dangerous offices.

He swallowed, wishing Hiroshige was there to advise him. The memory of his brother prickled at the corner of Masahiro's eyes, and he glanced away, blinking rapidly. There was nothing to be done.

Or was there?

"What is known of the rebels?" Masahiro asked.

"Very little." Otose inclined her head in apology. "They killed the local Crab lord and seized the western half of the province. I can only assume they hold Five-Dragon Gate and plan to move east."

Masahiro felt his lip curl at the pretentions of peasantry. For the low to rise up risked upsetting the whole Celestial Order. Next, mortals would question their place under the gods. Truly reprehensible.

Just like that, he knew what Hiroshige would do.

Masahiro ran a hand through his hair, throat tight. It was an audacious plan, but now was not the time for meekness. Otose had bid him flee, and he would, but even in defeat he resolved to position himself for victory.

The imperial expedition could not have been overcome by mere rabble. His brother had been betrayed from within, surely. If the rebels had slain the lord, there would be succession issues. Who better than a Crane emissary to smooth the transition of power? Restore order to a province in turmoil? Recover his ancestral blade? The other clans would be grateful when Masahiro winnowed out the traitor, obligation he could leverage to rebuild his strength in court.

Like a sword pulled glowing from the forge, anger chilled to steely resolve as Masahiro gazed out into the night.

Otose cocked her head. "Where will you go?"

"Do not trouble yourself on my behalf." He patted her hand. "I know exactly where I need to be."

CHAPTER EIGHT

The funeral pyre was visible even from Shiba Irie's modest rooms – exactly as Tomiko had intended, no doubt.

Irie could hear the low, droning chant, dozens of voices imploring gods and spirits to speed Master Masatsuge's soul onto its next enlightenment. The bitter irony that they burnt a Phoenix Clan fire priest in effigy had apparently been lost on Isawa Tomiko and the other senior disciples. Such was to be expected from those who lacked the courage to even attempt to recover their master's body.

Irie did her best to ignore the travesty of a funeral. A man of refined tastes, Masatsuge would have been scandalized by such spectacle. Irie had said as much to the others, her arguments but a candle against the roaring conflagration of Tomiko's grand ambitions.

It had been Masatsuge's disregard of status that had drawn Irie to the Heaven's Blaze Dōjō. To the rest of the clan, she was but the daughter of low-rank samurai, descendant of a line of unremarkable people stretching back to the Phoenix Clan's very founding. Had it not been for Irie's ability to commune with the spirits, she might have passed her life as a road warden or sandal carrier for some petulant lordling like Isawa Tomiko.

Irie had hoped her refusal to attend might embolden others among Masatsuge's disciples, but none wished to offend Tomiko, a scion of the most powerful priestly family in all of Rokugan.

And so, Irie mourned her master alone.

She leaned close to the small brazier, as if the crackling flames might conceal some last bit of wisdom. Irie's chant might not match the power of those surrounding the distant blaze, but it was no less earnest. Incense smoke filled the small room, scents of cedar and sandalwood hanging heavy in the early summer warmth.

To anyone else, the heat would have been oppressive, but Irie sought to move beyond such concerns, to cultivate the Empty Flame.

She reached out a hand as if to stroke the small fire. The pain did not bother her. If anything, she welcomed it. As if by scorching her flesh she might somehow scour away her griefs, her doubts, her remorse.

The other disciples could not understand, would not understand. Bound by softer elements, they thought only of conciliation, rectification. Earth, air, water, void – all content to simply exist.

Fire was the only element that must be *stoked*.

Letting her hand linger over the flame, Irie implored the spirits to watch over Masatsuge's soul. They twisted around her, a brush of invisible cobwebs tickling at the edges of her perception. She selected a bit of coal from the basket, its surface polished to a glassy sheen in preparation for the ritual.

The smell of burning flesh cut through the haze of incense.

Irie blinked back tears, willing herself to move beyond the blossoming agony. She studied the coal. Reflected flames danced before her eyes. Each thread of bright fire stood stark against the mirrored surface of the coal. Centering herself, Irie sought to reach into the darkness, to seek out not the fire, but its reflection.

Just as Master Masatsuge had taught.

The Empty Flame. Light without heat. Fire without fuel. Wisdom without judgment.

To even exist, fire needed to destroy, but Master Masatsuge sought a different way, a better way. By marrying flame with void, one could summon something that would endlessly burn, an inner blaze that nothing could quench, a perfectly controlled source of power, limitless as the heavens.

Irie reached for darkness and light, cold and heat, absence and all. Only by balancing herself might she achieve such a sacred union. But, as always, she could not seem to quell the roiling blaze of her thoughts.

She should have been there. She should have died with him.

Like a candle guttering out, Irie's concentration died, leaving her pinch-faced and gasping, burnt hand clutched to her chest as the gathered spirits slipped off to their elemental tasks. Only the brazier's flame remained – small, helpless.

Just like Irie.

"You really should be more careful." Tomiko's voice cut through the swirling morass of self-recrimination.

Irie opened her eyes to see the tall, sharp-faced woman kneeling just outside the open door, half a dozen of Masatsuge's other senior disciples in tow. They were too polite to grin at Tomiko's barb, but Irie could see mirth in their eyes, reflected like firelight.

She pushed to her knees, burnt hand a tight fist at her side. "I was not informed of your intent to visit."

"My apologies." Tomiko inclined her head in a way that was not the least apologetic. "Our ritual was successful. I thought perhaps you might want some of the ash."

She produced a small, lacquered box from the sleeve of her robes and set it on the floor before Irie.

"I know it is not the master himself, but symbols are important, don't you agree?"

"I am grateful for your consideration." Irie pointedly ignored the box.

"There is a school assembly tomorrow." Tomiko spoke as if discussing flower arrangements. Unstated, was the fact that Irie had not been informed.

She breathed against the flush of anger curling up her spine. Fire possessed no loyalty. Without control, it was just as likely to burn its wielder. Irie's angry calls for action had made her no friends among the pacifist Phoenix. Nor had her low status aided Irie's cause, a sore spot Tomiko never hesitated to prod. Although Irie was Masatsuge's most senior disciple, it was unlikely the others would elect her to fill his role.

As if she could.

"If you wish, I could speak to the others." Tomiko studied a fold of her ceremonial robe. Apparently finding it not to her liking, she extended a delicate hand and pinched it back to razor sharpness.

"I would not have you trouble yourself on my account."

"Oh, it is no trouble."

Irie despised the mask of servile politeness Tomiko forced her to wear. The puffed-up Isawa might possess status and wealth, but Irie remained Masatsuge's most senior disciple.

"I could see your name added to the invitation."

As part of Tomiko's entourage, no doubt. The younger woman's ambitions burned clear as a beacon. Was it not enough the Isawa possessed the largest, most powerful school in the clan? Now they sought to suborn all others.

"No." The word slipped from Irie's mouth, seemingly conjured from deep within her.

"No?" Tomiko's full lips made a small moue of surprise. She leaned in, as if to give the appearance of privacy. "Irie, I know we have not always stood on the same ground, but this petulance is unbecoming of a senior student. What would the master say?"

Irie narrowed her eyes. Tomiko accused *her* of petulance? The conceited wretch probably couldn't even dress herself without the aid of servants.

"You are not worthy of him."

Tomiko stiffened as if Irie had slapped her. "Such crass insults do you a disservice. They bespeak a poor upbringing."

And there it was. The difference in status coiled between them like a serpent, fanged and venomous. To Tomiko, Irie was but some up-jumped soldier, little better than the guards who warded the outer chambers.

Irie let the silence stretch, lest she say something she could not take back. Perhaps mistaking her quiet for contrition, Tomiko could not help herself.

"You see." She turned to the other disciples. "For all his wisdom, Master Masatsuge's coddling has ill-prepared Irie to lead. How can we expect her to represent us if she cannot even leash her own baser impulses?"

Irie surged to her feet. Anger thrummed in her muscles, her heart beating a furious rhythm upon her ribs.

For a moment, Tomiko only stared, her mask of cool courtesy slipping to reveal shock, almost fear. Irie was the stronger priest, they both knew it. Had Tomiko faced her alone, she would have been consumed like leaves tossed into a bonfire.

But Tomiko was not alone.

The Isawa priest stood slowly, calmly, her move mirrored by the six other senior disciples.

"Did you have something to say, Shiba?"

Hate seethed in Irie's breast, but even through her rage, she knew when she was overmatched. She reached for the void, letting it fill her – anxiety, remorse, anger rendered minuscule against the endless expanse.

Something in Irie's expression must have concerned Tomiko, because the Isawa priest took a small step back, as if seeking protection in the circle of her followers.

She seemed about to speak, but whatever new barb she planned to fling died on her lips at the hurried whisper of slippers on wood.

Both Tomiko and Irie turned to see a messenger rushing along the sheltered walkway. With a bow to the other disciples, the man dropped to his knees before Irie.

"Senior disciple." He bowed low. "A visitor has arrived from the Dragon Clan. An Emerald magistrate by the name of Kitsuki Naoki. She claims business with Master Masatsuge."

"Then I must inform her of his passing." Irie could not quite conceal her relief at the interruption.

"Would you like us to accompany you?" Tomiko asked, all simpering civility once more.

"That will not be necessary." Irie took no small pleasure in dismissing the other disciples. No matter Tomiko's pretentions, Irie remained senior disciple – at least for the moment.

Without a backward glance, Tomiko turned, head high as if she expected the others to trail after her like ducklings.

They did.

Irie realized she had bared her teeth at the Isawa priest's back, and lifted a hand to conceal her tactlessness from the messenger.

"Please, take me to our guest."

The Dragon magistrate waited in Masatsuge's outer chambers. Although the servant offered to announce Irie, she dismissed him with a distracted wave, preferring to study the guest through a small gap in the screen. It was not often the Heaven's Blaze Dōjō received visitors from other clans, its remoteness and modest standing conspiring to funnel most emissaries to the more prestigious Isawa academies.

Kitsuki Naoki appeared like no Dragon Irie had ever met. Far from her clan's reputation for solemn contemplation, the magistrate seemed distinctly uncomfortable, shifting her weight from leg to leg. She was a thin woman, dark-haired and dark-eyed, her features unprepossessing enough to leave almost no imprint. The guards had relieved her of weapons, so Irie could make little guess as to her martial ability, but her robes were high quality, if travel stained.

Naoki's gaze roamed the sparse antechamber as if to slip through cracks in the old screens. Meanwhile, her fingers worked at a bit of loose thread on the hem of her sleeve, picking and pulling without regard for the fabric.

She gave a little start as Irie slid the screen aside, quickly concealing her surprise with a low bow.

"I am Shiba Irie, Master Masatsuge's senior disciple."

"Mistress Irie, thank you for meeting with me." She straightened. "I have come to speak with your master."

"Alas, I must convey ill tidings." Irie tightened against the twinge of sorrow in her own chest. "Master Masatsuge has passed on."

"Oh." Naoki seemed to wilt. "How?"

"He fell with the imperial expedition to the Twilight Mountains."

The magistrate's eyes grew wide. "They are... gone? The Dragon as well?"

"I am sorry." Irie shook her head. "I thought news had reached even the northern mountains."

"My work has kept me far from court." Naoki glanced away, a strange quirk twisting the corner of her mouth. "It is what brings me here."

"Although my master has reached his next enlightenment, perhaps I may be of assistance?"

"Perhaps." Naoki withdrew several sheets of paper from her robes, laying each flat. The first bore an imperial seal. Irie was unfamiliar with the name, but it was clear Naoki acted on behalf of the Jade Magistracy. Interest blossomed in the back of Irie's thoughts. Dragon and Phoenix had always worked closely together. The gratitude of a magistrate would do much to advance her cause among the other disciples.

The other papers looked to contain poetry, although of a baser sort, the verse somewhat crude.

"These are but copies. The originals were written in blood." Naoki folded her hands. "I search for a murderer who has killed nine Dragon officials already. I believe he means to do worse."

"How is this possible?" Irie asked, surprised by Naoki's candor. By admitting to her inability to catch the villain, she insulted both her skills and her clan.

"I believe he has unnatural aid."

"A tainted sorcerer?"

"None of our priests found any evidence of Shadowlands corruption." Naoki pursed her lips, seeming to consider her next words. Instead of speaking, she withdrew yet another sheet of paper, passing it to Irie.

The contents were strange – a rambling philosophical treatise on realms beyond the spiritual, incorporating obscure formulations and barely cogent suppositions. Irie frowned down at the page, the various details roiling in her thoughts. Although technically possible, the wild theories verged on outright heresy.

"Do you not have priests in your own clan capable of unraveling this nonsense?"

"Of course." Naoki leaned forward to indicate the name scrawled upon the outside of the letter. "But the missive is addressed to your master."

Irie glanced down, surprised. Masatsuge's blending of fire and void was considered esoteric by even the Asako family, but she had never heard him utter such outright profanity as the letter countenanced – blood sacrifices and necromantic scryings meant to pierce the veils of heaven.

"I am sorry to have wasted your time." She handed the letter back to Naoki.

"But" – the Dragon investigator chewed her lip – "I was hoping I might review some of your master's correspondence."

"That would be ... highly irregular."

"I understand," Naoki replied. "I would not ask if the situation were not so grave."

Irie fixed her with a level stare, considering. The investigator seemed to be the sort to cause trouble. Masatsuge had no direct kin, and no heir. Although the master's effects were technically

Irie's to disburse or destroy, that would change if Tomiko was selected to lead Heaven's Blaze. The ambitious Isawa would not balk for a moment at making Masatsuge's letters public, especially if it might win her allies.

Better for Irie to allow Naoki access, if only to keep an eye on the investigator.

"Come with me." She turned, sliding open the door to Masatsuge's inner study.

Even now, the sight of the room burned like a fresh brand. Unprepossessing as Masatsuge himself, the room was unadorned, stone columns, woven mats, and richly burnished cedar panels without embellishment. Irie had spent many happy days here, poring over her master's writings or kneeling at his feet as she basked in the ageless wisdom of a true scholar.

Irie gestured Naoki forward, afraid her voice would crack should she speak.

The investigator slipped into the room, eyes sharp as she scanned the meager furnishings. A writing desk, several wall scrolls, a futon rolled in one corner, a chest of robes, and several small shelves bearing a profusion of books and scrolls. It was to this last Naoki went, running her finger along the spines as she mouthed the titles.

"Foundational texts on the elements." Irie joined her by the shelves. "Many written by Master Masatsuge himself."

"Would any contain similar theories to the letter?"

Irie felt her lip curl. "Of course not. My master pushed the bounds of knowledge, but he did not veer into blasphemy."

"Apologies, I meant no insult." Naoki inclined her head. "And your master's letters?"

"Here." Irie pointed to a heavy cedar chest.

"So few."

"He was not given to correspondence." She watched carefully as Naoki knelt to open the chest, sifting through the few dozen letters with increasing consternation.

"There is nothing here from the man I seek."

"I am sorry."

Naoki frowned at the chest, nudging it with her hand. It rocked on uneven legs, if only slightly.

"Master was never one for embellishment," Irie replied. "Simple tools for simple tasks, his mind occupied by weightier issues."

Naoki hunkered down. "It is not the chest. The floor is uneven."

"The dōjō is quite old."

"Would you help me?" Naoki made as if to shift the chest. Frowning, Irie joined her, and together they moved the heavy weight. Almost immediately, Naoki dropped to her hands and knees, picking at the corner of the woven bamboo mat.

Irie moved to stop her. "Please refrain from–"

Naoki managed to hook a finger under the mat, lifting it with a strained grunt.

Below was another chest, concealed within the heavy stone foundations. Irie blinked at the concealed vault, unable to hide her surprise. Master Masatsuge had never been given to keeping secrets.

"Would you help me?" Naoki said again, reaching down.

Slowly, Irie got to her knees. She felt as if she should have some explanation for the strange chest, but curiosity had kindled a fire in her hands.

With a bit of effort, they were able to lift the dusty chest from its hole. Made of dark, heavy wood banded with strips of rusted iron, it was unadorned save for a heavy lock – a strange affair of interlocking bits of red and black steel. There was no keyhole.

"We could break it open," Naoki said.

"That would bring the guards running." Irie shook her head, suddenly self-conscious. "And if Masatsuge has enchanted the chest, trying to force it open might destroy the contents."

"Shall we bring it to the other disciples?"

"No!" Irie's answer surprised even her. "If it was Masatsuge's, then it is now mine."

She bent to the lock, inspecting the strange webwork of colored steel. There was enchantment involved, of that she was sure. She had but to touch the metal to feel the thrum of power through the lock – the black strips of steel cold as ice, the red almost hot to the touch.

Fire and void.

The answer came in Masatsuge's voice, careworn and familiar. Irie swallowed against the thickness in her throat. Whatever the chest contained, her master had wanted it hidden. It felt like a betrayal to paw through his personal effects in the presence of an outsider, but Naoki had already seen the chest. Better for Irie to open it here, in private, than for the magistrate to make an issue for the entire dōjō.

"I believe I can unlock it." Kneeling, she placed her hands upon the lock, voice slipping into the intricate ritual chants necessary to entreat the spirits. Slowly, they responded to her call. One hand glowing with a warm inner light, the other lost in shadow. At Irie's touch, the lock unwove. Like fingers unlacing, it spread supplicating hands to Irie.

With a nod, she opened the chest.

There were perhaps a dozen letters inside, all written in the archaic, rounded hand of the murderer Naoki sought. More, the chest contained a theater mask. Lacquered in swirling patterns of gold and crimson, it was inscribed with strange characters. Unlike any script she had ever seen, they seemed almost to flow like high clouds across the cheeks and forehead. Although the mask wore no expression, Irie could not quite dispel the unsettling notion it was grinning at her.

Naoki went for the letters, but Irie was drawn to the mask. It seemed strange her master would hide such a relic away – perhaps it was dangerous, or cursed. Carefully, she examined the mask, but could find no hint of corruption. It seemed to vibrate in Irie's hands, radiating power, a roiling vortex of spiritual energy constrained by nets of careful enchantment.

Irie must have gasped, because Naoki looked up from her letters. "What is that script?"

"Names, I think. But not mortal ones." Irie turned the mask over in her hand. "I have heard of this. The Unicorn call it name magic, spirit binding. One of the more eccentric practices they brought back from foreign lands. Rather than entreat the spirits, practitioners of name magic seek out their true name, binding them to talismans and charms."

"How is that possible?"

"Names have power, especially in the Spirit Realms," Irie replied. "To speak a spirit's name is to call it, to claim their name compels obedience." She gave an uncomfortable frown. "It is a troubling practice."

"There are spirits... in there?" Naoki thrust her chin at the mask.

"Yes." Irie slipped it into the sleeve of her robe. "Master Masatsuge traveled widely in his younger days. He must have acquired it from the Unicorn."

"Indeed." Naoki frowned, lifting the parcel of letters. "But what about these?"

"Even my master cannot control who seeks to contact him."

"Then why keep the letters?"

"I cannot say." Irie shook her head, misliking the magistrate's line of questioning. Who was Naoki to insinuate the corruption of a Phoenix master? The magistrate had not even *known* Masatsuge.

Irie kept her expression calm, jaw tight against the upswell of fury that colored her cheeks. "Perhaps he sought to unmask the murderer?"

Naoki scanned a letter. "I am no expert in spiritual matters, but this appears to be a conversation. There is mention of the Twilight Mountains, a place of power. Is that not where the rebellion rages? Perhaps your master joined the expedition to investigate–"

"You will go. Now." Irie pushed to her feet, anger hot in her cheeks.

"I am afraid I cannot." Naoki gave a helpless shrug. "These are important evidence. They must be examined, catalogued."

For a brief moment, Irie considered setting the letters aflame. It would take only the slightest touch of a fire spirit to destroy the evidence of her master's potential heresy. She could not accept that Masatsuge would have corresponded with a creature such as the one Naoki sought. Let the magistrate call her a liar – without the letters there would be no proof.

"What are you doing?" Tomiko stepped into the inner study, frowning at Naoki and Irie.

The Dragon investigator made to speak, but Irie held up a hand.

"Master had friends among many clans. Magistrate Naoki sought some correspondence he had written to a Dragon Clan elder." The lie came almost too quickly.

Naoki cocked her head. Irie glanced at her, expression studiously blank, eyes pleading.

"I believe I have found what I am searching for." Naoki hefted the small folio, then turned to bow to Irie. "I am in your debt, mistress."

Irie inclined her head. "Shall I walk you out?"

"Please." Naoki nodded.

Tomiko's lips formed a thin, suspicious line, but there was little she could say, at least until Irie was removed. She stepped from the doorway with a bow, gaze never leaving the two.

Together they walked from the study.

"Thank you." Irie took Naoki's arm, guiding her along one of the older walkways.

"Who was that?" Naoki asked.

"Someone who would very much like to destroy me," Irie said. "But that is irrelevant. You cannot make those letters public. They could ruin my master's reputation."

"But I must return them to the Dragon Clan." Naoki shook her head. "There might be some clue as to–"

Irie gripped her shoulder. "By the time you return, the murderer could strike again. Is it not better you examine the letters yourself?"

Naoki shook free of her grip, eyes suddenly wary. "What do you mean?"

"I can help you decipher the theories." Irie's words came in a sudden torrent. "Search the text for valuable information. They speak of danger in Crab lands – I could accompany you. I am Masatsuge's senior disciple. If anyone can understand what he saw in your killer's ravings, it is me."

Naoki frowned. "This is highly irregular."

"Please." Irie spread her arms. "Masatsuge was a kind man,

a wise man. You must give me the opportunity to clear his name."

Naoki's throat bobbed. She studied Irie, eyes sharp as if to pierce the very heart of her. After a long moment, the investigator sighed. "Perhaps your insights *could* be of use."

"I am in your debt." Irie bowed deeply. "Truly."

"We travel south." Naoki looked her up and down. "Gather your things. There will be plenty of time on the road to study the letters."

"Yes, of course." Irie realized she was trembling like a new initiate and took a breath to steady herself. As if summoned by her attempt at calm, anxieties bubbled through the cracks in her resolve.

She squeezed her eyes shut. Departing the dōjō would essentially cede authority to Tomiko. Although the thought needled her, it was nothing compared to the censure they would all face if it was were discovered that their master dabbled in dark sorcery.

Irie could not believe Masatsuge guilty of such blasphemy. They would find evidence of his innocence, of that she was confident. Then she could return to Heaven's Blaze a hero, having preserved the good name of one of its most prominent scholars.

Irie opened her eyes, straightening. "I will require a half hour to gather my traveling gear. Then another to meet with Tomiko."

Naoki quirked a brow. "The disciple who wishes to destroy you?"

Irie smiled through her blush of anger. As distasteful as it was, she did what must be done – for Masatsuge, for the school.

"Tomiko will smooth over any ill feelings better than I ever could."

"And why would she do that?"

Irie turned away. "Because what I am about to say will make her very happy."

CHAPTER NINE

The two young warriors sweated and strained, muscles trembling as they sought to force their opponent to the ground. Matsu Chiaki could think of a dozen throws that would send one or the other tumbling, but it was not time to interfere.

Neither student was ready to learn.

With a cry of triumph, the larger grappler managed to bull her opponent to the trampled dirt of the training field. They hit the ground hard, limbs twisting as they scrambled for position.

Chiaki didn't wait to see who came out on top. Calmly, she stepped up to the struggling pair and pretended to slit both their throats.

"Dead. Dead."

Red-faced and puffing, they sprawled back, expressions caught midway between chagrin and anger.

"In battle, you never face a single opponent." Chiaki thrust her wooden practice sword back into her sash. "To manifest a duelist's focus is to blind yourself to a thousand other threats. Strength falters, muscles tire, the body weakens..."

Chiaki resisted the urge to rub her own aching knees. She had sat too long, inactivity creeping over her joints like morning frost. Although Chiaki was fit for a woman of nearly seventy winters, her bones remembered their age.

"In grappling, as in battle, the goal is to down your opponent quickly, expending the minimum of energy." Chiaki stepped between the panting students, helping both to their feet before turning to regard the rest of her class.

"What did Hisa do wrong?"

There were no answers, but she hadn't expected any. A score of broad-shouldered Matsu youths knelt before her, still fresh from their coming-of-age ceremonies. They may have spent their lives studying battle, but they did not yet possess the wisdom to survive it.

That was, if survival equated to wisdom. Even after all these years, Chiaki wasn't sure.

"Here." She stepped in to grasp Hisa, mimicking the position she and her opponent had held just a moment earlier. Accustomed to hands-on instruction, Hisa gave little resistance as Chiaki moved.

"They fought chest-to-chest, arm-to-arm, strength-to-strength." Chiaki surreptitiously hooked a foot behind Hisa's heel. "But there are other ways."

With a sharp twist, she drove her hip into Hisa's midsection. Breaking the larger woman's balance, she sent her tumbling to the ground. Hisa went with the throw, making it easier for Chiaki to toss her. Head-over-heels she hit the earth with a hard slap.

Chiaki was grateful for the assistance. Once, she could have broken Hisa like a dry twig, but skill could only take you so far. Had the bigger woman resisted, Chiaki might have been forced to resort to techniques more painful for both of them.

"Always fight at an advantage." She straightened with the

smallest of winces. "Hands are stronger than fingers, legs stronger than arms, bodies stronger than limbs."

Although none of the students questioned her, Chiaki could feel their discomfort. They had been trained in Matsu family schools, steeped in tales of glorious demise.

"Strength, valor, sacrifice – those are the Matsu way," she continued. "Few enemies can stand against a warrior who has accepted death. Is this not what your masters have taught you?"

This was met with nods from the assembled students.

"They did not lie." Chiaki took a slow breath. "But is it not better to win *without* dying?"

A tentative hand raised near the back of the group. "Mistress, the Lion Clan stands upon the shoulders of the Matsu family. We must never relent, never falter. Only–"

"Only death releases a samurai from duty," Chiaki finished the old parable, unable to blame the students for their single-mindedness. Their masters had taught them how to die well. Now, it fell to Chiaki to teach them how not to die poorly.

With a sigh, she regarded her students – her final class, although they did not know it. Her gaze drifted up, beyond the dōjō walls, to the ancient spreading boughs of the wide-boled camphor.

"That will be all for today." She gestured toward the barracks.

Bowing, her students departed.

"Thank you for your assistance, Hisa," Chiaki said as the large student took her leave.

"Sano, mistress."

"I'm sorry?"

"My name is Sano." She bowed to soften the disagreement. "Hisa was my mother's name."

Hisa. Yes. She had taken a Unicorn arrow to the ribs at the Battle of Singing Vale, then cut down six more enemy riders before the fight was over, including their one-eyed chieftain – ripped him right from his horse to drown in the crimson waters of the river valley.

None of which had saved Hisa when the wound festered.

The clan elders had called it a border skirmish, hardly worth mentioning let alone recording. Chiaki always meant to go back to see what the Lion had done with the river valley, but was afraid she might find it empty.

"Of course, of course. My apologies." Chiaki dipped her head, throat uncomfortably knotted.

"Thank you for your instruction, mistress." Sano rapped a fist against her breastplate in a warrior's salute. "Can I assist you back to your quarters?"

"I am not *that* old." Chiaki waved Sano away with a wry smile. She made her way across the practice field, head high, pace deliberate but surefooted. Chiaki had seen elderly monks, backs bent, heads bowed as they shuffled forward on the arms of their disciples. She would never be that old.

To be fair, she had never expected to be *this* old.

Her satchel was packed, her blades cleaned and oiled. Chiaki had never been one for trophies, the walls of her modest chambers decorated with the same paintings and wall scrolls they had boasted when she had come to the dōjō two decades ago, retired from a lustrous career in the Lion army, her reputation hard as steel.

Chiaki studied her old battle armor. Arrayed upon a stand of burnished oak, it still gleamed bright as the day the clan champion had bestowed it upon her. She pressed a hand to her midsection, frowning. Now, Chiaki's reputation was the only hard thing about her. Of all the enemies she had faced, her own body was the most cruel.

She ran quiet fingers along the crested helmet. Better to leave it all. The flash would only draw attention.

Calmly, she crossed the practice field to the dōjō armory. It stood empty, dinner having drawn all the students to the great hall. Frowning, Chiaki selected a scarred breastplate and pauldrons, a woven battle skirt without marking, and a solid iron helm, its steel dull and lusterless, battered almost shapeless in a thousand battles.

Just like Chiaki.

Her horse was already saddled. She often went for sunset rides, galloping across the wide fields surrounding the dōjō, the wind in her hair, wild cries snatched from breathless lips. Sometimes, if she rode fast enough, it was as if she had left all the aches behind. For a moment, it was almost possible to pretend she charged toward battle, comrades behind her – but only for a moment.

Chiaki's comrades were dead and burned long ago. Her enemies, too.

Truthfully, she could not say which saddened her more.

The gate guards ushered her past with respectful nods. They would have been children when Chiaki had last faced true battle. She did not glance back as her horse trotted from the shadow of the high walls. Although she regretted leaving her students, the dōjō held nothing for her, if it ever had. Like an ill-fitting suit of armor, the role of master had always chafed, only growing worse over the years. Despite the respect and status it carried, Chiaki could never seem to squeeze herself into the position.

Still, she could not help but pause at the old camphor, the

dirt around it packed and grassless, its bark scarred by years of futile determination. How many bull-headed Matsu youths had beaten themselves bloody on its unmoving bulk? Chiaki couldn't quite remember.

She greeted the tree like an old friend – the two of them made a fine pair after all. It may have been wishful thinking, but Chiaki thought she detected the slightest ripple of wind shifting the ancient branches. As if the tree were nodding farewell.

Smile tight, she turned her horse. Only to find a pair of burly Matsu samurai blocking the road. Ten years ago, they would have never gotten the drop on her, but that was ten years ago.

"You depart without your lord's leave?" Daimyo Matsu Akoya stepped from behind the broad cedar, her arms crossed, her careworn face tight with anger.

"I owe you no fealty." Chiaki reined in her mount. As master of the dōjō, she was technically outside Akoya's purview, but such distinctions might mean little to a prickly lord.

"I am not here as your lord, but as an old comrade." Akoya's reply came clipped and stern.

Chiaki clucked her tongue. "Here to chide me?"

"Here to *help*, you grizzled beast."

"How did you know I meant to leave?" Chiaki asked.

"You are not so clever as you think, old woman." Akoya's severe expression was spoiled by a slight uptick at the corner of her lips. "You should have told me."

"And have you send warriors? Tramping through the woods, snorting and stamping like boars. They'd bring every rebel in a dozen miles down on our heads." Chiaki glanced at the two guards. "No offense."

Unlike their lord, the samurai's scowls did not shift a hair.

"Katamori was my nephew."

"And *my* student." Chiaki left the rest unstated. Akoya knew how much pride she had taken in watching Katamori rise through the ranks. He had been the best of them, a Matsu general the equal of any Akodo strategist – strong in mind, body, and spirit. To have such a promising career cut short by treachery was the basest, most vulgar insult.

Akoya inclined her head to the dōjō. "What of your responsibility to them?"

"I have trained the other instructors well enough. I doubt the students will miss my sharp tongue."

"You might be surprised who misses you." With a soft smile, Akoya ran a hand through her hair. By the ancestors, when had it become so gray? Chiaki still remembered her as an unblooded captain, doubts poorly hidden behind a veneer of brazen bluster.

"I couldn't have a dozen young fools tromping after me. They are even worse than samurai." Chiaki nodded to the guards. "No offense."

Akoya drew in a deep breath. "I could stop you."

"You would have to break my legs." Chiaki leaned forward in her saddle, trying for a softer tone. "You know as well as I the Lion elders will not move. The rebellion is distant from our lands, and with the court in turmoil and rumors of treachery among the clans, we cannot risk dispatching a force so far away."

"The emperor may call upon us once again."

"The Son of Heaven is not long for the mortal world. It was a wonder he ordered the first expedition." Chiaki let the words hang. Although true, it boded ill to speak poorly of any emperor, even one as ineffectual as Hantei XXVI.

Akoya gave a thin-lipped nod, acknowledging, if not necessarily condoning Chiaki's remark.

"I must avenge Katamori," Chiaki said, hating her high, old-woman's voice. Once, her words had made lords tremble. Now, they sounded weak, almost pleading. "If it *was* betrayal, then I will unmask the traitor."

Akoya regarded her, arms still crossed. They both knew the only thing Chiaki was likely to discover was a hard and bloody death.

Then again, that was the point.

"Please," Chiaki said. "I cannot…"

She swallowed against the sudden hoarseness in her voice. The thought of spending another day, another *hour* wasting away amidst the dōjō's high-gabled armories and practice halls filled Chiaki with a misery she could not articulate. Doomed to usher class after class of fresh warriors onto the battlefield, their youth a constant reminder of all she had lost.

Throat tight, she gestured back toward her dōjō, her prison. "I simply *cannot*."

Akoya raised a hand, and one of the guards stepped forward. For a moment, Chiaki thought he was going to drag her from her horse. She turned her mount, forcing him back a step. Chiaki might not be able to match the man in strength, but she could certainly make him regret laying hands on her.

Instead of reaching for her bridle, he withdrew a small sheaf of papers from his breastplate.

"Travel documents," Akoya said, when Chiaki did not immediately take them. "They will see you safely through any guard post in Lion lands, and beyond if the local lords still obey imperial law. Just see you present yourself. I will not have it said our warriors skulk about like Scorpion thieves."

"I will." Chiaki took the documents, stashing them away in her saddlebags.

"Are you sure you wish to travel alone?" Akoya asked. "Even a few warriors might ease your journey."

"I am certain."

Akoya stepped forward, reaching up to clasp Chiaki's forearm in a warrior's grip. "May the ancestors watch over you, old master."

"And you, lord." Chiaki turned her horse away, kicking it into a canter. Farewells had always made her uncomfortable. She had become a blade long sheathed, her edge dull, her joints gone rusty from disuse. It felt good to ride toward battle, to have an enemy, again.

She would make the rebels regret rising up against their rightful lord. And if one of the great clans were behind the revolt, she would winnow out the truth or die in the attempt.

In truth, Chiaki didn't know which outcome would comfort her more.

CHAPTER TEN

Iuchi Qadan screamed. Not a bark of pain, nor a shout of rage, but a high, triumphant roar that burst from her throat like a stampede. She ran her fingers across the ancient stone door, hands tingling from the wild exhalations. After years of combing through dusty archives, months picking over the unkind peaks of the Twilight Mountains, dodging bandits, feral spirits, and the occasional Crab Clan patrol, at last, she had actually found the tomb.

"Careful, careful." Moto Jargal's customary smile flickered. Her bodyguard clicked his tongue, extending one callused hand as if he were attempting to calm a bucking colt.

"This has to be it." Qadan turned on him, still not quite able to catch her breath. "Archaic etchings, local stone, it even bears the Ki-Rin crest!"

She gestured toward the shapeless carving on the door.

"Looks like a buffalo to me." Jargal raised an eyebrow, seemingly unconvinced. He shook his head, blew a puff of air out his nose. "I just don't want to see you disappointed again."

"I won't be." Qadan pressed her palms against the door, as if she might move it through sheer force of will. "This is it. This is Shinjo Kantaro's tomb, I can *feel* it."

Jargal shrugged, leather armor creaking. "I'll get the workers on it."

"Tell them to be careful." Qadan squeezed her eyes shut. "My spirits did not detect any wards, but the ways of the ancients are powerful and mysterious. To think, this tomb might have been sealed by Iuchi himself."

"I'll keep an eye on them." With a bow, he turned back toward camp, his walk the peculiar rolling gait of those long to the saddle.

Qadan reached for her talismans. Nascent energy tingled up her arm as she rummaged through the collection of medallions, charms, and carefully sculpted jewels. Some seemed to twinkle with an inner light, the bound spirits almost visible in the early morning gloom. Others appeared wholly mundane, their power quiescent until called upon. There were those among the other clans who thought of name magic as foreign sorcery, that its priests profaned the elements by binding spirits within talismans. They did not understand. Rather than supplicate themselves before the elements, name magicians sought deeper understanding, a relationship in harmony with the arcane. It took more than ritual and petition to earn a spirit's true name.

It took trust.

Qadan took slow breaths, willing her heart back to calm as she whispered Gion's name. It had been a difficult rapport to build – spirits of earth and stone always proved hesitant to move, at least at first. The true challenge was getting them to stop.

Carefully, she asked the spirit to reach into the stone, feeling for the otherworldly tremors that would presage some manner of arcane warding. When Gion replied, it was not with a voice but rather a vibration. It traveled up Qadan's questing hands, her skull seeming to rumble with the low, sonorous response.

She frowned, drawing a circle of delicately woven silk from her satchel. Eruar, her first, the familiar name spilled easily from her lips. A spirit of air, they swirled about the door, seeking the smallest crack. Finding none, Eruar ruffled Qadan's hair, then slipped down to tug at the drawstring of the satchel.

Sweat beaded Qadan's brow as she implored the spirits to work together. Name became form, word became deed. She had hoped they might be able to impart some sense of the tomb's size and layout, but again, the spirits found nothing.

It was as if the tomb simply didn't exist. If not for the ancient door set into the side of the rocky overhang, Qadan might have believed them.

She stepped back, shaking her head. There were no wards barring entrance, no curses poised to strike down thieves. No spirits watched over the tomb, and yet it remained stubbornly resistant to Qadan's scrutiny.

Which only made her *more* excited to see what was inside.

Metal scraped on stone. She turned to see Jargal leading a few dozen laborers up the low switchback. Although the Crab Clan may have granted permission to search for ancient Unicorn tombs, their grudging acquiescence did not extend to actual aid. Qadan had been lucky to find even this many workers so far from civilization. The foothills of the Twilight Mountains were a rugged affair, cold and sharp as the people who inhabited them. Although they owed only nominal loyalty to the Crab, the laborers certainly possessed their lords' hard-eyed parsimony. With the western portion of the province in open revolt, Qadan had parted with far more coin than she would have liked to hire even these.

Despite their tattered clothes, the laborers seemed sturdy enough, peeling back the layers of earth and debris to slowly reveal the heavy stone door. Qadan paced back and forth like a wild stallion confined to a pen for the first time.

For his part, Jargal stretched out on a nearby shelf of rock and began to whittle, whistling some refrain he had picked up in the drinking halls of Khanbulak. It nettled Qadan that he could be so calm. But then, the Moto samurai hadn't spent years poring over ancient documents, weaving tattered threads of myth and legend into something tangible.

This wasn't just any tomb, it was the tomb of Shinjo Kantaro. A follower of the divine sibling Shinjo, he had been slain during the battle against the fallen god Fu Leng. For his valor, Kantaro had been posthumously adopted by Shinjo herself, his remains interred before the Ki-Rin Clan had begun its great exodus from the Empire. Qadan's heart pounded at the thought of what relics the tomb might contain. It was a window into the past, a priceless glimpse of what her people had been before the long, arduous journey shaped them into the Unicorn Clan.

Unable to restrain herself, Qadan tied back the sleeves of her robe and took up a shovel.

"Careful, mistress. The rock is treacherous." One of the workers stepped aside as she joined the line. Although clothed in shapeless gray robes, he had the look of an itinerant priest, face wrinkled as a dried persimmon, white eyebrows sprinkled with dirt and dust from the work. As if to punctuate his warning, some of the gravel shifted beneath Qadan's feet, and he caught her arm.

Nodding her thanks, Qadan found her balance and began

to shovel away centuries of debris that had built up around the tomb. She knew she should be conserving her strength. They had ridden for days, crossing from Unicorn, to Scorpion, and finally to Crab lands at speeds that would have given an imperial courier pause. With the imperial expedition defeated and the rebels holding Five-Dragon Gate, it was only a matter of time until the revolt pushed east and Qadan lost her chance.

A wave of queasiness bubbled up from Qadan's stomach. She blinked away the vertigo, surreptitiously glancing over to where Jargal sat. Her bodyguard seemed oblivious, attention focused on the wooden horse that was rapidly taking shape in his rough hands. Qadan slipped a hand down to her satchel, feeling for the nest of woven sticks that housed Kahenu, her fire spirit. The talisman left streaks of ash upon her fingers, scorched wood coarse against Qadan's palm, but as she whispered the spirit's true name, she felt a flush of hot energy course through her, muscles twitching as her heartbeat quickened.

"You promised you wouldn't do that again, mistress." Jargal's voice caused her to jump. How had he crept up so quickly?

"One last time." Qadan gave a helpless nod toward the tomb door. "We're *here*, Jargal. If I'm right, there will be time to sleep afterward."

Jargal sucked air through his teeth. "Sit down at least. This lot seem to be making good progress."

With the efficiency of lifelong miners, the laborers had cleared most of the rock away, piling dirt near the lip of the overhang, levering the boulders from their resting places to send them tumbling back down the rocky slope.

With a nod, Qadan allowed Jargal to guide her back to the flat shelf of rock. After seeing her comfortably settled upon a deer-hide blanket, he went back to whittling.

Qadan only meant to close her eyes for a moment. When she opened them, the sun was high in the sky, long shadows dwindling to tiny splotches beneath the feet of the workers. In a few minutes, Lord Sun would pass over the mountain, swathing the east-facing cavern in afternoon gloom.

Standing, Qadan scrubbed a hand over her face, her joints sore, her thoughts still fogged from sleep.

"You could do with another few hours of that, mistress," Jargal said without looking up.

"Later." Qadan waved absently at him, her gaze fixed upon the door.

Apart from a few stubborn rocks at the base, the workers had almost cleared it. Qadan threaded between the straining laborers, lips pursed as she looked up at the carvings.

Despite the shelter of the overhang, the etchings had become almost illegible in the millennia since they were first carved. Qadan caught up a torch from one of the makeshift brackets and held it so the shadows fell across the lower carvings.

She could just make out the soft curves of classical text, the style familiar, if not the characters themselves. Lips moving, she ran trembling fingers along the ancient carvings, too faint to decipher. The ones inside would be better protected.

With an echoing crack, the last boulder fell away. Qadan drew in breath to bid the workers take care, but she found she needn't speak. With the reverence of priests unveiling a sacred object, they worked long steel pry bars into the lip of stone, feet churning the loose gravel as they levered the great door open.

Qadan held her torch high, illuminating the round tunnel cut into the rock. Featureless except for the mark of ancient pick and shovel, it delved back into promising shadow. Qadan was seized by the sudden urge to dash inside, her muscles trembling with excitement. So little remained from before the Unicorn Exodus; such a find as this would be a great boon to her clan.

"Shall we?" Jargal stepped to her side, torch in hand.

Qadan gestured the workers back, blinking against the sudden sting of tears. This was it. She could feel it in her bones.

Together, they followed the tunnel, which extended perhaps forty meters into the solid rock. Qadan frowned at the walls. She had expected carvings, bas reliefs, some paintings at the very least. But the walls were unadorned, their wide expanse barren but for a series of strange linear gouges that gave the tunnel an odd, fluted quality. Together with the roundness of the passage itself, Qadan felt almost as if she were walking down the throat of some massive, petrified beast.

The tunnel leveled, and they found themselves in a central chamber. At last, the torchlight revealed carvings, although not nearly so many as Qadan had hoped. Despite having been constructed long before the Empire began burning its dead, the chamber was empty.

A hollow opened in the pit of her stomach. It seemed impossible that tomb robbers could have found the crypt, let alone breached the door. And yet it seemed the place had been raided.

Jargal shook his shaggy head. "Mistress, I–"

Qadan waved him to silence, not trusting herself to respond. It was a blow, yes. But she had found the tomb when no one else could. Turning away so Jargal could not see her tears, she squatted to examine the carvings on the rear wall.

Far better preserved than those on the door, they were a mix of words and images. Rather than the rounded edges of classical characters, the words were sharp, almost angular.

"This was written around the time of the Unicorn's return." She gestured at the script. "This style was popular a few centuries ago."

"Who would build such a thing?" Jargal turned to regard the vaulted ceiling. "The Crab?"

Qadan shook her head. "They possess the architectural ability, although certainly not a predilection for elaborate burials."

She squinted at the words, which described a long trek through the jungle, encounters with ravening beasts and local tribes, the exploration of hidden valleys, ancient temples, an army ravaged by terrible disease and unknown curses.

"Impossible." The word slipped from Qadan's lips.

"What is it, mistress?"

Qadan ignored the question. Bending close, she reread the lines, unable to believe what they said.

"This describes the journey of the Green Horde."

"But they never returned," Jargal said. "Lost in the vast jungles of the south."

"According to this, some came back." Qadan indicated a carving which depicted a small group of riders, framed by strange, long-leafed trees. Led by Iuchi, a powerful spiritualist and disciple of the divine sibling Shinjo, the Green Horde was one of the five armies that departed Rokugan during the Ki-Rin Clan's ancient exodus.

"How is that possible?" Jargal asked. "How could the Unicorn not know of this?"

"I cannot say." Qadan followed the story, which showed the green riders constructing this tomb – no, not a tomb, a reliquary.

"There is more, but it is concealed." Neck tingling, Qadan

drew forth her talismans, calling upon her various spirits to illuminate and reveal. The walls glittered as if studded with buried gems, spiritual sigils burning with a pale, heatless flame.

"What is it?" Jargal asked, open mouthed.

"A name." Qadan's voice broke. "A true name."

"Mistress, I don't–"

The arrow took Jargal in the throat.

Qadan blinked as her bodyguard wheeled, dragging his blade from its hide sheath even as he choked on blood.

A dozen shadowed forms stood just beyond the circle of torchlight. Some carried bows, others axes and picks. Their expressions were cold as stone, eyes like dark smudges in faces steeped in cruel regard. They moved with calm surety, silent as they spread out to surround the chamber. Such was the change in their manner and bearing, Qadan might not have recognized the workers if not for their dirty, dust-stained clothes.

She shook her head as if to deny the sudden violence. It made no sense. The laborers had been paid well, with more promised upon Qadan's return to Unicorn lands. Perhaps they thought the tomb held ancient treasures? With a silent snarl, Qadan swept the questions from her thoughts.

It did not matter *why* her workers had turned bandit, only that they had.

With a gurgling shout, Jargal charged the two workers nearest the door. They moved to meet him, but even mortally wounded, the Moto samurai's blade was quicker than sunlight. He cut the chest of the first, ducking the second's axe to drive his blade up and into the traitor's murderous heart.

"Mistress, go!" The words were almost unintelligible, but Jargal's plan was clear enough as he lowered his shoulder and bulled aside a charging worker. The path to the door was clear.

Qadan took one quick step, flinching back as an arrow slashed past her face.

Bellowing like a wounded ox, Jargal tackled the archer, only to have two more attackers leap upon him. They struggled on the ground, a mass of blood-slicked shadows.

Qadan drew forth her burnt-stick talisman, Kahenu's secret name springing to her lips. Fire filled the air, a twining serpent that sent two of the attackers reeling back, robes alight, their hair limned in brilliant flame. Even dying, they made no sound, the chamber empty but for the crackle of fire and the stink of burning flesh.

Snarling, Qadan made to turn Kahenu upon the others, only to see the spirit flicker and fade.

"Enough of that." One of the workers stepped forward. A slash of his wrinkled hand sent the flame spirit slipping back to its talisman.

Qadan tried to summon it once more but could not seem to find the words. It was as if a cold hand had closed about her throat, squeezing the life from her voice. There was a flash of light, a sense of cold pressure at Qadan's side. She glanced down to see oily smoke rising from her satchel. It seemed impossible, but somehow her talismans burned. Qadan tried to beat out the pale flames, but found she could not move.

"Your spirits cannot aid you now." She recognized the elderly worker by his bow-legged walk, but that was the only familiar thing about him. He moved like a stalking spider, each jerky motion imbued with deadly purpose. A necklace of bone dripped from his right hand, the circular tokens tugging at Qadan's gaze. She recognized them as talismans, but of a strange, ill-fortuned sort. There was no sense of elemental force about the necklace, no hint of earth, fire, air, water, or even void. Name magic, but frighteningly twisted, it roiled with a cruel and terrible power, the air about it seeming to shift as if in a heat mirage.

The old man glanced about the tomb, posture changing to one of distinct irritation.

"Not the one." He grunted. "Pity."

Qadan's lips moved in a ward against corruption, but the little man only chuckled.

"You take me for a cheap conjurer? Some fawning servant of a vile and petulant god?" He spread his arms like a performer basking in applause. "I bow to no one."

A furious grunt from Jargal caught both their attention. Impossibly, the Moto samurai had shaken off his attackers. Painfully, he struggled to his feet, wobbling on unsteady legs as he threw himself at the dark priest.

The little man skipped back. Raising his bone talismans, he shouted a name that blistered the air. One moment, Jargal was running, stocky legs pumping as he reached for the murderous monk, then he was gone. It was as if the air simply folded around him, as if he had slipped through a crack in reality itself.

With a scream of wounded rage, Qadan charged. Her furious rush caught the little priest off balance, sending him careening from the rear wall of the chamber. Out of the corner of her eye, she could see other laborers moving.

There was a flash of bright pain as an arrow sank into her upper shoulder.

"Alive!" the monk shouted. "I need her alive for the seeking ritual!"

If they heard, the laborers gave no sign, advancing on her with weapons raised.

Names spilled from Qadan's lips as she backed away, one

hand raised. But her spirits had departed, their talismans destroyed, along with their trust in Qadan. Somehow, the horrid little monk had severed her bonds.

Hard stone pressed against Qadan's back, a circle of bandits slowly closing. Without her spirits, without her names, Qadan had no hope of overcoming so many. Her desperate gaze flicked around the chamber, searching for something, anything.

Like stars in shadowed firmament, the strange symbols glittered on the vaulted roof. Qadan drew in a deep breath. The little monk may have stricken her names, but there were others.

It was like plunging her face into oil. Slick and viscous, the strange name rolled off Qadan's tongue, seeming to cling to her like an insect.

A shadow shifted behind the swirling dark, not within the stone, but somehow *outside* it. Qadan had the feeling of a great, ponderous shape, turning to regard her. Like a deep-sea leviathan, its merest movement set ripples through the air.

Qadan felt something press into her hand. Sharp as broken glass, it cut into the flesh of her palm, her fingers suddenly slick with blood as its name burned in her thoughts.

"Take me from here!" she shouted.

The monk flung out a clawed hand, but it was too late.

Space seemed to flex and bend, the heavy stone above parting like dusty curtains. Qadan did not move so much as stretch, her body slipping through the unyielding rock, reality stretched tight as a drumhead as she slid along an unnatural seam.

There was a moment of profound disorientation, a feeling as if Qadan had been turned inside out. The strange spirit's name burned itself into her thoughts, her blood, her bones, etching itself into every part of her even as the bladed talisman chilled her hand to the bone.

Still screaming, Qadan found herself back at camp. The afternoon sun hung low overhead, the air heavy and warm. A half-dozen horses placidly cropped scrub near the circle of felt tents. One raised its head to regard her, chewing.

Qadan drew in a deep shuddering breath, seeming to slip back into herself.

A furious howl echoed down the mountain. "I will inscribe the walls with your blood!"

Moving quickly, she untethered the horses. Taking her horse, Marrow, and Jargal's stocky bay mare, she sent the others running off with shouts and slaps. Rocks skittered on the slopes above, shadows already visible against the afternoon glare.

The surviving laborers loped down the sharp slope, seemingly unconcerned for their own safety.

Breath rasping in her throat, Qadan mounted up and kicked Marrow into a gallop.

An arrow hissed by. Not close, but still Qadan ducked, the move sending a flare of pain down her side as it jostled the barb in her shoulder.

Teeth gritted against the urge to scream, Qadan rode on.

CHAPTER ELEVEN

Doji Masahiro was beginning to suspect he had made a terrible mistake.

"This is it." The porter stopped before the low wall, dropping Masahiro's bundled effects as if they were a sack of offal.

To call the sprawling, ramshackle collection of cracked stucco and drooping eaves a manor would have been extremely charitable. If anything, it reminded Masahiro of one of the haunted temples travelers often blundered into in the ghost tales Hiroshige had read him when they were children. His older brother had always delighted in scaring Masahiro – not because he enjoyed watching him squirm, but because he would often crawl over to Hiroshige's futon after the servants had put them to bed. When he was younger, Masahiro had thought it was a means to control him. Now, he suspected his elder brother just hated being alone.

He certainly wasn't alone now. A thousand Crane samurai had accompanied Hiroshige into death.

"Should I air the place out, lord?" The porter scratched his patchy beard and spat, seemingly ignorant that he was in the presence of nobility.

Masahiro let the discourtesy slip past his thoughts. At least the man was willing to help. Masahiro had known the situation was dire when he took the position of court emissary – easily acquired, given half the province was in open revolt. At best, it was a rustic backwater dotted with hardscrabble villages and filthy mining camps, the closest thing to civilization a dilapidated trade town with the uninspired name of "Crossroads." Even so, Masahiro had expected the remaining peasantry to possess at least some modicum of respect. Instead, the locals ranged from insolent to openly contemptuous. It had been all Masahiro could do to acquire the services of his current porter, a rather odious fellow named Kichibei.

Masahiro peered past the open gate, its doors loose on rusty hinges. "Where are the guards?"

"Most died with Lord Tadamune." Kichibei shrugged. "The rest went with your lot."

"My lot?"

"The other ones." Kichibei mimicked a noble's mincing walk. "They came through a month ago along with every samurai in Rokugan."

"Hardly." Masahiro kept his expression studiously blank. The expedition had been a mere fraction of the Empire's might, although he could see how that might seem overwhelming to a simpleton like Kichibei.

"And the servants?" he asked, trying to hide the note of pleading in his voice.

The porter gave a noncommittal grunt. "They ran away."

Masahiro followed him into the garden, twisting to avoid a prickly rosebush that had outgrown its bed. At first glance, it seemed like the servants had done more than run away. True to their baser natures, they had made off with anything of value – if this wretched place had ever possessed such things.

Kichibei stumped over to one of the nearby villas. Rather than slide open, the entry door simply fell from its setting. Kichibei set it aside, then made a show of dusting the broken screen.

That, more than anything, hammered home the hopelessness of Masahiro's predicament.

He had left court just ahead of his rivals' knives, barely able to gather a few personal items, let alone the meager remnants of his family's fortune. His attempt to secure guards had been met with deferment from the clan. Their warriors were needed elsewhere, it seemed, even the ones that had guarded Masahiro's manor. But if he would just wait a day, perhaps two, they assured him they could find some worthy samurai.

Masahiro had fled the Imperial City in a tawdry palanquin, fine robes concealed beneath a rough straw cape. Fortunately, it seemed his flight had thrown off any pursuit; that, or Masahiro's enemies no longer considered him worth killing.

"Where would you like me to put your things, lord?" Kichibei slouched over and shouldered the bag.

"In there, if you don't mind." Masahiro gestured toward the least dilapidated villa. Only after Kichibei had slipped inside did Masahiro allow himself to weep.

Silent tears streaked his cheeks as he wandered through the garden. In addition to his other failings, Tadamune had been a Crab lord, his attention to aesthetics predictably lacking. Arranged in a ninth-century Kayushiki style, the garden would have been outdated even if well-tended. Left to grow wild the foliage had become truly hideous.

Although the wall ringing the manor grounds was in good repair, most of the villas seemed on the verge of collapse, and those that remained were beyond archaic, with tar and tile roofs and cracking pine beams that wouldn't have looked out of place on some low-class bath house.

It was a terrible place to live, an even worse place to die.

Rumor was the rebels were only a few days away. Already the outlying villages had gone over, and if Kichibei was any measure of local sentiment it wouldn't be long until Crossroads joined them.

A rising tide of self-pity swept away the last vestiges of Masahiro's composure. From the heights of the Imperial Court, he had been reduced to squatting in the manor of a dead Crab lord.

He threw himself to the ground, face cradled in his hand like some desperate pillow-book heroine. Such conduct was unbecoming of any noble, let alone a Crane.

Masahiro hardly cared. The clan had as much as disowned him. His ancestral blade was lost along with his brother. There were no nobles here, no samurai, only rebels and those who would soon become rebels.

What need had Masahiro to cling to decorum?

Distantly, he heard a rapping at the gate, but could not bring himself to answer.

Kichibei's loud breathing announced the peasant long before he shambled into view. Masahiro made the vaguest attempt to comport himself, rising to his knees and turning away so it seemed he was admiring a weed-choked bed of lavender and hydrangea.

"Lord, there's an old woman at the gate. A samurai. Says she is with the Lion Clan."

"Tell her to come back later." Masahiro didn't turn, unwilling to let the peasant see the puffiness around his eyes.

"As you wish." Kichibei crunched off through the overgrown gravel.

Flowers surrounded an algae-covered pond. Frowning, Masahiro plucked a long sheaf of grass and flicked it across the surface. It would have been lucky to find a koi or two, but it seemed the fish were as dead as Masahiro's prospects.

He dolefully inspected the rock garden beyond the pond. Ivy had invaded the western half, larger stones completely covered. Patches of white sand were still visible on the eastern side, little islands of calm amidst the weeds and wild grasses poking up through the garden.

Masahiro knuckled his eyes, sorrow turning to irritation. If this place was to be his grave, he could at least try to make it presentable. Heedless of the soil staining his travel robes, he bent to rip up great clumps of weeds, winding long ropes of ivy around his arms like some itinerant farmhand.

The mindless work lifted the pall of distress that had weighed down Masahiro's thoughts these long days past. He abandoned the weeding to fetch the last bit of paper from his effects, jotting down what little he had been able to glean from the surly Crab nobles at whose desolate towers and smoky halls he had been forced to tarry on his journey west.

Even trapped beneath a veil of recrimination, Masahiro's courtly reflexes had bid him peer into the murky political landscape. Amidst the tasteless dinners and grunted conversation that passed for Crab hospitality, he had managed to glean some sense of who remained – mostly merchants, village elders, and local mine bosses. Everyone of note had been slain with the expedition, but, unlike many Crane, Masahiro had never balked at working with lower orders. Next to each name, Masahiro added several questions and notes.

When he had finished, he called for Kichibei. "Can you read?"

"Yes, lord." The peasant winced. "If it isn't too flowery."

"Good." Masahiro handed him the list of questions. "Ask around discreetly. If you can find the answers I seek, there will be silver in it for you."

With a bob of his head, Kichibei hurried away. Feeling a rumble in his stomach, Masahiro waved the servant back, requesting that he also purchase whatever passed for food in this bucolic nightmare.

After that, Masahiro returned to the garden. Sweat matted his pale hair, his hands cut and blistered, muscles sore from unaccustomed exertion. He found a cracked rake near one of the outbuildings, its head missing two tines. Still, one must work with what one was given, and Masahiro applied himself to raking the sand back to some semblance of respectability.

It was almost dark when Kichibei returned bearing dried meat, pickled vegetables, and a modest jug of sake. Seeing Masahiro's work, he grinned a fool's empty smile.

"Looks good, lord."

A compliment from a pig was no compliment at all, but Masahiro accepted the praise with a polite nod.

Kichibei set the provisions down along with several small parcels. He handed a rumpled sheet of paper to Masahiro. "I was able to find some answers, lord. As well as some of the things you requested."

"I suppose that will have to do." Masahiro took the paper. "Keep at it."

The servant shifted from foot to foot. "If you don't mind, I'd best be getting home."

Masahiro eyed the food warily. His hunger was such he

might enjoy even such rustic fare, but he had no wish for Kichibei to see him eat.

"Go on, then."

The servant lingered, expression flickering between embarrassment and a nervous smile.

"Yes, what is it?"

"There's the matter of payment, lord."

"Oh, yes, my apologies." Masahiro fished two silver coins from his money pouch, pressing them into the servant's callused hand. It was certainly more than the man deserved, but Masahiro could afford to be magnanimous. Even had his death not been certain, there was nowhere to spend what little remained of his family's fortune.

"Thank you, lord." Grinning like a fool, Kichibei bobbed his head in a rough approximation of a bow. "I'll be back tomorrow morning."

"I'm sure you will."

Masahiro waited for the creak of the gate before going for the food. To his surprise, the meat was actually well-seasoned, its salty tang a fine complement to the sharp, vinegary bite of the pickled vegetables. The meal was over far too soon for Masahiro's liking, so he helped himself to a healthy pull from the jug of sake, finding it equally pleasing.

Kichibei had left a lantern, and Masahiro lifted it, intending to explore the remainder of his rustic domain. It seemed a shame to leave the sake, so he took it with him, commiserating each distasteful discovery with another drink. The liquor soon filled his stomach with warmth, making his lips buzz.

Masahiro wandered through the manor grounds like a wayward spirit, voice raised in half-remembered song. If anything, the place seemed all the more dismal in the dark – a collection of dusty rooms and creaking walkways. Rather than dull his maudlin sentiments, drunkenness whetted them to razor sharpness. Songs became dirges, then incoherent reproach.

With Masahiro's planning and Hiroshige's talent at court, they should have been able to guide the Empire into a golden age, perhaps even broker a lasting peace between the Great Clans – or at least grudging respect buttressed by Crane dominance.

"I promised to follow you anywhere, brother." Masahiro gestured to the empty air, almost shouting. "Here I am. Poised to join you in the world beyond."

It seemed right that Masahiro compose his death poem. He spent some time looking for brush and paper, but the manor remained reticent to provide even the barest trappings of civilized life, so Masahiro settled for scratching it into the floorboards of his sleeping chamber.

He had just begun to refine the first line when the silken cord slipped around his throat.

At first, he thought it mere imagining, some doleful figment conjured by rough food and even rougher drink. Only when the cord drew tight did Masahiro realize he was about to die.

Contrary to his earlier thoughts on the matter, he found himself quite reticent to join Hiroshige in the Realm of Waiting. He tried to stand, but his attacker had a knee on Masahiro's back, breath heavy as Kichibei's as he kept pressure upon the cord cutting off Masahiro's air.

Masahiro tried to flail back with his dagger, only to have the man rudely stomp on his wrist and kick the weapon away.

He clawed at the assassin, but face-down on the floor, could muster little force. Masahiro's blows fell weakly, the throb of blood in his ears drowning out the murderer's grunts of exertion.

He felt himself slipping from his body, a leaf drifting from the boughs of a tall tree. A small tickle of pride wormed its way through Masahiro's fading awareness. The man used silk instead of cheaper fiber. This was an assassin from the capital, at least, and not some bucolic brigand after Masahiro's few remaining coins.

Apparently, someone in the Imperial City still considered him worth killing.

Dimly, he heard a distant crash. The sound of running feet.

The assassin gave the cord a sharp jerk, as if hoping to break Masahiro's neck. But although it cut into his throat, Masahiro's spine remained blessedly intact. He even managed to slap a numb hand against the floorboards.

Someone kicked the door from its moorings.

Masahiro gulped down a wheezing breath as the pressure on his throat relaxed. There was shouting, although he could not tell whose. A blade glittered in the dim lantern light. Wood cracked as someone went tumbling through one of the thin walls. Masahiro felt he should assist his savior, but could do little save lie on his side, gasping in breath after grateful breath.

By the ancestors, it felt as if all the demons of Fu Leng had carved a fiery trail down his throat, and when Masahiro coughed, he tasted blood.

A shadow darkened the ruined doorway, heavy footsteps creaking toward him. It was all Masahiro could do to raise his head, half-expecting it was the assassin come back to finish the job.

Instead, he saw a gray-haired woman in battered armor. Her cheeks were red from exertion, a pale webwork of scars faintly visible against the flush. She knelt to turn him over, hands surprisingly strong.

"Are you well?"

"Hale and hearty." Masahiro managed a pained smile.

"Have you no guards?"

"Not as such, no."

"No servants?"

"There is Kichibei." Masahiro gave an absent wave, almost toppling from the exertion. "But I gave him the night off."

"You are lord of this place?" she asked.

"No. Although it seems I am the ranking noble." He levered himself up onto his elbows, rubbing his raw neck. "Until the rebels finish the job."

She offered him a terse bow. "I am Matsu Chiaki."

Masahiro returned her politeness reflexively, wincing at the pain in his head. Her name was familiar, although his thoughts were too foggy to dredge up specifics.

"I bear travel papers signed by Lady Matsu Akoya," she continued as if Masahiro were not lying, half-dead, on the floor at her feet. "She bid me present myself."

The name Akoya unlocked some shadowed vault in Masahiro's memory. He raised a hand as if asking to be helped up. When Chiaki obliged, he turned her hands, revealing the long vertical scar across both palms.

"So it is true." He got unsteadily to his feet. "Chiaki Steelgrip. Is it true you can snap blades with your bare hands?"

She gave an uncomfortable grimace.

"May I inquire as to why a lauded Lion warrior has chosen to grace this humble manor with her presence?" Masahiro attempted to rearrange his travel robes, only to find his near-murder had left them in hopeless disarray.

Chiaki's jaw pulsed as if she did not wish to answer, but a lifetime of discipline apparently won out.

"Matsu Katamori was my student."

"My condolences," Masahiro replied. "Doji Hiroshige was my brother."

She regarded him for a long moment, still as a leafless oak.

Discomfited by her scrutiny, Masahiro sought to gather his jumbled thoughts. The arrival of a famous samurai, even one of such advanced years, could be turned to his advantage – if only he could find the proper lever.

"We both owe the rebels a debt of vengeance." He nodded. When speaking to Lion samurai, it was best to use words they understood – revenge, battle, duty, death.

"So it would seem."

"Tell me, how do you plan to seek justice for Katamori?" he asked.

"Find the rebels." She shrugged. "Kill them."

"Even a warrior such as yourself cannot hope to overcome thousands of traitors. All you are likely to find is an uncomfortable end."

If anything, the prospect seemed to cheer the Lion samurai.

So she had come to die. Masahiro could use that.

"Perhaps we might help each other," he said.

Chiaki glanced at the livid bruise on Masahiro's neck. "I doubt that, Crane."

"You know as well as I the rebels could not have achieved victory alone," he continued as if she hadn't spoken. "It will take more than blades to uncover their true benefactor, and I have much experience with… more subtle forms of inquiry."

"How do I know you aren't their patron?"

Masahiro pointedly rubbed his neck. "Because they just attempted to kill me."

Chiaki did not exactly smile at that, but her scowl did seem to relax a fraction. "What do you propose?"

"As you can see, I am woefully undefended."

She snorted. "Find a Daidoji."

"Alas, my clan's forces are required elsewhere," Masahiro replied.

"I am no Crane lapdog."

"I am not asking for your oath." He raised what he hoped was a placating hand. "Only your protection. Keep me alive, and I shall help you find the truth."

She narrowed her eyes.

"Work with me, at least for the moment." Masahiro ventured a smile. "The rebels will be here in a few days. You can have your glorious death then."

"I've had my fill of glory." Chiaki crossed her arms. "But you speak sense." She looked him up and down, then nodded as if to herself.

"I will keep you alive for the time being."

Masahiro bowed, grinning. "Then it is settled."

"Nothing is settled." It seemed impossible, but Chiaki's smile was more distressing than her scowl.

"But it will be, Crane. On that you can depend."

CHAPTER TWELVE

Naoki had been raised among mountains. The high, snow-dusted peaks of the Great Northern Mountains had been a constant in her life, their sharp crags and deep roots like a comforting hand on her shoulder, a heavy, reassuring weight to ground her racing thoughts.

On the roughly two weeks of their frenzied journey south from Phoenix lands, Naoki had looked forward to being among mountains again. They had taken a courier ship down the coast, the wide, alluvial plains and valleys of Crane lands discomfiting in their sameness, as if some giant hand might reach down and sweep away the profusion of rootless villages. The ride west had been no better, the high trees of the Shinomen Forest crowding out the light, seeming to hem them in on all sides. Naoki's magisterial credentials had been enough to see them through the various guard posts and patrols with only a modicum of delay, but the Crab lands were as unwelcoming as their owners.

Naoki had felt her heart swell as they rode into the broken foothills, the first mist-shrouded crests coming into view. But, even in the light of morning, the Twilight Mountains were not reassuring.

Not at all.

They seemed a rugged, reckless place, hard as the clan that governed them. Rather than comfort Naoki, the peaks seemed to loom like carrion crows, waiting for her to slip so they could swoop down and pick her apart.

"The cavern should be close." Irie squinted at the nearby cliffs, head cocked as if listening to a voice only she could hear.

For all Naoki knew, she was.

Despite her assistance in deciphering the corrupted monk's esoteric ramblings, the Phoenix priest largely kept her own council. Even so, Naoki could see the creases on her forehead, the hollow shadows below her eyes. Their journey had been difficult, a hurried flight down sea, road, and river, but Irie's exhaustion seemed far more than physical. Naoki understood the root of her companion's anxieties.

The monk's letters spoke of blood rituals and terrible sacrifice, of forbidden relics and long-buried stores of dreadful knowledge. It was clear he meant to seek them out, that the murders were part of some vile ritual to glean insights into the location of various crypts and catacombs. What remained unclear was what role Irie's master had played in all this.

Masatsuge had clearly corresponded with the monk, but they had only one side of the conversation. Were the Phoenix master's letters admonitions or evocations?

Irie noticed Naoki watching her and scowled. "I wish you wouldn't do that."

"Do what?"

"Watch me as if I am an errant spark."

"Are you?"

"Have I not answered all your questions?"

"You have responded to my questions," Naoki replied.

"Whether you have answered them remains to be seen."

Irie reined in her mount, fixing Naoki with a level stare. "I wish to catch this murderer. If only to prove Master Masatsuge's innocence."

"And if he is not innocent?"

"He is." She kicked her horse into a trot. "He must be."

Naoki followed, shaking her head. Irie's loyalty to her dead master might be laudable, but it would complicate matters should Masatsuge prove corrupt.

They rode in silence for some time, along the twist of a rocky goat path winding up a shelf of shale thrust from the mountain like an accusatory finger. Naoki found herself studying every shadow, every brooding overhang. She had been warned about this place – tales of bandits, foul spirits, and worse. The Crab warriors at the last guard post had reviewed Naoki and Irie's travel papers with the air of men preparing prisoners for execution. They had received word that the rebels had crossed Five-Dragon Gate and were even now marching east. The Crab were preparing for a siege.

Then again, the Crab were always preparing for a siege.

"There." Irie raised a hand to indicate a shadowed overhang perhaps a hundred yards ahead. "The spirits say that is the cave."

A dozen tents dotted the rocky earth just beyond the entrance. Some had fallen; others remained half-pitched. Even at this distance, Naoki could see tools scattered about, the remains of abandoned cook fires black upon the stone.

Naoki peered into the gloom. Unable to distinguish anything inside the cave itself, she noted the boulders and rock piled beneath the sharp slope. "Someone has excavated the cavern, recently by the look of those pick marks."

"The cave may hold answers," Irie said.

"More likely, it holds danger." Naoki scanned the surrounding cliffs, barren of shadow and movement – which meant nothing, of course. There could have been an army concealed behind the rocky escarpments, and Naoki would have been none the wiser.

"This whole place holds danger." Irie dismounted. Kneeling to press one palm to the stone, she muttered a low prayer, eyes squeezed shut in concentration.

"Nothing moves beyond the cavern." She stood, dusting her hands.

"And inside?"

"The spirits do not say."

"Then I suppose we must have a look." Naoki flicked her reins. The camp had been abandoned relatively recently, ashes cold, but not yet smeared by rain or wind. In the lee of a flapping tent, Naoki noticed a streak of blood upon the fabric and more rusty red speckled upon the stones.

Not an encouraging sign.

Dismounting, she inspected the spatter. "Someone was wounded, but not killed." She turned to point down the gravel slope. "They rode that way in quite a hurry."

"And what of the others?" Irie asked. "This camp must have held dozens of laborers."

"If they died, it was not out here." Naoki glanced toward the yawning darkness. Something else caught her eye, a snatch of purple amidst the drab browns and grays of the tents.

She picked the bit of torn fabric from amidst the stones. Running it through her fingers, she gave the swatch a sniff. "Unicorn."

"How can you tell?"

"This purple dye is from a berry bush found on the western

steppes, and the fabric is wool and horsehide. Either the wearer was Unicorn, or they bought it from them."

"What would the Unicorn Clan be doing here?"

"Perhaps the same as the Dragon and Phoenix Clans?"

Irie gave a tight-lipped nod toward the cavern. "Let us find out."

Helping themselves to lanterns near the entrance, they crunched up the rough gravel slope and into the cavern. It resolved into a long, high tunnel, scored by regular marks along the walls as if some massive worm had burrowed through the rock.

Beyond lay a round chamber, a wide dome overhead. Once, it might have borne carvings or inscriptions, but someone had been at the walls with picks, marring the stone with great, irregular gouges.

Although the floor was empty of bodies, Naoki noted old blood amidst the debris. Kicking some stones aside revealed a streak of dried gore, a curving line that seemed to intersect with another.

"Help me with this." She stooped to brush away more of the fallen rock. Together, they cleared most of the wreckage to reveal bloody words written across the floor.

Naoki stood, letting out a low, unconscious groan.

> *Winter's killing frost.*
> *Cherry or Chrysanthemum?*
> *Flowers have no say.*

"He dares threaten the emperor?" Irie scoffed. "The man must truly be corrupt."

Naoki massaged her forehead, trying to quiet the furious

whirl of thoughts. Chrysanthemum was the imperial bloom, just as the cherry blossom was the flower of samurai, but who would be so arrogant as to compare himself to a force of nature?

She raised her torch to peer around the ravaged chamber. "Whatever he sought here, let us pray he did not find it."

Irie knelt to examine one of the larger bits of masonry. It had clearly been part of a mural, depicting the armored sleeve of a warrior.

Naoki felt her shoulders slump. She had arrived too late, again. "We would need every antiquarian in the Imperial City to reassemble this mess."

"This was a place of power." Irie turned the shard over in her hands, her gaze fixed on the middle distance. "Although not a type known to me."

"The Twilight Mountains stretch to the Shadowlands," Naoki said. "Perhaps it is some corrupt spirit?"

"Perhaps." Irie frowned, eyes narrowing, her whole face twisted in hard concentration. "Although there *is* something familiar."

She drew in a sudden breath. After rooting around in her satchel for a frenzied moment, she drew forth a theater mask.

Naoki recognized it as the one they had found in Master Masatsuge's hidden chest. She had often spied the Phoenix priest studying the mask when she thought Naoki was resting. But Naoki's attention had always been as fitful as her slumber, and it had been easy to feign sleep. At first, Naoki had thought Irie might harbor the same eccentricities as her erstwhile master, but the Phoenix priest's expression had not been one of interest, nor even curiosity. If anything, Irie had looked as if handling the relic caused her physical pain.

Irie blew out her lantern, then tossed it aside. Holding the mask tight, she muttered intricate callings under her breath. After a moment, she opened her eyes.

"Shutter your lantern."

Naoki cocked her head.

"Just for a moment."

Grudgingly, Naoki drew the shade.

She blinked in the sudden dark. No. Not dark. Not exactly. At first, she thought it might be daylight from outside, but the tunnel's slope was too sharp for even a glimmer to reach the central chamber.

The stones themselves seemed to shed a faint, flickering illumination, not enough to read by, but enough that Naoki could make out Irie's shape amidst the darkness.

"Name magic," Irie said softly. "A spirit was bound here. The whole vault seems to be some form of vast geomantic talisman."

"The Unicorn!" Naoki made a tight fist. What little she knew of name magic and spirit binding had come from Irie, and that filtered through the Phoenix priest's disdain for the practice. "What could they have bound here? And why?"

"I cannot say." Irie spoke in an uneasy whisper. "But it was powerful."

"Can you track this spirit?"

The Phoenix priest shifted uncomfortably. "I think so."

"Then we must move quickly." Naoki unshuttered her lamp, already moving for the tunnel. Irie followed silently behind. After a rather graceless descent, they mounted up. For a moment, Naoki thought she detected movement among the ruined tents. But upon turning, she saw only the flap of unsecured canvas, loose poles rattling in the mountain wind.

Irie lifted a trembling finger to point in the direction of the blood trail, and they were off, riding as quickly as the broken ground would allow.

Naoki could not believe the Unicorn had a hand in the murders, but from what Irie had told her of name magic, its practitioners were an eccentric lot.

Thoughts awhirl with signs, possibilities, and theories, Naoki did not mark her companion's silence until they had covered several miles. Only when Irie reined up did she notice the tightness around the Phoenix priest's eyes, the way her lips made a thin, anxious line as she nodded toward a rocky outcrop.

"Up there." Irie winced. "I think."

"You are troubled?"

Irie looked away. "This whole situation is troubling."

"Do you believe your master dabbled in name magic?"

"If he did, I am sure it was for a good cause." Irie's whole posture spoke of a rope drawn taut – shoulders high, head low, back hunched as if Irie expected Naoki to strike her. With conscious effort, Naoki bit back her urge to interrogate the priest. There would be time for hard questions later. For now, she needed Irie's knowledge.

"Come, let us prove your master innocent." Naoki tried for a reassuring smile, but Irie only looked to the rocks. Dismounting, Naoki drew her jitte. Their solid weight felt right in her hands.

"A moment." Irie's fingers moved in ritual motion, her chant soft, but insistent.

A breeze ruffled Naoki's hair, chill swirling down through her robes.

She shivered. "What was that?"

"The spirits will muffle our footfalls."

Naoki nodded, once again glad she had decided to allow Irie to accompany her south.

They picked their way carefully up the boulder-strewn slope, pausing as a faint whicker echoed from behind the outcrop. Something stomped, metal on stone – once, twice.

"Horses," Naoki whispered.

They half-scuttled, half-crawled up the hill, the air seeming to swallow the rattle of loose stone beneath their feet. Just before they crested the rise, she looked to Irie.

The priest held the mask in a white-knuckled grip, her jaw tight.

With a nod, they went over the hill.

The spear thrust almost took Naoki in the throat. She threw herself to the side, rocks skittering as her ankle twisted. All was dust and rocks for a sickening moment, then Naoki struck hard stone, the blow sharp enough to drive the air from her lungs.

She twisted, expecting another strike. But Naoki's attacker stepped back with a pained hiss, spear wobbling as if for balance. Beneath the dirt and blood, her robes were Unicorn purple – heavy, serviceable cloth, yet trimmed with soft white fur that spoke of high status. Strange for a Unicorn noble to be traveling without an entourage. That, and her apparent injuries spoke to dire events back at the ruined tomb.

Irie's voice rose. Sharp and clear, her chant echoed from the rocks, which gave a threatening rumble.

Their attacker made as if to hop back, only to find the stone beneath her feet had become sucking mud.

Snarling, she hurled her spear at Irie, but the priest calmly sidestepped, hardly a break in her call as she drew more spirits into the fray.

"Demons! Blood sorcerers!" the Unicorn woman shouted.

Snatching a dagger from her belt she grabbed Irie's robe, dragging the priest close. Struggling madly, they fell to the ground. The Unicorn twisted to bring her knife to bear, only to let out a scream as Irie drove her fingers into the woman's bloodied shoulder.

Still gasping, Naoki pushed to her knees – she had tumbled down into a makeshift camp. Two horses were tethered to a twisted tree. Still saddled, their harnesses boasted the silver accents and white-edged purple livery favored by the Unicorn. Several wads of bloody cloth lay discarded near an open pack. At first, Naoki suspected it the makings of some dark ritual, until she saw the needle and bloody thread, a short stick nearby with deep teeth marks, as if someone had bitten hard upon it.

The woman had obviously been trying to stitch her wound. Hardly the act of a dark sorcerer. Nor did she resemble an aged monk.

"Stop! Wait!" Naoki turned to struggle up the low hill.

Despite the Unicorn's wound, Irie appeared to be getting the worse of the struggle. It seemed no words would part them, so Naoki stepped up to deal the woman a ringing blow to the head. Even though she pulled the strike, the heavy steel jitte set the Unicorn reeling.

Irie shoved the woman aside, and she slumped back, moving limply. The priest surged to her feet, fingers crooked as if to call down Lord Sun himself upon her foe.

"Stop." Naoki caught her shoulder. "This is not our quarry."

Irie turned, a snarl half-frozen on her lips. "How can you know?"

"Look around." She gestured at the threadbare camp, the blood, the woman's wound. "Does this appear the work of dark sorcery?"

"What of the foul presence I sensed?" Irie turned as the woman gave a low groan, shifting on the rock.

Naoki had no answer for that, but before she could respond, the woman spoke.

"You seek the monk." Her voice was rough as raw silk.

"We have been on his trail for weeks." Naoki pushed past Irie to kneel next to the woman, interest overwhelming her sense of threat. "Who are you? What do you know of him?"

"I am Iuchi Qadan, and I know only that he killed my friend." Qadan gave a pained swallow. Her gaze flicked to the crest of the hill, and she gave a jagged laugh – almost a sob. "But I will know more, soon."

"Why?" Naoki glanced up, uncertain.

"Because you fools have led him right to me."

CHAPTER THIRTEEN

Matsu Chiaki was beginning to suspect she had made a grave error.

She had spent the night inspecting the decrepit Crab manor, searching for potential hiding places, of which there were many, and avenues of assault, of which there were blessedly few. With typical Crab single-mindedness, the lord had focused on external defense, shoring up the walls while the rest of the manor rotted from within.

Just like the Crab Clan themselves.

After several rounds of stretches, Chiaki jogged loops around the manor grounds, varying her route to catch potential assailants off guard. Fortunately, she found no sign of the assassin – who was almost certainly waiting for nightfall.

For his part, Doji Masahiro acted as if he had not almost died. The Crane noble slept until midmorning, awakening only when a rather scruffy servant made an appearance with a roll of blank paper. They spoke for the better part of an hour, Masahiro educating the peasant on the finer points of pickled plums and wall hangings. Then he sent the man off with a list, a sheaf of calligraphed letters, and a pocket full of silver. Hardly the actions of a man dedicated to seeking vengeance.

Chiaki would have abandoned the pompous Crane, but she had given him her word. Not to mention, she would need all her strength when the rebels came. Younger Chiaki would have charged off after the traitors, but she had learned the value of patience – hard, bitter lessons beaten into her over and over at sword point, or a comrade's pyre.

At last, Masahiro emerged from his quarters, only to don a straw hat and putter about in the manor's sad excuse for a garden.

"What are you doing?" Chiaki asked, unable to contain her irritation.

"Moving sand." Masahiro drew the lopsided rake in lazy whorls across a barren patch.

"And how does that help us?"

He bent to pick a bit of ivy from between two moss-covered rocks.

"Shouldn't you be seeking information on the rebels?"

"And just how would I do that?" He straightened to regard her, a lazy smile nestled at the corner of his lips.

"You're the self-proclaimed savant," she replied. "You tell me."

"I just did." He set the rake aside, sidling over to the nearest pavilion before turning to observe the garden.

"I am in no mood for games."

"Have you ever been?" He arched one carefully plucked eyebrow. "Rest assured, I am taking this *very* seriously."

Chiaki snorted. "Rebellions cannot be fought with poetry and moon-viewings."

"Nor with blades and warriors, as Katamori discovered."

Masahiro slid the entry screen aside and proceeded to lay out several sitting pillows.

Chiaki fumed as he dusted the uneven floorboards, changed robes, then unrolled some insipid wall scrolls to hang in various alcoves. At last, he glanced back, looking her up and down.

"You don't happen to have anything… more presentable?"

"Apologies." She spat the word at him. "I left my dress armor back at the dōjō."

"Ah well, your reputation's luster shall have to suffice." He turned away. "Although that breastplate could certainly do with a bit of polish."

Chiaki watched him go, shaking her head. It was as if the fool *courted* death.

A flush crept to her cheeks as Chiaki realized she and Masahiro might have more in common than she suspected.

They came just after midday, a procession of merchants, elders, and local pillars of the community, all dressed in what passed for finery among the lower classes. Chiaki had spent little time at court, but she knew enough to recognize their rustic manner would have seen them laughed out of even the lowest functions.

Even so, Masahiro treated the peasants as if they were imperial nobles, plying them with amusing anecdotes, gifts, and inquiries concerning the health of family members. Had she not known the Crane noble arrived only a day before, Chiaki would have thought the man had spent months in the province.

"Please, allow me to introduce famed warrior and general, Matsu Chiaki – hero of Longbow Bridge, first over the wall at the Siege of Cold Harbor, veteran of a hundred desperate battles, known as 'Steelfist' for shattering the blade of Burning

Pine, one of the most fearsome bandits ever to ravage the Spine of the World."

Chiaki had been so intent on scanning the crowd for potential threats that the introduction surprised her. The peasants crowded forward, eyes wide as silver coins.

"Go on." Masahiro nodded. "Show them your palms."

Taken aback, Chiaki held out a hand.

"There, you see." Masahiro's voice dripped with reverence. "Snapped Pine's flaming sword with her bare hands."

"It was already badly bent," Chiaki muttered, although no one seemed to notice. Once, she would have reveled in the recognition. But, like the strength in her sword arm, such bravado seemed to bleed away with age. Now, such talk just made Chiaki uncomfortable.

"She is my advisor for defense of the eastern reaches," Masahiro continued, apparently oblivious to Chiaki's shocked glare. "All military matters shall be within her strong, capable hands."

There were whispers among the crowd. Although some of the younger merchants appeared nonplussed, Chiaki could not help but note they were far outnumbered by white-haired elders, all nodding sagely. She opened her mouth to speak, but Masahiro had already whisked his guests away to the garden pavilion for tea and sweet bean cakes.

What followed was an afternoon of polite conversation – all present acting as if there were not a horde of murderous rebels marching toward them. Although the peasants chewed their cakes loudly and did not hold their cups in the correct hands, Masahiro treated them as visiting lords, sifting compliments from the dross of their rough manners.

As the afternoon drew to a close, he deftly extracted funds

from merchants, promises of militia and fortification from the various elders. It would've been fascinating to watch, had not Chiaki known the villagers were doomed.

"What are you playing at, Crane?" she asked after the last elder had tottered through the manor gate.

"You fight your battle, I shall fight mine."

"These farmers cannot win." She crossed her arms. "Not if I had a year to prepare them."

"Winning is not important." Masahiro flicked a stray fleck of dirt from the sleeve of his robe. "All that matters is they *believe* they can win."

"They will be slaughtered."

"Unfortunately, yes." He frowned. "But they also won't be joining the rebels, will they?"

Chiaki could not help the grunt of surprise that slipped through her lips. She had thought Masahiro a preening peacock, helpless outside his gilded nest. Now, Chiaki realized how truly dangerous he was.

"I am not in the habit of sending farmers to their deaths."

"I thought you came here to kill rebels?"

"Not like this."

"Noble, warrior, peasant – all must sacrifice for the Empire. Is that not what you Lion say?" He gave an airy wave. "We can beg the ancestors for forgiveness later. For now, the more we can frustrate the rebels, the more chance we have to dig deeper. For instance, were you aware the rebel leader is a sorcerer?"

"How do you know?"

"Several of the elders are sheltering kin from the west," Masahiro replied. "They spoke of seeing this 'Bent-Winged Shrike' summon shadowed flames and biting darkness."

Chiaki took a steadying breath. This changed matters. There had been no mention of unnatural foes.

Masahiro tapped his cheek with a thin finger as if trying to recall the words of a poem. "Wasn't Burning Pine an elementalist?"

"She was." Chiaki felt her palms tingle at the memory. She pushed down the jagged recollections – screams and shouts; fire in the trees, among the ranks; bodies twisting in flames so bright the night was like high noon. Chiaki had meant to die when she'd thrown herself at Burning Pine, if only to spare herself the pain of burning alive. She didn't even remember grabbing the sword, didn't remember breaking it. Others said she had, much later, once she could walk again, once the wounds had healed.

Most of them, at least.

"I promised to help you, did I not?" Masahiro mounted the low steps up to the villa, kneeling upon the dusty pillow like a magistrate about to pass sentence. "Keep me alive, and I shall do all I can to see you face this Shrike with as much advantage as I can muster."

Chiaki regarded him for a long moment, duty and concern warring in her chest. What did it matter if this Bent-Winged Shrike was some self-important demagogue or corrupt elementalist? He would know who betrayed the imperial expedition.

If another great clan was behind the treachery, then the Lion would be duty-bound to act. Then, at last, her disciple's spirit would find justice.

She remembered Katamori as a child, focused in a way even veteran warriors found hard to achieve. He had come to her an orphan, both parents lost to fire in the high pines. Lady Akoya had provided for his training, but she could not raise the child, not with her responsibilities.

At first, Chiaki had seen it as a challenge, a way to pass on all the sharp lessons she had accrued over a lifetime of battle. Katamori had learned all she had to teach, taking to even the most intricate techniques with a casual competence that made Chiaki proud. She couldn't pick the exact moment when the serious, sad little lad had gone from student to son, but she did remember the first time he smiled.

She was telling the story of when she had challenged her old friend Sana to a mock duel, each trying to one-up the other with outlandish dares. What had started with a score of open-hand slaps gradually escalated to tightrope walking across latrine pits, the wrestling of greased animals, and scaling the barracks walls. Chiaki had just reached the point where Sana dared her to drink a quart of sake from her dirty boot, when Katamori finally grinned.

It had taken Chiaki six months to make Katamori smile again, another year before he laughed at one of her foolish stories. His joys came rare as summer snows, all the more beautiful for their scarcity.

The memory conjured a twinge of pain in her chest, sharper than a sword thrust.

By the ancestors, how she missed him.

"Do I still have your protection?" Masahiro asked.

"You do," Chiaki replied, jaw tight against sudden thickness in her throat.

"Then get some rest." He gestured toward one of the pavilions. "I doubt this afternoon holds any more hidden daggers, and I will need you sharp for the days ahead."

Chiaki did not bow. No matter their relationship, Masahiro

would never be her lord. For all his playacting and subterfuge, the Crane represented the clearest path to vengeance. If he would use her, Chiaki would use him as well.

She had come here to die, but that did not mean she need die poorly.

CHAPTER FOURTEEN

Peasants swarmed over the ridge. Dirty and dust-streaked, their threadbare clothes sporting bloodied tears from where they had scrambled, unheeding, over sharp stone, Irie might have mistaken them for refugees if not for the look upon their faces – eyes glinting with singular focus, the barest lilt of a smile on their lips.

It was not the expression that unsettled her; rather that they all wore the same one, as if the whole group had been captivated by a beautiful melody.

They made no sound as they came, the hill silent but for the skitter of rock and the high skirl of wind through the cliffs above. Like the roughest sort of bandit, they were armed with staves and clubs, barely a bow or blade to be seen.

"Stop!" Naoki raised one of her jitte.

The foremost of the peasants swiped at her with a misshapen club, and the magistrate ducked to drive the dull blade of her weapon into his midsection. He folded without a sound, two more peasants stepping around him.

Irie did not need her spiritual senses to know foul magic was at work. It coiled about their attackers like smoke, a thick miasma of corruption that seemed to cling to Irie's skin. She raised her arms, voice pitched to thread the distant wind.

The spirits came in a gusting torrent, plucking at clothes and hair, a swirling maelstrom that whipped the loose scree into the faces of their attackers. Several stumbled and fell, but the rest came on, heads down, bodies angled against the wind, not even a flicker of fear in their eyes.

"They are the monk's followers!" Iuchi Qadan shouted, face twisted in pain as she bent to retrieve her spear.

Although Irie did not trust the Unicorn, she could see the truth of Qadan's words clear enough.

Her voice the howl of a rising gale, Irie stoked the wind, a wild, shrieking chant entreating the air spirits to greater force. Villagers tumbled back down the slope. Others dropped to their knees, still crawling toward Irie and the others.

Sweat slicked Irie's forehead, tickling between her shoulder blades. The local spirits were as hard and cold as the mountains through which they gusted. They snatched at her exhalation, every indrawn breath seeming to bring less and less air into Irie's lungs.

Other spirits moved along numinous currents. Colder, darker, they darted amidst the elemental gyre, their twisted shapes like pennants caught in the gale. The spirits of air shrank from their corrupting touch. A sharp fleck of rock carved a painful gash across Irie's cheek, a stone striking her shoulder with such force that it drove her back a step, her arm buzzing with pain.

Kansen. Corrupted spirits. Qadan had been right.

Centering herself, Irie tried to renew her call, but whoever had summoned the kansen was powerful indeed. The words seemed to slip from her lips, unspoken, unheard. With a low moan, she fell to one knee, the icy gale cutting her to the bone.

The cultists lurched to their feet.

Naoki sent one woman stumbling with a kick to the knee, then turned to help Irie to her feet.

"More behind us!" Qadan shouted.

Irie glanced back to see that a half-dozen attackers had skirted the base of the hill.

The Unicorn tucked the spear under her wounded arm and took several stumbling steps toward the horses. As if aware of her need, one of the mounts lowered its head, turning so Qadan could catch the saddle pommel and drag herself up. Twisting, she brandished her spear at the oncoming attackers, then kicked her mount into a charge.

Irie lost sight of the Unicorn as nausea swept over her like a rising tide.

"Can you stop them?" Naoki dragged her a few steps back as the peasants began to close on them once again.

Irie nodded, but in truth, she was not sure. Master Masatsuge had warned her of such sorcery – corrupt rituals, blood magic and the like – but Phoenix territory was far from the Shadowlands, and she had never encountered true kansen.

With a soft grunt, Irie pulled free of Naoki. Willing her knees not to buckle, she centered herself, reaching for the Empty Flame, attempting to cultivate an inner fire that would let her reach spirits of fire and void.

There was a flicker, heat without light, a moment of weightless energy, but Irie's concentration was not sufficient to hold the mantra in her thoughts, and it slipped away, leaving naught but fire.

It would have to be enough.

Fingers interlaced, Irie reached for the blaze.

Bonfire bright, the spirits of fire twined from the empty air.

Heat washed over Irie, forcing her back a step. She bent her knees, pushing into the scorching wave, determined, unafraid.

For the first time since Masatsuge's death, Irie was in her element.

The kansen were strong, but only loosely bound. Whoever had bid them aid the assault had either fled or not been nearby in the first place. Her words the crackle of burning cinders, Irie entreated the fire spirits to scour their blighted foes.

She felt as if gripped by fever, limbs trembling, her forehead hot as a forge. But Irie did not relent, pouring all her anger, her fear, her rage into the spinning maelstrom of elemental energy. The kansen scattered like burning leaves. Seared by a coruscating glow, they slipped back to whatever mystical blight housed such corrupted energies.

Irie would have fallen had not Naoki caught her.

Two cultists came in, clubs swinging. Naoki released Irie to crush one's fingers with her jitte. The other struck Irie with a ringing blow across the shoulders. She hardly felt it, the spiritual conflict having rendered her thoughts slow, her limbs numb and sluggish.

She hit the ground hard. Words came, rituals for aid, but the fall had knocked the wind from her. It was all Irie could do to push to her knees. She labored to draw breath, vision blurred from exertion. She saw Naoki struggling with two cultists, Qadan riding in small circles as men and women thrust bamboo spears at her horse.

Irie turned, hands digging into the rocky scree as she sought to entreat the elements in her defense. Although she felt the spirits move, those of the earth were always slow to rouse. Her attacker stepped forward, hateful gaze upon Irie as he brought his club down.

A samurai in gray and blue stepped from behind a nearby boulder. He caught the arm of the cultist mid-swing. Breaking it with a casual twist, he drove a fist into the man's jaw, dropping him like a sack of millet.

The samurai's armor looked to be of the heavy, overlapping design favored by the Crab, its breastplate embossed with the Kuni family crest. He was so large Irie at first thought him some manner of ogre or underworld demon.

Two other cultists turned on him. His backhand sent the first reeling away, face bloodied. The second he simply lifted bodily from the ground and tossed down the hill.

The samurai moved among the cultists like an ox through tall grass. One struck at him with a stave, and he twisted, expression almost workmanlike as he caught the blow on one armored shoulder, then snatched the staff from his opponent's grip easily, as if he were pulling reeds. Bamboo shattered over the peasant's head, the Crab samurai turning from his poleaxed opponent to bury the jagged haft in the chest of another. He helped himself to the man's club, which he applied to the other three cultists with brutal results.

Finally, Irie's lungs responded to her will, and she drew in a whooping breath, stumbling to her feet. In barely a few seconds, the Crab samurai had disposed of all the cultists on the rise.

"Thank you for the rescue, friend," Naoki panted, hands on knees.

The large samurai turned on them.

"I am Kitsuki Naoki. Might I inquire as to your–"

Irie saw the samurai shift. Acting on instinct, she grabbed the back of Naoki's robe, dragging the investigator back as their erstwhile savior brought his club down in a vicious swipe.

Shock bled into anger, Irie's arms prickling at the thought of one who could kill so indiscriminately.

The Crab followed with a looping backhand, almost too quick for the eye to follow, but Irie was already chanting, her voice the low rumble of a distant avalanche. With a sharp crack, a finger of stone thrust up from the ground, blocking the samurai's advance.

He moved around it, but Irie summoned another, and another, the earth spirits answering her plea to craft a hedge of rock between her and the hulking samurai.

"I don't understand." Naoki shook her head. "Why is he–"

"What do his motives matter?" Irie tugged her down the hill toward Qadan's remaining horse.

The Crab rounded the rough wall. Rock shifted under his boots as he descended the hill, walking with the calm, unhurried stride of a man on an evening stroll. Irie could sense no evidence of the supernatural about him, nor did his broad-featured face betray any malice, and yet there was a hollow intensity about his deep-set eyes, like a butcher carving cuts of meat.

Irie stumbled toward Qadan's other horse, which was tugging at its reins. Stones turned under Irie's foot, and she fell to one knee. She glanced back as Naoki helped her up. Despite his measured pace, the samurai had covered a surprising amount of ground. He would have overtaken them, had not Qadan's charge driven two cultists into his path.

"Stay away from him!" Irie shouted as the samurai dashed a cultist's head against a nearby boulder.

Qadan gave her a confused look but turned away.

Hands trembling, Irie untied the second horse's reins and dragged herself up into the saddle.

She bent, hand extended for Naoki to grasp. The Dragon

investigator watched, open-mouthed, as the Crab knocked the second cultist's legs from under him, then finished the man with a heavy stomp to the chest.

"Hurry!" Irie's shout seemed to break Naoki from her horrified stupor, and she reached up to catch Irie's hand, clambering up behind her.

"This way!" Qadan jerked her head toward a cleft between two cliffs.

Naoki's arms tight around her stomach, Irie kicked the horse forward. The ground was too uneven for a full gallop, but they cantered down the narrow switchback into a canyon studded with thorny trees.

Irie had always considered herself a good rider, but it was all she could do to keep pace with Qadan. Despite her wound, the Unicorn threaded the rocky bluffs with almost preternatural skill.

It crossed Irie's mind that Qadan could be leading them into a trap. But whatever the Unicorn planned could be no worse than what they had just escaped. So she rode on, following Qadan for what seemed like hours.

At last, the Unicorn raised a hand for a halt. Nodding toward a rocky overhang, she turned her horse in the direction of shelter. Irie followed.

"I am Shiba Irie, first disciple of Master Asako Masatsuge." She nodded toward Naoki. "And this is Kitsuki Naoki, investigator and Emerald Magistrate. We seek–"

"There are brushes in the bag." Dismounting with a pained wince, Qadan began to see to her horse, seeming unconcerned by rank and title.

"Why is the monk after you?" Naoki asked. "What is a Unicorn doing in Crab lands?"

"We may need to flee in a hurry." Qadan untied a waterskin and poured some into a bowl for her mount to drink. "Horses first. Talk later."

Irie and Naoki slipped from the back of their mount, taking care to check the horse's hooves for stones and loosen the tack and saddle straps to let it breathe. Despite their hurried flight, Irie's mount seemed to calm faster than she did, her heart continuing to race as her mind spun with questions. Only when they had finished watering and caring for the horses did Qadan turn to them.

"I was searching for the resting place of a hero of my clan," she offered. "What I found was… them."

"What do they want?" Naoki asked.

"What do any dark sorcerers want? Blood? Power?" Qadan shrugged. "Their leader spoke of a tomb. A place of great evil, I imagine."

The magistrate's excitement was obvious. "The leader, what did he look like?"

"Older man, perhaps seventy summers." She sucked her teeth. "Attired simply, but his head was shaved like a monk. His command of blood magic was… horrifying."

It was as if a trickle of meltwater bled along Irie's spine. Somehow, she had let herself believe they would find no one. Despite the letters, despite the concerns of dark magic. It would have been better for it all to simply fade away.

Naoki clapped her hands, glancing to Irie. "It's him. It has to be."

"You know this man?" Qadan asked.

"My companion and I have been tracking him since–" Naoki paused as Irie raised a warning hand.

"When we first found you, I was following a trail of

corruption." Irie tensed, unsure of how the Unicorn would respond.

"The crypt was not what I thought." Qadan glanced away. "It held something dark, something foul. They murdered my bodyguard. I sought to confront the monk, but he destroyed my talismans."

"Talismans? You practice name magic?" Irie had not meant the question as an accusation, but the Unicorn seemed to bridle at her tone.

"I will not be interrogated by one who knows nothing of our ways." Qadan's scowl was as sharp as the surrounding peaks. "Your rituals entreat the spirits, begging, bullying without regard for what you interact with. We forge a *bond*, a relationship. When that fiend broke my talismans, I didn't just lose my spirits, I lost part of myself."

"Fine words, Unicorn." Irie found her own temper rising. "But it was not I who reeked of corruption."

Qadan glared at her. "And what do you sense now, Phoenix?"

Truth be told, Irie sensed nothing. Although there was a lingering wisp of taint, it hung about them all. No one who stood in the presence of kansen could come away without contamination. Unless one embraced it, however, such foulness could be easily cleared through ritual purification.

"We can discuss the finer points of spirits later." Naoki stepped between them, hands raised. "Lest you forget, the cultists almost killed us. Not to mention that creature in Crab armor."

"The monk invoked kansen," Irie said. "He must follow some manner of demon."

"I am not so sure." Qadan seemed troubled. "The monk unleashed foul spirits, but he was untouched by them."

"It was the same when he murdered the Dragon officials," Naoki added. "All the trappings of dark magic, but no lingering corruption."

Qadan gave a soft sigh. "In the crypt, he used a relic – a necklace of bone inscribed with strange names."

Naoki glanced at Irie, but she gave a quick shake of her head. She could feel the weight of the mask in her satchel, resisting the urge to grasp it. If Master Masatsuge possessed a similar charm, it was surely only to determine how to destroy it.

"He used name magic?" she asked.

"It is not the same." Qadan balled her fists. "We name keepers commune with the spirits. It takes time to forge such a close relationship, but in learning their elemental nature we are gifted with names." She squeezed her eyes shut, teeth bared. "To exploit such names is a mockery of our ways. The monk had no bond, no connection. What he did was horrible, vicious – a betrayal of everything we hold sacred."

Irie had read of such corrupt sorcerers. In all cases, they had been tainted, evil things, their workings reeking of the Shadowlands. Without the medium of ritual and prayer, those who dealt with spirits opened themselves to darker forces. No matter Qadan's beliefs to the contrary, Irie knew name magic to be a fraught practice.

"How could he wield such power without consequence?" she asked. "Surely the corruption must go somewhere?"

"The monk is a Bloodspeaker." A man's low, rasping voice came from behind Irie. He spoke slowly, as if testing each word.

Irie turned, hands coming up reflexively, her mind full of fire. Naoki stepped to her side, jitte hissing from her sash, Qadan's spear already pointing toward the interloper.

"He follows a cruel path." The Crab samurai stepped into the shadow of the overhang, footfalls quiet as a plague. "One that leads beyond death."

CHAPTER FIFTEEN

Shosuro Gensuke watched the rebels with growing irritation. They had descended on Crossroads in late midmorning, trickling down from the surrounding hills in ragged mobs. Gensuke was no strategist, but he had infiltrated enough army camps to know when a force was poorly organized. Although there had been much talk of this "Bent-Winged Shrike," the architect of the revolution had yet to materialize.

Which suited Gensuke just fine.

Since he had disposed of that Crane fool at Five-Dragon Gate, his thoughts had been troubled by the porcelain-masked abominations, their dread presence dredging up things Gensuke preferred to leave buried in the muck of his subconscious. Two centuries was long enough to blur all but the most important details, but it was not enough to erase the memory of the betrayal that had almost scoured the Scorpion Clan from Rokugan. The masked creatures at Five-Dragon Gate bore an unsettling resemblance to those described in Scorpion poems and stories of the Battle of Sleeping River.

The dead had come in their thousands. Spurred by dark sorcery and aided by a traitor from the Shosuro family, it had taken the combined might of all the Great Clans to beat back the invasion. A desperate, brutal affair culminating in Sleeping River, it had almost doomed the Empire – and yet, almost no records remained. It was as if Rokugan did not *want* to remember.

Had the traitor not been of Gensuke's own family, the Shosuro might have forgotten as well. Could the traitor Akifumi have returned? He would be centuries old, but such longevity was not beyond the reach of dark sorcerers.

Gensuke dug his fingernails into his palm, using the pain to focus his mind. A coincidence, surely. The Twilight Mountains dipped down into the Shadowlands where such twisted creatures hid behind every rock and tree. A coincidence, yes. Terrible, tragic, but ultimately not Gensuke's fault. He had done as he was ordered to do. After tying off one loose thread, Gensuke would be back to Scorpion lands. He could make a full report and let the clan elders debate the danger.

The future was a distraction. For now, he need only focus on Doji Masahiro.

Gensuke had hoped to use the chaos of the rebel assault to kill the Crane, but Masahiro's Matsu bodyguard had proven surprisingly adept. Seemingly overnight, she'd had barricades thrown across the roads, knocking holes in dams to flood the rice fields and turning the town outskirts into a sodden, sucking morass. Armed with axes and bamboo spears the villagers had held off the rebels' piecemeal assault far longer than Gensuke expected.

At least there had been no sign of the dead. Gensuke prided himself on always finishing a contract, but after the horrors he had witnessed at Five-Dragon Gate, he was beginning to suspect there was more at play than clan politics.

He shifted amidst the baled hay on the upper floor of the

storehouse. A quick sprint from the manor walls, it provided good visibility with little chance of being spotted. Studying the manor, Gensuke counted heartbeats. The Matsu woman had posted guards along the walls. Although better armed than the rabble at the barricades, Gensuke had no doubt he could slip by with little trouble. They hadn't even bothered to vary their routes.

Good news for them, as it meant he wouldn't have to kill any. Good news for Gensuke, too. Only amateurs left bodies in their wake, and Gensuke was nothing if not professional.

Shouts rose from the western barricade as rebels tried to overrun the position. Gensuke couldn't believe the villagers opposed them. Could they not see they had more in common with the rebels than some conceited Crane diplomat?

Not that Gensuke felt any ill-will toward Masahiro. The Crane had attempted to suborn imperial succession with a handpicked candidate. The ploy was nothing new; more than one Hantei had been the puppet of one clan or another. Except Masahiro and his brother had failed. And failure carried consequences.

Consequences Gensuke had been sent to mete out.

The moment came. One guard rounded the far corner of the wall. The next guard, a large man with a pronounced limp, would not come into view for another five heartbeats.

Gensuke tucked his legs to absorb the shock of hitting the hard-packed dirt. In a moment he had sprinted across the intervening distance and leapt to catch the lip of the wall. From previous forays into the manor, Gensuke knew the interior boasted a patch of overgrown camellia bushes. But as he slipped soundlessly over the wall, he found the ground bare save for a few hacked stumps.

That damned Matsu had cleared away all the brush, flowerbeds bare as harvested fields. It would take the Fortunes' own luck to make it across the garden unspotted. With an irritated sigh, Gensuke dropped back over the wall, slipping into the shadows of the warehouse.

Only fools depended on luck. Professionals created opportunity.

Gensuke checked to see his short swords were still in place. Sharp as a courtier's tongue, they would have made quick work of Masahiro, just as they had his brother. But while the contract stipulated Hiroshige be bloodied, Gensuke's lord had insisted Masahiro die "as a criminal," denied a warrior's death by the blade, or even a courtier's poisoning.

All of which conspired to make Gensuke's task more difficult.

He clucked his tongue as the second guard limped into view. Despite the poor tools provided, the Matsu woman had managed to craft a credible defense. Gensuke needed to distract Masahiro's guard dog, draw her away from the Crane or, failing that, engage her with other foes.

He frowned under his mask, considering.

Perhaps the rebels might be of use after all.

Gensuke headed toward the western barricade, taking care to keep to the afternoon shadows. It was helpful that Crossroads was a trade town, storehouses and stalls crowding the main streets like hungry refugees. Gensuke had paced the maze of backstreets on his first night in town. To know the terrain was to know the best means of attack, not to mention escape. Gensuke might respect his own abilities, but he was not so arrogant as to believe himself flawless.

Such pride was for Crane and Lion; the Scorpion were far more practical.

Some rebels were attempting to set the barricade alight. Defenders doused the wall with buckets of water, draping wet clothes over smoking logs and broken crates. With typical peasant timidity, the remaining combatants prodded at each other with bamboo spears.

Gensuke squatted in the shade of a blacksmith's stall, studying the conflict. Despite much shouting and clamor, he noted few wounds on either side. The rebels who attacked Crossroads seemed a different species than those who faced the imperial expedition – unsettled, almost afraid, casting worried glances over their shoulders.

These must be the dregs. The fiercest rebels had opposed Katamori's assault. Even then, they would have been quickly defeated had not Gensuke forged those false orders in the general's name.

It had been laughably easy to stoke mistrust among the clan forces. All would have gone to plan had it not been for Bayushi Kogoro. For all his preparation, Gensuke could never have foreseen the Scorpion contingent would be led by the one Bayushi possessed of a conscience. With Katamori discredited and Hiroshige doomed, the situation was ripe for Kogoro to take control, but the Scorpion commander had demurred. Unaccountably, he had even seemed discomfited by the impending assassination of his Crane colleague.

The fool had almost given the plan away. Fortunately, Gensuke was a quick thinker.

His gaze roamed across the muddy street, drifting over houses, storefronts, and carts piled with goods. With a nod, Gensuke rose from the shadows, his strides quick, but not panicked. He was dressed as a local, in drab browns and grays, blades concealed beneath bulky work clothes, his roughspun mask easily mistakable for a scarf tied to ward off the smoke.

Gensuke stooped to grab an empty water bucket, then joined the scattering of villagers dashing back and forth. Rather than empty his bucket upon the barricade, he helped himself to a flaming bit of wood, concealing it in the bucket as he hurried back toward the well.

With a quick glance around to ensure none were paying attention, Gensuke tossed the flaming brand into a nearby stall. The canvas caught quickly, dry wood and thatch feeding the blaze as fire spread among the closely packed dwellings. Within a score of breaths, it had grown to a credible conflagration, and Gensuke absconded to the far side of the street to watch.

The first panicked shouts rose above the din of combat, defenders rushing about with water, unsure whether to see to the barricade or their own homes. Attentions divided, they could not resist the rebels, who spilled over the barricade in a shouting, clamoring throng. Some peasants remained, either too foolish or stubborn to retreat, and were cut down. Fortunately, the majority showed sense and fled.

Gensuke stood with a sad tilt of his head. The deaths were regrettable, but he consoled himself with the knowledge the defenders would have been overwhelmed eventually. If anything, he had spared them undue suffering by hastening the inevitable result.

Their garb almost identical to the villagers, the rebels distinguished themselves only through a coal-stained armband – no doubt some ill-conceived nod to the dead miners at the heart of their movement. Fortunately, Gensuke had availed himself of a similar accoutrement earlier in the day. Slipping it onto his arm, he joined the flood of rebels, most of whom also wore masks.

After some halfhearted looting, he was able to steer a relatively sizeable contingent toward the manor. They arrived to find the newly reinforced gate barred and blocked with heaps of half-rotted furniture.

"Over the walls, comrades!" A bristle-bearded man with a missing hand waved what looked like a butcher's cleaver. "Make the tyrants pay!"

No doubt the man's grievance was legitimate, but Gensuke could not allow for the possibility of Masahiro being slain by some overzealous peasant. He needed a distraction, not a slaughter.

"They have guards, warriors!" Letting his voice slip into the low drawl of the far-mountain dialect, Gensuke called from the back of the crowd. "Why not smoke them out?"

The man peered into the milling crowd, but Gensuke had already slipped behind a red-cheeked woman in a leatherworker's smock.

"Let the murderers choke on ash." Gensuke pitched his voice higher. "They'll come out soon enough."

"Been here too long already. You all know he's coming." Bristle-Beard tried to quell the crowd, but others had already taken up Gensuke's call. Like a murmuration of starlings, the mob had shifted with blinding speed, wheeling to gather up tinder and broken wood to pile against the gate.

Within a span of minutes, the manor gate was cheerily ablaze. Gensuke was just about to slip over the far wall when a shiver went through the air. That was the only way to explain it, as if heat from an invisible conflagration had suddenly turned air to water.

A man stepped from nowhere.

He was clad in embroidered robes, dyed a crimson so dark

they seemed almost black in the smoky light. Long-sleeved and flowing, they were gathered at the waist by a simple sash. His face was shadowed by a wide-brimmed straw hat; even so, he could be no other.

The Bent-Winged Shrike.

With a wave of his hand, the Shrike quelled the flaming gate, smoke slipping away as if caught in the grasp of a mighty wind.

The rebels flinched back, faces pale, stolen weapons clutched in white-knuckled grips.

"I told you the nobles were to be brought to me." The Shrike's voice was that of an old man, someone more accustomed to archives than assaults.

"We are not dogs, to hunt or heel." Bristle-Beard rose from behind a pile of broken barrels, red-faced and furious. He glanced to the others as if for support. "When we rose, we swore there would be no lords, no masters."

"Such high-minded ideals mean nothing to a sharpened blade. Where would you be without my guidance?" The Shrike chuckled, casually walking toward the man. "Rotting in a field, your heads on display as a warning to others who might think to reach beyond their station."

Despite the obvious shaking of his legs, Bristle-Beard displayed laudable resolve. "We will not trade one oppressor for another."

"And do you all feel this way?" The Shrike glanced about.

A few score of the other rebels rose, moving to Bristle-Beard's side, albeit hesitantly.

Gensuke considered slipping away, but feared any movement might bring attention. So he simply endeavored to make himself as unobtrusive as possible. The Shrike was clearly a creature of dark and terrible power, almost certainly the architect of the slaughter at Five-Dragon Gate.

Gensuke squinted at the dark sorcerer. There were no paintings or statues of Shosuro Akifumi, nor had any descriptions survived. The Shrike seemed old, but not two centuries old. Even so, he might know of the traitor. Not that Gensuke had any means to compel him to part with that knowledge.

"Alas, I had much higher hopes for you." The Shrike glanced toward the manor gate. "Fire is an easy tool to use. Far harder to use well." He turned to regard Bristle-Beard. "Shall I show you?"

A tongue of bruise-purple flame licked from the Shrike's outstretched finger, seeming almost to caress the big man's cheek. Nothing happened for a moment, then Bristle-Beard began to cough. Red-faced, he doubled over as a torrent of smoke and soot poured from his mouth.

The man's body began to glow, as if his chest hid a festival lantern, a skein of pale red skin and shadowed bones barely able to contain the growing light. His skin blackened, peeling back as flames crept along the outline of his skeleton. There was no time to scream, no time to flail, no time to even fall. He simply went up like a wisp of paper in a bonfire, nothing more than a smear of greasy ash upon the hard-packed dirt.

Only then did Gensuke realize he had taken several steps back, one hand pressed to his mouth. Like water slipping through cracks in ancient stone, Gensuke's self-assurance began to crumble. He had seen the opportunity to remove a stain on his family's reputation. Now, he only wished to flee from this horror.

"I tire of this pretense. Kill them." The Shrike tilted his head, and the street descended into chaos.

Gensuke could not restrain the soft moan that slipped past his tightly clenched teeth when dozens of masked dead scuttled from the shadows. They fell upon the rebels like hungry dogs, ripping and tearing as the living tried to flee.

One of the dead noticed Gensuke, limbs almost spiderlike as it scrabbled across the rubble. He knew his blades would be of little use – what was a slit throat to a thing like that?

He leapt up to catch the lip of the wall, pulling himself over just as the creature lunged. Without a glance back he hopped down into the ruined garden, almost twisting his ankle in his haste to get away.

The garden was full of smoke, guards little more than panicked shadows running this way and that. He could hear the Matsu woman yelling – curses mostly.

In all this confusion, the Crane would be easy to kill. Then Gensuke could slip back to Scorpion lands and warn his clan. Now that the dead had passed Five-Dragon Gate, the Shrike could either march east into heavily fortified Crab lands, or north into the Shinomen Forest and beyond into Scorpion territory.

Gensuke knew which direction he would go.

More than the shock of realization was the growing understanding he was on the wrong side of something more dire than clan politics. It seemed too much of a coincidence that his mission coincided with the Shrike's goals. Perhaps the sorcerer had agents within the Scorpion Clan. Gensuke could not believe any of his fellows would help such a vile creature, but he was not so foolish as to think his clan proof against promises of wealth or power.

Akifumi had proven as much.

Even should Gensuke warn the Scorpion, it was clear they

could not stand alone. All of Rokugan must be told – the courts, the legions, the clans, the emperor – but Gensuke was under no illusions as to how much credence they would give to the word of a Scorpion assassin.

Dodging through the shadowed smoke, Gensuke wrinkled his nose. Masahiro had friends in the Imperial City. If anyone could make those in power take notice, it was the pompous Crane courtier.

"To the gate!" The Matsu woman's shout cut through the confused babble.

Baring his teeth, Gensuke made for the strident voice. Let spirits and sages ruminate about the future, Gensuke could only do as best he could in the present. Whatever the Shrike planned, it boded ill for both Rokugan and the Scorpion Clan, and that was enough to act upon. Gensuke had always prided himself on a job well done, be it a perfectly sharpened blade or the slow strangulation of an exiled Crane noble, but this went beyond simple assassination.

No matter the cost, he could not allow another Sleeping River.

Professionalism be damned.

CHAPTER SIXTEEN

Qadan's uninjured hand dropped to the satchel at her side, unconsciously reaching for her talismans. Rather than the comforting power of old friends, there was only a dire emptiness, as if Qadan had clenched her jaw only to find her teeth gone.

Wood scraped on stone as she fumbled for her spear, wounded shoulder stiff and painful as she pointed it at the samurai in Crab armor.

Stepping back, Naoki drew her jitte with a low hiss, while Irie extended a hand toward the samurai, palm out.

"One more step, and I burn you where you stand."

"I thought Phoenix were pacifists." The Crab squatted, forearms on knees, calm as if they discussed the cost of rice.

"There is a time and place for peace," Irie replied coolly. "This is not it."

Qadan leveled her spear at the Crab, careful not to jostle her wounded shoulder. The fight and hard ride afterward had torn her inexpert stitches. Jargal would have done a better job, but Jargal was gone. The memory of his disappearance came as sharp as the pain in her shoulder. She did not even know if her bodyguard was dead, or if the monk's terrible summoning had sent him somewhere worse than the Realm of Waiting.

"Why did you attack us?" she asked through gritted teeth.

"I thought you were Bloodspeakers," he replied.

"They were trying to kill us!" Qadan almost shouted the words.

He gave a noncommittal grunt. "Evil often battles evil."

"So, you would simply have murdered everyone without knowing the reason for our battle?" Naoki asked. "Is that wise?"

"In my experience, yes."

"And what now?" Qadan edged around Naoki, spear angled toward the Crab's throat. She had seen how fast he could move and felt much better with eight feet of steel-tipped ash between them.

"Now, I know differently."

"How?" Irie asked, hand still raised.

"The cultists told me. Some were not dead." His voice held no emotion. "They are now."

"How are we to trust you?" Qadan asked.

"We seek the same thing, although you do not know it."

"And you do?" Irie asked.

He made no reply, only watched them, unblinking, his eyes the color of wet shale.

"How do we know you will not try to harm us again?" Irie asked.

"Because you are still alive." He stood, head cocked as if listening.

Qadan heard nothing but the low wind threaded with a distant trickle of water over rock. The strange samurai seemed touched, or tainted; certainly not the first of his unfortunate clan to succumb to the terrors that lurked beyond the Carpenter's Wall.

"I do not trust him." Irie stood with the uneasy aspect of a woman anticipating sudden violence. Qadan did not blame her.

"Nor I," Naoki added, although from the magistrate's thoughtful expression, Qadan suspected there was a "but" to follow.

The Crab did not give her the chance. "Then we have nothing more to discuss."

Qadan tensed, gathering her legs for a thrust. But the Crab samurai only walked back down the hill.

"Should I detain him?" Irie asked.

"He doesn't seem one to volunteer information, even at dagger point." Naoki frowned, then cupped a hand to call after him. "You haven't told us your name."

The Crab paused. "Kuni Tetsuo."

Knowing the samurai's name only deepened Qadan's concerns. The Kuni were a family who walked in shadow, ostensibly to better combat it, but Qadan had heard of many who succumbed to the lure of forbidden knowledge.

Even so, Tetsuo seemed perhaps her best chance at discovering what corrupt magic had ruined her talismans. She could still feel her spirits, if only faintly. Eruar, Gion, Kahenu, relationships she had nurtured over years reduced to a few tenuous threads. The spirits' names yet remained to her, but to invoke such power without regaining their trust would be the cruelest betrayal. It was best to accept her talismans were gone, at least for the moment.

No. That wasn't quite right. One remained.

Qadan could feel it in her satchel, edges sharp even through the layers of quilted leather. She had invoked its name in the crypt, read it from the great dome without nurturing even the barest connection. And yet, there had been no resistance, no anger. The spirit had come willingly, almost gleefully.

Which was troubling.

"Where are you going?" she called after Tetsuo.

"To kill more Bloodspeakers," came the gravelly reply.

She glanced at Naoki and Irie. The Dragon magistrate seemed troubled, lips downturned, her weapons held close to her chest as if she were weighing them. By contrast, Irie watched the Crab with almost desperate longing, as if he bore away some treasured object.

"What do you know of the Bent-Winged Shrike?" Irie called after him.

"I know he shall soon die," Tetsuo said without slowing or looking back.

Qadan frowned at his armored back. She did not trust the Crab, but neither did she trust Irie or Naoki. The magistrate's motives seemed solid enough – if the monk had murdered several clan officials, it made sense the Dragon were tracking him. But it did not explain why a Phoenix elementalist had become involved. Irie was holding back, perhaps even lying. Although Qadan had no way of unearthing the Phoenix's truth, she could at least test the Crab.

The Kuni were not the only ones who dealt with Bloodspeakers.

"Wait!" Qadan called down the hill.

Tetsuo paused.

"What can you tell us of those who attacked us?"

"Nothing if you don't follow me." He slipped around a canted boulder and disappeared.

Qadan clucked her tongue, then winced inwardly as she recognized it for one of Jargal's more irritating mannerisms. With a sigh, she turned to Marrow, tightening straps before taking up the reins and leading him down the hill.

"Where are you going?" Naoki asked.

"We are days away from the nearest Crab castle, and I doubt the Bloodspeakers have given up their search."

"Their search for what?" Naoki asked.

"Perhaps he knows." Qadan nodded at the cleft where Tetsuo had gone. "Perhaps he doesn't. Either way, I am not simply going to wait for them to find me." She had gone twenty paces downhill before she half-turned. "You may keep my bodyguard's horse for the time being. Treat him like family."

"You have my word." Naoki grinned. Even Irie's veneer of cold mistrust seemed to thaw slightly, her scowl relaxing into pensive regard. Naoki leaned close to Irie, their whispered exchange punctuated by gestures and glances at Qadan. She affected not to notice, shoulders tickling as if Irie and Naoki held bows aimed her back.

After a long moment, she heard the creak of harness, Jargal's horse giving a low whicker followed by the clack of hooves on stone.

Tetsuo did not even glance over as they came up beside him.

"What do you know of the Bent-Winged Shrike?" Irie asked before Qadan could speak.

"Little," Tetsuo replied. "He is a Bloodspeaker, like the monk. A follower of Iuchiban."

"The dark sorcerer?" Naoki asked. "I thought he was just a myth."

"Iuchiban is real enough," Tetsuo said.

"Then why is there nothing written about him in the High Histories?" Naoki asked.

The Crab shrugged. "I am no scholar."

Irie sniffed. "Even if we assume the stories are true, were

not Iuchiban and his followers slain at the Battle of Sleeping River?"

"Iuchiban cannot be killed so easily," Tetsuo replied.

Qadan tried to hide her surprise at the discussion of Iuchiban. She had read of his corrupt name magic – distant, thirdhand reports of blood sorcery and risen corpses, of impossible power over death itself. A shadowy figure even at the time, Iuchiban's crimes had only grown murkier in the intervening centuries. But why would his followers be seeking out Unicorn burial places? And what role did the Green Horde play in all this?

Qadan glanced at her companions. Although Irie seemed focused on the Crab, she noticed Naoki regarding her with a thoughtful expression.

"Our Unicorn companion first encountered the monk in an ancient tomb." Irie nodded at Qadan before turning her gaze on Tetsuo. "Could he be seeking to raise another army of demons?"

"Not demons," Tetsuo replied. "Risen dead."

There was a moment of tight-lipped silence as everyone worked through the dire implications. Most Rokugani dead were burned; most, but not all. Especially this far from civilization, older practices might still survive.

"It could not be the monk." It was Naoki who replied. When the others regarded her, the magistrate gave an uncomfortable shrug. "He would not wield such a blunt instrument."

Tetsuo nodded. "Other Bloodspeakers might."

"The Shrike?"

"Perhaps."

"Might they be one and the same?" Irie asked.

"Not unless Bloodspeakers can travel across the Empire in a heartbeat." Naoki frowned, seeming uneasy. "Can they?"

Tetsuo shook his head.

"Good." Naoki straightened. "An army of the dead, that would explain how the rebels overcame the imperial expedition."

The Crab samurai grunted in affirmation, eyes on the path ahead as he continued to walk.

"My master must have suspected Bloodspeaker involvement." Irie nodded. "He would have sought to uproot such foulness."

Naoki seemed about to respond, but a sharp glance from Irie caused the Dragon magistrate to run a hand through her hair, glancing away.

More secrets.

Qadan frowned, an uncomfortable suspicion tickling at the back of her thoughts. "The monk spoke of other crypts."

"They seek the Tomb of Iuchiban," Tetsuo said. "Just as I do."

"If Iuchiban cannot be slain, how can he have a tomb?" Naoki asked.

"A prison, more like." It was Irie who responded. "It is said Iuchiban's body was sealed in a warded tomb, its location unknown even to the architects, but that his spirit escaped to plague Rokugan once more. He was only defeated through the combined efforts of all the Great Clans at the Battle of Sleeping River, to be sealed away once more."

"Lies." Tetsuo's reply was matter of fact.

Irie glared at the hulking Crab samurai. "My information comes from a sacred scroll inscribed by ancient Phoenix masters."

"My information comes from Bloodspeakers." Tetsuo shrugged. "Iuchiban's tomb was not built by mortal hands, but by servants of the dark sorcerer himself."

"You would trust cultists over clan records?" Naoki asked.

"I have ways of finding the truth." Although the Crab's response was delivered in the same flat tone, Qadan could not ignore the implication of his words. Tetsuo did not seem a man given to more gentle methods of inquiry.

Naoki chewed her lip, brows knitted in confusion. "If the tomb was not built to contain Iuchiban, then why?"

"It is said to contain terrible secrets – relics and spiritual lore collected over many lifetimes," Tetsuo replied.

"How do you know this?" Qadan asked. The others might trust the Crab samurai's words, but the monk's betrayal still ached like a fresh wound. She had been blind to the danger of the hired laborers, and it had cost her Jargal and her spirits.

"My order was founded after Iuchiban was defeated at Sleeping River," Tetsuo replied. "We have interrogated many Bloodspeakers in the centuries since. Many spoke of this tomb, hidden, powerful. Several of my predecessors sought it. None returned."

"Why would Iuchiban conceal the tomb from his disciples?" Qadan asked.

"He is a cruel and jealous master." Tetsuo regarded her for the first time since leaving the overhang. Qadan met his gaze boldly, as if daring the Crab to question her.

Whatever Tetsuo saw in her eyes must have satisfied him, for he gave the slightest of nods.

"The tomb also contains Iuchiban's heart. The only way to destroy him."

"That must be what my master sought. A way to banish the dark sorcerer forever." Irie seemed genuinely relieved, her pinched face relaxing into an expression that appeared almost grateful.

Although the realization seemed to satisfy both her companions, it only heightened Qadan's concern. There were simply too many coincidences. The Bloodspeakers' corruption of name magic, the secretive return of the Green Horde, the similarity between Iuchiban's name and that of–

"You have been quiet, Iuchi." There was a focused intensity in Naoki's tone, as if the magistrate were interrogating a suspect. "Have you no questions for our Crab friend?"

"Apologies." Qadan inclined her head to hide the flush creeping up her neck. "My wound troubles me."

"I can see to it." Irie glanced at the others. "If you will all consent to a short rest."

"That might be wise." Naoki looked to Tetsuo.

The Crab gave no response, only halted, arms crossed over his broad chest.

"I'll take that as a 'yes.'" Naoki nodded.

Qadan gritted her teeth, pale and trembling as they peeled back the blood-encrusted silk from her shoulder. It was all she could do not to snarl as Irie prodded the ragged stitches.

"Had the monk not destroyed my talismans, I could have seen to this myself."

"Of course." Irie's tone held only mild condescension. Still, her ritual worked well enough. The smooth, flowing motions lured spirits of water from the parched air. They flowed around Qadan's wound, cool touch knitting flesh and calming ragged nerves. It was strange to be ministered to by spirits with whom Qadan had no connection, but she nodded her thanks, even as the sharp pang of loss made her eyes sting.

Whether it took weeks, months, or even years, she would rebuild her spiritual connections, prove herself worthy of their names once more.

Apparently mistaking Qadan's tears for physical discomfort, Naoki laid a hand on her arm.

"It is nothing." Qadan scrubbed a hand across her eyes, then flexed her shoulder. The spirits had left little more than a livid scar, and only echoes of pain.

"I am in your debt." She offered a grudging bow to Irie and Naoki.

"Then tell us the truth." The magistrate's turn came quick and sharp. "Why were the Bloodspeakers tracking you?"

"I saw the monk, witnessed his sorcery firsthand." Qadan shrugged. "They must wish me silenced."

"And the taint Irie sensed?"

"As I said, he corrupted my talismans," Qadan said. "It will take time and purification to make them whole again."

"What of Iuchiban?" Naoki continued. "Surely I cannot be the only one to have noticed the similarity between the name of an infamous dark sorcerer and that of your family's founder?"

"Iuchi died in the south, lost with the rest of the Green Horde." At least that was what Qadan had believed until recently. Now, she wasn't so sure.

Iuchi had been a powerful name keeper, perhaps the most skilled ever. If any were capable of such dark sorceries, it would be him. Rokugani history was littered with tales of seekers who had pressed too far, sought too much, and whose quest for knowledge had led to corruption.

"But both were name keepers?" Naoki asked, irritating in her doggedness.

"To liken blood sorcery to name magic is like comparing friendship to slavery." Qadan was growing tired of having to explain herself, especially with the wound of her own broken bonds still so fresh. "Name keepers cultivate their spirits, Bloodspeakers compel them."

She turned on Naoki, letting raw emotion bleed into her voice. "The monk took something from me in the tomb. He tore asunder relationships that took a lifetime to build." Qadan moved so she was almost face to face with the magistrate. "I will see him punished if I have to tear the very mountains from their roots, of that you can be sure, Dragon."

Naoki did not flinch at Qadan's closeness, only studied her face as if searching for some hint of deception.

Apparently satisfied, Naoki gave a soft sigh, a grin spreading across her face. "I believe you will." She clapped Qadan on her newly healed shoulder. "Come, let us track this Bloodspeaker together."

"My path leads elsewhere." Tetsuo spoke for the first time since they had stopped.

"I don't understand?" Qadan turned to regard him. "Do you not seek the monk as well?"

"The monk will reveal himself eventually," the Crab replied, voice level. "The rebellion has been corrupted. It represents the greater threat."

"And if the monk unearths Iuchiban's tomb?" Qadan asked. "If he gains access to its dark secrets? If he manages to empower his master?"

Tetsuo shrugged. "If."

Naoki looked from Qadan to Irie, as if either of them might possess some means of shifting the implacable Crab samurai. Qadan could but shake her head. Tetsuo clearly cared nothing for supposition.

"He's right." It was Irie who spoke. "The Shrike must possess dark sorcery. If so, he is the more powerful of the two."

"But… the monk, the letters?" Naoki asked.

"This monk has slain a few low-ranking officials. The Bent-Winged Shrike murdered a Phoenix Clan elder." Irie's hands tightened to fists at her side.

"What letters?" Qadan ignored Irie's outburst. "I have told you both all I know, and yet you hold back. What role did Irie's master play in all this?"

The Phoenix priest shifted uncomfortably. Whatever answer she might have given was lost as, apparently tiring of discussion, Tetsuo began to walk once more.

Irie half-turned, gaze flicking to the departing Crab.

"You can't mean to accompany him," Naoki said. "He's… he's…"

"I'm sorry." With a stilted bow, Irie hurried after Tetsuo.

Naoki watched them go, open-mouthed.

"Perhaps you aren't as good an investigator as you believe, Kitsuki," Qadan said with a wry tilt of her head. She held nothing against the Dragon, but it felt good, for once, not to be the one surprised.

Grinning, Qadan clapped Naoki on the shoulder, mimicking the smaller woman's tone. "Come, let us track the Shrike together."

As Naoki glanced over, Qadan let the smile fall from her face.

"But first, tell me all you know of Irie's master."

CHAPTER SEVENTEEN

If Doji Masahiro had ever been in a worse situation, he certainly could not recall. It was like the warrior stories Hiroshige used to tell – all smoke and shouting and flashing blades. Unfortunately, what had been thrilling on the page proved distressingly chaotic in person.

"Back to your posts!" Chiaki's rough voice cut through the crackle of burning wood. "Buckets to the pond!"

Thank the Fortunes for the Matsu. Chiaki's face might be as scarred as a teahouse table, but she had managed to bully the local mob into a reasonable approximation of defense – at least until the fires started.

Masahiro scrubbed a hand across smoke-stung eyes. Although practiced with blade and bow, he maintained no illusions concerning his ability to hold a line. Chiaki seemed to be doing an admirable job of that, so it seemed best for him to stay out of the way.

At the moment, Masahiro's only goal was to die well.

To be fair, the idea of dying did not appeal to him in the least, but it seemed far more fitting to be struck down in calm repose rather than in a sweating straining mob of peasants, his body trampled into the bloody muck.

It wouldn't do for the hero of a warrior tale, and it *certainly* wouldn't do for Doji Masahiro.

He knelt upon the central pavilion's creaking tatami mats, trying to maintain some semblance of decorum. Fortunately, he had managed to convince Chiaki to spare the stone garden and reflecting pond. An adequate view, at best, if somewhat spoiled by smoke and screams, but needs will as needs must.

At the moment, Masahiro's only real hope was that someone would finish him before the smoke ruined his kimono. A gift from Hiroshige, it was a fine weave of blue and pearl silk, embroidered with scenes of wings fluttering among shadowed branches, the moon picked out in pale silver thread, striking but understated.

He regarded one of the perfectly hemmed sleeves, wondering if he should remove the robe. It would be a shame to see such artistry spoiled by an errant spray of blood.

At least the smoke was clearing. Chiaki and the others must have gotten the fire under control. Masahiro was grateful for that. Once it had tainted the fabric, the smell of woodsmoke never really went away.

"Form up!" Chiaki's voice boomed like a battle drum. "They're through the gate!"

This was it, then. Masahiro congratulated himself on showing such composure in the face of death. Outnumbered, surrounded by traitors, the ancestors would still be pleased by his bravery. A true Crane to the very end.

An arm slipped around Masahiro's throat. Jerking him back, hard, it drew tight, cutting off his air and sparing him a very undignified squawk.

"If you desire to live, listen carefully," a man's voice hissed into Masahiro's ear. "In a few moments, the Bent-Winged Shrike will come. He is a dark sorcerer of great power. If you remain, he will take you, torture you for information, and possibly devour your soul. Do you understand?"

The attacker let up on his hold just enough for Masahiro to gasp out an affirmative.

"I can lead you from this place, but you will carry a warning to the Imperial Court: the dead walk – in their hundreds, their thousands." The man tightened his grip. "Or I can kill you right here. Either way, the Shrike will not have you."

Masahiro's breath came as a throaty wheeze. Assassins, dark sorcerers, walking corpses – it was all getting to be a bit much. Still, one of the most important parts of any scheme was knowing when to walk away, and he had *certainly* done all he could here.

He stopped struggling. "I'd prefer to live if it's all the same to you."

"Good, then you must do exactly as I–"

The manor gate exploded from its hinges. Such was the force that, even forty paces distant, they were both knocked sprawling. Masahiro scrambled to his feet, only to see his erstwhile attacker spring up a few paces away.

The man was dressed as a peasant, his mask little more than a loose bit of fabric. The cut of his hair, the curve of his jaw were so unremarkable as to almost beg for some distinguishing scar or birthmark. Even so, Masahiro recognized the way he moved, the sinewy strength of his arms, the long-fingered hands that had held the garrote.

"*You!*" Masahiro drew his blade.

The assassin's gaze flicked over Masahiro's shoulder. A trick, of course, to get Masahiro to lower his guard. If so, the man seemed truly committed. He stared, wide-eyed, at something beyond Masahiro, not moving, not speaking, hands low at his sides, his whole body tensed as if preparing for a sprint.

Against his better judgment, Masahiro glanced over his shoulder, and gaped.

The Bent-Winged Shrike floated into the courtyard.

His face was shadowed by a farmer's wide sun hat, but the man's robes wouldn't have looked out of place at the Winter Court save for the strange sigils on the silk. Not so much embroidered, they seemed almost cut into the robe – as if the fabric were the hide of some strange beast, the symbols carved into its flesh. The robes rippled in the breeze, causing the writing to shift and swirl, tugging at Masahiro's gaze.

He might have stood there for some time, spellbound by the strange interplay of symbols, had not Chiaki come charging from the fading haze, lips drawn back from her teeth, blade held parallel to the ground. Despite the gray hair loose beneath her helm, she moved like a woman half her age, sword slashing toward the Shrike's shadowed throat.

He caught the blade between thumb and forefinger. Masahiro could see the strain in the Matsu's bearing, the way she leaned into the blow, but the Shrike seemed as solid as a castle wall. With nightmarish ease, he stripped the sword from Chiaki's hands and sent it spinning into the churned earth.

Undaunted, the Matsu drove a fist into his midsection, then pivoted to hammer the other into the side of his head. She might as well have been throwing herself against a temple pillar.

Dark flame twisted from the Shrike's hand. Seeming to claw at the light, it struck the Matsu's breastplate in an explosion of gnarled shadow. The Lion samurai tumbled back, somehow finding her feet even amidst the lightless fire.

From the ruined gate came a dozen figures in torn and bloody clothes, their faces concealed by masks of pale porcelain. They moved with an erratic, loose-limbed gait that put Masahiro in mind of drunks stumbling home from a sake den. He might have mistaken them for rebels if not for the obvious wounds – sword cuts and missing limbs, broken spears thrust through their ribs.

"*The dead walk.*" Masahiro whispered the assassin's warning.

With a wave, the Shrike set his creatures upon Chiaki. She drew her short sword, blade flashing in the smoke as she cut at the grasping limbs. Despite her skill, she was driven back by the fury of the onslaught, retreating toward the pavilion where Masahiro stood.

He did not realize he was backing away until he bumped into the assassin. Reflexively, he swiped at the man. The blow was halfhearted, almost an afterthought.

The assassin swayed away, hands raised. "Come with me."

Masahiro fixed him with an appalled glare. "You tried to murder me!"

"I did." He thrust his chin at the Shrike. "So imagine what it would take to change my mind."

Masahiro chewed his lip, gaze darting to the Shrike. Blessedly, he had yet to enter the fray, and was standing, head cocked as if listening for a sound on the wind.

"There are more dead," the assassin said. "An army of them, poised to march. You must warn the courts."

Masahiro worked his tongue around his mouth. It was clear the killer had been sent by his political opponents. It seemed unlikely they would employ someone with a surfeit of conscience – which meant the man had some use for him.

Finally, a motive Masahiro understood.

If the Shrike represented a true threat to Rokugan, Masahiro needed to know more. A dire warning, delivered properly, could provide just the leverage he needed to regain his position in court.

And there was also the offer of rescue. Masahiro had been prepared to die, but now as another path presented itself, he found himself wholly ready to take it.

There was a clatter from below. Chiaki retreated to the stairs at the front of the pavilion, several of the dead clutching at her with mangled hands.

Masahiro nodded to the assassin. "Help me retrieve my bodyguard."

They descended the few steps together. Masahiro didn't bother with refined sword-work, settling instead for a two-handed chop that sent one of the masked heads rolling. The assassin stepped to Chiaki's side, a pair of short blades suddenly in his hands.

At any moment, Masahiro expected them to be scoured by dark fire, but the Shrike only glided to the rubble-strewn earth, gaze fixed on something beyond the manor wall. Rather than summon some new horror, the sorcerer turned and strode from the gate, looking for all the world like a man late for an appointment.

"Chiaki, fall back!" Masahiro cut at a pair of ragged corpses, their hands little more than nubs of bone.

"You are not my lord." The Lion samurai's reply was almost a snarl, but she did retreat to the nominal shelter of the pavilion. One of the dead scrambled after her, and she sent it tumbling into its fellows with a solid kick to the chest.

Masahiro and the assassin followed, sliding shut the manor's heavy screen. Although he had never found much to commend the Crab for, even Masahiro could not deny they erected quite adequate fortifications.

Chiaki blinked at the assassin. "Is that–"

"Our only way out of this mess." Masahiro nodded.

As if to punctuate his point, something threw itself against the door with a rattling boom. Already, Masahiro could hear the dead scrabbling at the walls.

Chiaki bared her teeth. "You can't seriously intend to trust this murderer?"

"All samurai are murderers," the murderer responded. "Have you not killed at the behest of your lord, your clan?"

"I have, but as a warrior, face to face – not like some goblin spider skulking in the shadows."

"So you admit to being a killer." He nodded as if Chiaki had complimented him. "We only disagree on methods."

"Do not twist my w–"

"This may be a conversation better had later." Masahiro laid a hand on Chiaki's shoulder. "Unless you'd like another go at the Shrike?"

Chiaki lowered her eyes.

"We will find a way. You have my word." Masahiro used the voice he employed when cajoling truculent courtiers – low, direct, with just the slightest edge of emotion.

Chiaki regarded the assassin from beneath storm cloud brows. "Why are you aiding us?"

"Because I was at Five-Dragon Gate when the imperial expedition fell. I saw what the Shrike would unleash upon Rokugan." He tapped his nose, then pointed at them. "I oppose him. You oppose him. The decision was simple."

The door gave an ominous creak.

Chiaki thrust her chin at him. "You're a Scorpion."

"Shosuro Gensuke." The man returned the slightest of bows. "At your service."

Masahiro wrinkled his nose. "Oh, I very much doubt that."

"Flee with me or die here," he replied. "Either way, you serve my needs."

"He can help us escape," Masahiro said to Chiaki.

She clucked her tongue. "And have that killer stick a dagger between my shoulder blades at the first opportunity? I think not."

"If the Shrike is as dangerous as I believe, it is our duty to warn the court." Masahiro did not add that the court would be grateful for such a warning.

Chiaki frowned, considering.

"Better a knife in the back than the Shrike," Masahiro continued. "We cannot face such foul magic alone. If we wish to avenge Hiroshige and Katamori, we must seek what aid we can."

Chiaki uttered a frustrated oath, and Masahiro knew he had her.

"You're going to get me killed, Crane."

Masahiro grinned. "I thought that was the point?"

There came a shuddering boom from outside. Not the door, nor the walls, but further out in the village. It was accompanied by a flickering crimson and gold light, watery and strange, like fire reflected on bronze.

Masahiro flinched at the glow. "What–"

Chiaki held up a hand. Both she and Gensuke had gone very still, their tense regard the wariness of a half-drawn blade.

"Do you hear that?" Gensuke asked softly.

"The explosion?" Masahiro replied.

"No." Chiaki nodded at the door. "*That*."

Only then did Masahiro realize the scraping and rattling had stopped. "They're gone?"

"Or they're waiting for us to open the door," Chiaki said.

"I have seen them fight," Gensuke replied. "The dead are single-minded, but far from clever."

There was a flash outside. Like distant lightning, it flickered through cracks in the villa walls, a series of muffled explosions trailing behind like body servants.

"What was that?" Gensuke asked.

"A fine distraction," Masahiro said.

"It came from the north." Chiaki turned, quick as a hunting hawk. "Just inside the barricade."

"Then we should head south." Masahiro peered through one of the cracks in the wall. There were more than a few corpses strewn about the wreckage of the garden, but fortunately none moved.

"The way is clear."

From the north, a gout of red-gold flame bloomed, just visible over the manor wall. Masahiro glanced back at his dubious allies.

"If they battle the Shrike, we should aid them," Chiaki said.

"And if it is another dark sorcerer? Or a Shadowlands demon?" Masahiro shook his head. This was no time for deliberation; he needed to quash Chiaki's misgivings, and quickly. Straightening, he fixed her with what he hoped was a steady stare.

"It is our duty to warn Rokugan."

Chiaki stiffened, just as Masahiro had known she would. The Lion liked to think themselves the best warriors in the land – strong, steady, uncompromising – but pride cut as sharply as blades, obligation bound tighter than any chain.

In the end, Chiaki was a Matsu. Her selfish quest for vengeance was as nothing before a lifetime of service. Masahiro knew she would do as he desired, not because she wished to, but because responsibility dictated no alternative.

He dearly wanted to smile but knew it would ruin the moment. Instead, with the somber gravity of a high-court official, Masahiro turned to Gensuke.

"Lead us from this awful place."

CHAPTER EIGHTEEN

The screams had stopped some time ago, which was a mixed blessing. When they had sighted the rebel scouts, Tetsuo had asked whether Irie had any means of enjoining the local spirits to draw information from unwilling captives. She'd explained such rituals trod dangerously close to corruption, but now Irie wished she did possess the power.

Whatever harm the spirits inflicted upon their unfortunate captives, it could not equal Tetsuo.

The Crab approached interrogation with the same callous precision he brought to all endeavors. As if the half-dozen rebels they had apprehended were bits of unworked stone from which Tetsuo intended to carve a bench. Irie had excused herself long before the Crab began, which was somehow worse than staying to watch.

She was a coward. That much, at least, Irie understood.

When she had vowed to clear her master's name, she had imagined following a trail of clues to some witness or document that would expunge all doubt concerning Masatsuge's questionable interests. She had very much not expected to be kneeling, head bowed, trying to maintain some semblance of calm while her comrade murdered a handful of peasants.

The worst thing of all was that, even now, Irie did not regret leaving Naoki and Qadan.

She ran her fingers over the mask, lingering on each contour like a string of prayer beads. There was comfort in the Crab samurai's single-minded focus. Although Irie might disapprove of his methods, she knew Tetsuo would take her exactly where she needed to go.

Irie knew the peasants to be traitors, killers, perhaps even servants of a dark sorcerer. If there was truth to be found, Tetsuo would discover it, would do what Irie could not bring herself to do... not yet, at least.

As always, she sought the Empty Flame, attempting to conjure a spark from nothing, a conflagration of perfect calm, raging tranquility, power without price.

And, as always, it eluded her.

"The Shrike follows Iuchiban." Tetsuo's voice cut through the roiling tempest of self-recrimination.

Irie opened her eyes, grasping for composure. She knew little of Iuchiban, but she knew of other dark sorcerers. All Phoenix were told of fallen priests and elementalists, spoken of in hushed tones behind high walls and warding trigrams, as if corruption might spread through the very mention of their name.

Questions surfaced in Irie's thoughts, flickering like leaves caught in a fast stream. What kansen did the Shrike control? What were his plans? Had he killed Masatsuge? How could her master have fallen to some rustic warlock?

But like before, like always, Irie said nothing, fearing that to benefit from such brutal means would somehow make her complicit – even though she already was.

For all its benefits, a life of study and ascetic contemplation had ill prepared Irie for the endless vulgarities of the real world. She had thought herself above such things, an observer, a critic, the harms and cruelties of the unenlightened reduced to little more than words on a page, topics of discussion. She and her colleagues had spent days debating the nature of war, of vengeance, of desire, but they had not understood, not really.

"He searches for his master's tomb, as does the monk," Tetsuo continued, blind to Irie's struggle.

"To what end?" Her voice came as a rough croak. It was a simple enough question, but one that struck at the root of her fears. The Shrike, the monk, were they merely ambitious fools, driven by a lust for power, for control, or was there something more? Some deeper understanding that might appeal to a student of philosophy, a true seeker of knowledge?

Someone like her master.

"The captives did not know. They were fleeing the Shrike." Tetsuo shrugged. "The rebels are nothing, a blind to conceal the true hunter. The Shrike promised those fools a way to overthrow their betters. As with all such corrupt paths it leads only to slavery."

Irie regarded the Crab samurai for a long moment, wondering if by choosing to accompany him, she might have set foot upon such an ill-favored road.

Her hands tightened around the mask. No. Irie did only what must be done, for her school, for her clan, for her master. There was but one path, and though it might lead into shadow, it would preserve everything she knew.

Irie drew in a slow breath, holding it as she stood. "And now?"

"The Shrike approaches a town called 'Crossroads.' A few days west." Tetsuo turned, moving off without another word.

Irie followed silently. There was no need for elaboration; she knew where they were going.

They crossed a series of low hills, patches of scree and goblin pine like the mottled skin of a plague victim. More than once, Tetsuo's dogged march crossed a way or footpath, but the Crab samurai did not veer from his course, though it led over sharp stones and rocky escarpments.

They ate on the move, stopping only for a few hours' rest. Tetsuo did not sleep, at least not that Irie could tell. The Crab only propped himself against a boulder or the bole of a tree and sat, slack-faced and staring.

It was early on the fourth day when Crossroads came into view. Irie knew she should be exhausted. They had walked most of the night without cease, but when the first tepid rays of sunlight painted the mountains, Irie found herself suffused with a strange sense of excitement.

No more equivocating, no more questions. At last, she would have her answers.

Crossroads was a wild, scraggly town, a patch of weeds rooted in unkind soil. A few score houses, hovels, and barns clustered around the intersection of trade roads from which the town no doubt took its name. The only building of note was a fortified manor, stone walls surrounding a huddle of blocky villas, the whole structure appearing more like a windbreak than a lord's abode. The sparse rice fields to the town's north and south were flooded, its throughways piled with rubble. Although they were perhaps a mile distant, Irie could pick out shadows running here and there – fighting, fleeing, frolicking, she could not say.

Also, the town was on fire.

Tetsuo moved from a brisk walk to a steady jog. Irie kept pace. Although unsettled by the normally placid Crab's sudden hurry, she knew any questions were like to receive little more than shrugs and noncommittal grunts. Like a hunting hound, Tetsuo had scented his prey – and that would have to suffice.

Irie moved in his wake, already calling to the local spirits. Like the land they inhabited, the elementals were hard, pitiless things – spirits of jagged stone and barren defiles; of wind sharp enough to cleave through fur and flesh; of storm-blackened trees, and the slow, cutting drip, drip, drip of icy water.

Irie called to them nonetheless, her voice a half-feral screech.

There was fighting in the town. No, not fighting. *Slaughter.*

Townsfolk and rebels scrambled through smoking streets, a crowd of clutching shadows in their wake. Amidst the chaos, Irie saw soot-streaked masks, porcelain glinting white through fire and ash. Some of the masked were missing limbs; others sported ghastly wounds, the brown of old blood framing bits of broken bone. They moved through flames to rip and tear at fleeing folk.

Disgust and horror made a tight fist in Irie's throat. The creatures were hollow, empty. It was not the calm of the void, but something far crueler. Dark, malignant, grasping, a shadow not content to simply echo and mirror, but to grow and grow until it consumed its maker. They were not people, not anymore.

They were abominations.

Tetsuo shouldered his way through the press like a warship

cutting through rough surf. Every move sent folk sprawling, but they might have been windswept grass for all the attention the Crab samurai showed.

He met the rush of corpses head-on, blows sharper, hands harder than the masked dead. Irie heard spines snap, bones break, porcelain crack under Tetsuo's cold-eyed assault. There was no fury in his strikes, no ferocity, only the calm, almost languid movements of a master artisan practicing his craft.

There came a moment, quick as an indrawn breath, where Irie thought the Crab would overmatch the creatures through sheer violence. Like waves crashing on the beach, they pulled back, leaving behind a jumble of broken bodies upon the sandal-churned earth.

But waves are endless.

More dead surged from a fire-blackened hovel, ripping aside wattle and burning straw to fall upon the Crab samurai. In their dozens, their scores, they came from all directions, not a wave but a flood. Like a breached dam, Tetsuo began to crumble beneath the sheer weight.

Calling upon the blaze, Irie stoked the hungry flames into a conflagration. The sweep of her hand sent a wave of coiling heat over the mob of dead. Ragged robes caught flame, hair like candle wicks in the smoky gloom. Fires spread, whipped into a terrible frenzy by Irie's elemental convocation.

The local elemental spirits had resented Crossroads since the Crab Clan first hacked it from the unlovely scarp. It was a blight upon their empty land, a constant reminder their home could be shaped and changed no matter how unwelcoming they made it.

Irie gave the town to them.

Her invocation coaxed forth an apocalypse in miniature, a

swirling, crackling torrent of fire that scattered the dead like burning leaves.

More came scrambling from the shadows. Irie drew in breath to call again, heedless of her shaking legs, her trembling arms, the war-drum rattle of her heart.

But something stopped her.

It came not as opposition, as ward or counter-ritual; rather, it was the feeling of being watched, regarded, judged, as if the heavy clouds above had parted to reveal some great eye gazing down upon Irie's works.

The Shrike.

Her ritual guttered, spirits fading, their anger spent. Dimly, Irie heard Tetsuo fighting, his soft grunts punctuated by the hollow thump of fists striking flesh, the wet snap of bone. It tugged at Irie, but could not hold her.

The dead were but shadows.

She picked her way across the smoking cobbles, careful not to stray near the fallen lest one grab her leg. Irie could feel the Shrike, sharp as a fresh burn, his power seeming to scorch the very air.

He was waiting for her outside the lord's manor, hands folded in his sleeves, head bowed so his wide-brimmed hat covered shoulders and face. Dark incantations inscribed his robes, seeming to slip from the fabric to bend the edges of his being, the body within as insubstantial as shadowed flame. But he could not hide from Irie, not after she had come this far.

The Shrike raised his head to regard her, smile as sharp as a broken oath.

"You found me." His voice rang in Irie's bones, as familiar as her own. "I knew you would."

She met his gaze, unsure whether to bow or weep.

"Master."

CHAPTER NINETEEN

The tomb was empty, just like the others. The monk's followers had defaced the walls, marring the stone with pick and hammer. Bloodstains spotted the debris, flecking the stone with bits of rust brown. Although it was clear the monk had conducted some manner of foul ritual in the chamber, no bodies remained.

Qadan rested her hand on the wounded stone. So much had been lost.

"He must not wish anyone to learn these secrets." Naoki paced the burial chamber, occasionally pausing to pick a bit of stone from the carpet of rubble. Like the other tombs in Qadan's notes, this one was relatively unassuming. In the style of the pre-exodus Unicorn, it was bored directly into the mountainside, little more than a long downward stair connecting one or more burial chambers.

"He is jealous of his secrets," Qadan said.

"There is malice in this." Naoki ran her fingers along a rough stone. "He did not simply destroy the etchings, he *obliterated* them."

Qadan frowned, considering. "If both he and the Shrike

seek Iuchiban's tomb, it would make sense for him to erase the path."

"From what little I know of Iuchiban, he seems someone not given to cooperation." Naoki squatted to poke through the debris. "No doubt, his followers are the same."

"No doubt." Qadan clenched her jaw against an upswell of hopeless anger. She and Naoki had spent days combing the harsh mountain slopes. Back in Khanbulak, Qadan had noted many promising sites. Now, they found only barren rock and ruined crypts, the monk always seeming one step ahead.

With her spirits, she could have searched the rubble, perhaps even reconstructed some semblance of events. It was as if the monk had plucked out her eyes, taken her ears, her hands.

Qadan reached for the pouch in which the talisman rested, careful to use only the lightest touch. From even a single use, she knew the thing to be sharp, hungry. A nest of edges, it would cut at the slightest provocation. It was something to be handled with care, both for its age, and for the dangers it might conceal. As Jargal always said: "Blind charges yield nothing but broken legs."

Naoki clucked her tongue, breaking Qadan from her spiraling grief.

"What is it?" Qadan asked.

"That's the wrong question." She stood, shining her lantern across the tomb's marred ceiling.

Qadan tried to hide her irritation. The magistrate was genial enough, but her thoughts were as arrows fired high into the sky. Qadan never knew where they might land.

"Do you see?" Naoki glanced back.

Qadan shrugged. "I see the work of a petulant sorcerer."

"He is losing patience, yes." Naoki nodded. "But this is sloppy, hurried."

Qadan nudged a pile of rubble with the tip of her riding boot. "It seems quite thorough to me."

Naoki shone her lantern around, as if to illuminate some previously unseen evidence. "There is no poem."

Qadan blinked. She had thought only to look for what was, not what wasn't. "What does that mean?"

"I don't know." Naoki's shoulders rounded.

Qadan frowned at the debris. If only she had Eruar or Gion. Their senses were keen beyond measure. Once again, she found her fingers working the straps of the pouch containing the strange talisman, and once again she drew back.

Only as a last resort.

She clenched her jaw, considering. They had ranged west across the Twilight Mountains on the murderous monk's trail. Although Irie had healed her shoulder, Qadan's strength had yet to fully return. They had reached the final tomb her research had uncovered, the last she and Jargal had hoped to explore.

Now, at last, there was time.

"I might have a path forward." Qadan turned, hurrying from the tomb.

"Where are you going?" Naoki called after her.

"*Out.*"

The horses were tethered outside, busily cropping at a ragged thatch of snakebrush near the cavern entrance. Marrow reacted quickly to her touch, tossing his head as she mounted, eager to put some distance between them and this awful place.

"We ride." She patted his neck. "But not away."

She guided Marrow down the rocky path. When

approaching the tomb, they had passed a promising gulley. It was there Qadan headed, ignoring Naoki's confused calls, echoing from back in the cave.

The valley was a narrow affair, a long strip of stone and earth nestled between the roots of two looming mountains, but it was flat and windy enough for Qadan's purposes.

She rooted around in her saddlebags. It was still painful to draw forth the small, oilcloth-wrapped bundle that had housed Eruar's new talisman. Her first spirit had always been a playful, enthusiastic presence, and she still felt their absence deeply.

Eruar's talisman was a bundle of woven cloth. Made from cavalry pennants, they had tasted the wind, snapping in brilliant charges, almost alive. Qadan had threaded the strips into a prayer circle, silken streamers dangling from every knot.

Jaw tight, she kicked Marrow into a gallop, wind pricking the corners of her eyes. Faster, faster Qadan rode, until her hair streamed behind her, until the air seemed almost to lift her from her saddle, until the frenzied joy filled her chest, bright and cold as a winter moon. She drew great whooping breaths, letting the chill mountain air roll across her tongue like a mouthful of fine arak.

Spirits' names could be rendered in speech, written in mortal tongues. It was a direct path, one born of necessity, for even the most skilled name keepers did not possess the fortitude to meet a spirit on their own terms every time. But Eruar's name was not truly a word; rather, some collection of disparate sounds given voice by brush or tongue.

Spirits were older than language, their names older still.

Eruar was the ripple of wind through Qadan's hair, the wild chill that rushed down her spine as she seemed to fly across the rocky ground. They were a feeling, a sense, elemental and eternal.

Only when the breath caught in her throat, when Marrow's hooves seemed almost to leave the ground did Qadan call to her old friend.

The answer came, faintly. Little more than the whisper of wind through tall grass, evident only by its passing.

Qadan reached out, calling to Eruar in hope, in pain, in sorrow. Their connection had been cruelly rent asunder, the loss multiplied a thousandfold across the spirit's numinous form. Mortals gave names, changed names, took names. Spirits *were* names – they could no more shift than could a stone become a bird, or a tree a cloud.

Eruar's name spilled from Qadan's lips in a wild, exultant shout. She held the talisman high, streamers unfurling, seeming almost alive in the gale of her charge.

Wind buffeted Qadan from all sides, almost tearing her from her mount. The tempest of Eruar's broken form surrounded her. It snatched the words from her lips, the sweat from her brow, tugged at her hair, her clothes, threatening to send Marrow careening into the broken cliffs.

Qadan screamed, her own voice threading through Eruar's aggrieved howl. The spirit clung to her, battered by their own wounded name. Qadan leaned close to the saddle, every muscle tensed as she fought to grip the talisman. She sang to Eruar of the high plains, of open spaces and wide horizons, of grass so high a thousand riders could simply disappear beneath the windswept blades.

Gradually, the wind died, Qadan's heaving mount slowing to a canter, then a trot. She patted Marrow's neck, whispering thanks into his ear.

Swallowing against the thickness in her throat, Qadan dismounted. It took an effort of will to unclench her fist from around the talisman. Empty no more.

"Welcome home." She pressed the knotted circle to her chest, tears cutting hot tracks down her wind-chapped cheeks.

After Qadan had seen to her horse, they walked back.

It was evening when Qadan reached the mouth of the tomb. The dying light cast the mountains in deep reds and browns, the serried peaks like a row of pitted spear blades thrust from the earth.

Naoki was waiting outside, tending a pair of small pots bubbling merrily over a wisp of a fire.

"Tea and soup." She dipped a spoon into one of the pots, tasted, and winced. "Or my best approximation."

"Thank you for not coming after me," Qadan said.

"I'm no stranger to unlikely inspiration." Naoki waved the spoon in the air. "I figured whatever you were doing must be important."

"It was." Qadan held out Eruar's talisman. "The seeking wind. With this, I may be able to–"

Naoki held up a hand. "Eat first. You look about to faint."

Qadan did as she was bid, almost collapsing on a nearby stone. The ritual had sapped what little strength remained, and it was an effort to even take the proffered bowl. Although relatively bland, the soup of dried vegetables and beans filled the hollow in Qadan's stomach, just as the weak tea spread warmth through her body. Like a parent with a newborn, she found herself checking on Eruar's talisman, fingers gently probing for the whisper of breath, terrified the spirit had slipped away once more.

They were there. They would always be there.

Qadan smiled softly. In time, the others would return as well. With Eruar back, they would see it was safe, that she could be trusted. By destroying Qadan's talismans the monk had created room for new understanding, new strength. She would make new talismans, better, stronger.

Next time, they would not be so easily parted.

She clutched Eruar's talisman to her chest, drawing comfort from the way the silk flowed through her fingers. Jargal might be forever lost, but not all her friends were lost forever.

Qadan didn't know she had dozed until Naoki shook her awake. She rolled over, pawing at the blanket the Dragon magistrate had spread over her.

"How long was I asleep?"

"The better part of the night."

Qadan rubbed her eyes. Standing, she worked her tongue around a mouth gone sour with sleep. "You shouldn't have let me."

Naoki snorted. "Your horse needed rest."

"In that case, I forgive you." Stretching her stiff shoulder, Qadan started down the rocky escarpment and into the tomb. "Come, let us see what we can see."

There was a brief commotion as Naoki relit the lanterns, then a skittering of rocks as she followed Qadan.

The tomb was just as they had left it, but now Qadan saw with new eyes. Grasping the talisman, she spoke Eruar's name, grinning as the spirit flitted free in a swirl of silken streamers.

"Seek what is concealed," Qadan whispered. "See what we cannot."

Naoki gave a surprised cry as Eruar whipped by in a swirl

of ancient dust, plucking at the hem of her robes. She seemed about to speak, but Qadan hissed her to silence.

Qadan did not see so much as feel the disturbance. Like a deer on a muddy riverbank, the monk's ritual had left deep impressions on the spiritual fabric of the place. Eyes squeezed shut, Qadan spread her arms, a tiny maelstrom of sense memories twisting within her.

Such terrible callings left equally terrible scars, and yet the tomb held only the barest hint of corruption. It seemed impossible that the monk could commit such atrocities and remain unscathed, so Eruar dug deeper, broken stones rattling as the wind grew. Naoki bent low over her lantern, one hand shielding the guttering flame, but Qadan cared little for light – her eyes saw more than stone and shadow.

She felt the echo of the monk's kansen, stolen names passed about like copper coins. She clapped her hands to her ears, their keening wail almost sharp enough to cut.

"What do you see?" Naoki's question rose above the shriek of wind.

"He bears something." Qadan forced the words through gritted teeth. "An artifact, a name. Blood is the key. Dark rituals. The corruption bleeds into the relic."

"That must be why our priests found no evidence of taint."

"He possesses the key, but not the map." The words came without thought. "That is why he searches."

"For Iuchiban's tomb?"

Qadan's nod was reflexive. She saw beyond the chamber, beyond the tons of soil and stone, beyond the clumsy fetters of mortality. This tomb was not one, but many, the center of a web that stretched across the whole of Rokugan, its strands meant to snare, to trap.

But a web could also be a guide, if you were searching for a spider.

Qadan reached for the invisible strand, knowing it would lead her to the center. For a moment she saw the path, then the world seemed to shift around her, air stretched tight as a drumhead as something moved in the inchoate darkness. It came nearer, growing like evening shadow until it seemed to fill the whole of the chamber.

Dimly, horribly, Qadan realized it was aware of her, that it *sought* her.

Qadan gasped, falling to her knees as Eruar's pain burned up her spine. Fingers grasping at the air, she called the spirit back, hoping it was not too late, that they had not ventured too far.

Naoki had her by the shoulders. But Qadan could not move, could not breathe. It was as if she were deep underwater, the air pressing in around her with terrible weight. Like a drowning woman, Qadan clung to Eruar's talisman, lips moving soundlessly as she repeated the spirit's name, pulling against the hideous strength that gripped them both.

Naoki was dragging them. Sunlight kissed Qadan's cheek. Like a swimmer surfacing after a long dive, she gasped in a ragged breath, the world seeming to snap back into focus as Eruar slipped back into their talisman, free of the clutching grasp of whatever dwelt at the center of the web.

"I will never abandon you. *Never.*" Qadan clutched the talisman to her chest, hugging it to her like a small child.

"Are you well?" Naoki's concerned face swam into view. "What happened?"

"The monk draws closer to Iuchiban's tomb." Qadan's words came breathless with exertion.

"Then we must intervene." Naoki pressed something to Qadan's brow – a wet rag, blessedly cool. "Can you track him?"

"No." Qadan clawed the water gourd from her belt and took a long, painful swallow. "But I think I know where he is going."

CHAPTER TWENTY

"I hoped you would come." Masatsuge removed his hat, then gently placed it on the wheel of an overturned cart. "The ground might be fertile, the weather kind, the gardener meticulous, and yet it remains for the seed to grow."

"Spare me your proverbs." It was as if Irie were gripped by a fever, alternately freezing and boiling, her robes damp with sweat. "I thought you were *dead*."

"In a manner of speaking, I was." His reply came soft, voice frustratingly calm.

"You lied to me."

"Never." Masatsuge's voice held no reproof, no guile, only the kind patience that had circumscribed the breadth of Irie's education.

"Then what is *this*?" Irie flicked her fingers at the cruel tapestry of symbols upon his robes, the corpses spread around the plaza, still twitching with vile life.

"An unfortunate necessity." He sounded almost pained. "A crime inflicted upon humanity by those who would bind us to a broken wheel, in this life and the next."

Irie gave a violent shake of her head, as if to deny his very presence. "I don't understand."

"You do." He took a slow step toward her. "You always have."

"Stay back." She raised a warding hand, lambent flame curled in the palm.

"A Phoenix elementalist, powerful and clever." He ignored the implied threat. "Forced to bow to your lessers by dint of birth alone. How can this be right? How can this be just?" He tapped his nose. "Only I saw your promise. Only I saw your future. Nurtured you. *Guided* you."

"Into this nightmare?" Irie's question was almost a snarl.

"It is gruesome, isn't it?" Masatsuge glanced around, his expression rueful. "But no less gruesome than villages ravaged by plague, than starving peasants, than the mountains of corpses left by the clans, the courts, the emperor, the gods – all so that they may cling to power for another year, another decade, another century."

He ran a hand through his beard, an amused tic Irie recognized from their long discussions. Even now, it comforted her. She felt a reflexive smile twist her traitor lips, and glanced back, hoping Tetsuo would burst into the plaza. The Crab would leave no room for deliberation. He would strike Masatsuge down without a moment's hesitation, would do what Irie could not.

"The Phoenix consider ourselves above the fray, but I ask: is it crueler to defend a broken world? Or to benefit from death and pain while taking no action to prevent it?" He sighed. "Inaction is complicity, and the Phoenix are worst of all. At least the other clans embrace their brutality."

Irie closed her hand, wisps of smoke slipping between clenched fingers. Masatsuge's logic made a terrible sense. She had spent her life in contemplation, debate, but her recent travels had shown the world to be a far more vicious place than she could have imagined.

"The Crab would have slaughtered these rebels, burned their homes, culled their families," Masatsuge said. "A peasant's only real choice is to die quickly or by inches."

He took another step, close enough to touch. "I would change that. I would make Rokugan better, kinder, fairer."

"With blood magic?" Irie's rebuttal sounded weak, even to her.

"A tool, no more horrible than a bared blade, a scouring flame."

"You surround yourself with kansen!"

"And yet I am not corrupted." Masatsuge spread his arms. "See for yourself."

And Irie *did* see. Despite the roil of tainted energy around Masatsuge, the man himself remained untouched. It was as if something shielded the old master, a liminal void crackling around the edges of his being, dark and impenetrable.

"*The Empty Flame,*" Irie whispered.

"Now you understand." His grin held a teacher's pride, the joy of a parent seeing their child excel at a difficult task.

"The kansen are foul, but blood magic is a tool, a weapon." Masatsuge held up a finger. "Like any weapon, it is neither good nor evil. Only in acting do we give it weight. A blessed dagger may be used to strike down a child. A corrupt ritual may save a village. Who are we to say what is right and what is wrong?"

Irie pressed a hand to her forehead, Masatsuge's words swirling about her like a fog.

"Here." He drew something from his robes, held it out to her. A sheaf of papers, carefully bound with ribbon.

"What is this?" Irie asked.

"What you have been searching for." Masatsuge pressed the papers into her trembling hands.

"Your letters." She regarded the bundle, a mix of curiosity and disgust warring in her breast.

"Copies of them, at least." He gave a conciliatory nod. "I doubt that fool monk will part with the originals. Even so, they should help you on your way."

"My way to where?" Irie shook her head, gesturing about. "To *this*?"

"That is for you to decide. I have taught you to see clearly, Irie, to question, to examine. Do not cling to the world's lie." He gripped her arm, shaking hard. "Think for yourself!"

"And what would you have me do?" She pulled free, turning away. "Join you in raising an army of abominations? Overthrow the emperor? The gods?"

"I would have you try." His voice was soft, almost hopeful. "Iuchiban has revealed the way, just as I have shown you. The hidden path – one the gods would conceal from us. He is beholden to no petty lord, no spirit, no Fortune, only to knowledge, only to *truth*."

Irie could not help but understand. Had Masatsuge not spent a lifetime paving the way? Had she not spent a lifetime following it?

"What is the Empty Flame?" she asked.

"You have always known."

Irie drew forth the mask. It felt slick in her hand, as if she stroked a chill candle flame, power without heat, without light.

"Name magic."

"Of a sort." Masatsuge nodded. "But one that leaves us beholden to none."

"Why did you not take this with you?" She turned, holding it out.

He smiled that kind smile. "I needed you to bring it to me."

She knelt, dipping the talisman in a smear of blood near a sprawled body. The mask seemed almost to leach the blood away, names glowing crimson in the reflected firelight. Irie's fingers traced them, unbidden, the swirling sweep of ancient script seeming to shift at her touch.

Standing, she regarded her master, his careworn face, his patient eyes, the soft curve of his bearded lips – never judging, never accusing, never angry. He had taught her to look beyond the real, beyond what Irie was told, beyond what she believed. Knowledge was the only path to truth, she felt that in her bones – even now, even here. But could she take this step? Was this the truth, or simply another belief repeated by one in power?

In the end, Masatsuge was right.

Irie needed to think for herself.

The ritual spilled from her lips like blood. Ancient and powerful, it flowed through the plaza, seeming to fill the smoky air until it inhabited every breath, every thought.

Masatsuge's smile faltered. He took a step back, hands coming up, an arcane call already on his lips. Too late. Far too late.

The mask burst into flames.

Irie blinked back sharp tears, unsure whether they came from sorrow or relief. She need not kill her master. Masatsuge had done a fine job of that on his own.

Freed of their arcane bonds, the bound kansen fell upon Masatsuge in a nightmare torrent. The old master's flesh became as coiled ribbon, his bones as windswept twigs.

The whole of him stretched before Irie, a spiraling line of incarnations without start or end. Through it all, her master did not cry out, did not flinch, only held Irie's gaze, his pale brown eyes heavy not with pain, nor fear, nor even anger, but a strange species of pride.

"I forgive you." Masatsuge's lips formed the words, all sound lost amidst the shrieking maelstrom that consumed him, body and soul.

Through it all Irie stood still as a temple column, every muscle tensed against the urge to hide her face. To turn from her master's death would be to admit he had been correct about her, about everything.

But blood magic was not a weapon, it was a curse. Masatsuge's quest for knowledge was rooted in pride, in the mistaken belief that he was equal to any challenge, that he could not be tainted. If Irie had learned anything at the Heaven's Blaze Dōjō, it was the peril of arrogance.

The Empty Flame may represent power, but it did not light the way. That, Irie would have to discover on her own.

She realized she still held the mask, the lacquer scorched and cracked, names scoured from the pitted wood. Cool to the touch, wisps of smoke rose through the eye holes, the smile that was not a smile seeming even more pronounced.

Irie turned the talisman over in her hands, unsure of whether to cast it away or press it to her face.

There was a crash at the rear of the plaza, a smashing, cracking clatter of broken wood and splitting bamboo. Irie slipped the mask into her sleeve, turning to see Tetsuo stagger from the wreckage. She watched him come, chest tight with concern and relief in equal measure.

Blood streaked the Crab samurai's armor, dribbling from

a trio of jagged gashes in his cheek to trace crimson shadows along his breastplate. He held a broken spear in one hand, little more than a long-hafted dagger. The other gripped a length of chain, links threaded with hair and broken bone.

Expressionless, he watched the last of Masatsuge's death throes. By the time Irie looked back, her master was little more than blackened bones, his body so thoroughly disjointed that, had Irie not known better, she might have mistaken it for the remains of a campfire.

Tetsuo stepped to her side, and for a moment Irie thought he would strike her down. But the Crab only dropped his weapons, wiping soot-covered hands upon blood-covered armor.

"The Shrike is dead," Irie said softly.

"The monk remains." He nudged the bones with his boot, then nodded like a craftsman inspecting fine work.

A shuddering crack echoed from the north end of the village, sparks swirling heavenward.

Tetsuo spat a gobbet of blood upon the scorched stones. "More dead come."

Irie frowned, confused. "They should have ended with the Shrike."

"Cut the head from a serpent, it dies." Tetsuo's response came flat as a frozen pond. "Cut the crest from a wave, it still crashes."

"There are more Bloodspeakers?"

"Always."

Something glimmered in the back of her thoughts – a lie, or a truth, Irie wasn't sure. "What is the use of hunting disciples when the master still teaches?"

Tetsuo glanced at her, a thoughtful frown creasing his scarred slab of a face.

"You know the tomb's location." It was not a question, and Tetsuo did not treat it as such, he merely regarded her, eyes as cold as the corpses sprawled about them.

"Have I not proven myself?" She gestured at the pile of bones.

"There is no proof that will suffice."

"So we destroy the monk. What then?" Irie asked. "You crawl back to your mountains? Wait for another Bloodspeaker to rise?"

He nodded.

"You said the tomb holds Iuchiban's heart." She shook her head, willing him to see reason. "We have a chance to finally end this, while he is weak."

"Iuchiban is never weak."

"To accept the invincibility of one's opponent is to admit the inevitability of defeat." It felt somehow wrong to use one of Masatsuge's maxims, but nothing else came to mind. "It has been centuries since Iuchiban last threatened Rokugan. It may be centuries more before he does again. Where will you be?" Irie kicked the bones, scattering them farther. "The same as these. Dust. Forgotten. You may not wish it, but you cannot deny that whether we succeed or fail, now is our only chance."

Tetsuo studied her for a long moment. "Agreed."

He strode through the smoldering rubble. Irie followed, unaware she had been holding her breath until she began to feel light-headed.

Tetsuo had not seen Masatsuge's face. There was nothing to link her master to this corruption but the suppositions of one flighty Dragon magistrate. Irie could go back to Heaven's Blaze dōjō and accept a place beneath Tomiko, or she could return to her family. With a dearth of elementalists, the Shiba would certainly find a use for her.

But terrible though his methods might have been, Masatsuge's arguments were not wrong. This world was corrupt. By showing Irie a problem, her master had imparted one final lesson.

Iuchiban might be impossible to destroy, but his collection of lore was not. Irie was not so arrogant as to believe herself immune to the lure of forbidden knowledge, but she was certain Tetsuo would kill her long before she succumbed.

Irie glanced around the ruined village, old dead and newly dead spread about the bones of a once prosperous town. The Empty Flame might be yet another lie, but if it held even the faintest glimmer of something better, Irie had to seek out the truth.

She owed her master that much, at least.

CHAPTER TWENTY-ONE

There were no paths, no trails. There was barely even a scrap of flat rock for them to rest upon. If not for Qadan, Naoki would have pressed her mount, the urge for speed overcoming concerns over a fall or broken leg. If the monk managed to discover Iuchiban's tomb, the lives of a few horses would be nothing compared to the horrors he might unleash.

Qadan seemed not to care about the looming threat, stopping several times a day to meditate and work on talismans. Naoki understood they needed every weapon at their disposal, but it was torturous to have to wait, pacing and muttering while the Unicorn buried herself up to the neck in stones, or stood beneath an icy mountain waterfall, teeth chattering as she coaxed back wayward spirits.

More than once Naoki wished she still traveled with Irie. If not for her burning need to bring the monk to justice, she would have.

The Phoenix elementalist might have been sullen and secretive, but at least she understood the need for haste. It felt as if there were an executioner's blade hanging above Naoki's neck, every moment bringing her closer to decapitation. She tried to review her notes, to consider other ways to defeat the monk, but her thoughts were like scraps of paper seized by autumn wind. No sooner had Naoki pinned one down, than another fluttered by, demanding her attention.

If only the imperial expedition remained, if only the Crab would bring an army west. She would even be pleased to see the Scorpion. Should Naoki even be tracking the monk? Would it not be better to warn the clans? Any of them could send word to the Imperial City. But would the courts respond? With the emperor barely clinging to life and his heir dead from the plague, the capital was sure to be rife with plots and paranoia. Even if someone believed Naoki's tale of dark sorcery and walking dead, it was unlikely they could do anything about it. Any attempt at marshaling forces would be viewed as a threat by their rivals. In trying to prevent Rokugan from being overrun, Naoki might very well plunge the Empire into civil war.

"You're muttering again." Qadan opened one eye.

Naoki tossed her head. "So are you."

"If I am, it serves a purpose." Qadan stood, rubbing at her soot-stained robes. She had insisted on rooting around in the remnants of their campfire. Naoki hadn't wanted to light one in the first place. They had seen shadows on the high hills: bandits, rebels, or worse. The lands around were lawless even before the revolt. None who roamed these heartless peaks were likely to be friendly.

"My spirits have begun to return." The Unicorn's smile held a hint of sorrow. "But I must show them it is safe."

"And is it?" Naoki asked.

Qadan's expression soured. She stalked across their tiny campsite and began to saddle her horse. For lack of a better option, Naoki did the same.

She hated not knowing what lay ahead, placing her trust in a woman she had met mere days ago, but try as she might, the path held no branches. If Naoki wished to deliver justice to the man who had murdered so many of her clan, the man who sought to bring a new darkness upon Rokugan, then she must follow Qadan.

At least until she could find a better way.

Rocky hills leveled out into a low valley, broken goat paths becoming something like a road. Naoki saw signs of civilization among the sedge and pine – a dam of piled stone across a stream, the remains of felled trees, a trail of ox prints in the dried mud along the bank. Against her better judgment, Naoki began imagining the possibility of a hot meal, perhaps even somewhere dry to rest, if only for an hour or two.

All such hopes guttered when the town came into view.

Ruined farmland surrounded a collection of burnt homes and storehouses. A waterwheel had fallen from its moorings to lie amidst the shallows of the stream. The road they were on crossed another heading north, the intersection marked by the blocky remains of a fortified manor, the approaches piled with makeshift barricades, all broken and blackened.

Nothing moved amidst the ruins. The fields to either side of town were flooded, a mass of mud and bamboo stakes. To ride around the town would have taken hours, so they were forced to follow the central road. The smell of woodsmoke and scorched earth came eye-wateringly sharp, threaded with the sickly undertones of decaying flesh. Naoki could still see embers, thin wisps rising from the larger buildings.

"This fire was recent," she said. "Half a day, perhaps less."

Qadan did not respond, only sat stiffly on her mount, expression hard.

Naoki had seen more than her share of corpses. Even so, she could not help but bring a hand to her mouth as the first bodies came into view, scattered like rotten fruit amidst the wreckage. Walls of scorched stone stood to either side of the ruined gate, its heavy iron hinges bent as if by the hand of some blood-maddened ogre. Beneath the streaked ash, Naoki recognized the battered sigil of the Crab Clan.

"This was the lord's manor." She shook her head, unbelieving. "Could the rebels have done all this?"

"Lord Hiruma Tadamune died west of Five-Dragon Gate, months ago." Qadan's tone was dismissive, almost curt, but Naoki noted she kept her gaze fixed on the far mountains, pointedly not looking at the slaughter. "It must have been the monk."

"This isn't like him," Naoki surprised herself by answering. "The monk moves quietly. His kills are brutal but contained."

"The Shrike, then."

"Do you think Tetsuo and Irie were here?" Naoki peered about.

"I think you ask too many questions."

Naoki reined up her horse. "We should look for them."

"They made their choice." Jaw tight, Qadan scanned the low hills to the north. "Whoever did this may still be about."

She kicked her mount into a canter, and Naoki was forced to follow or be left behind. Their horses moved through low drifts of ash, bits of soot and glittering embers swirling behind them like a cloak.

Once past the town, they rode hard. Naoki could not help but cast nervous glances about, but the scrub was silent save for the echo of hooves upon hard-packed earth.

The road wound between a series of craggy hills, twisting

like a snake along a series of narrow switchbacks. Despite its obvious age and disrepair, the path remained relatively wide, the work of ancient Crab artisans evident in the occasional stone buttress and graded slope. Although possessed of a fearsome aspect, the Twilight Mountains were rich in ores and coal. The Crab must have once planned to settle this region. It discomfited Naoki to imagine what might have stopped them.

They were wending through the hollow of a narrow gorge when the monk struck.

With an avalanche rumble, a wedge of crack-spidered granite thrust from the path ahead of them. Naoki blinked at the wall of stone, so taken aback by its sudden appearance she almost ran into Qadan when the Unicorn reined in.

A dozen arrows came arcing from the graveled rise to their right. Naoki's mount pitched forward. She threw herself from the saddle, tucking as she had been taught. The rocky ground tore bloody rents in Naoki's robes, but she was able to turn her fall into an awkward roll, getting far enough away that her dying horse didn't land atop her.

Expecting more arrows, Naoki scrambled toward the safety of a nearby boulder, only to hear Qadan scream. She turned as the Unicorn rose from her own fallen horse, her shout more anger than pain. Tears glittered in Qadan's eyes, whipped away by a sudden gust.

More arrows slashed down as Qadan turned, the high skirl of her voice accompanying the rising wind, a tangle of silk streamers in her hand. Arrows tilted drunkenly in the gale, rattling harmlessly from the rocks and boulders below.

"Show yourself, coward!" Qadan's shout echoed from the rocks. Her only answer was another flight of arrows. She swept them aside with an almost contemptuous flick of her wrist, wind gusting along the little valley.

"Get down," Naoki hissed at her, but the Unicorn seemed not to hear. A coil of purple-green flame rose from the cliffs to their left, uncoiling like a centipede as it slipped silently down the incline, almost invisible in the afternoon shadows.

"Behind you!" Naoki cried, but Qadan was still shouting. Three quick steps brought Naoki to the Unicorn's side, and she dragged Qadan back just as the ribbon of dark flame sizzled through the air above.

Snarling, Qadan tore free of her grip, her gaze tracking the stream of fire back to its source. With an almost feral grin, she pressed a hand to the earth, which issued a series of racking booms. Cracks spread up the cliffside, dust and rock raining down as stone split like rotten fruit.

A rain of gravel was Naoki's only warning as the monk's surviving followers charged down the hill.

There were barely a dozen, armed with sickles and broad-bladed brush knives. Their emaciated faces gleamed with ecstatic glee, smiles sharp and eyes hooded, like drunks swept along by a raucous tavern song. Uncoordinated, without planning or finesse, it was exactly the sort of backstreet assault Naoki had been trained to frustrate.

Turning from Qadan, Naoki met the stumbling rush.

The first woman stepped in with an awkward overhand chop. Naoki slapped the blow aside with her foremost jitte, pivoting to hammer the heavy, blunt length of her other into the woman's collarbone. She stumbled back, still trying to swipe at Naoki, but a solid blow to the knuckles sent the brush knife skittering from her hand.

With an unceremonious kick, Naoki set her sprawling into

the two behind, who tumbled past in a spray of limbs and gravel. The others came on in a disorganized mass, more fury than forethought, seeking to bury Naoki in a press of bodies.

She gave ground, aiming for small bones – wrists, ankles, ribs, fingers. The monk's followers might be beyond pain, but a broken hand was a broken hand.

Teeth gnashing, the cultists screamed like wild animals, almost climbing over one another in their haste to reach her.

"Qadan, we need to stay together!" Naoki glanced back, but the Unicorn was striding up the opposite rise. A blizzard of dark shale came cutting down the hill, almost knocking Qadan from her precarious ascent. She responded with a twining pennant of wind-carried flame.

One of the remaining cultists aimed a cut at Naoki's head. She stepped into the blow, hooking the man's arm with her jitte. Pivoting to thrust her hip into his midsection, she dragged him from his feet and sent him face-first into a boulder.

The last of the monk's followers crumpled as Naoki leveled a punishing kick to his knee. Teeth gritted, he tried to slash at her with his reaping hook, but she stepped into the blow, dropping him with a heavy chop to the neck.

A quick survey showed one straggler limping on a broken leg. A few of those Naoki had downed were crawling toward her, bloody teeth bared. With a disgusted shake of her head, she backed away. It was one thing to defend herself, but this would be slaughter.

Qadan raged atop the crest of the cliff, scouring the stone with cruel winds and blasts of scything flame. Of the monk, there was no sign.

"Qadan, stop! He's not there!" When the Unicorn did not relent, Naoki cupped her hands and called again, and again.

"Where are you, demon?" The Unicorn's voice was raw with helpless fury. She stormed along the rise, talismans clutched in white-knuckled fingers, her spiritual allies bending the air like a heat mirage.

Naoki took slow breaths, trying to will her shaking hands to something approaching calm. The monk was not on the cliffs; she knew him better than that. He was canny, clever, deadly as a rock adder – it made no sense for him to waste his few remaining resources on a halfhearted ambush. His poems had been arrogant, cruel, but his actions had shown pride tempered by caution. The monk was not the Shrike. He moved at oblique angles, only confronting foes when no chance remained to them.

Slowly, Qadan's fury calmed. She descended carefully, scanning the gorge with narrowed eyes, talismans in hand.

"He is here." She spoke through gritted teeth. "I can feel the corruption."

"I don't understand." Naoki shook her head. "Why come for us?"

"We're the only ones who know what he is."

"But he has escaped me before." Naoki scrubbed a fist across her forehead, sure there was something she had overlooked. "Why put himself in danger just to remove two pursuers?"

"He knows we can stop him."

"Can we?" Naoki glanced at Qadan. Something in the Unicorn's expression gave her pause. She frowned. "He has had ample opportunity to strike me down, which means he must want you. But why?"

Qadan glanced away.

"What aren't you telling me?" Naoki took a slow step back. Why did the Fortunes continue to curse her with unreliable allies?

Qadan chewed her lip, gaze flicking to Naoki, then back to the cliffs. "He wants a name."

"What name?"

"I do not know." She winced. "I found its talisman in the tomb where he ambushed me. It is a spirit, powerful and ancient."

"A kansen?"

"No." She frowned. "I don't know. I cannot sense corruption, but it isn't like other spirits."

Naoki drew in breath to speak, only to find she could not move her lips, her jaw, her tongue. It was as if a frigid hand had gripped her skull. She tried to move and found her limbs unwilling to respond. A flush of cold panic filled her, hairs pricking along her arms and neck.

Naoki heard a voice in her head, slipping through her mind like mist. Unbelievably, Naoki felt her mouth move, lips forming words not of her making.

"The talisman… where is it?"

"Safe." Qadan glanced down, swallowing. "I'm sorry for keeping this from you. After the attack, I wasn't sure who to trust."

Naoki pressed against the invisible weight, muscles trembling as she struggled to raise an arm, to widen her eyes, to do anything that might give Qadan warning, but Naoki's body felt distant, numb, as if she had been entombed in frozen earth. She could not will herself free of the terrible grip upon her mind.

"*I have read of such talismans. Perhaps I could help?*" It was her voice, but it wasn't her. The monk had trussed her tight as a web-caught dragonfly.

Qadan dropped a hand to her satchel. "Yes, perhaps."

Naoki felt the monk's excitement, the smothering weave of

his power as it flexed around her thoughts. She was no priest, no Shinseist master; she could not slip free, could not force the monk to release her. Helpless recriminations whirled through Naoki's mind like storm blown seeds.

"There has to be a way," she muttered.

Qadan turned, head cocked. "What was that?"

Although the smile could not reach her lips, Naoki felt a lightness bubble up within her chest. It seemed the monk could no better grasp Naoki's tangled thoughts than she could.

Grinning her invisible grin, Naoki let her mind wander.

Possibilities, permutations, a wild jumble of interests and fascinations dragging her in a thousand, thousand directions. It was as if she peered through a cloudy window, her mind awash with all manner of speculation. Like wave-tossed flotsam, one would rise, snapping into sharp focus until it seemed to devour the whole of her attention, only to be suddenly swept below once more, another dozen taking its place.

She could feel the monk's hold on her slip, her thoughts seeping like water through the gaps in his tightly woven snare.

"He wants the talisman," Naoki said. "He has… me."

At last, Qadan seemed to notice Naoki's rigid posture, her body trembling with the effort of resisting the monk's dire sorceries.

Qadan's jaw pulsed, once, twice, and her gaze snapped to a jumble of rocks near the entrance of the gorge. A hard smile tugged at the corner of her lips.

"*There* you are."

The monk rose from behind the stones, perhaps twenty paces distant. It was as if someone had run a knife across the invisible bonds that held Naoki's mind. She drew in a sharp breath, her limbs her own once more.

The monk was a small man. Shaven headed, he wore loose robes of undyed cloth. Although his face was weathered as an old map, he moved with the easy confidence of a man a quarter his age.

"It would have been easier this way." He shrugged, slowly retreating into the shadow of the cliff. "But I am patient."

"We are ready for you," Qadan hissed through clenched teeth. "You will not escape."

"I do not need to."

A skitter of rock behind them caused Naoki to turn.

A samurai stood near the entrance of the gorge. Although his armor was spattered in blood and filth, Naoki recognized the lines of battle plate, his cleft helmet ringed with the distinctive mane of a Lion Clan general. One of his arms was gone, little more than a nub of ragged bone protruding from his shoulder. In the other he gripped a broken katana, held low by his side, as if the weapon were an afterthought. He took a step toward them, moving quickly despite his wounds.

More shadows filled the approach to the gorge, armored outlines blurring into a mass of terrible forms. Corpse pale, they stalked forward with silent menace.

"What have you done, monk?" The question sprang to Naoki's lips unbidden.

"These are not my work." His chuckle was distant, as if from the end of a long tunnel. "But they serve my purpose well enough."

CHAPTER TWENTY-TWO

The dead were relentless. They moved in ragged groups, wading through icy streams and clambering up sheer cliffs with the ease of crag spiders. Twisted shadows stretched across the stone, long-limbed and boneless.

Chiaki and her companions were not so agile.

Gensuke set the pace, a brisk jog that led them from Crossroads into the broken foothills girding the Twilight Mountains. They had tried to head east toward Crab lands, but found only more dead – peasants and samurai both. Remnants of the imperial expedition, the walking corpses seemed a mix of Dragon, Phoenix, and Unicorn soldiers.

Chiaki did not know what she would do when they found the Lion Clan.

The way north proved similarly untenable, which had sent them scurrying back into the mountains like wild foxes.

Chiaki was fit for her age, but she found herself pushing against more than the normal number of aches. Fortunately, Masahiro's stamina waned long before Chiaki was forced to admit defeat.

"I need to rest." He mopped his sweaty brow with one long

sleeve, then regarded the fabric as if it were stained with blood.

"Rest and die." If anything, Gensuke increased his pace. Despite the teeth-grinding stab every time she came down hard on her left knee, Chiaki was beginning to like the Scorpion assassin – if only because he knew how to remain silent.

"Run and die tired." Masahiro stopped to lean against the bole of a stunted goblin pine, rubbing at one thigh with exaggerated motions.

"We are close to Five-Dragon Gate. Once through the pass we can skirt the foothills north to Scorpion lands." Gensuke turned, nodding toward a score of relentless shadows on the stony embankment perhaps a half-mile distant. "They will overtake us if we stay."

Masahiro waved a tired hand. "Let them come."

Although Gensuke's expression remained bland, almost disinterested, there was a sudden shift in his bearing, a cold, understated menace that set Chiaki's warrior impulses on edge.

"If you are intent on death, I can oblige." He took a step toward the Crane.

"Go on, kill me." Masahiro grinned his courtier's grin, the one Chiaki had come to despise, the one that said he thought he was being clever. "We'll see if the court believes a Scorpion assassin raving about walking corpses and blood magic."

"They would believe *me*." Chiaki very much enjoyed seeing Masahiro's self-important smirk curdle.

"This, from my own bodyguard?" He pressed a hand to his heart. "You wound me, Lady Matsu."

"I am not your bodyguard." Chiaki took the opportunity to stretch her shoulder, bruised when the Shrike's demon flames had sent her tumbling. "And I am no lady."

"Fine." He pushed off the tree. "By my estimation we're at

least two days from the nearest Crab fort, longer to Scorpion lands. Even if we could somehow slip past the dead, do you plan to run the whole way? Because our pursuers certainly do."

Gensuke shook his head. "There must be some limit, even to them."

"The Shrike seems to have peopled this whole province with the dead," Masahiro replied. "What use is running if there is no path out?"

Chiaki bared her teeth. She hated it when the Crane made sense.

"The cliffs are no safeguard," Chiaki said. "They climb faster than we do."

"Faster than *you* do." Gensuke regarded them through callous eyes.

"Even so, I think the mountains are–"

There came a chest rattling boom from beyond the rise. A series of sharp cracks followed, each accompanied by the sound of shifting earth and stone. Wind whipped the scrubby trees into a frenzy of thrashing limbs, a distant swirl of dust kicked up by the miniature whirlwind.

"I wonder what that could be?" Masahiro cocked one sculpted eyebrow.

"Nothing we want any part of." Gensuke stepped behind a craggy shelf of stone as another burst of wind rolled along the rise. Even a hundred strides distant, the fury of it still made Chiaki deepen her stance.

"It seems to have gotten their attention." She thrust her chin toward the dead that had dogged their trail since Crossroads. The corpses had made a sharp turn and were now scrabbling toward the disturbance.

"Then we should take advantage of the distraction," Gensuke said.

"I'm no expert on spiritual matters, but that has the look of elementalists' work." Masahiro pursed his lips, as if considering. "Could it be the same magic we saw back at Crossroads?"

"We are wasting time," Gensuke said.

"I'm not so sure." Chiaki disliked agreeing with Masahiro, but the uproar had piqued her interest as well.

"Only fools seek danger," Gensuke said. "It is our duty to warn the court."

"Fine words from a man who makes his living killing courtiers." Masahiro raised a calming hand before Gensuke could respond. "The fact remains *something* drew the Shrike away from us."

"And it could do so again," Gensuke replied.

"They might be allies," Chiaki said.

"Or more enemies."

Chiaki squinted at the rise, hoping to distinguish something amidst the wind and cracking stone. Only belatedly did she realize Gensuke and Masahiro were both staring at her.

"We should investigate." Chiaki spoke firmly, more to convince herself than the others. She nodded toward Masahiro. "You and I will make for the ridge. Gensuke, stay here."

"Wouldn't it be better for Gensuke to have a look?" Masahiro frowned. "He's the fastest."

"Which is why we need him to hang back." Chiaki hated having to explain herself; no Lion would nurse so many doubts. Couldn't Masahiro see they were in the midst of a war?

"But why me?"

"Because we need someone to report back to Gensuke if things go badly."

The Crane looked unconvinced but acquiesced to follow along with only a modicum of petulance.

They made their way up the rise, careful not to dislodge any rocks. Whatever elemental force had seized the cliffside seemed to have abated, but Chiaki saw scores of dead rounding the ridge.

They crawled to the lip and peered over the edge. The cliffside below was scoured clean, rocks ripped from the earth as if by the hand of some ill-tempered god. Two women stood in the canyon below, one in scarred Unicorn armor, the second in what looked to be the robes of an Emerald magistrate. Both were staring at the far end of the gorge, but it was not the women that caught Chiaki's attention.

The dead had reached the canyon entrance. Not peasants, nor even low-rank samurai, they wore Lion armor. Beneath the blood and filth, beneath the grinning porcelain masks, despite gaping bloodless wounds, missing limbs and broken bone, tattered manes and broken helms, Chiaki could not help but recognize them.

She had trained each and every one.

At their fore stood Katamori, a leader even in death. Chiaki blinked against the prickle of tears, letting sorrow give way to fury. It had smoldered in her chest for years, faded to embers in the long, slow march of time. But despite her aching bones, her slack muscles, the gray in her hair, Chiaki was still Matsu, and the Matsu *burned*.

She was on her feet in a heartbeat, already sliding down the uneven slope before Masahiro could even draw breath. His anxious call was distant, little more than wind through leaves. The magistrate shouted something, but her words were eclipsed by the hammer of blood in Chiaki's ears, the furious roar building in her throat.

It had been a long time since the killing rage had gripped Chiaki, longer than many who wore the Lion crest had been alive, but she welcomed it like an old friend, arms spread as she skittered down the hill.

They had made a mockery of her children, of her clan.

She would set things right.

The first of the dead was Matsu Haruka – last to roll call, first to volunteer. There was no recognition in Haruka's dead eyes as Chiaki's blade removed her head.

She bulled the falling body aside, already hacking into the packed ranks behind. It was better this way, to think of them as things rather than people, as demons rather than the children she had sparred with, laughed with, loved.

Kazuya, who had adopted a one-eyed dog from the local village and fed it his rations. Chiaki had been furious when she discovered the animal, but the other students had leapt so quickly to its defense, she couldn't muster the will to toss it back. The hound had accompanied Kazuya for years, scrappy to the end.

He was still wearing one of its fangs on a little cord around his neck when Chiaki cut him down, the brutal sweep of her backswing ensuring Kazuya did not rise again.

They came for her then. Emi, with her thoughtful eyes. Motoharu, who Chiaki had caught crying over a small cameo of his parents, and promised never to tell. Kaori, who had such a temper Chiaki had been forced to knock the wind from her lest she take an axe to the old camphor tree behind the dōjō.

Chiaki's memories came like shattered blades, dull, broken, but still jagged enough to cut. For the first time in years, her aches faded to nothing, burned away by hopeless fury. She felt nothing as Kaori hammered a heavy spear shaft into her side, the dull crack of ribs little more than sullen accompaniment to the anger that raged through her.

She caught the awkward swing of Motoharu's fist on an upraised arm, the force of the blow knocking her back a step. The dead may have forgotten every lesson she had taught them, but they were quick to take advantage, swarming like ants over the body of a fallen wolf.

Chiaki had been in the press many times, knew it was pointless to struggle, her long blade useless as a willow switch. She worked a hand to her belt, dragging her short sword from its sash. This was different, though. Neither a slit throat nor slashed belly was likely to stop the dead. Even so, they possessed ligaments, muscles that must move, eyes that must see.

Chiaki laid about with her blade, aiming for wrists, for arms, for faces. But there were simply too many. They clutched at Chiaki's arms, crooked fingers clawing at her. She could feel the spiky press of their armor as they crowded in. Pain blossomed in Chiaki's side as one of them worked the edge of a broken dagger between the plates of her armor. She felt the blade scrape along her ribs, then slip between.

There was no time to gasp. Cold hands closed about her throat, tight as a noose. She recognized Kenjiro by his hair, so long and fine. He had spent hours oiling and combing it, even going so far as to fill his helmet with incense smoke so whoever took his head would have a pleasant gift to present their lord.

He leaned close to her, face obscured by the terrible mask. Beneath the rot she could smell sandalwood and rose oil. A racking moan worked its way up Chiaki's throat, strangled by Kenjiro's cold grip. Her vision curled up at the edges, blackening like burning paper. She had thought to avenge her students, but, in the end, she had forgotten her own lessons. This was no warrior tale. Chiaki was no hero.

This would be a very poor death indeed.

Through the blacksmith hammer of her heart, Chiaki heard a ringing clatter. Steel flashed, and the pressure on her throat eased. She drew in a sharp gasp and cried out, the pain in her side finally rising through the furious haze. Blood pooled in her breastplate, seeping down into the silk bindings. It was agony to breathe.

"You were supposed to be cautious." Masahiro stepped past her, his own sword transcribing a tight arc that sent Kenjiro's head tumbling.

"And you were supposed to be clever." Chiaki spoke through pain-gritted teeth.

"I am." Masahiro thrust his chin at the two women Chiaki had marked earlier. "The Unicorn is a name keeper. She was about to set you all aflame." Although Masahiro's face was streaked with grime, his infuriating grin never wavered. "I convinced her to wait."

Blades swinging, they retreated from the scrabbling onslaught. Masahiro's style was typical of a Crane, less concerned with what one did than how one looked while doing it. Even so, Chiaki was glad to have him at her side.

"Down!"

Chiaki glanced back to see the woman in magistrate's robes gesturing wildly. Pulling Masahiro with her, she ducked as a bright banner of flame whipped over their heads, carving smoky ruin through the packed ranks of the dead.

Chiaki stumbled to her feet, light-headed from blood loss. She squeezed her arm tight to her side to stop the flow, and grimly staggered after Masahiro.

"My gratitude for your forbearance," he said as they reached the two women.

The one in Unicorn armor seemed not to hear. Her eyes were squeezed shut, her cheeks flushed. She swayed on her feet, voice slipping from a low thrum to a howl as wind whipped about her in a tangle of streaming silk cords.

The woman in magistrate robes crawled toward them, shouting to be heard over the wind. "I'm not sure how much longer she can continue!"

Chiaki glanced back. Although the Unicorn's conjurations had scattered broken bodies across the canyon, more dead jostled at the narrow mouth. For a moment, she dared hope Katamori had been destroyed in the blaze, but she saw him stand, one arm raised as if to signal a charge. It burned Chiaki's heart to think even some tormented echo of him might remain.

"How many are there?" the magistrate asked.

"Too many," Masahiro replied.

The Unicorn shuddered, her chant stuttering. Wind died. Fire guttered. The earth grew silent. She took a quick step to the side, as if to catch her balance, only to have her ankle roll.

The magistrate was quick to catch her, Masahiro moving to support her other arm.

"Our companion waits just over the rise." Chiaki nodded toward the rear of the gorge. "He can guide you from the mountains."

"Not until we stop *him*." The Unicorn shivered like a plague victim, cheeks flushed, her lips pale and bloodless.

"Stop who?" Masahiro asked. "The Shrike?"

"Now is not the time for questions," Chiaki shouted.

Relentlessly, mercilessly, the dead began to rise. Chiaki fixed her eyes upon Katamori, glad she could not see his face behind the mask, could not see what they had done to her boy.

"We can't outrun them," Masahiro said. "Not carrying her."

"I am fine." The Unicorn tried to shake free, only to have one of her knees buckle.

"I will hold the gap," Chiaki said.

"Unacceptable." The vehemence in Masahiro's voice surprised her.

"Spoken like a spoiled Crane pup." Chiaki filled the words with as much venom as she could muster. "Run back to your poetry readings and perfumed sheets."

"I know what you're trying to do," Masahiro replied, his voice uncharacteristically soft. "It won't work."

"I came here to die, Crane." Chiaki lifted her arm, letting him see the blood that soaked her side. "Let me be about it."

He nodded, throat bobbing as he blinked several times in rapid succession. "I shall see your sacrifice memorialized."

"Do that, and my spirit will come for you." Chiaki pressed a hand to her ribs, wincing. She let the pain turn her voice into a rough growl. "Now go, before I have to break my promise and cut you down."

Masahiro said something else, but Chiaki wasn't listening.

Her attention was only for Katamori.

He led the assault, limping on a leg that bent the wrong way, his remaining arm waving the broken katana like a banner pole. Behind came a wedge of Matsu warriors, pale bone showing through rents in their armor.

Dimly, she heard Masahiro and the others stumbling away. Chiaki widened her stance, blades at the ready. Although she knew better, some small part of her still expected the sense of stoic calm that was said to come over those awaiting death. In truth, Chiaki's hands were sweaty, her lips chapped and sore, and her wounded side stung like a fresh burn. She would have traded her helmet for a cup of cool water.

Hardly the stuff of legend.

The dead were only a dozen paces away. If she squinted just so, Chiaki could almost pretend it was one of the hopeless charges the Matsu sagas were always going on about – a few brave warriors facing impossible odds for the glory of clan and empire.

A smile tugged at the corner of Chiaki's lips, her chuckle the pained croak of a dying crow.

Perhaps warrior tales had some use after all.

CHAPTER TWENTY-THREE

Paper crackled under Irie's nervous fingers. She did not need to read the letters to know what was inked upon them – two score pages, half covered in Masatsuge's careful hand, the other in the monk's archaic scrawl, correspondence, a back-and-forth between two master Bloodspeakers. Amidst the taunts and cruel barbs coiled veiled secrets, meditations on the nature of the gods, the spirits, the worlds. Like epistolary vipers, they waited for the unwary to stumble into reach, filling Irie's head with venomous thoughts.

She should destroy the letters, but she could not escape their terrible logic. Perhaps it was exhaustion. It seemed that no sooner had Irie quieted her troubled mind than Tetsuo shook her awake. Her robes were torn and dirty, her hands covered in scrapes, her legs a mass of bruises, and still Irie pushed forward, terrified by the knowledge that if she faltered, even for a moment, the Crab would leave her behind.

It wasn't the dead Irie feared. She and Tetsuo had burned their way through dozens of the walking corpses already. With Masatsuge gone, the dead roamed the hills like hungry wolves, drawn to noise, to movement, to life. Irie did not fear them; rather, it was the idea of being left alone with her thoughts, Masatsuge's words choking the life from Irie's flimsy justifications.

The world was broken. The Empire was a lie. There were realms beyond this, locked away by the whims of cruel and petty gods. Again and again, Irie told herself these were the arguments of a corrupt mind, but had she not seen the evidence with her own eyes? Had she not witnessed Masatsuge's power firsthand?

Doubt cut at her like an enemy blade.

Irie shook her head as if to dispel the cloud of clinging apprehension. No decision ever suffered from too much information. Whatever her questions, the answers lay in Iuchiban's tomb. She would see, she would understand, and then she would act.

"We are near." Tetsuo's voice came rough from disuse. He fixed Irie with an appraising stare. He had been doing much more of that lately. "Are you well?"

"Just tired." It was not a lie, not quite.

With a low grunt, he gestured toward the cliffs ahead. "Five-Dragon Gate."

They stood at the edge of a tattered pine forest, the air sharp with the tang of bleeding sap. Perhaps a hundred yards beyond, the slope became more pronounced, trees giving way to the sweep of ancient stone. Although it was midmorning, the sun bright in a steely, cloudless sky, Irie could not help but feel the shadow of the mountains, cold and deep.

Drawing in a shaky breath, Irie regarded Five-Dragon Gate. The pass seemed to shed light, a dark, ragged crack in the cliffside, as if the mountains sought to shy from what lay within.

Masatsuge had spoken of destroying the gate, of freeing Iuchiban's power. He had known the tomb's location but had not opened it. Had he been waiting for something? For her?

"The Shrike's creatures have been here for weeks." Irie could not tell Tetsuo *how* she knew. "How could the tomb remain shut?"

"Its door is not a door." As usual, Tetsuo's terse reply only raised more questions.

Irie burned for elaboration, illumination, but knew further inquiries would elicit nothing but silence. Instead, she simply followed Tetsuo into the pass, trying to keep her balance amidst the shifting stones.

Although the way was wide, perhaps fifty paces across, the road was little more than a trampled line of earth, warded on either side by outcrops of fallen rock. It smelled of the mountain, of cut pine and cold earth, of streams and wet stone. But as they descended, other scents threaded the air, sharp and sickly. The place reeked of rust, of rot, of sorrow and mildewed bones. Irie knew this was where the imperial expedition had met its end, but she saw little evidence of the slaughter – a streak of old blood on the underside of a canted rock; the remains of a banner pole, its flag little more than bleached tatters. Bits of discarded armor and broken weapons poked from the scree, but no bodies.

Not that Irie had expected any. Unbidden, she found herself trapped by ruinous arithmetic. The rebels, the villages, the imperial expedition – her master had commanded a sizeable force, enough even to threaten a great clan.

"Here." Tetsuo nodded toward a patch of scorched stone. No, not stone, some manner of carving – cracked and weathered.

Irie bent to rub a hand across the soot. A low hiss slipped

through her lips as she recognized the sheen of polished jade beneath the grime. She stood, throat tight as she regarded the broad expanse.

Perhaps ten paces wide, the shattered jade seal had been set into the rock. From the cracks, and charred, broken bits scattered about, it looked to be easily a foot thick, the surface carved with images of the five elemental dragons, surrounded by an intricate series of trigrammatic wards. The prayers were marred beyond comprehension, but from their placement, and the fact that the seal had gone so long unmolested, Irie guessed they were wards of stability and concealment.

She swallowed heavily. "This must have cost an emperor's ransom."

"Every clan contributed," Tetsuo replied. "So that what occurred might never happen again." He drew in a slow breath. "But mortals die, records are lost, children forget the struggles of their ancestors."

Irie waited, hoping Tetsuo would elaborate. He did not.

"This wards the entrance to Iuchiban's tomb?" She studied the corrupted seal. "I see nothing."

"The door is not a door."

"You said that already." Irie pressed her lips together, leashing her rising irritation. "But can you open it?"

"We were not told how," Tetsuo said. "For our protection."

"What *do* you know of the door?"

Tetsuo gestured toward the seal. "It is here."

Irie could not help the annoyed groan that worked its way up from her chest. Now she knew why Masatsuge and the monk had been searching for more information. If the Five-Dragon Gate was a ward, then finding and destroying it should have revealed the entrance to Iuchiban's tomb.

But there was no door, at least not in a physical sense.

Irie upended her satchel upon the stone, sorting through the letters and notes.

"What are those?" Tetsuo asked.

"Research," Irie replied. She had been worried the Crab would see, but now she realized it hardly mattered. Tetsuo's knowledge of the occult was that of an artisan, skilled at his calling, but blind to more scholarly aspects.

She paged through the correspondence. Both Masatsuge and the monk had been caught up in their struggle. Like duelists, they thought only of how to best their opponent. They had been too competitive to see the knowledge hidden within the teeming flurry of taunts, feints, and veiled insults. But Irie possessed both distance and ability.

She may not have committed the letters to memory, but she understood the implications. Masatsuge had taken her under his wing, had prepared her for years, for decades. She was his favored disciple – how could she not follow his reasoning?

It was like when her master had taught Irie to read. Although time blurred the details, she could still recall a time before – when words had been nothing but incomprehensible symbols. Now, they had substance, meaning.

But there was a trap in literacy: once you had the skill, you could never look at a word without understanding it.

Irie had been given a glimpse of a greater reality, and now she could not help but see the shallowness of her surroundings, a world circumscribed by the clumsy grasp of elemental fetters. Earth, air, fire, water, even void – illusions, all. There was no truth to be found. Only lie heaped upon lie.

With a start, Irie realized she understood. Iuchiban had crafted this tomb. There was no door, not in Rokugan, not that any mortal, nor even any spirit could see. Masatsuge had sought it like he sought everything, with ritual and scrutiny, but elemental magic was as useless as feeling about with one's hands. The door was elsewhere.

After carefully folding and putting the letters away, Irie sat cross-legged, back straight. Centering herself, Irie reached for Masatsuge's mask.

"What is that?" Tetsuo asked the question she had known he would.

"The Shrike's mask." There was no use in lying.

The Crab's mountainous shadow fell over her, but Irie did not turn.

"It is the only way." She spoke softly.

"The mask is tainted."

"Since when do Kuni shy from employing the tools of darkness to combat it?" It was a fair question, one Irie knew Tetsuo could not answer with words. Either he would strike her down or he would not.

The Crab stood for a long moment, simply breathing. Then his shadow retreated.

Eyes closed, Irie pressed the mask to her face. It was surprisingly light, although the inside was rough with splinters, gouging dozens of scrapes and tiny punctures. There were no straps, but when she took her hands away, the mask remained affixed.

Irie opened her eyes and called the Empty Flame.

Unlike all the other times, she did not attempt to thread fire and void – for the flame was neither. Rather, it dwelt beyond such clumsy considerations, in the space between moments, the realm outside of thought, of hope, of desire. It was a thing apart, unlike any power she had ever called upon.

Unbidden, words spilled from her lips, chants learned from the contentious exchange between master and monk, sifted like flecks of gold from the endless flow of enmity. The answer had been before them the whole time, had they but looked beyond their rivalry, their ambitions.

Had they but sought the truth.

The Empty Flame filled Irie's body, burning away the mask in a burst of lightless heat. She let the tainted relic go. It was no longer necessary.

Like sunset, there was no single point of change, only a growing sense of power – outside the feeble bonds of reality, corrupting but not corrupted, touching all, but untouched. Irie's muscles relaxed, her heart ceasing its wild flutter. She seemed to sink into the earth, to move beyond fear, beyond exhaustion, beyond time. The Empty Flame was limitless.

She felt Tetsuo shift. The Crab samurai was watching her, his hard features betraying nothing of his thoughts. Only a few hours ago, his scrutiny would have filled her with dread. Now, she knew she had nothing to fear. Tetsuo was as blind as the others. Only Irie could see what must be done.

No decision ever suffered from excess knowledge.

"Are you ready?" she asked.

He rumbled wordless affirmation.

Irie let the Empty Flame grow beyond her, the barest splinter of its limitless scope sufficient to cover the surrounding cliffs in invisible fire. The sun seemed far away, little more than a tarnished bit of bronze swallowed by a sky dark and lustrous as a crow's wing.

She understood why Masatsuge had sought in vain. His was a sharp mind, steeped in knowledge. It was long used to being in control, used to understanding. There was no problem he could not unravel, no secret he could not winnow out through careful consideration.

And that had been his undoing.

The door could not be found, could not be illuminated. It was privy to neither insight nor knowledge, for it was not something that could be revealed, not something that could be sought.

The door must find you.

There was no light, no darkness, no heat nor chill. The Flame could not be seen, but it could reveal. The door came to Irie. Like a vast ocean predator surfacing beneath a ship, it seemed to rise from murky depths, not becoming clearer so much as growing closer. Only when she heard the sharp intake of Tetsuo's breath did Irie turn.

The door was behind them. It had always been behind them.

Carved of pitted basalt, it was an elaborate affair, heavy slabs of stone incised with thousands of prostrate figures, hands raised in supplication, their faces pointed heavenward. Irie had seen such carvings upon temple walls, the object of worship ranging from divine to enlightened. Here, however, there was no image of Shinsei, no Fortune, no honored ancestors, no inkling of heavenly panoply.

The sky above the worshipers was a mirror, each kneeling figure twinned to one above, their blind obeisance rendered in intricate, almost mocking detail.

Tetsuo stepped up to put a hand on the stone, only to flinch back, hands bunched into fighting fists.

"Let us be done with this."

Irie rose, arms raised as if to push the portal wide. "Open."

The door did not move.

She summoned the Empty Flame, sending invisible tendrils

coiling along the door's pitted surface. Jaw tight, she implored them to throw the entrance wide, but the portal remained frustratingly shut.

Again, Irie reached out, voice hard, spirit straining as she enjoined the dark fire to rip the stubborn doors from their moorings.

Nothing.

It was as if the door were not even there. Which, of course, it wasn't.

"Open it!" Tetsuo shouted, the first emotion Irie had ever seen from the Crab.

"I don't understand." She wilted like summer grass. The weight of past exertions, physical and spiritual, seemed to press down on her. Her master had not been waiting, for Irie, for anything. Masatsuge had broken the jade seal, slaughtered the imperial expedition, filled the province with unquiet dead, and yet none of it had allowed him entrance. If he did not possess the key, what hope had Irie of finding it?

Tetsuo towered over her, hands clenching and unclenching. "Why won't it open?"

"I have not the key." Irie shook her head, eyes stinging with shameful tears. To have come so far, sacrificed so much, only to fall short.

Truly the ancestors must have abandoned her.

"Where is it?" Tetsuo ground the words through gritted teeth. "Tell me, and I shall rip it from the very earth."

Irie bowed her head. "I do not know."

CHAPTER TWENTY-FOUR

The path was clear, empty but for a few thrushes flitting amidst the tangle of thorny shrub. Little more than an abandoned goat path. Masahiro was nonetheless grateful. He didn't know if he could manage another sprint across broken ground. To say the flight from Crossroads had been punishing would be akin to calling the Emerald Champion a passable duelist.

He moved, half-jogging, half-stumbling down the stony path, focusing on his breathing, his balance, anything but what had occurred in the pass a few hours ago. Chiaki was gone, that much was certain. Even unwounded, there was no way the Matsu could have held back the swarm of corpses.

And yet, he hadn't seen any on the slopes behind them.

Masahiro still could not quite believe he had followed Chiaki into the battle. He had not been thinking right. No doubt a result of the numerous tortures heaped upon him over the past weeks. It troubled Masahiro to think that some of the doddering Lion samurai's single-minded truculence may have infiltrated his decisions.

Exhaustion, that was it. Had to be.

Even knowing Chiaki was dead, he still expected to hear her

creaky admonitions every time he stumbled or slowed. He had not liked the Matsu – her self-destructive impulse ran counter to everything Masahiro believed. And yet, in the moments between labored breaths, amidst the tumult of fear and raw nerves, he could not help but miss her. Again and again, he would glance back, expecting to spy her on the path behind, her weathered features craggy as the peaks through which they fled.

Such hopeful thinking was a waste. Masahiro had long ago learned to work with what he was given, not with what he wished he had. The hard truth was he had lost an unwilling protector, traded Chiaki for two suspicious strangers and a man who had, until quite recently, been trying to murder him. There had barely been enough time to get their names.

The smaller woman, Naoki, wore the robes of an Emerald Magistrate, the Dragon Clan and Kitsuki family crests picked out between the shoulders. She ran like a palanquin bearer, slow but steady, her breathing punctuated by the occasional curse as she slid on gravel or kicked a stone. The Kitsuki were famed investigators, so it didn't strike Masahiro as odd for one to become a magistrate, nor for her to be mixed up in the affairs of a dark sorcerer.

The other he was less sure about.

Iuchi Qadan had the hard-eyed, rustic look Masahiro had come to expect from Unicorn Clan nobility, no doubt exacerbated by days or even weeks in the shadow of these horrible mountains. Masahiro had seen her call down flame and cutting wind to destroy a number of the dead. Definitely a priest, although not of any type he was familiar with. Her power had been a strange, sudden thing, a far cry from the chants and elemental invocations of elementalists back at the capital. It was odd to see a Unicorn this far from their territory, even more so one of their idiosyncratic priests. Qadan certainly bore watching, not that Masahiro was in any position to act should her motives prove suspect.

Currently, it was all he could do to keep his feet.

"A moment, please." Masahiro's voice came as a jittery rasp.

"Five-Dragon Pass is just ahead." Gensuke did not even turn.

"What's the use of reaching the hinterlands if we drop dead from exhaustion?" Masahiro glanced back, again. "The path is clear behind us, the mountainside bare. We will see them long before they see us."

Gensuke stopped. "A moment only."

Naoki paused, hands on knees, face red as she puffed and panted. Masahiro braced himself for a barrage of questions from the magistrate, but it was Qadan who spoke first.

"Who are you and what are you doing here?"

"Doji Masahiro, at your service." He began a bow, only to have his head swim. Rather than risk a tumble he leaned against the rocky cliff face, striking what he hoped was a casual, and not at all desperate, pose.

"I know you." Naoki waved a tired hand. "When I was last at court during the Autumn Reconciliation, we met at a moon viewing. Weren't you part of Otomo Yasunori's entourage?"

"He was part of mine," Masahiro replied. "But close enough."

"Yes, yes, I remember." Naoki nodded. "You were with young Prince Tokihito. He ate a bad persimmon and began to cry."

"Quite a dreadful affair," Masahiro said. "The poor lad was inconsolable."

Qadan fixed him with a truly belligerent stare. "You still haven't answered my questions, Crane."

"I am but a humble diplomat," Masahiro replied. "Dispatched

by the Imperial Court to smooth the transition of power in these lands after the unfortunate and untimely death of its Crab lord."

"How is that going?" Qadan asked.

Masahiro shrugged. "There have been some setbacks."

"And the Lion samurai back at the pass?"

"Chiaki, my bodyguard." He gave a sad shake of his head. "To her discredit, perhaps."

"What is a Crane doing with a Matsu bodyguard?" Naoki asked.

"I'm more interested in what a Crane is doing with him." Qadan looked to Gensuke.

Masahiro nodded at the little man. "That, my friend, is Shosuro Gensuke, the man my enemies sent to kill me."

Gensuke frowned at the three of them. "If you have enough breath for pleasantries, you have enough breath to run."

"Not until I know where we're running to," Qadan said.

"Five-Dragon Gate." Gensuke thrust his chin ahead. "It's the only pass for miles. The eastern province is swarming with dead, but we can lose them in the hinterlands then head north to Scorpion lands and warn the court."

Qadan crossed her arms. "Quite noble, for an assassin."

"Gensuke is nothing if not practical," Masahiro said. "I have friends in the capital, individuals who would be quite vexed to learn of an army of walking corpses." He gave a thin smile. "Now, if I might inquire … what has brought a Unicorn ritualist and Emerald Magistrate to such disastrous surroundings?"

Qadan glanced at Naoki, who fixed the Crane with an appraising look. After a long moment, she nodded to herself.

"We are tracking a killer. A dark sorcerer of tremendous power."

"Ah, I knew it!" Masahiro clapped his hands, glancing at Gensuke. "They *were* the ones who confronted the Shrike in Crossroads."

"The burnt village?" Frowning, Qadan shook her head. "We passed through after the battle. And we do not seek the Shrike."

"There is more than one dark sorcerer?" Masahiro blinked, unable to conceal his surprise.

"So it seems," Qadan replied.

"The village – what did you see, exactly?" Naoki asked.

"Flames, mostly," Masahiro replied.

She glanced at Qadan. "Do you think it was Irie and Tetsuo?"

"There are more of you?" Masahiro asked.

Gensuke sucked air through his teeth. "There won't be *any* of us if we don't start moving."

Masahiro was about to argue, when Qadan collapsed. It was a sudden thing – limbs limp, head tilted back, eyes little more than pale whites. Had Naoki not stepped forward to catch her, the Unicorn might have cracked her skull on the rough stone.

"What is the matter?" Masahiro asked.

Qadan's eyes fluttered, head rolling on a neck gone limp as loose silk. "The door has been discovered."

"Is it open?" Naoki asked.

"I cannot say."

"What door?" Masahiro asked.

The Unicorn seemed to be regaining her bearings, a distinctly uncomfortable looking Naoki still gripping her arm. Masahiro gave Qadan a moment to collect herself before repeating his question.

"With all due respect." Qadan fixed him with a level glare. "Tell us why we should trust a disgraced courtier in the company of a Scorpion assassin?"

"We did save your lives." Gensuke stepped to Masahiro's side, showing interest for the first time.

Masahiro's grin was positively venomous. "My would-be murderer makes a compelling point."

"A moment, if you will?" Naoki led Qadan a short distance away. It was clear she thought them beyond earshot, but any courtier who intended to last even a few days in court learned to read lips, and Masahiro was better than most.

"You would face the monk and Shrike together, just the two of us?" Naoki asked.

"I am not alone." Qadan gripped her talismans. "Not anymore."

"I like this no more than you, but we almost died back there." Naoki clucked her tongue like a disapproving parent. "You cannot simply charge ahead like a wild mare. If the Bloodspeakers have truly found the tomb, we do not know what lies ahead."

"Look at them." Qadan shook her head, gaze flicking back to Masahiro and Gensuke. "You would clutch an adder and a scorpion to your breast."

Masahiro lifted a hand to his face to smother an aggrieved sniff at the Unicorn's uncharitable portrayal. Truly she must have received a double helping of her clan's rustic backwardness if she could not distinguish between an avowed murderer and Crane nobility.

"I am not saying we should put our lives in their hands," Naoki replied. "Only that they may be of use."

"Do what you will." Qadan chewed chapped lips, her expression almost pained. "But should either of your new pets show the slightest hint of treachery, I will burn them where they stand."

"I would expect nothing less." Naoki nodded, heading back toward them.

"I hope your conversation was edifying." Masahiro spoke as if he hadn't understood the whole thing. He had little interest in facing *any* number of dark sorcerers, but had even less confidence in his ability to navigate this demon-haunted nightmare on his own.

"We can talk on the move," Gensuke said, gaze fixed on the path behind. No dead yet clambered down the daggerlike ridge, but they would come. Of that, Masahiro was sure.

"The man we seek, the dark sorcerer," Naoki said as they began to descend once more. "He wishes to unleash a great evil upon Rokugan."

"Worse than an army of walking dead?" Masahiro asked.

"Much worse." Naoki gave a ragged sigh. "Tell me, what do you know of Iuchiban?"

CHAPTER TWENTY-FIVE

Qadan felt like half a corpse already. Although she could walk without aid, there hadn't been time to recover her strength after their stumbling flight from the canyon. The dead had fallen by their scores, and yet there seemed no end. Although it was Eruar, Gion, and Kahenu who ravaged the walking corpses, to summon such power took a toll upon Qadan's already overtaxed body.

Almost without thinking, her trembling hand crept into her satchel, feeling amidst the talismans for Kahenu's nest of scorched branches, the spirit's name already on her lips. Jargal would have chided her for drawing upon the fire spirit to prop up her failing strength, but Jargal was gone.

Like stepping into a shaft of summer sunlight, Kahenu's power flowed into Qadan, her muscles jittering, her aches and pains lost against the rapid beat of her heart. She straightened almost without thinking, vision clearing, exhaustion boiling away like morning mist.

Freed from the smothering weight of fatigue, if only briefly, Qadan took a moment to collect her frayed thoughts.

Someone had found the door to Iuchiban's tomb. The knowledge had gripped her like a demon reaching from the underworld, one hand clutching Qadan's stomach, the other worming a sharp claw into her forehead. Back in the crypt, the feeling had been muted, distant, but now it seemed to surround her, pressing down with an almost physical weight.

Loath as she was to agree with Naoki, the magistrate was right. They would need every advantage to defeat the Bloodspeakers.

Qadan regarded Gensuke. The small assassin was dressed as a peasant but did not move like one. Surefooted as a mountain goat, no stones turned beneath his feet, no spray of dust marked his passing. He seemed almost to float down the mountain. Although Gensuke appeared to carry no weapons, Qadan noted several suspicious bulges beneath his roughspun tunic. Throughout Naoki's explanation of Iuchiban and his disciples, the Scorpion had raised neither comment nor question, merely regarded the magistrate, the pinched look on his face that of a man having his worst fears confirmed.

The Crane had reacted with predictable bluster, as if by displaying the proper amount of outrage and disbelief he might somehow scandalize the Bloodspeakers back into hiding. Naoki had responded to his flustered banter with surprising patience, elaborating on the search that had brought them here without dwelling on specifics. At last, Masahiro had lapsed into sulky silence, his seemingly endless dialogue silenced by ragged breaths as they ran.

Now, the Crane looked as tired as Qadan felt. His once fine robes were streaked with grime, stitches pulling free along the shoulders, delicate embroidery concealed beneath soot and dried blood. His hair had pulled free from its binding to wreathe his head like a cloud, bits sticking to his sweaty forehead and the back of his neck as he cast glances behind.

Qadan could have told him to spare the trouble. If the Bloodspeakers had found Iuchiban's tomb, then there were likely enemies ahead as well.

"There." Gensuke nodded at a dark cleft in the mountains. Just beyond the ragged tree line, it had the look of an ill-omened place – a sharp break gouged into the cliff as if by the sweep of some demonic blade. Even worse was the feeling of wrongness that clung to the shadowed walls. It was not corruption, not quite. But Qadan knew what lay beyond was the work of neither gods nor spirits.

She could not help but shiver, hand thrust deep in her satchel for comfort. Her fingers brushed the strange talisman. Like a nest of adders, it drew blood, hot against Qadan's cold skin. With it came a sense of recognition. The talisman was somehow connected to the power that coiled within Five-Dragon Gate.

"Are you well?" Concern threaded Naoki's question.

"The door." Qadan gave a brisk nod. "It's in there."

The magistrate chewed her lip, staring into the cleft as if to pierce the shadows through will alone.

"So why are we walking toward it?" Masahiro asked. "Isn't our goal to warn someone capable of actually fixing this mess?"

"There is no time." Qadan felt her lip curl. She misliked everything about the Crane – his robes, his condescension, his self-important smile.

"All the more reason to hurry back to civilization," Masahiro replied. "Unless I misheard our Dragon friend, the last time Iuchiban rose it took several armies to beat him back." He gestured at the others. "Not to insult the skill or dedication of our fine companions, but we stand before the tomb of an immortal sorcerer. One, might I add, who has had *centuries* to prepare."

"Coward." Qadan spoke through clenched teeth.

Masahiro seemed to take the insult in stride, another mark in his disfavor. "If you wish to add your shambling corpse to Iuchiban's legions, I shall not bar your way."

"We are days from safety, longer if we must avoid the dead." Always the peacemaker, Naoki stepped between them. "If the monk gains access to Iuchiban's power, all is lost."

Masahiro glanced to Gensuke, who tilted his head. "They make a fair point."

"I'd expect such foolishness from a Matsu, but you always struck me as a sensible man." The Crane pressed a hand to his head as if to dispel a sudden ache.

The assassin shrugged. "You're welcome to find your own way out of the mountains."

"You know I cannot."

"Then it seems there is no decision."

"Fortunes spare me from heroic sentiment." Masahiro pulled back his hair, straightening his much-abused robes with exaggerated care. "The least I can do is leave a handsome corpse."

Naoki laughed, a wild, bubbling titter that seemed equal parts humor and nerves. Qadan spared her a withering glare before stepping up beside Gensuke, talismans at the ready. The magistrate had the decency to look a bit embarrassed as she drew her jitte.

They made their way down into the pass.

"Watch the rocks," Gensuke whispered, knives suddenly to hand.

Qadan nodded. "If the Shrike is here, we can expect more dead."

"And if it is the monk?" Masahiro asked.

"Then we don't know what to expect," Naoki replied.

Although the pass was wide enough for a dozen people to walk abreast, they moved in a tight knot, gazes flicking from shadow to shadow. It seemed impossible that the pass was empty, and yet Qadan saw nothing but the occasional flicker as a spiny lizard darted amidst the rocks. All the while, Iuchiban's power bore down on Qadan, as if she galloped through a driving rain, cold droplets sharp as knives upon her skin.

They had descended almost a half-mile when a shadow rose from behind a boulder just upslope. It hefted a heavy rock, poised to throw.

Qadan had Kahenu's name upon her tongue when Naoki ran forward, arms raised.

"Wait, wait!" The magistrate flailed like a frightened child. "Tetsuo! It's me! We've come to help!"

Unbelievably, Naoki's skull remained uncrushed.

Like some ancient terracotta guardian coming to life, the Crab samurai stepped into the light.

"You know this… fellow?" Masahiro asked.

"He is Kuni Tetsuo," Qadan replied. "A witch hunter."

"*Finally*, a professional." Masahiro stepped by her, sword low as he picked his way up the slope. "Allow me to introduce myself. I am Doji Masahiro, ambassador of the Imperial Cour–"

Tetsuo walked down the far side of the rise, disappearing from sight.

Masahiro blinked, glancing back. "Is it safe to follow?"

"No." Qadan pushed by him, enjoying the Crane's confused mutter as she climbed the rocky embankment. At Masahiro's insistence, Naoki relayed the details of their brief meeting with the Crab witch hunter, although Qadan noted she left out the part where Tetsuo had almost murdered them all.

Although relieved to see little more than Tetsuo and Irie waiting for them on the far side, Qadan could not help but feel an upswell of apprehension as she beheld the massive iron gate set into the side of the cliff.

"It was here all along." Irie spoke without preamble. In the days since they parted company, the Phoenix priest seemed to have aged decades, her hair wild, her eyes sunk in bruised hollows, her face crisscrossed with scabbed cuts.

"How did the Bloodspeakers not discover it?" Naoki asked.

"Five-Dragon Gate." Irie thrust her chin at the remnants of what had been a truly prodigious jade seal set into the rocky floor. "But more than that, the door is not here, not actually."

There was an almost frenetic intensity about her movements, Irie's fevered gaze hot as a forge as she paced back and forth. Concern sparked in Qadan's thoughts. In the days since she last saw the Phoenix, Irie seemed to have frayed both physically and spiritually. Qadan would have suspected corruption, if not for Tetsuo's presence.

Even so, the Phoenix bore watching.

"I cannot be sought, only found," Irie continued. "They could not see, could not understand."

"Who?" Naoki asked.

"The Shrike, the monk, all of them." She flicked a hand as if to brush away an irritating insect. "But I found it – beyond the elements, beyond the spirits, beyond *everything*."

Qadan glanced at Tetsuo, but the Crab only stood, arms crossed, his expression cold as a funerary obelisk.

"Then we had best see it hidden again," Gensuke said.

"The Shrike's creatures come on our heels," Naoki added. "And the monk not far behind."

"The Shrike is dead," Irie said. "Burnt at Crossroads."

"So it is *you* we have to thank." Masahiro offered a courtly bow. "Were it not for your swift action, I fear my dear friend Gensuke and I would have joined the shambling throng."

Irie regarded the Crane as if he had begun reciting bawdy limericks.

"That is good news." Qadan felt something uncoil within her shoulders. Only one master Bloodspeaker remained, although by far the more dangerous.

"Why seek the tomb and not the monk?" she asked.

It was Tetsuo who answered. "To end it."

"I discovered the tomb entrance, *manifested* it." Irie seemed to slump, her burst of energy expended. "But it will not open."

Qadan stepped toward the door. Although set back into the cliffside, it loomed over her. She could pick out the expressions of the supplicants carved into the metal. They wore a uniformly wide-eyed look, hands stretched toward those mirrored above, mouths open in what might have been laughter, or screams. The sight conjured a chill in Qadan's chest, her burgeoning anxiety hard and unyielding as the pitted iron of the door itself.

Qadan laid a hand upon it. The metal felt warm, almost alive. She could feel the spirits at her side recoil from the gate, withdrawing deeper into the comforting weave of their talismans.

All but one.

A static tingle traveled down Qadan's arm, an almost spiritual pulse of energy, echoed by the strange talisman in her satchel. It was what the monk had been searching for, not a door, but a key.

Breath coiled in her lungs, Qadan withdrew the talisman, not even flinching as it cut her. She knew how to open the tomb, had *always* known, but something held her back.

She looked at the others, their expressions ranging from confusion, to apprehension, to fascination.

"Is this… right?"

"You have seen what Iuchiban's followers are capable of." Naoki winced as if the very mention of his name might summon the dark sorcerer. "Imagine what horrors the dark sorcerer himself has planned."

"We must destroy his heart," Tetsuo said.

"And his knowledge," Irie added.

Gensuke shook his head. "I cannot allow another Sleeping River."

"And I cannot seem to talk any of you out of this foolishness." Masahiro cast a pensive frown back up the path. "Best open it before the dead arrive."

Qadan drew in a slow breath, steeling herself. Whatever dwelt within the razored talisman was very old and very powerful and very cruel. Although Qadan sensed no corruption, she could not stem the flood of doubt that set her hands trembling. Had there been any other way, Qadan would have snatched at it like a drowning woman, but there was no time.

The monk would not hesitate, neither could she.

Muscles tense and humming, Qadan turned back to the gate, a name on her lips, a name she had promised herself she would never speak again.

Qadan spoke.

And something answered.

CHAPTER TWENTY-SIX

Naoki could not restrain a shudder as they entered the shadowed gate, the shock snatching the breath from her lungs. There was a sudden sense of movement, not a step, so much as a plunge. Although she could feel stone beneath her feet, Naoki's stomach lurched as if she had leapt from a great height. They had taken only a few steps into the tomb, but when Naoki glanced back, she saw nothing but a gyre of swirling mist beyond the entrance. She gripped her jitte, struck by the uncomfortable realization they were no longer in Five-Dragon Pass.

The passage was perhaps ten paces wide, arrow straight, the ceiling high enough Naoki could just make it out in the flickering light. Heavy blocks of unmortared limestone made up the walls and floor. Cut to wildly differing sizes, they fit together less like a structure than a woodblock puzzle. The light came from small sconces cut into the wall every five paces. Within each burned a small blue flame. Absent of fuel or wick, they bathed the hall in unnatural light, casting long shadows and giving Naoki's companions a sickly look.

"Can you close the gate behind us?" Irie was the first to

speak, her hollowed cheeks and darkly circled eyes making her appear almost skeletal in the half light.

Qadan shook her head, frowning. "What gate?"

They peered into the shifting fog. Naoki stretched out a hand, then snatched it back with a hiss.

"What is it?" Gensuke asked.

"Cold." She flexed her numb fingers, the feeling beginning to return. "Like meltwater."

Gensuke gave a sharp nod. "Then we must assume the monk will follow."

Tetsuo was the first to move. After an appraising look backward, the Crab samurai stalked down the hall.

"Wait, where are you going?" Masahiro called. "There could be guards, traps. We had best stay together."

When Tetsuo ignored him, the Crane wrinkled his nose. "Is he always like this?"

"Yes," Irie replied. "And we would do well to follow."

With a nod, she moved off after the Crab, Gensuke and Qadan close behind. After the unsettling display at the tomb entrance, Naoki resolved to keep a better eye on the Unicorn name keeper. Qadan had spoken of the differences between name and blood magic, but the calling she had worked to open the gate looked suspiciously like the latter.

Naoki frowned, considering. If any of their dubious company had knowledge of darker arts, it would be Tetsuo and Irie. They had, by their own account, destroyed a blood mage, after all, but neither the Crab nor Phoenix seemed the least troubled by Qadan's display – not that Naoki wholly trusted them, either.

She was about to follow when a bit of odd stonework caught her eye. About knee level, wedged between two curving ribs of limestone, was a small circle of etched basalt. There were other oddities nestled amidst the walls, but this seemed to be the only one that bore any sort of engraving. The etching was faint, barely noticeable in the pale light.

Naoki rummaged in her satchel for paper and a bit of chalk, which she used to make a quick rubbing of the carving. About the size of a clenched fist, the stone was carved with a diamond pattern of interlocking stone, as if someone had removed a section from a castle wall – one stone above two, above three, above two, above one. Superimposed over the stonework was a human hand, curled like a bird's talon, fingers spread across the stones.

"What have you got there?" Masahiro leaned in to study the rubbing. "Looks like the sigil of the Kaiu family." He touched the stylized hand. "Although their banner bears a claw."

Naoki blinked. "Could the Crab Clan have built this place?"

"Perhaps." Masahiro glanced around. "The architecture is certainly ugly enough."

He touched her shoulder, nodding toward their companions, who had dwindled to little more than shadows.

"We must go."

Nodding, Naoki followed. "Should we show the others?"

"You know them better than I."

"Hardly."

"Then it might be best to keep this between us," Masahiro said with an uncomfortable tilt of his head. "I am hesitant to upset our Crab friend. He has the look of someone who would rather break bones than ask questions."

Naoki could summon no argument to that.

They hurried down the hall, limestone gradually becoming marble, then brickwork, then thick cedar beams. The tomb seemed to have been constructed with no care for material or style, wood, stone, and even bits of smoky glass fitted together seemingly at random.

The others stood at an intersection, passages leading in either direction. The rightmost seemed grown of old wood, gnarled roots and limbs jutting from the walls, the floor covered in dark, rich soil. The left tunnel was of roughly cut glass, its walls studded with sharp edges, spines of crystal hanging from the ceiling like stalactites, the floor glittering with fallen shards. Naoki could only shake her head. She had not known what to expect when they stepped through the iron door, but even her wildest imaginings could not compete with the strange architecture of Iuchiban's tomb.

Masahiro thrust his chin toward the wooden passage. "That one certainly appears more inviting."

"Perhaps it is meant to," Gensuke responded.

Even Tetsuo seemed at a loss. The hulking Crab's gaze flicked from side to side, his hands flexing as if to crush the life from the walls themselves.

A low grinding sound echoed through the tomb, stone vibrating as if shaken by some distant stampede. Naoki turned, searching for the source, but it seemed to come from all around. Branches rustled to her right, bits of glass falling from the tunnel to her left to shatter upon the floor in sprays of tinkling shards. She took an unconscious step back, drawing her jitte almost by reflex, her gaze flitting about the chamber, shoulders high in anticipation of assault.

But none came.

After perhaps a dozen heartbeats, the grinding stopped, the tomb once again silent. With a start, Naoki realized her companions had formed a tight knot in the center of the hall, weapons raised. Despite her anxiety, it was strangely reassuring to discover the others knew as little about the tomb as she.

"What was that?" Irie whispered.

"Nothing good, I'd wager." Masahiro sighed. "We should have taken our chances with the corpses."

"Can you sense anything?" Naoki asked Qadan and Irie.

The name keeper shook her head, scowling. "This whole place is steeped in dark sorcery. It's like trying to hunt on a starless night."

"More like a hall of mirrors." Irie ran a hand through her hair. "I see only us, reflected into infinity."

"Here is something." Gensuke squatted near where glass met wood, tapping the wall with his dagger.

Set into the wall was a small silver coin engraved with the number five, writ in classical style. Gensuke prodded it with his knife, but the coin seemed solidly set into the wall.

"Perhaps it's a marker," Qadan said. "Or a direction indicator."

"What map has five directions?" Masahiro cocked his head.

"We're underground," Gensuke replied. "There could be up and down as well."

"I doubt it's telling us to burrow through the ceiling." Masahiro sniffed.

Gensuke narrowed his eyes at the Crane but didn't argue.

"Could it represent the gods? Or perhaps the great clans?" Naoki could only speculate. "We know Iuchiban has designs on Rokugan. Perhaps if we track the order in which the clans joined the Empire to their holdings on a map, we can discern a direction to–"

"The elements." Irie spoke softly, but with the force of conviction. "The five elements."

Naoki turned away to hide her reddening cheeks as the

others nodded agreement. As usual, she had gotten wrapped up in conjecture and overlooked the obvious.

"The elements don't convey direction," Masahiro said.

"They don't need to. The choice is obvious." Irie gestured to the crystal tunnel. "Glass is made, constructed from sand, and fire, and air. It reflects light, not shadow. Trees grow from the earth, nurtured by water and air. They provide fuel for fire, leaving nothing but dark ashes behind." She turned to the wooden tunnel, interlacing her fingers. "Five elements, together."

The others exchanged questioning glances, but no one offered up a different solution.

With a soft grunt of acknowledgment, Tetsuo headed right.

They followed carefully, gazes roaming the network of twining roots, weapons at the ready. As before, Tetsuo and Gensuke took the lead, the two priests in the middle, with Masahiro and Naoki in the rear. Although the tendrils did not move, there was something unsettling about the twisted snarl. The tunnel sloped upward, twisting like a dying snake. More than once they were forced to climb a steep incline, thick soil shifting beneath their fingers. Once, Tetsuo reached out to grip a protruding root, but quickly snatched it back, teeth bared in a pained snarl.

Blood spotted the Crab's palm, the flesh of his fingers gone the color of old driftwood. By contrast, the wood had taken on a warm, almost burnished glow.

Irie took the Crab's callused hand. Studying it, she wiped away the blood, but there were no visible wounds.

"There is nothing I can do. They have drunk of your very soul." She pursed her lips. "Fortunately, the contact was brief. With time and meditation, you will heal."

Tetsuo gave no response but to clench his injured hand and continue ahead.

Naoki regarded the bloodied roots, wondering what other terrible powers they might possess. Although the snarled mat of vegetation remained still, she was unable to shake the feeling that if she glanced away, even for a moment, they would writhe to unnatural life.

"Five elements, indeed," Masahiro muttered, although soft enough that only Naoki heard.

They were more careful, taking pains to avoid the coiled roots and hack down any protruding branches. Fortunately, the limbs seemed to lose their malicious hunger once separated from the main trunk.

They had been traveling for some time when Gensuke clucked his tongue, pausing to regard a cluster of roots. As she caught up to the Scorpion, Naoki saw the reason he had stopped.

Bones.

Woven through the roots and vines looked to be dozens of skeletons, some little more than yellowed ribs, others almost wholly intact, bones fresh and white almost as if they had been licked clean. Naoki could not hold back the sharp intake of breath, unable to dispel the image of her own bones lining the earthy tunnel, roots slithering like serpents through her cracked ribs, nesting in the empty hollow of her skull.

"I thought we were the first to set foot in this place for centuries," Qadan said.

Gensuke sucked air through his teeth. "Perhaps not."

"Who were they?" Irie asked. There were no clothes, no armor, no weapons, nothing but aged bone.

"Fools," Masahiro replied. "Like us."

As if in answer, the grinding came again, dust and soil sifting from the webwork of branches above, leaves shaken by the tremor. At first, Naoki thought it was the vibrations that moved the vines, but they did not seem to simply shake like the other limbs. Instead, they almost uncoiled, crawling like worms through the desiccated bones, weaving rib to spine, to shoulder, to skull, wrapping around joints to stretch and contract like ancient tendon.

"They rise!" Naoki shouted as the first skeleton stood, a terrible amalgamation of twisted vine and pale bone. She lashed out reflexively, training coming to the fore as her jitte knocked the thing's clutching claws aside.

The others were quick to heed her warning. Masahiro's blade flashed in the gloom, removing one of the creature's grasping arms. Undaunted, it lunged forward, only to stumble to the side as Gensuke drove a heavy kick into its midsection. The Scorpion gave a yelp of pain, hopping back on a leg gone suddenly limp and wooden.

"They're still connected to the trees!" Qadan shouted, one of the skeletons clawing down the length of her spear as she fumbled at her talisman pouch.

With a quickness belying his size, Tetsuo swayed between two of the creatures. Although they could not seem to lay a hand on the Crab, it would only be a matter of time until they caught him.

More rose from among the roots, vines slithering in their dirt-caked skulls, poking from ribs and hollowed eye sockets. A gnarled hand brushed Naoki's cheek, its touch like cold fire. She flinched back, hammering her jitte into the side of its skull. Bone parted before the heavy steel blade, but the skeleton only stumbled, more vines writhing from the crack in its skull.

"Fire!" she shouted. "Irie, Qadan, we need fire!"

The Phoenix priest was quick to respond. Arms crooked, fingers splayed, her words blistered the air, a sheet of white-hot flame scything from her outstretched hands. Bones burned and cracked in the heat, vines unweaving as they sought to escape the expanding blaze.

Qadan spoke into being a serpent of crackling fire, sending it among the roots with a flick of her fingers. Vines coiled as if in agony, squirming like dying snakes amidst the spreading inferno. Great plumes of oily black smoke rose from the coiled roots. It filled the tunnel, sharp as razors in Naoki's lungs, her eyes red and stinging.

Coughing, she retreated with the others. Faces blackened with soot, their robes singed, they fled back through the tunnel of earth and wood, pursued by scouring smoke. Although they had come this way only recently, the twists and turns seemed unfamiliar to Naoki – as if the passage had rearranged itself behind them.

At last, the smoke thinned, their stumbling flight slowing to a trot, then a shambling walk. Once more they found themselves at an intersection, the passage of trees at the back; but instead of stone and glass, the tunnel at their left was studded with glazed tile, the other seeming carved from solid ice.

It was some time before any could breathe easily, let alone summon the wind to speak.

"Wrong way." Although Tetsuo's gravelly baritone held little in the way of reproach, Irie raised a sleeve to cover her face.

"I am sorry. I was so sure that–" She shook her head, shoulders rounding. "The elements failed me."

"Iuchiban is clever and cruel, a creature with centuries of forbidden knowledge." Naoki laid a hand on her shoulder. "We all believed the wooden passage was correct."

The Phoenix elementalist gave a stilted nod. "Then which way do we go?"

Gensuke gave a low chuckle. When the others looked over, he thrust his chin at the intersection between the tiled and frozen tunnel. Set into the wall was a small silver coin, this time etched with the number two.

"Not directions, not clans, and *certainly* not elements." Masahiro threw up his hands. "What is the meaning of all this?"

"Five, two." Naoki chewed her lip as she sought for some connection. Thoughts fluttered like moths to a lantern, clamoring for her attention. Amidst the nerves, the worry, the frustration, a thought glimmered like gold tossed into a well. She glanced down at her own hands, fingers hooked into anxious claws.

And then she had it.

She drew forth the rubbing she had made of the stone near the entrance, spreading it so the others could see.

"What is that?" Gensuke asked.

"I took it from a symbol near the gate."

"Is that the Kaiu crest?" Qadan glanced to Tetsuo.

"Not quite." He thrust his chin at the hooked fingers.

"Five fingers," Naoki said. "Look how they touch the various stones, some on the left, some on the right. The last intersection bore the number five, and we know the wooden passage was the wrong choice. If we count the fingers right to left, it brings us to the thumb, which is touching one of the leftmost blocks on the wall. This makes sense knowing now we should have taken the crystal passage on the left."

"And the second finger?" Qadan asked.

"Here." Naoki indicated the hand's second finger. "It's pointing right."

As one, they looked down the frozen hall.

"Certainly the less inviting of the two." Masahiro drew up the collar of his robe as if to ward off the cold. He favored Naoki with a small grin. "But I don't hear any other ideas."

There was a moment of silence, everyone weighing their options.

"The way back is lost." Gensuke shrugged. "We can only move forward."

The Scorpion's words seemed to settle the others, and they busied themselves retightening armor straps and readying weapons. A few moments, and they were ready once more.

Naoki glanced at the rubbing, then the silver coin marker. This *must* be the solution. There was no other option.

Or perhaps there was, and she was too caught up in conjecture to see it.

"Shall we?" Masahiro gestured toward the frozen tunnel like a noble displaying a new wing of his manor.

The Crane's attempt at humor failed to summon even the barest smile from the others. Naoki could not blame them. All they had was vague supposition. Even so, she could not help but feel a strange sense of pride. Although their belief might be rooted in desperation, it was comforting that the others were willing to trust her.

Naoki only hoped she did not lead them to their graves.

CHAPTER TWENTY-SEVEN

Irie stood, head low as the others inspected the newest coin marker.

"Four." Naoki consulted her rubbing. "Left."

She nodded toward a circular passage, its pinkish-red walls glistening with thick excrescence. Mucus dripped from luminous nodules of flesh on the arched ceiling, ribbed bands of striated cartilage running along every surface.

The grinding came again, a blast of humid, reeking air washing over them as Iuchiban's terrible labyrinth rearranged itself once more.

"Why do I get the feeling we're about to be swallowed?" Masahiro asked no one in particular. Normally, the Crane's chatter would have annoyed Irie, but now she hardly noticed. She had thought herself clever, learned, that she could trust the elements. Instead, they had betrayed her.

She had thought as herself, and failed.

Now, she must learn to think as Iuchiban.

Gensuke tested the floor with one foot, frowning as his sandal sank into the fleshy expanse.

"This is no time to be squeamish." Irie ducked into the

low tunnel, teeth gritted against the foul odor of the place. It seemed to cling to her, seeping through robes, oily against her skin. A dollop of something vile splashed against the back of her neck, frighteningly warm as it oozed between her shoulder blades.

Seeing that the first portion was safe enough, the others followed. With a nod, Gensuke slipped by her and into the lead. Irie did not protest. Although Naoki's calculations had spared them further encounters with deadly vines or walking dead, the passages had been far from safe. The Scorpion assassin had proved remarkably adept at avoiding sudden falls of ice, or false floors, or near-invisible tripwires set to unleash crushing stones and sprays of envenomed arrows. Irie was happy to let him take the risk, so long as it brought her closer to Iuchiban.

There had been hints of true genius amidst the cruelty and danger, marvels of enchantment and engineering that had left Irie speechless with wonder. Even now, as they shuffled down into the gut of some demonic leviathan, Irie could not help but respect the terrible artistry of the place.

Imagine if such power were turned to good, used to repair Rokugan rather than exploit its weaknesses. In a way, Masatsuge had been right: with such knowledge they *could* make this world a paradise.

Without a sound, Gensuke hopped back, barely avoiding Irie in his haste. The reason for his concern became evident as the tunnel contracted ahead, muscles clenched tight enough to crush bone. After a moment, the passage relaxed, the way clear once more.

"Tread lightly." Gensuke's whisper came sharp in the gloom. "It seems… sensitive."

"If it reacts to weight, perhaps we should spread out?" Naoki asked. The magistrate was stooped, her body angled away from one of the glowing nodules. Unlike the walls of the hall of roots, these seemed safe to touch, but that did not mean it was pleasant.

"If the tunnel shuts, it might separate us," Qadan said.

"Better than it pulverizing all of us," Masahiro replied. Even more than Naoki, the Crane looked supremely discomfited by the humid confines, his face screwed up in a pained expression, gaze flicking from left to right as if searching for a way out.

Irie nodded her assent. To be honest, it might be good if some of them were cut off – she barely trusted Qadan, Tetsuo, and Gensuke, and Masahiro seemed little more than a liability.

They all looked to Tetsuo. Bent almost double, the hulking Crab samurai half-crawled down the damp passage, his armored shoulders almost brushing the fleshy walls. Unspoken, however, was the assumption that if the Crab refused to see reason, nothing could compel him short of violence.

Irie let out a sigh of relief as, with only the slightest narrowing of his eyes, Tetsuo retreated a dozen paces down the hall.

Spreading out seemed to quiet the passage's delicate sensitivities. Although it trembled ominously several times, the tunnel did not close. It did, however, narrow, the passage's ceiling growing lower, its walls seeming to close in step by step until Irie was forced to stoop, then crawl.

"We should turn back if it gets any tighter." Gensuke was visible only as a pair of legs squirming up ahead.

"But this is the correct way." Naoki's voice came from somewhere behind.

Irie could but shake her head. The magistrate still trusted logic. The tomb would break her of such arrogance soon enough. They had only what Iuchiban chose to give them. To succeed, they would have to study the undying master.

"This isn't where I die." Panic edged Masahiro's words, his voice high and strained. "Not here. Not in this filth."

There was a scuffle from behind Irie. She tried to turn, but only succeeded in bunching up her robes.

"Stop!" Qadan spoke in an urgent whisper. "You'll irritate the tunnel."

"Move again, Crane, and I will snap your neck." Tetsuo spoke as if remarking on the weather.

Masahiro went silent.

Irie swallowed, throat tight with disgust. So this was what Iuchiban wished, to make them skulk through filth, prostrate before his cruel majesty.

If so, Irie would oblige him. She had no pride. Not anymore.

There was nothing for it but to crawl. Irie was forced to her belly, inching forward on knees and elbows, the terrible tunnel pressing in on all sides, slowly crushing the life from her. The air was hot and thick. It was a struggle to draw more than shallow breaths, the passage seeming to fight the expansion of her lungs. She pressed on, the soles of Gensuke's sandals just visible in the constricted gloom.

The Scorpion gave a sharp, surprised cry, his feet sliding from Irie's view.

Panic filled her as the passage became too tight to move. She wanted to scream, to call upon the spirits and burn her way from this terrible place. Only there was no ritual Irie could use. To open her mouth would be to have it fill with vile fluid. One of her arms was pinned to her side, the other extended uncomfortably ahead. Somehow, she knew by calling upon the spirits, she would fail Iuchiban's hateful test.

If he wished them to crawl, Irie would crawl.

She wormed forward, knees and hips, inch by painful inch. Whatever had taken Gensuke, it could be no worse than this.

She was surprised by light up ahead. Not the bilious glow of the fleshy nodules, but the steady flicker of lamplight. Irie redoubled her efforts, anxiety lending strength to her tired muscles.

Something moved ahead. Irie recoiled, then realized it was a hand.

"Take it. I'll pull you free." Gensuke's voice was as welcome as an old friend. Not caring if it was a trap, Irie gripped his hand, worming free of the tunnel and into the glow of lamplight. She gasped in a racking breath, glancing around the chamber.

Steam filled the air, humid as the tunnel, but without the horrid odor. It was clean, scented with herbs and dried flowers. The chamber was spacious, floor and walls tiled like an imperial bath house, its upper reaches lost in swirling mist. In its center sat a deep, recessed pool, steam rolling across the placid water like one of the hot springs Irie used to visit with her master. The pool conjured fine memories of days spent in exercise and scholarly debate, nights relaxing in the springs – tired muscles, tired thoughts seeming to bleed away into the warm water.

That had all been a lie as well.

"Help me with the others." Gensuke stood next to the wall, shoulder deep in the horrible tunnel. Irie hurried to his side, and together they were able to extract Qadan, who gazed around the chamber in obvious shock, and Masahiro, who lay with eyes screwed shut, curled upon the floor like a dying insect. The Crane sported a black eye, no doubt from his scuffle with Tetsuo.

It was an effort to drag the Crab from the tunnel. He had shed his helm and armor, but even so, Tetsuo's broad body would not fit through the opening.

"Dislocate my shoulder." His words came muffled.

Although the tunnel had been undeniably terrible, it had cured Irie and the others of any lingering squeamishness. The three of them gripped Tetsuo's arm, pulling until they felt the pop of it slipping from the joint.

The Crab made no sound as they heaved him from the tunnel, only stood, and slammed his shoulder against one of the cedar beams, hard enough that Irie could feel the vibration.

Apparently satisfied with the result, he lifted his arm, flexed it, then turned to the others.

"What is this place?"

"A bath house." Masahiro had apparently regained his composure. To look at him, one might never guess he had been on the verge of collapse mere moments earlier.

As if to overcompensate, Masahiro cocked his head, sniffed the air, then peered into the pool. "A Crane bath house, unless I am mistaken."

"How do you know?" Gensuke asked.

"The scent." He swirled a finger through the misty air. "Wisteria and heron grass blended with notes of chamomile, and… silver-nettle pine – reputed to be the favorite of Kakita Shimizu."

When no one responded, the Crane clucked his tongue. "One of my clan's most famous iaijitsu masters, Shimizu was founder of the Kakita family, and the Second Emerald Champion – quite the illustrious pedigree. He was said to use this particular blend to focus his mind before a contest. Even the most hapless Crane duelist would recognize it."

Qadan wrinkled her nose. "That is quite a lot to base on odor."

"Indeed." Masahiro thrust his chin toward the pool. "Fortunately, the Kakita family sigil is emblazoned on the floor."

They glanced into the pool. Despite the steam, the water was clear enough for them to make out the vague image of a crane picked out in blue tile, one wing curled around a bared blade.

"And *why* would we find a Crane family crest deep within the tomb of a blood sorcerer?" Naoki asked.

"How am I to fathom the whims of an immortal warlock?" Masahiro shrugged. "Perhaps he meant it to drive a wedge between us. If so, Iuchiban miscalculated, for I am Doji, not Kakita."

"Iuchiban does not miscalculate," Irie said, surprised at the vehemence in her voice. Somehow, she had crafted a picture of Iuchiban in her mind. Sharp and canny, cruel and wise, a mind long removed from base human concerns, leaving only pure intellect.

"Whatever it means, this is very clearly a trap." Gensuke's assertion was met with nods all around.

"I don't see an exit," Naoki said. "We should search the walls."

"I, for one, could use a warm bath." Masahiro gingerly dipped a foot into the pool, frowning. "A bit tepid, but it will do."

"Are you possessed by a demon?" Qadan chopped a hand through the air. "That water could be poisoned, or worse."

"If it's poisoned, we have been breathing the fumes." Masahiro chuckled. "There is one thing I've learned about this place: we have *no idea* what is dangerous. Bathing is no more risky than running your hands along the walls."

"The Crane has a point," Irie said, provoking a few surprised looks from the others. "If he wishes to go into the water, I say we let him."

And if it *was* poisoned, Irie would have one less problem to worry about.

"If I must die, I would prefer to do it clean." Masahiro stripped off his outer robe. Sitting on the edge he dangled his legs in the water to scowls and stares from the others.

After a long moment of nothing, he began to wash his robes. "A little cooler than I prefer, but much better than this filth."

Shaking her head, Irie turned her attention to the walls. Although the tiles were a uniform cobalt blue, they seemed to have no common shape. Ranging from the size of a thumbnail to little more than a fleck of enameled porcelain, they were arranged at random, the whorls and eddies seeming almost to mirror the billowing steam.

Irie mopped a sleeve across her brow. A vain effort to keep the sweat from her eyes. The chamber seemed more oven than bath house.

"There are no trips or triggers I can see," Gensuke said.

"Is the chamber enchanted?" Naoki asked.

"The whole tomb is enchanted," came Qadan's curt reply. For all her talk of bonding with spirits, the name keeper had proven surprisingly shallow with regards to theological matters, but such bluntness was to be expected from a Unicorn.

Brushing back a slick strand of hair, Irie turned her attention to the wall, fingers twitching into interlocking trigrams as she muttered a seeking ritual. It was like dipping her hands into pitch. The spirits of the tomb were wan, pale things, imprisoned or corrupted by Iuchiban's blood sorcery. Irie had made a mistake calling upon them back in the hall of roots, and her flames had raged beyond control.

She was more circumspect now, careful to call only upon those spirits who seemed free of taint. It did not mean they would tell her the truth, but they were more likely to accede to her ritualized requests.

Irie's sight expanded as spirits of air swirled at the edges of her vision. The walls radiated enchantment, diffuse spiritual energy seeming to accentuate the swirling pattern of the frescos – and they *were* frescos, she could see that now.

Images appeared and fell apart like crashing breakers, vague forms seeming to assemble themselves from among the patterned tiles. Irie stepped back to better take in the scene and had to press a hand to her mouth.

The figures were *her*.

She saw herself as a child, tears fresh in her eyes as she first set foot in the Heaven's Blaze dōjō. Masatsuge had been younger then, his hair more gray than white, his posture a little straighter, but his smile had never changed, nor had the kindness in his deep-set eyes.

Someone was talking, Qadan or Naoki. Irie thought she heard her name, but ignored it, staring deeper into the nested frescos.

The scene shifted, mandalas of interconnected meaning glittering like light refracting from water. There Irie was with the other disciples, hands folded in her lap as she debated esoteric Shinseist philosophy. Now, she stood by Masatsuge, a basket of steamed buns in the crook of her arm. They were in a village, one of many the dōjō cared for – Masatsuge had always seen compassion as the highest mortal virtue.

She watched him watching her, pride glimmering in his

careworn face whenever he thought she wasn't looking. It had been that pride which proved his undoing.

Now they stood in the burning rubble of Crossroads, he in his robes of shifting sigils, her smoldering with betrayed indignation. Even in the full fury of her power, Irie seemed a brash, brutal thing, a blaze threatening to burn beyond control.

Masatsuge's face showed no fear, no concern, only the well-worn regard she had come to trust. He had trusted Irie as well, believed in her, and she had seen him torn cruelly asunder for that mistake.

Or was it a mistake?

Masatsuge was many things, but foolish was not one of them. Had he known she would destroy him? Had he sacrificed himself?

The tiles shifted again, hinting at more. Irie redoubled her efforts, hoping to peer into her master's motivations, his very thoughts. Truth lay just beyond her grasp, she only needed to dig deeper.

Absently, Irie wiped a hand across her cheek, blinking against the steam. It seemed thicker now, heavy as the fog that sometimes settled in the valleys below Heaven's Blaze. She began a more intricate ritual, one meant to pierce illusions.

Someone grabbed Irie's shoulder. She tried to shake free, but the grip was firm, drawing her back as if from deep underwater.

Qadan's face snapped into focus. Blood spotted the name keeper's cheeks and forehead, but Irie could see no wounds.

"The mist." Qadan's teeth were crimson. "Blood magic."

Irie blinked, glancing about. She could barely make out the others. Gensuke, Naoki, and Tetsuo stood in a tight group, weapons bared although there seemed no foe. Masahiro remained in the pool, little more than a vague shadow in the mist.

Irie glanced down at her own hand, bloody flecks seeming to seep from her skin, threading the swirling steam with ribbons of bright crimson.

"Help me." Qadan dragged her toward the others. Drawing forth a talisman of woven ribbons, she sent a breeze cutting through the hungry mist. The sirocco spun a tiny cocoon of clear air around Irie and the others. Coils of steam edged around them, predators searching for an opening. Irie could see shapes in the fog, taloned hands, fanged maws, spines and stingers streaked with veins of corruption.

Kansen.

They must have slipped up on the others while Irie stood transfixed.

Furious at being misled so easily, Irie called into being a torrent of icy air. She set it slashing through the steam and saw the kansen recoil. But they were back a moment later, a questing claw slipping through Qadan's barrier to cut at Tetsuo.

Although he made no sound, Irie saw the ephemeral claw cut a ribbon of crimson across the Crab's chest, droplets of blood bubbling from the wound to spiral up into the clutching mist.

Gensuke slashed at a snapping maw, only to have his blade pass through without effect.

"Steel cannot harm them." Naoki gave a pained grunt as the razored edge of fog opened her cheek to the bone.

"Irie, do something!" Gensuke called. "Before these demons bleed us dry!"

She summoned another gust of cutting wind, scattering the kansen like windblown seeds. But they were back a heartbeat later.

"There are too many." She spoke through gritted teeth.

Something glimmered in the fog, steel bright in the lantern light. Like a diving hawk, it cut through one of the kansen, dispersing the tainted spirit into harmless ether.

With a flourish, Masahiro stepped from the coiling mist. The Crane was naked but for a loincloth, his white hair slicked back, skin still wet and glistening.

Surprised, Irie could not help but notice the Crane did not bleed. Also, his black eye had healed.

"The water harms them!" Masahiro set his blade through a series of whirling cuts, droplets arcing through the air. Kansen flinched back as if the Crane had spattered them with melted bronze.

"Into the pool!" Naoki shouted.

Irie sent a crescent of wind arcing toward the pool, gouging a corridor through the thicket of clutching hands. Masahiro led the way, katana bright amidst the steam as they dove into the water.

All but Irie.

The tomb had stoked her curiosity – another trap, or perhaps another test? Iuchiban had wished for Irie to crawl, now it seemed he wished for her to bleed.

But she was no longer a cloistered scholar, blind to the truths of the world. She had seen suffering, seen death, seen the terrors of dark magic made manifest. This was not a time for philosophy, for study – it was a time for action.

Irie would have been hard pressed to call upon spirits of fire within such a sodden place. Without fuel, without dry air, they would have been quickly overwhelmed by kansen. But the Empty Flame needed nothing. It simply was.

She stepped to the edge of the pool, glancing to the others

in the water. "When I give the command, duck beneath the surface."

Naoki shouted a breathless question, but Irie had already turned away. There was no time for discussion. The magistrate could either trust in the Empty Flame or die.

A nebulous talon raked along Irie's arm, the wound cold as it drew her blood into the terrible fog. Irie barely felt it, her thoughts already slipping away, replaced with the hollowed shadows necessary to draw upon the flame.

It came more easily this time, a tide of rootless power rising to eclipse conscious thought. Bloodied arms outstretched, Irie called it into being, not darkness, not light, but something outside of either.

"Down!" Her voice came as a strained rasp. She could only hope they had heard.

Kansen swept in, a torrent of snapping jaws and clutching claws seeking to overwhelm Irie's defenses.

They were as nothing before the Empty Flame.

The tangle of corrupt forms melted like salt in the rain. Irie's mortal senses could not encompass the sights before her. Tiled walls warped like old wood; time, place, direction reduced to mere distractions. Such was the power of the Empty Flame, Irie feared it would destroy her as well, not through intention or malice, but through its very existence.

She threw herself back into the pool as the incomprehensible inferno raged through the chamber. Unable to do more than gulp a stilted half-breath, she plunged below the water's surface. It was warm, but not uncomfortably so, very welcome after the cloying heat of the bath house.

Eyes open, she could just make out the others, little more than shadowed smudges set against the formless blaze above.

And then it was over, the Empty Flame slipping back along some impossible angle.

Irie surfaced, sputtering. The pool was far too deep for her to touch bottom. Her robes clung to her, heavy as stone as she kicked her legs, working to stay afloat.

Masahiro was the first to rise. He glanced around, swallowed.

"Well done."

Qadan came up snorting water. Naoki and Gensuke bobbed up a moment later, Tetsuo surfacing like a boulder at low tide.

"What was that?" Naoki asked.

"The kansen were corrupt spirits of water and air," Irie replied. "I boiled them away like morning mist."

The explanation did not seem to satisfy the Unicorn. Rather than suffer a renewed inquisition, Irie made a show of looking around. Although the air was clear, there yet remained no obvious way forward.

"Will the kansen return?" Gensuke asked.

Irie shook her head.

"Then we should get out of this pool, before–"

There came a booming echo from below, ripples spreading across the surface. Irie looked down to see the Kakita sigil had fallen away to reveal a deep, dark hole. She tried to paddle away, but was already caught in the current, her heavy robes like chains as she swirled round and round.

Any plan of escape was driven from Irie's thoughts as she crashed into someone. A hard knee drove the breath from her lungs, a flailing arm hammering into her nose hard enough to send flickering motes of light across her vision. She drew in a shocked breath, half-air, half-water.

Her foot struck hard stone, and Irie tried to push off, but

the pull was too great. She clawed at the lip of the hole, fingers slipping across slick tile as she was sucked into darkness, the pale glow of the bath chamber receding to a single flickering star overhead.

Then it, too, was lost.

CHAPTER TWENTY-EIGHT

Half-naked, half-starved, half-drowned, and still Masahiro had to admit he felt better than he had in weeks. After a rather aggressive egress from the Kakita bath house, he and the others had been deposited in the collecting basin for a large marble fountain.

Masahiro cast about for his blade and robes. Public baths were common throughout Rokugan, and he had little concern over a bit of exposed skin, but some degree of propriety must be maintained, even in the tomb of an immortal necromancer.

The others were slower to rise. Even that beast Tetsuo seemed winded by the fall, kneeling in the water, loose hair dangling like a cowl as he drew in slow, measured breaths. Such was to be expected – the others had been in the miraculous water for a shorter time than Masahiro.

He had but dipped his legs in the Kakita pool when he'd begun to feel his muscles loosen, the painful litany of physical indignations bleeding away like spilled ink. Masahiro had tried telling the others, but it was clear they thought him a fool.

Well, they would have to acknowledge his cleverness now. He had, after all, saved their lives.

Although still quite soaked, Masahiro's kimono was almost spotless, the water having washed away not only the feculence of that horrid living tunnel, but also weeks' worth of grime and dust. His blade shone like a crescent moon, silver in the watery light of the new chamber.

Masahiro suspected the tomb only waited to heap some new humiliation upon him, but for the moment, it felt good to be clean.

The chamber appeared to be some manner of gallery, stone columns disappearing into the vaulted shadows, the floor tiled in smoky marble like the audience chamber of some high official. There was even a dais at the far end: seven steps leading to a platform upon which stood seven statues arrayed around a central pedestal.

Wringing out the sleeves of his robe, Masahiro regarded the statues warily. Attired as clan nobles, they bore the weapons, robes, and armor of generals preparing for war. He did not need to approach to recognize the beautiful lines of Crane battle kit on the second statue from the right, a long, curved blade held in classic guard. After that, the others were easy to pick out – the Crab samurai shaped like a rocky crag, the Scorpion concealed beneath robes of carved granite, the Lion with arms raised as if caught in mid-charge. They were all there – seven statues, seven clans.

No doubt they would presently spring to life, or breathe fire, or explode.

Masahiro considered stepping from the fountain but decided it might be better to let one of the others prod that particular peril.

They had mostly collected themselves, standing unsteadily amidst the gently swirling water. Unlike the pool above, it was only waist deep, and so appeared to offer little risk of conveying them somewhere worse.

"Where are we?" Naoki asked – as if *any* of them could provide an answer. Truly, the magistrate could learn a bit more circumspection. It was as Masahiro's poetry master, Abe, had always said: "Better to remain silent and be thought a fool, than speak and remove all doubt."

So, Masahiro remained silent.

Gensuke was the first to step from the fountain. The wiry assassin sucked his teeth, studying their surroundings with a well-practiced eye.

"The light comes from these." He nodded toward a series of glowing glass panels set into the walls at about shin level. "Which means we aren't meant to see what's up there." He cast his gaze toward the shadows above.

"Can you summon more light?" Naoki turned to Qadan. Masahiro noted the magistrate hadn't asked Irie, and took a sidling step toward the Phoenix priest. It never hurt to befriend someone who could call up scorching doom.

Surly as always, the Unicorn huffed a bit, sliding a not-so-subtle glare toward Irie as she muttered about uncontrolled spirits and creeping corruption. For her part, the Phoenix affected not to notice. If anything, she seemed even more withdrawn, hands concealed in her dripping sleeves, eyes hidden beneath a fall of wet hair.

Masahiro coughed to get her attention. "Thank you for that, back there."

He spoke more from the desire to break the tension than anything. Also, if the others acknowledged Irie had dispersed the kansen, they would *also* have to admit Masahiro had saved their lives.

They did not.

It was clear none of them trusted Masahiro, but at least they wouldn't discount him. After that incident in the tunnel of flesh, he was just happy to be in a place that wasn't trying to swallow him whole.

In the glimmer of Qadan's serpentine flame, the upper reaches of the chamber appeared perfectly banal, an expanse of arcing stone faced by dark wood, like the vault of some ancient ancestor temple. The empty ceiling did not comfort Masahiro. It only meant danger would come from someplace else.

The others moved about the room, careful not to touch the pillars or tread too heavily upon the tile. Growing weary of wet sandals, Masahiro joined them in studying the statues.

"Seven clans." Naoki once again stated the obvious.

"And here, another sigil." Masahiro bent to regard the symbol carved into the first step. Picked out in red sandstone, it appeared to be a weave of crimson cord, knotted lines giving the vague appearance of masks, or hooked claws.

"That's the Shosuro crest, if I'm not mistaken. Isn't that your family, Gensuke?" Masahiro glanced at the assassin.

"We cannot all possess the integrity of the Crane." His erstwhile assassin's icy glare told Masahiro everything he needed to know. "There are rumors of... traitors. Individuals fallen to the lure of power or dark knowledge. It was one such creature who helped unleash Iuchiban's hordes upon our lands."

"And this could be the mark of one such traitor?" Masahiro kept his tone light, preferring not to antagonize a professional murderer.

Gensuke's nod was terse, but unthreatening.

"Why did you come here?" Qadan stepped up to regard the Scorpion, who returned her stare with cold menace. Masahiro swallowed a frustrated groan. Sometimes it seemed the Unicorn *wanted* to have her throat slit.

"I can attest to the fact he came to kill me." Masahiro raised his hands.

"But why enter the tomb?" Qadan nodded at the others. "I know why they are all here, but you… what business does a Scorpion assassin have with Iuchiban?"

"I cannot allow another Sleeping River," Gensuke replied.

"You could do that by reporting back to your clan," Naoki said. "Why risk it all by coming here?"

The assassin's gaze flicked away, as if he were judging his chances of flight.

"Whoever designed this room," Masahiro said softly, as if to a small child, "they were your ancestor, weren't they?"

Gensuke's hands tightened into fists, then slowly relaxed.

"Shosuro Akifumi, a clever, curious man who delighted in exploring the limits of morality and human nature. They say he constructed elaborate scenarios to gauge the reactions of those around him – some were simple tests, others more deadly." Gensuke spoke as if reciting from a historical scroll. "None know how he came to serve Iuchiban, only that he played a role in circumventing the Scorpion information network, leaving our lands open to Iuchiban's assault. In return, Iuchiban made him a favored disciple. Now it seems he's had a hand in designing this tomb as well."

Gensuke would not meet anyone's eyes. "Akifumi is a stain upon my family. If the dark sorcerer once again marshals forces, I cannot allow the Shosuro to aid him."

"Sleeping River was two centuries ago," Naoki said. "You believe Akifumi still lives?"

"I believe he is still here," Gensuke replied. "Whether he draws breath is irrelevant."

"What about the statues?" As usual, Tetsuo's gravelly rasp made Masahiro jump. For a lump of walking, talking basalt, the Crab could move with surprising stealth.

Gensuke regarded the dais. "I cannot say."

With a flick of her wrist, Qadan sent her pet fire spirit arcing up the stairs. It wove around the statues' heads, their stone expressions visible for the first time.

Masahiro drew in a strangled breath.

"What is it?" Naoki asked.

He realized he had taken an unconscious step back, one hand raised to his mouth. There was no time to recover, nor could Masahiro think of anything else to say.

"The Crane statue…" His voice sounded distant, strange. "It is my brother."

Hiroshige stared down at Masahiro, the curve of his jaw, the arch of his brow, even the knowing smile that perpetually curled the corner of his lips.

"How is this possible?" Masahiro turned to the others, seeing his confusion mirrored. Even Gensuke's usually dour expression flickered with uncommon emotion. Surprise, yes, but something more. It was a small tick, barely more than the glimmer of sunlight off a distant temple spire, but Masahiro noted it all the same.

The assassin *recognized* Hiroshige, Masahiro was sure of it.

"The others seem familiar as well." Naoki mounted the first few steps to peer up at the graven faces. She brought a finger to her lips in thought, eyes widening. "Mirumoto Hakka!"

Masahiro had heard the name before but could not quite place it. "Was she not a Dragon Clan diplomat?"

"One held in high regard by the Imperial Court," Naoki replied. "Her career was on the rise, only to be cut short by an unfortunate illness. It struck during winter, ravaging her body before the passes cleared and aid could arrive."

"And that is Master Isawa Kichinosuke." Irie nodded toward the Phoenix statue, a well-kept, bearded man in scholar's robes. "I attended one of his talks at the Moon River dōjō. I heard he disappeared while on pilgrimage."

"Suspicious." Masahiro studied the other statues, unsettling recognition prickling at the back of his neck. "The Lion is Akodo Saigen. I met her at Winter Court. She was slain fighting bandits in the Twilight Mountains." He glanced at Gensuke, who stood as if anticipating a strike. "I'm sure you recognize the Scorpion."

"Bayushi Sōji," The assassin's reply came cold and sharp.

"Not a bad fellow for a Scorpion noble." Masahiro watched Gensuke for any reaction, but the assassin remained as still as the statues on the dais. "We crossed paths several times in the Imperial City – a man of ambition if I recall."

"What happened to him?" Naoki asked.

"He backed the wrong conspiracy." Masahiro could not help the twinge of regret that caused his heart to flutter. "The official word was that he died of the plague, a polite fiction – more likely he was assassinated."

"As was Kakita Kōgoro." Tetsuo nodded at a Crab in heavy war plate, a wide-bladed polearm balanced on his broad shoulders.

The name was unfamiliar to Masahiro, but no one seemed willing to compel Tetsuo to elaborate.

"And Lady Iuchi Gerel was thrown from her horse while hunting steppe wolves." Qadan's tone made it clear the Unicorn's cause of death was considered suspect.

"Seven murdered nobles." Masahiro crossed his arms, jaw tight as he worked out the implications.

"There is something written on the wall behind them." Gensuke mounted the dais to squint up at the words etched into the stone. "*From high to low, not wealth, nor blades, nor rank can open the path to heaven. Who among the clans stands highest in virtue?*"

"You said Akifumi liked to test those around him?" Naoki asked.

Gensuke nodded.

"Does he expect us to array ourselves upon the steps?" Qadan asked.

"Not us." Gensuke nudged one of the statues. Despite weighing multiple tons, it glided across the stone as if carried on a gentle breeze. Light as a wind-carried seed, it settled upon the second step.

"There is a hole in the pedestal." Gensuke knelt to peer inside. "I see some manner of lever."

Naoki nodded. "No doubt we are to reach inside and pull it once we've settled on the proper configuration."

Qadan bared her teeth. "I mislike this."

"Oh, and I have *so* enjoyed the other chambers." Masahiro waved a dismissive hand as Qadan turned to glare. "Shall we begin? Or would you prefer to spend more time commenting on the merits of traps conceived by murderous necromancers?"

As was her wont, the Unicorn lapsed into brooding silence.

"The Dragon and Phoenix walk closest to the Way of

Shinsei." Naoki mounted the dais, brow furrowed as she pushed the statues to the forefront. "The Lion follow Akodo's Code, which is principled, although not exactly moral."

"The Crab defend the Empire," Tetsuo said.

"But they also tread closest to corruption," Gensuke replied.

The Kuni gave a low rumble but did not deign to disagree.

Masahiro studied his companions. Tired, battered, suspicious, they had no reason to trust one another. Masahiro did not know which clan was the most virtuous, but he understood people – and everyone here was ripe for conflict.

Which may have been the point all along.

"What morals? What virtue?" Qadan tossed her head. "We cannot simply accept the Way of Shinsei as objective morality."

"The Little Teacher brought the clans together," Irie replied as if by rote. "Only through his teachings may we achieve true enlightenment."

Qadan's scowl deepened. "This world holds more truths than are enumerated in some ancient scrolls."

"The path your clan treads is hardly virtuous," Gensuke said.

"Very rich coming from a Scorpion." Qadan rounded on him. "It was a member of your family who built this monstrosity, after all."

Gensuke's eyes narrowed.

"I feel as if I should say something in defense of the Crane." Masahiro glanced about, hands spread as if to calm a herd of skittish colts. "But I think that is what Akifumi desires."

When no one spoke, he nodded toward the dais.

"Consider not objective virtue, but subjective." He tried for his usual, easy smile, but found it elusive. Even so, it seemed best to forge on before any of the others thought to silence him with a fist. "This test was not designed by the gods, it was designed by a blood sorcerer. How would Akifumi rank the clans in virtue?"

"He was a traitor," Gensuke said, voice strained with uncommon sentiment. "A monster."

Naoki sucked air through her teeth. "A man like that would not ascribe virtue to *any* clan."

"So we remove all the statues from the dais?" Qadan asked.

"It seems worth a try," Naoki replied.

Shifting the statues took almost no time at all. After a bit of discussion, each of them pushed the one representing their clan, with Tetsuo moving both Lion and Crab.

Masahiro could not help but study his brother's face. Hiroshige looked as he always had – proud, clever, strong – a man who did not bow before the whims of the world, but who worked to shape all around him into something different, something better.

Hiro could have been emperor in all but name. Now, he was little more than a note on some archivist's scroll, an unfortunate contender in a burgeoning secession crisis.

Hiroshige deserved better. They both did.

As if caught within the current of a river, Masahiro's gaze was swept toward Gensuke. The Scorpion struggled with his statue, light, but awkward due to its flowing robes.

Masahiro stepped up to lend a hand, earning a nod from his erstwhile assassin.

The others might have forgotten, but Masahiro had not, *could* not. These statues were murdered nobles. Masahiro could not believe their placement was merely random, some cruel jest by one of Iuchiban's twisted disciples. There was truth here, even in shadow.

"Which of us pulls the lever?" Naoki asked, although Masahiro knew the answer had already been decided. He could see it in their faces, the way their gaze flicked in his direction when they thought he wasn't looking. That the others considered him expendable was evident. In their place, Masahiro might have felt the same.

That did not mean he forgave them.

"Shall I spare us the farce of deliberation?" Masahiro mounted the steps, back straight as the others surreptitiously moved away. Let them cower, Masahiro would show them who stood highest in courage, if not virtue.

The lever was a small affair, tucked back in the pedestal far enough that Masahiro had to reach in almost to his shoulder to grasp it.

Jaw clenched, he pulled, trying not to flinch as the wall behind the dais cracked open in a spray of ancient dust.

Coughing and waving his hand to dispel the cloud, Masahiro saw that a new tunnel had opened. Thankfully, it was of cut stone, lit by lanterns spaced every dozen paces. If anything, the passage appeared wholly mundane – which was also a concern.

With a courtly bow, Masahiro turned back to the others. "Gensuke, I believe you should take the lead?"

The Scorpion assassin slipped up the steps. After a long, appraising look at the passage, he stalked into the gloom, every step carefully balanced to spring in any direction. He would be a hard one to kill, far beyond Masahiro's ability. And still, Hiroshige's spirit cried for justice.

But the tomb held more than danger. Masahiro had learned much in the courts. Advancing one's cause owed as much to recognizing opportunity as it did to clever stratagems. His chance to dispose of Gensuke would come, of that he had no doubt.

Iuchiban would give Masahiro his vengeance.

All he had to do was wait.

CHAPTER TWENTY-NINE

Qadan had but to close her eyes to feel the wrongness of the place. Spirits writhed in the shadows, their anguish suffusing the air, the stone, the glimmering crystals spaced around the wide, circular chamber. The floor was incised with a dozen concentric rings, each inscribed with layers of interlocking trigrams. The slope was gentle but obvious, each circle placed a bit lower than the one before, the whole descending toward the center, where a deep stone pit promised a bone-breaking fall.

"What new underworld have we stumbled upon?" Masahiro surveyed the room, his thin lips drawn into a look of vague disgust.

"Underworld, indeed. This one is inscribed with the sigil of the Hell of Black Thread." Qadan squatted to study the closest ring, one hand extended. Perhaps a pace wide, it radiated a sense of abject terror. Dark spirits moved within the ring, beaten around the armature of sigil and sign by the cruel hammer of blood magic. There must have been dozens, *scores* of trapped spirits here, their names stolen. Arm clasped protectively around her talisman satchel, Qadan could not find words to describe the horrors on display.

"The Chamber of Even Blades." Irie nodded toward the name inscribed above the door through which they had entered. Below it was the Shosuro family crest.

"It seems we have your ancestor to thank once more, Scorpion," Qadan said.

Gensuke did not even have the courtesy to look abashed, regarding the sign as if it were a road marker upon a country lane. Despite his skill, Qadan did not trust the wiry assassin's motives. Since when did Scorpions concern themselves with the truth? More likely he had come to steal Akifumi's power; that, or convince the ancient warlock to return.

"It is a model of the underworld – part of it, at least." Leaning forward, Naoki frowned at the descending rings. "The underworld is said to contain endless layers of torment, but there only seem to be a few dozen here – Hell of Burning Blades, Hell of Carving, Hell of Raining Knives, Hell of Eight Thousand Piercing Trees, and more."

"Why might your ancestor choose these?" Irie asked Gensuke.

The Scorpion only shook his head, jaw tight and shoulders high.

"The Chamber of Even Blades." Tetsuo repeated the name. "All of these hells cut."

"Hardly a comforting realization." Masahiro sighed. "But I suppose we must forge ahead."

"Can your spiritual senses discern anything more?" Naoki looked to Irie and Qadan.

"There is power in these rings," Irie replied. "Although what I cannot say."

"The bindings are motivational." Qadan scowled at the Phoenix priest. For one who claimed extensive knowledge of spiritual matters, Irie's understanding seemed remarkably shallow. "The spirits' names are woven into this place, allowing them to manipulate physical space without manifesting."

"So, the rings are meant to move?" Masahiro asked.

"It would seem that way," Qadan replied.

Tetsuo gingerly extended one sandalled foot to nudge the nearest ring. It rotated as if affixed to some central ring, trigrams clicking by. Qadan felt the captive spirits stir. A moment, and the whole chamber was filled with a metallic rattle as the other rings began to spin.

Qadan took an unconscious step back as a circular stair spiraled up from the pit, rising toward the chamber's ceiling, where a hidden trapdoor sprang wide, a golden glow filtering down from above. Upon the stair was carved a short phrase:

Let the guilty step forward and confess.

Masahiro glanced about, his smile rueful. "It seems we are to ascend from the underworld."

"It cannot be this simple." Naoki shook her head. "Akifumi desires to trap us, but how?"

Qadan ignored the Dragon magistrate, instead studying the layout of the rings. Rather than a jumble of trigrams, the inscriptions had formed a series of words, one character on each ring, radiating out from the center stair.

"One must not contravene the will of heaven." She read the inscription aloud, gesturing to draw the others' attention.

"That is a line from the *Teachings of Shinsei*," Irie said. "Specifically, *The Book of Duties*. It is third of Shinsei's two hundred and twenty-five Rules for Virtuous Conduct."

"And I suppose your master had you memorize them all, Phoenix?" Qadan could not keep the edge of scorn from her voice.

Irie drew herself up. "We spent many months contemplating the true path. I know Shinsei's maxims like I know the mountains of my home."

"So Akifumi would have us recount our sins?" Masahiro sniffed. "Seems somewhat hypocritical."

Naoki bared her teeth, more snarl than smile. "I suspect the irony would be lost on him."

"Who among us is guilty of acting against heaven?" Qadan let the question hang, uncomfortable silence settling about them like a heavy cloak as the others scowled and glanced away. Confessing such wickedness was tantamount to admitting corruption – not something to be taken lightly, especially with an imperial magistrate present.

"Gensuke is a murderer," Masahiro ventured, at last.

"Murder falls under a different proscription." The assassin glared at the Crane courtier. "And besides, I never killed anyone of note."

Masahiro sniffed. "You were about to."

"Hardly," Gensuke replied, an ugly grin curling his lips. "Perhaps you should enlighten the others regarding exactly *why* I was sent to dispose of you."

Masahiro crossed his arms, face reddening.

"This one sought to manipulate the line of imperial secession," Gensuke continued, still smiling. "Place an infant on the throne so he and his brother could act as puppeteers."

"Tokihito recently celebrated his eighth birthday." Masahiro tossed his head like a surly colt. "Hardly an infant."

Qadan could not restrain her surprise. She had known the Crane frequently involved themselves in court politics, but to undermine the emperor's will seemed beyond arrogant.

"Climb the stairs, Crane." Tetsuo stepped behind Masahiro.

Although the Crab's arms remained at his sides, there was an air of unstated menace in his bearing.

"So, I am to be the sacrifice, once again." Masahiro raised his hands, derision dripping from every word. "And after I saved all your lives back at the pool."

"Irie's summoning saved our lives," Gensuke said.

"Ah, but whose quick thinking bought time to call the spirits?"

"Enough talk." Tetsuo shoved the Crane forward. Masahiro stumbled onto the first ring. He teetered like a child's top, arms spinning as he tried to regain his balance, only to tumble down the incline and roll to a stop several paces from the stairs.

The rings remained motionless.

Face red, Masahiro stood, not even deigning to glance back at the others as he straightened his robes. Qadan held her breath as, gingerly, he placed one foot upon the staircase. When nothing happened, Masahiro ascended several stairs, then turned and sat down, favoring Qadan and the others with a truly venomous glare.

"Come, let us see what *you* are guilty of." He leaned forward, head on hands like a child eagerly awaiting a tale.

At Tetsuo's touch, the rings began to move once more.

Honor thy master as thy parents.

Qadan drew in a deep breath. She had learned name magic from Erhi, a truly ancient priestess who made her home amidst the sea of grass that flowed across the Unicorn lands. The old woman had been demanding, even cantankerous at times, but Qadan had always followed her commands.

"It is me." Irie's voice was soft, as if the very act of speaking might condemn her spirit to the underworld. She turned, fingers plucking at the sleeves of her robe.

"I should have accompanied Masatsuge, should have died with him."

Naoki stepped up to place a hand on her shoulder. "No master would wish such a thing for their disciple."

Irie pulled away. Shaking her head, she stepped upon the first ring. The reaction was almost instantaneous. Rather than remain still as when Masahiro had trod upon them, the ring became as mist beneath Irie's feet, disappearing into the dark to leave a roughly three-foot wide void behind. She would have followed it had not Naoki caught the back of Irie's robes. Qadan hurried forward to join the others in hauling Irie back from the edge.

From within the pit there came an awful cacophony, a sound of metal on metal that reminded Qadan of the clatter of combat. There was movement within the shadows, a hint of razored edges, of bared blades seething down in the dark.

Even Masahiro surged to his feet, his earlier mockery washed away by an expression of nervous concern.

"I-I don't understand." Irie shook her head.

But the rings were moving once more, the remaining eleven rotating to form new words.

Comrades are as precious gold. Burnish your friendship with loyalty and sacrifice.

"Shinsei's wisdom is timeless," Masahiro mocked from the safety of the stairs.

Qadan ignored him. True, they had treated the Crane poorly, but Masahiro was hardly a comrade, and certainly not deserving of loyalty. Of all her so-called companions, only Tetsuo and Naoki seemed remotely dependable, and that was more a result of predictability than trust. Qadan's true comrades were the spirits who had trusted her with their names. No, that wasn't quite true.

There had been Jargal.

He had given his life for Qadan, perhaps his very soul, yet the monk still drew breath. Even now, he was no doubt making his way deeper into this horrible place while Qadan wasted time. There was no choice but to move forward as quickly as she could, else the monk would become too powerful to stop.

She drew in a deep breath, gathering her legs for a leap.

Naoki gave a strangled yelp, one hand outstretched as Qadan cleared the narrow pit, not daring to glance down for fear of what she might spy below. It was a short leap. Qadan needed but a half-step to catch her balance. She straightened, all the while expecting the stone beneath her feet to slip away and send her plummeting into a maelstrom of piercing blades.

The ring remained.

Qadan's breath hissed through her lips, her stomach roiling with a mixture of relief and self-recrimination.

She *had* failed Jargal.

Masahiro greeted her with a tight-lipped nod. "Welcome to hell."

The clatter of moving rings drove all replies from Qadan's mind. Neck prickling, she turned to see what new maxim the chamber sought to inflict upon them.

Every moment is a chance for enlightenment. To rob another of life is to empty your own coffers.

"Alas, we seem to have been blessed with an embarrassing surfeit of killers," Masahiro announced to no one in particular.

Qadan favored him with a hard-eyed glare. It was as if the Crane *wanted* someone to wring his scrawny neck.

On the far side of the chamber, the others stood in conversation. Qadan could understand their concern – neither Tetsuo nor Gensuke seemed one to balk at murder.

"Shinsei's admonition does not equivocate." Irie shook her head, eyes downcast. "To take life is to take life. Whether by a lord's command or to rid the world of evil, it matters not."

"Perhaps they should both go?" Qadan pitched her voice to carry.

Tetsuo glanced at the wiry assassin, who shrugged. "It seems as good a chance as any."

They leapt together, easily clearing the pit and the ring beyond, but no sooner had their feet touched stone then Qadan felt the trapped spirits shift within their ethereal cages.

She cupped her hands around her mouth. "Jump, quickly!"

Both men reacted seemingly without thought. Gensuke sprang a half-dozen feet forward, tucking into a tight roll as he hit the shifting floor. Tetsuo pushed off with heavily muscled legs as the ring gave way. His jump was far less graceful but carried him farther than the small assassin.

Beneath them, other rings snapped down into grinding shadow, almost giving the appearance that the men were skating over the surface of an icy winter lake. Gensuke was first to reach the stairs, springing forward to catch the lowest stair with one hand.

Qadan threw herself down, Masahiro at her side as they caught the Scorpion assassin's arm.

"Pull me up." He looked down, eyes widening. It was the closest thing to fear Qadan had seen on Gensuke's face. Blades clashed and clattered below his feet.

Qadan gritted her teeth and pulled, but Masahiro had the better grip.

"Help Tetsuo!" The Crane's normally cultured voice came as a strangled rasp.

Qadan glanced about for the Crab. Impossibly, Tetsuo had

caught himself upon the round base of the stair. Just visible on the far side of the column, he hugged the smooth stone pillar like a shipwrecked sailor clinging to a mast.

"I've got him. Go!" Masahiro shouted.

Qadan rounded the stairs. Snatching up Eruar's talisman, she bid the earth spirit make a shelf of stone extend from the column below Tetsuo's feet. The Crab samurai released his hold with a grateful sigh.

She felt the captured spirits react to Eruar, their agonized energies reaching a fevered pitch. Like a fish leaping from a churning sea, one of the blades detached from the mass to spin toward Tetsuo. It struck the Crab samurai several inches below his shoulder blade, sinking deep into his ribs.

Tetsuo's expression owed more to irritation than pain. Another blade flashed past his face, tracing a bloody line from cheek to forehead.

"Up." The Crab's slate gray eyes caught and held Qadan's.

She glanced about, almost losing her leg as a dagger-sized hunk of metal pinged from the stairs just below her. To call upon her talismans would only antagonize the captured spirits.

Unwinding her sash, Qadan quickly braced herself and lowered the makeshift rope. Tetsuo was heavier than Qadan had dared imagine. Her shoulders and back screamed as she took the brunt of the Crab samurai's weight, silk cutting into the palms of her hands. It was as if she were the worst of criminals, her limbs tied to snorting horses, condemned to be torn apart by their exertions. Just as Qadan feared her body might come apart, one of Tetsuo's callused hands caught the edge of a stair, and he hauled himself up to lie gasping at Qadan's side, blood pooling on the stone.

Barely able to catch her breath, Qadan hurried back to

Masahiro, only to find the Crane sitting upon the stairs, hair loose, one arm clutched to his chest, fine robes spattered with blood.

"I almost had Gensuke, but…" Masahiro looked up at her, pale face streaked with crimson.

"What happened?" Qadan grabbed the Crane by the front of his robes, dragging him to his feet. He gave a pained bleat, like an arrow-struck deer. Qadan could not restrain her sharp inhalation when she saw the source of the Crane's concern.

His right hand was missing, cleanly severed just above the wrist. Masahiro had cinched a makeshift tourniquet around the wound, but blood still leaked from the raw flesh.

"The blades…" He shook his head, seemingly dazed. "They *took* him."

CHAPTER THIRTY

Naoki's cry was lost amidst the horrible shriek of steel on stone. She clutched at Irie's sleeve, willing Tetsuo and Gensuke to glide above the sea of slashing blades. Wherever one foot touched, the ring would fall away, providing just enough footing to leap once more.

Gensuke was the faster of the two. He dodged and dove, seeming light as a windswept leaf. For all his strength and size, Tetsuo could not match the wiry assassin's speed, and was left to teeter on such rings as remained before they, too, became as mist.

Naoki stood rigid, muscles tense, one hand held to her mouth as Gensuke's final leap carried him to the edge of the stairs, Qadan and Masahiro diving to catch his outflung hand. She saw Tetsuo stumble on a shifting ring, almost disappear into the cutting shadows, but the Crab hurled himself forward, striking the stone column below the stairs. It was an awkward jump, more strength than finesse, and Tetsuo hit the stone with bone-jarring force.

And still, the Crab managed to hang on.

Masahiro shouted at Qadan, who moved around the stairs to help Tetsuo.

Naoki finally found her breath, turning to Irie. "Is there nothing the spirits can do to help?"

The Phoenix priest stood as if transfixed, although not by the struggle on the stairs. Instead, her gaze seemed fixed upon the golden glow above, her lips moving as if Irie were parsing a riddle.

"I did not betray him." The words were lost to the infernal grinding, but Naoki was close enough to read the Phoenix priest's lips.

"Help them!" Naoki shook her.

Irie blinked as if roused from intense study. She glanced around the chamber, eyes widening as she finally took in the scene.

Qadan had summoned a shelf of rock for Tetsuo to stand on, but the calling seemed to drive the blades below into a frenzy. Daggerlike shards of metal flicked up from below to ricochet off stone.

Naoki dragged Irie from the edge of the nearest pit, lest they be cut to ribbons.

Desperately, she looked to the stairs. Qadan was lowering a sash to Tetsuo while Gensuke clung to Masahiro's dangling arm. Face red from exertion, the Crane courtier hauled at the assassin. He spoke to Gensuke, teeth bared in an almost feral snarl, the distance too great for Naoki to make out what was said.

Blades pinged from the stone around them. One cut across the Scorpion's side, and he almost lost his grip. Rather than attempt to climb, Gensuke's free hand flew to his sash. He drew a wide-bladed knife from his robes and launched a heavy, overhand swing at the Crane.

Masahiro flinched back, his face and neck out of reach. But he could not free his hand from Gensuke's grip. The blade cut deep into the Crane's exposed arm. Masahiro's scream was swallowed by the grating cacophony. Gensuke brought the blade back and hacked again; once, twice.

He fell back, still holding Masahiro's hand.

Naoki squeezed her eyes shut rather than watch the carnage. When she opened them, Masahiro was standing, his wounded arm clutched tight. The look on his face was neither shock nor pain, but a strange species of satisfaction.

He slumped back to the stairs, bloodied fingers working his sash as he sought to staunch the bleeding. Qadan appeared around the stairs, shouted at the Crane.

Then the knives quieted once more, the Chamber of Even Blades silent but for gasped breaths and soft moans of pain.

Naoki cast about for some sign of Gensuke, knowing there would be none. Not even a smudge of blood marked the assassin's passing. Blades glittered in the darkness like the fangs of a hungry predator.

Gensuke and Tetsuo's frenzied flight had left many gaps. Most were the span of a single ring, but one or two had doubled, the pit easily six feet across with only the width of a single ring to leap from. It would have been difficult even without the threat from below.

As if to mock her anxiety, the remaining rings began to rotate once more.

Following false light only leads deeper into darkness.

Irie made a soft sound of denial, her eyes fever bright in the reflected light from above.

"It cannot be you," Naoki said. "You slew the Shrike, avenged Masatsuge. Your master smiles down on you from the Realm of Waiting."

"He does, yes." Irie's nod was quick, little more than a twitch.

Naoki studied her companion. The Phoenix priest had weathered like an ocean pier, waves of privation and anxiety stripping the flesh from her bones, the confidence from her bearing, leaving something that barely resembled the woman Naoki had met back at Heaven's Blaze Dōjō.

Irie had never behaved treacherously, had summoned her strange flames to burn away the vine-woven skeletons, and again in the bloody mist. She had saved all their lives. Even so, her bearing spoke of one racked with guilt. Naoki would have doubted Irie destroyed the Shrike had not Tetsuo confirmed her claim. For all his air of thoughtless menace, Naoki doubted the Crab would protect a blood mage, especially one so vicious and powerful as the Shrike.

"Then it is I who have followed false light." Naoki pressed her lips together, considering. It seemed impossible. She had tracked the monk across half of Rokugan, hounded him at every turn. Even now she sought to prevent him from claiming Iuchiban's terrible knowledge.

Either Irie was lying, or there was something Naoki had missed.

Frowning, she studied the Chamber of Even Blades – concentric rings like a mouth with missing teeth, blades below promising a gruesome end to those who confessed the wrong sin. But who judged sin? Surely not heaven. Akifumi had already shown he thought little of the gods or virtue. In the Chamber of Statues, he had as much as stated his contempt for the divine. Now, he had constructed a room that forced all who entered to reveal their wickedness?

It did not make sense. Akifumi cared nothing for Shinsei, and no doubt thought the Little Teacher a fool and liar.

Naoki ran through events in her head, ticking her

companions off on her fingers. Masahiro had passed, Irie had not, Qadan had passed, Tetsuo and Gensuke had not – even though both were avowed murderers.

Realization came like a winter squall, cold and biting.

"None of it mattered." Naoki swallowed, her mouth as dry as tanned leather.

"What do you mean?" Irie asked in a small voice.

"Akifumi believes the gods lie to us. Heaven, the underworld, the Realm of Waiting, he would have us rise beyond them," Naoki replied, her voice gaining strength as the blocks fell into place. She flicked her fingers at the rings, the stair. "Akifumi would have us speak our transgressions for all to hear, pit us against one another. But he cares nothing for the Teachings of Shinsei. To one like Akifumi, the path to enlightenment must seem brutal and arbitrary."

"Then what is his goal?" Irie's question was almost pleading.

"The Chamber of *Even* Blades." Naoki turned to glare up at the name. "Brutal. Arbitrary. It murders every second person who attempts to cross."

"And these?" Irie thrust her chin at the rings. "They meant *nothing*?"

"A lie," Naoki replied. "Just as Iuchiban and his followers believe the world to be."

"None… none of it matters?" Irie drifted to her knees, face slack.

Naoki gripped her shoulder. "If I am correct, we can cross without danger."

"But you said every second person."

"The blades came for Tetsuo and Gensuke both," Naoki replied. "I believe it makes no distinction for size, only the number of attempts."

"And if you are wrong?"

"Then only one of us may cross." Naoki drew Irie to her feet. "And I would not sacrifice any more of our company to Akifumi's cruel games."

Lips tight, the Phoenix nodded.

Holding hands, they leapt the first pit, little more than a pace wide, landing on the other side with only the slightest shift in balance.

The ring remained solid, the blades blessedly quiet.

Irie squeezed her hand. "You were right."

"Praise the ancestors." Naoki let out a long, hissing breath.

It was slow going. More than once Irie or Naoki almost didn't bridge the distance, but together they were able to leap the missing rings, secure in the knowledge no more dangers awaited them in the Chamber of Even Blades.

Upon the stairs, Qadan was seeing to Masahiro's wound, Tetsuo a brooding presence on the higher stairs.

She gave a grateful nod as Irie and Naoki hopped to safety. "I have done what I can, but my spirits are not healers."

Irie nodded. Kneeling next to the panting Crane, she muttered a few words of invocation, hands moving as if to trace the path of gentle waves. Slowly, Masahiro's breathing evened, and the flow of blood ceased as a thin film of skin crept across the stump.

"I cannot return what was taken, in flesh or bone." Irie stood, arms spread to finish the ritual. "But you shall not bleed out."

"My gratitude." Masahiro gave a tight-lipped nod, his gaze seeking Naoki's. "I only regret I had not the strength to save Gensuke."

Naoki held her tongue, regarding the Crane through narrowed eyes. She could not say what had happened to the

Scorpion, not really, but there was already enough mistrust among the others; it would not help to pick at threads already frayed.

Irie saw to Tetsuo's wounds as she had Masahiro's. He made no sound as they drew forth the blade lodged in his ribs, holding still as Irie closed the many gashes that pitted his flesh. If not for the bloody rents in his robes, the paleness of his face, the strain around his mouth, Naoki might not have suspected the Crab had ever been wounded.

"You said you had Gensuke." Qadan's words came sharp as Akifumi's blades.

"I did." Masahiro gave a weak nod. "Then knives started flying."

Tetsuo spoke, deep and remorseless. "Qadan retrieved me. Gensuke was not a large man."

"You haven't cared about any of us before," Masahiro said. "Why the sudden concern?"

The Crab crossed his arms. "Gensuke was useful. You are not."

"It is convenient the man who tried to murder you is now dead," Qadan added.

Masahiro waved the stump of his right arm. "Had I wanted him gone, I would have chosen a less… uncomfortable method."

Qadan looked to Irie. "Did you see what occurred?"

Irie made no response, her gaze distant, hands bunched in the sleeves of her robe.

"What of you, magistrate?"

Naoki could not help her anxious frown. She weighed her concerns. None of the others had seen Gensuke strike at the Crane, but to accuse Masahiro of murder would only cause more strife. The Scorpion had been an assassin, accused and admitted. Perhaps, seeing death approach, he had made one final attempt to fulfill his contract.

In the end, motive did not matter. By law and custom, Masahiro was well within his rights to seek vengeance against the man who had attempted to kill him. As a magistrate, Naoki had no cause to question his version of events.

If only she could quiet her personal doubts so easily.

"I cannot be sure." That, at least, was the truth. Although discomfort prickled the back of Naoki's neck, this was neither the time nor place for accusation, not when greater evil abounded.

Qadan's scowl could have etched glass, but the name keeper had no choice but to move on. None of them did.

"I will go first. Tetsuo, behind me. Then Irie." Qadan nodded at Naoki. "You watch the Crane. I do not want him anywhere near my back."

Naoki nodded, stooping to assist Masahiro. Although he could walk, the Crane remained weak from shock and blood loss, leaning heavily on Naoki as they ascended the spiral stairs.

"Thank you," he whispered.

"Gensuke tried to murder you." Her reply was almost a question.

"He did." Masahiro's breaths came short, pained. "And he killed my brother."

"How do you know this?"

The Crane gave a ragged smile. "The tomb told me."

Naoki would have dearly wished to ask more, but Qadan was chanting, her talisman of woven silk held as if to ward off danger. A light, twisting breeze ruffled their robes as her bound air spirit slipped into the golden light above.

"A large chamber," Qadan said, eyes squeezed shut. "Filled with many things – bits of wood, skin, paper, cloth, stone. I am sorry, Eruar does not see things as mortals do."

"Anything living?" Masahiro sniffed. "Or I should say, anything *moving*?"

"No." Qadan shook her head. "Although I cannot be sure. The chamber is quite complex, and it would take hours for Eruar to examine the whole of it."

"We have little choice," Naoki said with a glance back at the blades. "Unless we wish to search for some other means of escape."

They mounted the stairs slowly, careful for even the slightest warning of impending danger.

What they found was a wonder.

The room was easily the largest they had encountered since entering the tomb. The walls were of worked stone, the ceiling high and vaulted. Daylight streamed from high windows, cut glass seeming to magnify and diffuse the brilliance into a thousand glittering motes. Intricate mosaics covered the floor. Countless bits of stone, tile, and polished gems formed complex interwoven patterns that seemed to multiply into infinity.

Naoki couldn't see the far wall, not because the chamber was impossibly large, but because of the profusion of beautiful screens, paintings, and hangings spread about.

She cast about for the maker's symbol and found the Kakita crest high above the lintel. Strangely, the sight conjured in her a vague sense of relief – Naoki did not know if she had the strength for another of Shosuro Akifumi's tortures.

As with the bath house, this chamber displayed an artist's sensibilities. Ranging in size from waist-high to massive multi-paneled constructions large enough to cover a palace wall, the screens were painted with a staggering profusion of subjects. A line of portraits zagged to Naoki's right. All of the same woman, they seemed to chart her life from birth to death, the first of a red-cheeked infant, smiling and plump; a child, kite in hand; a young woman in coming-of-age robes; and on, and on, the last showing a wrinkled matron, holding court over many generations of progeny. So lifelike were the depictions, they seemed almost to breathe. The work was beautiful. If not for the look of frantic desperation in the woman's eyes, Naoki would have ranked them among the finest paintings she had ever seen. As it was, the unblinking, terrified regard just made her want to throw a sheet over the art.

To her left were hunting scenes, nobles riding after deer and lions and other prey. Temples and mountains, warriors with glittering blades and stern demeanors, gold leafed palace scenes, delicate vases that would not have been out of place in the emperor's court. They spread about the room in a labyrinth of glittering filigree and polished wooden frames, bright silken draperies gently stirred by the passing of Qadan's wind spirit.

"Ah, I understand." Masahiro swayed at Naoki's side, the comment seeming to tax his weakened constitution.

Qadan glanced back at them. "What is it now, Crane?"

"Kakita Tsutomu." He nodded at the nearest of the paintings – a court scene in autumnal reds and golds. "Smooth lines, flowing brushwork; the style is unmistakable."

Masahiro drew in a shaky breath. "Tsutomu was a much-lauded artist several centuries ago. He created a number of murals and mosaics that adorn several high manors to this day. Tsutomu would have surely joined the ranks of the imperial luminaries if not for his temperament. When some of his murals were deemed... impolitic by the Crane Champion,

Tsutomu stormed off in a fit of pique. They say he sought a patron who would not compromise his vision." Masahiro clucked his tongue. "It appears he found one."

"A fine art lesson," Qadan replied. "But do you know anything that might aid us in navigating this illustrated maze?"

"Alas, no." Masahiro gave a tired shake of his head. "As I said, Tsutomu lived long ago."

"Context is never worthless," Naoki said, unsure as to why she felt the need to defend the Crane.

"These 'walls' are but paper and ancient wood," Tetsuo said. "We could cut a path."

"Tsutomu was an artist before aught else," Naoki said. "I doubt he would place his work in danger."

"There is enchantment here." Irie cocked her head. "Powerful, subtle. Can you not feel it?"

"Yes." Qadan gave a tight-lipped nod. For all her doubts and suspicion, Naoki was grateful the Unicorn could yet recognize reason. "We would do well to avoid damaging the work."

"Look, here." Something akin to wonder infused Irie's voice as she knelt to indicate the foot of the nearest screen – a line of sharp peaked mountains wreathed in winter pine. Although the frame looked carefully carved and burnished, it did not sit upon the floor, but rather seemed to grow from between the tiles, thin roots disappearing amidst the swirling mosaic tiles.

"They're everywhere." Naoki shifted her grip on Masahiro to regard the frame. "Like the hungry roots in the earthen hall."

"Another reason not to touch." Masahiro's chuckle was raw as an open wound. "I have little enough blood left as is."

They moved carefully through the maze of murals, court scenes giving way to gardens, to battle scenes, to summer landscapes. More than once, the path came to a dead-end, forcing them to double back. Fortunately, unlike the tomb itself, the paper labyrinth seemed neither to shift nor change. Naoki came to dread any mural with human or animal subjects. There was an air of watchful intensity about them, their eyes seeming to follow her with an air of malevolent intent.

As they walked, the scenes seemed to take on depth and dimensionality. So perfect were the renderings that more than once Naoki felt as if she might stumble into one by mistake. The outdoor scenes in particular tugged at her thoughts, making her wonder if she would ever lay eyes on true trees or mountains ever again.

More likely Iuchiban's tomb would become her grave.

The third time they doubled back, Qadan found the chest. It was tucked amidst a stand of painted trees, the dark wood almost invisible against the deep greens and browns. An impossible breeze blew cool on Naoki's forehead, the tree limbs seeming to beckon invitingly. So real was the scene Naoki swore she could smell cedar and pine, sharp in her nose.

The chest was large and square, with footings of burnished bronze, and loops affixed to either side so that it might be borne by bearer poles. Unlocked, the lid ajar, it sat in the painting as if someone had recently placed it there. Inside, Naoki could make out the glimmer of gems and polished gold and silver.

Qadan stretched out a cautious hand. "There is no paper, no barrier. I can feel the air beyond."

"Could it be another room?" Naoki asked.

Qadan shifted to peer through the gaps in the screen, then shook her head. "It is a painting."

"A painting that holds an emperor's ransom," Naoki said.

Masahiro's chuckle was strained. "More than one, by the look of it."

"Iuchiban is immeasurably old," Irie said. "Time enough to amass a thousand such fortunes."

"An obvious trap," Qadan said.

Naoki sniffed, shaking her head. "Who would be so foolish as to want anything from this terrible place?"

No one replied.

"We should move on," Irie said, seemingly unwilling or unable to meet the eyes of her companions.

They passed more treasures. Paintings of coins spilling from overflowing chests, piles of rubies, amethysts, and emeralds twinkling like captured stars. There were gilded statues of gods and heroes; scrolls and ancient, leather-bound books; glittering blades and battle armor; filigreed chalices and masterful carvings; delicate vases that would not have been out of place in the emperor's court. Impossible treasures caught the light in a labyrinth of gleaming brilliance, glittering reflections bathing the murals in gold and silver.

All within the paintings, just out of reach.

"Could this be some manner of illustrated vault?" Naoki asked, unsure if the treasure was real or illusory.

"He seeks to tempt us with wealth." Qadan frowned. "Fool."

"Perhaps it is a lesson," Irie said. "Shinsei teaches all wealth is but an illusion."

The Unicorn wrinkled her nose. "And we know what Iuchiban thinks of Shinsei's teachings."

For all her misgivings, it was Qadan who first succumbed.

They had rounded a gallery of grinning portraiture and stood at the intersection of several paths. Suddenly, the Unicorn gave a little moan, one hand creeping to her mouth.

Before any could raise a question, she had all but thrown herself to her knees, reaching into a painting of a cave. Within stood a small glass display of carved figurines.

Naoki tried to peer around Tetsuo. "Qadan, what–"

Tears glittered in the Unicorn's eyes as she turned, her hands cupped around a tiny carved horse. Hardly a treasure at all, it was roughly shaped, knife marks still visible on the wood.

"It is his." Qadan held the carving close, head shaking as if to deny her own words.

"Who?" Naoki asked.

"Jargal, my bodyguard." Qadan knuckled her eyes.

"The one the monk murdered?" Irie asked.

"Not murdered. No." Qadan glanced around, expression going hard. "That monster must have sent him here. He could yet be alive."

"Nothing lives in there," Tetsuo replied. "Nothing good."

Naoki tried to catch Qadan's arm, but the Unicorn turned, eyes bright with pain and fury.

"What of the tomb?" Naoki asked. "What of Iuchiban?"

"They can both be damned." Qadan cupped a hand to her mouth. "Jargal!"

The murals seemed to swallow her call, Qadan's voice seeming unable to penetrate even the thin paper screens. She called again, then gave a helpless snarl.

"Follow me or don't." Her eyes burned hot as braziers. "I *will* find him."

With that, Qadan stalked into the painting, seemingly deaf to questions or logic.

"That was ... unexpected." Masahiro blinked.

Panic bubbled through cracks in Naoki's resolve. Iuchiban's

tomb had been deadly enough when they were together. To wander off alone was beyond foolish.

"We should follow her," Naoki said.

"And stumble into whatever trap Kakita Tsutomu has planned?" Irie gave a tight-lipped shake of her head.

Naoki looked to Tetsuo for support, but the big Crab was studying one of the murals ahead, a strange look on his face.

Without a word, he started off, head cocked as if to parse some distant call.

"Where are you going?" Naoki called after him.

"The bell calls," came the rumbling reply.

Naoki looked to the others, finding her confusion mirrored in Irie and Masahiro's face.

"We *cannot* separate." Naoki hated the tremor in her voice, but there was nothing she could do to stop her companions. She glanced down the corridor in time to see Tetsuo step into a mural of a long stone hall. It seemed impossible, but Naoki swore she could make out the sound of a temple bell.

Frantic, she turned back to Irie, but the Phoenix priest had already moved a dozen paces away.

"It cannot be." Irie stared into what looked to be an ancient archive, head tilted as if to test the air.

"What now?" Masahiro asked.

"His knowledge." Irie's voice was distant, breathless. "I can feel its power. We do not need to face Iuchiban, do not even need to venture further. It is *all* here."

"It's a trap," Naoki said.

But the Phoenix priest had already stepped inside.

"Should we follow?" Naoki could hardly believe her eyes. For all their faults, none of her companions were fools. It made no sense for them to simply step into one of Iuchiban's illustrated snares.

She felt Masahiro tense at her side.

"*Higekiri*," the Crane whispered.

He pushed away from Naoki, stumbling toward the curve of a long corridor of interwoven forest scenes. Naoki saw nothing but more screens. She moved to grab Masahiro, but he moved surprisingly fast for a man on the verge of collapse.

"My family's ancestral blade. I thought it lost with my brother." His words came quick and feverish. "Can you not see?"

And Naoki did.

The screen just at the end of the curve showed a Crane lord's armory, the helm, breastplate, and blade arrayed upon a beautifully etched rack. The sword itself was sheathed, although from the careful wrapping of the handle and the expertly worked guard Naoki could tell it was a thing of danger and beauty. So perfect was the brushwork that the scene appeared real – no, it *was* real.

She could not abandon the Crane, or perhaps it was Naoki who could not bear to be alone in this terrible place. Either way, she found herself following Masahiro.

They had gone but three paces when Naoki stopped, recognition a sharp prickle at the back of her neck. A new hall stood to her right. Lined by paintings of offices, bridges, and market scenes, it painted a picture of bustling urban life, a riot of townsfolk, merchants, samurai, work animals, and artisans jostling with raucous life. But it was not the scene that gripped Naoki, nor was she transfixed by the familiar mountain villages, nor Dragon Clan greens and whites.

There, in a painting of a familiar post station, stood a small wooden table. What sat upon it was as unmistakable as it was unbelievable.

Her hourglass.

Behind it stood a tall unadorned screen, a short tanka poem upon it written in the monk's violent hand, bloody letters still wet and glistening.

Life is no river,
rushing in crimson torrent.
It is a still pond.
All of us but autumn leaves.
Join me, we sink together.

CHAPTER THIRTY-ONE

Masahiro could not believe it. *Did* not believe it. And yet, being an unerringly practical man, he could also not deny that somehow, some way, this crypt of autopsical art had somehow acquired his ancestral blade. Conjured from Hiroshige's cold hands, Higekiri sat upon a silken cloth but a dozen steps away, there for the taking.

It was a trap, of course.

Even so, Masahiro could not swallow the upswell of agonized desire that worked between his gritted teeth. Higekiri was more than a sword, more than his birthright, it was a tangible link between Masahiro and his ancestors. Even should he escape this wretched tomb, somehow regain his position in court, the loss of Higekiri would forever remain a mark against him, something for courtiers to mock behind closed doors, tittering and jeering, their eyes sharp as arrows.

Masahiro knew he should not go, but in that moment, the need to touch the blade was all-consuming, almost physical in its strength.

He tried to move, only to find Naoki holding his arm in a

death grip. The magistrate was surprisingly strong, or perhaps Masahiro was surprisingly weak – either way, he could not pull free.

She seemed transfixed by a bit of bad poetry. Scrawled in a barely passable hand, it stood within a nondescript office. The only thing of note was a well-made hourglass. It seemed to have been turned some time ago, as perhaps only a few fingers of sand remained in the top.

"My blade–" Masahiro stumbled as Naoki released him to draw her jitte. He caught himself on the frame of a nearby screen. Although the wood was warm to the touch, it thankfully seemed to have little interest in murdering him.

He made a weak grab after Naoki, but the magistrate was already stepping into the painting, weapons at the ready. Masahiro pushed upright, vision swimming at the sudden strain. By the time he got his legs to cooperate, Naoki was kneeling by the little table, gaze flicking around the room as she bent to retrieve the hourglass.

Despite her obvious wariness, she could not see the gradual shift in color. When the magistrate had entered, the office had seemed normal enough, wooden walls, a floor of tatami mats a half-dozen paces square. The scene had shown morning color, sunlight slanting in through the slatted windows to paint the floor in tiger stripes of gold and gray. Now, the light took on sunset hues, flooding the office in purples and deep reds. More, the very wood had changed, light mountain pine now the hue of burnished cherry.

Masahiro's unease blossomed to true concern as he saw Naoki strike at something. The attacker's form was obscured as crimson seeped along the edge of the frame, rivulets trickling down to obliterate detail. He cast a desperate glance at Higekiri, just a few shambling paces away. Even in his enervated state, Masahiro could reach the blade and come back for Naoki.

He took an unsteady step, then swayed, more irritated than anxious. What good would a blade be to a man who had lost his sword hand? Hiroshige had always been the better warrior.

Shame was a silken cord around Masahiro's throat, seeming to draw tighter with each breath. He had failed Hiroshige. He had failed Chiaki. He had failed his family, his clan, his empire. Now, he stood poised to fail the only person in their ridiculous company who had shown him even the slightest respect.

With a strangled groan, Masahiro tore his gaze from the sword. The painting darkened, becoming little more than ink on paper. He saw now it was not Higekiri, but some lesser blade. It sat in a Lion armory in some modest dōjō, surrounded by battered breastplates and practice weapons, the Matsu crest picked out on the wall above.

Masahiro moved toward Naoki's painting. She had her back to the view, pressed against the screen as if the paper were the fourth wall of the office. She still battled, although what Masahiro could not see – almost all the view had been swallowed by turgid crimson. It was also clear that the edge of the painting had become invisible to Naoki.

With a rueful shake of his head, Masahiro regarded his remaining hand – recently elevated to the rank of favorite. It was not as if he had any chance of survival without Naoki's help.

Masahiro unwound his bloodstained sash. Tying one end to a nearby frame and the other to his waist, he waded into the painting. It was like sinking into warm oil, thick and viscous.

A red blur resolved into a giant grinning face, wrinkled like old bark, but long-toothed as a skull, and possessed of a manic hunger Masahiro found unsettling. Although he had yet to make the old demon's acquaintance, it was clear enough this was the monk who had vexed his companions so.

The huge visage snapped at Naoki, who lashed out with her jitte. Heavy steel bludgeoned a bloody cheek, but the blow seemed not to slow the terrible visage. Naoki would have been snapped up had not Masahiro snatched at the back of her robes and tugged with all his might.

Lips peeled back from his teeth, he bent back, dragging Naoki toward where his sash disappeared into the crimson wood. There was a sensation of suction, as if the painting were loath to relinquish its prey, then they tumbled forth in a rude jumble of flailing limbs, the monk's horrible shriek of rage echoing in their ears.

Masahiro expected relief, even gratitude. Instead, he had barely untied his sash from its mooring when Naoki caught the front of his robes, dragging him upright.

"The monk was waiting!" She half-marched, half-dragged him down the corridor. "He means to destroy us one by one."

"Perhaps that was what Tsutomu's painting wanted you to think," Masahiro replied.

"No." She shook her head. "I felt him. It was just like before."

"Before?"

"When you first came upon us." She spoke quickly, as if concerned the words might slip from her grasp. "The monk, he… gripped my thoughts. I could not move, could not speak, it was as if my body were not my own. I could feel his mind, dark and hungry. It was the same in the painting."

"How can he possess the images?" The answer came to

Masahiro before Naoki could reply. "Tsutomu painted not with ink, but blood."

Naoki's eyes were wide and wild. "We must retrieve the others."

The screen through which Qadan had passed was closest. Where before it had shown the interior of a cave, now it was little more than a jumble of red-inked lines, vague shapes barely visible amidst languid brushstrokes.

"Where is she?" Naoki's words came rough with anxiety. "I cannot make her out."

"Eightfold Mountain Style." Masahiro was panting. It was hard to focus. "Abstract. Seventh-century school, they sought to capture natural phenomena without human artifice."

"How does that help us find Qadan?"

"In your painting, you were the only thing not crimson. We must search for what does not belong." He swallowed, blinking. "Look for straight lines, right angles, anything unnatural."

"Here?" Naoki frowned at a tangle of sharp points. Like some child's sand palace, it faded beneath the swirl of soft brushstrokes, disappearing before their eyes.

Masahiro shrugged. "Could be."

"Help me pull her free." Naoki reached into the painting, the upper half of her body dissolving into a web of rough hachures.

For lack of a better option, Masahiro handed her the end of his sash, wrapping the other end tight around the stump of his right arm as he gripped the edge of the screen with his good hand and followed Naoki.

All around were lines of bloody thread. Like the web of some tainted weaver, they flexed and crossed with no eye toward balance. But what drew Masahiro's horrified gaze were the thousands upon thousands of spiders that crawled along the threads.

Masahiro did not consider himself particularly averse to spiders, even the ugly, long-legged ones that scuttled through those parts of his manor the servants had neglected. But these were truly an abomination. Roughly the size of a clenched fist, their segmented bodies glistened wetly in the half-light, eight long, sinewy legs tipped by human hands. Although their pinched faces were a mix of human and arachnid, their baleful eyes were like chips of obsidian, the monk's unmistakable malice reflected from all corners.

A blade of yellow-orange flame slashed through the web, cut threads parting like severed arteries. But instead of blood, more spiders spewed from the broken bits of web. They crawled about the damage, weaving new strands from the congealing morass.

"Qadan!" Naoki shouted as the flaming blade lashed out once more, spiders falling with wet pops.

The Unicorn name keeper waded through the slashing blaze, her spirits close to hand. Gouts of wind and flame and cutting stone drove the spiders back, but for every dozen she destroyed, a hundred more descended on crimson thread.

"I will burn him to ashes," Qadan shouted as if passing a generational curse. "Scatter his bones for the vultures and worms."

"You cannot face him here!" Naoki cried.

"The monk commands the paintings." Masahiro added his own weakening voice to the magistrate's call. "If you wish to defeat him, it must be outside his realm."

With a grunt of fury, Qadan sent a hail of sharp stones

pinging through the web. She ducked through the flailing strands, wreathed in crackling flames like some demon fresh from the underworld.

There was a sharp pain in Masahiro's hand, and he glanced back to see one of the spiders had latched on to his wrist, the terrible, old-man's face wet with blood as it reared back for another bite. Screaming, Masahiro tried to shake the crawling abomination free, but it clung to him like a leech.

Steel flashed crimson as Naoki stepped up to bat the creature away, its body cracking like old pottery before the hard edge of her jitte. Then Qadan was with them, and together they pushed through the edge of the screen.

Masahiro fell hard, head bouncing from the tiled floor. Bright moths fluttered across Masahiro's vision, and he tasted blood.

It took longer than he would have liked to regain his bearings. Masahiro had just gotten his knees under him when someone gripped his arms, dragging him upright. He was growing quite tired of being treated like some child's plaything.

Although Qadan's cheeks glittered with tears, her expression spoke of cold rage. As usual, she did not thank Masahiro, but he thought it better not to press the issue.

"Let us fetch the others." Her voice came as the first breath of winter. "Then I shall deal with the monk."

Tetsuo's screen had become a glistening landscape of hazy vermilion, as if the painter had swirled paint upon the canvas. There were only the slightest hints of forms, as indistinct as waves seen from a high vantage.

"Masahiro, do you recognize the school?" Naoki asked.

"Running Water Style." It was hard for Masahiro to fill his

lungs. "They sought to evoke depth of field by layering paint and ink while still wet. Only scenery, no people. Tetsuo would be buried beneath the layers. Search for somewhere dry upon the page."

"There." Qadan nodded toward the lower right corner of the massive screen. To her credit, the Unicorn did not question Masahiro's artistic knowledge. "The paint looks old, cracked. You can almost see it flaking."

"Hold hands." Naoki formed a bridge between Qadan and Masahiro, lashing her forearm to his. "Do not let go or we are lost."

Grimly, he hooked one leg around the edge of the screen, hanging on as Qadan, then Naoki entered. Although only partly submerged in the screen, Masahiro was more than privy to the horrors within.

A sea of clutching hands spread in all directions, fingers caked in dried blood. Knee deep, they scrabbled and clawed at one another, as if fighting to reach Tetsuo. The Crab had fallen into the grip of a particularly massive hand, its bony fingers wrapped about his waist even as its smaller brethren scrambled about like ants, twisting and tearing at Tetsuo. Unaccustomed pain colored the Crab samurai's features as he laid about with clenched fists. Even so, it was clear he was overmatched, the huge, blood-caked hand squeezing tighter with every labored breath.

Qadan's aggrieved call sent a spear of white-hot flame into the thumb of the giant hand. Flesh sizzled, scorched ligaments unfurling like overtaxed tent ropes. There came a howl of pain and rage, and the hand momentarily relaxed its grip.

Tetsuo was quick to seize the opportunity, prying loose of the terrible grip to lunge toward Qadan's outstretched hand.

The blood-caked claws went into a fury, boiling up like ants from a kicked hive. Masahiro felt hundreds of tiny pinpricks as the hands clutched at his lower leg. He tried to kick out, but only succeeded in almost losing his balance.

Naoki gave a rough jerk as Qadan caught Tetsuo's arm. They waded back toward the opening, bodies angled as if they were walking into ocean surf.

Like a whale surfacing from a sunset sea, the great hand reared from the scrabbling morass, palm flat, fingers spread as if to slap down upon the interlopers.

With a pained groan, Masahiro hauled at Naoki's arm. Feeling like an indigent fisherman dragging in some dubious catch, he threw himself back through the screen. This time, he had the presence of mind to step aside before his companions came stumbling forth, and so was spared another ignominious tumble.

Despite his rough demeanor, Tetsuo had the courtesy to offer them all a quick nod of gratitude. Masahiro silently reconsidered his initial assessment of the Crab. Naoki was quick to explain their predicament as they stalked toward the screen through which Irie had disappeared. Tetsuo merely grunted an affirmation, seemingly unconcerned by the dark forces arrayed against them.

What had been a picture of ancient archives now showed the manuscripts themselves. Thick columns of characters girded row upon row of text, long lines seeming to shift and change even as Masahiro watched.

The others glanced at him, but he could only shake his head, frowning. "I was never one for literary pursuits."

"Perhaps the answer lies in the text?" Naoki asked.

They set themselves to the task, poring over the tangled

manuscript like dusty archivists searching for a bit of half-remembered lore.

The ramblings were arcane, referring to all manner of esoteric rituals. Masahiro struggled to make sense of it, the lines shifting like windswept grass, their subjects becoming more threatening as characters changed meaning. Soon, Masahiro found himself reading descriptions of his own death, slow and brutal.

"Regretfully, it seems Irie is lost to us." He ran a hand through sweat-streaked hair, only dimly aware of the tangles and grime.

"Something of her must remain." Naoki shook her head, scowling. "Look closer, a description, a name, anything."

"Is this part of her name?" Qadan touched a character, then recoiled. Masahiro saw a bead of blood well from the pad of her finger, twinned to the crimson droplet that even now spread along the lines of the character. It grew larger, sinking through the jumble of text like a coin tossed into a fountain, gradually coming to rest at the bottom of the screen.

"I saw her sign several letters before leaving Heaven's Blaze Dōjō," Naoki said. "This is the other character."

She touched the screen, wincing as it drew another drop of blood from her finger. As before, the character grew larger, sinking to join up with the other.

"Irie, 'To Place in Favor'," Masahiro read. "An auspicious name for such an inauspicious endeavor."

"Quickly, find the characters of her name." Naoki touched another, and another. In a moment, the others joined. Even Masahiro found himself pawing at the screen, teeth gritted against the tiny stabs of pain as it drew his blood, drop by drop.

Slowly, name became form, not so much conjuring Irie as inscribing her into being. For a moment, she was laid bare before them, all her life spread like the length of some vast, impossible scroll. It flashed by too quickly for Masahiro to pick out individual words, coiling into a robed figure, bent almost double, her face covered by her hands.

"You must put me back." Her voice came like a whispered prayer, terrified and reverent. She turned and would have sprung back into the screen had not Qadan interposed herself.

"Get ahold of yourself, Phoenix."

"It was an illusion." Naoki gripped Irie's shoulder. "The monk laid a trap."

"No, not the monk." She looked almost frenzied, eyes red, skin the waxy pallor of a plague victim. "It was Iuchiban. Please, you must let me go back. I was so close to finding the truth."

Several responses came to Masahiro's tongue, none of them polite. But before he could give voice to even the most urgent concern, Naoki made a terrible noise.

Like the croak of a dying crow, it seemed to resonate from deep within her chest, her head thrown back, her limbs quaking as the cry became a gurgle, then a wet cough as she bent to vomit a torrent of blood upon the tiled floor.

Masahiro knelt to throw his arm around the quaking magistrate, even as a creaky laugh echoed through the chamber.

The monk stepped from behind a tripartite screen showing the underworld, the Mortal Realm, and Heaven.

He seemed hardly the stuff of nightmare, a small, unassuming man sliding into creeping venerability. Masahiro had seen a thousand such monks swarming the temple and religious precincts of the Imperial City. Even so, there was an intensity about him, a calculating malevolence that shone like a funeral lantern from behind his deep-set eyes. Judging from the monk's tattered robes and the many, many bloody cuts that crisscrossed his exposed arms and face, it seemed Iuchiban treated his servants no less harshly than his enemies.

"You are for me to dispose of." The monk spread thin arms, shadows seeming to bend and warp at his touch. "Then, the Deathless Master will finally know my worth."

CHAPTER THIRTY-TWO

Irie watched, spellbound, as dark force raged around the monk, whipping his ragged robes into a fury as he flung out one gnarled hand. Lips peeled back to reveal bloody teeth, the whites of his eyes crimson with burst capillaries. Corruption gathered about the Bloodspeaker. Irie could see tides of vile kansen lapping over him, their taint twisting the air like a heat mirage, but as with Masatsuge, the monk remained untouched – as if he stood beyond such tawdry concepts as purity and corruption. Irie could only stand speechless, her tongue tied partly by horror, partly by awe.

Tetsuo was the first to act, striding toward the Bloodspeaker, his movements possessed of terrible urgency. Irie could have told him brute force would have no effect, but the Crab was unlikely to listen.

Also, it was fascinating to watch.

Tetsuo blurred into sudden motion, his punch almost too fast for Irie to follow. The Crab's fist was large enough to remove the monk's head from his withered neck. But the blow never connected. Instead, Tetsuo struck the invisible sea of kansen swirling about the Bloodspeaker. They swarmed up the Crab's brawny arm, blood boiling and flesh blackening, bones twisting like water. Tetsuo's breath turned to poison in his lungs. By stubbornness or sheer idiocy, the Crab managed another step, his kick sinking into the invisible morass.

The monk's laugh was the creak of old iron, cold and brittle.

Tetsuo stood for a moment longer, muscles trembling against the strain of dark magic, then he collapsed without a sound, simply folding at the middle, his knees buckling like rotten wood. Irie had thought the Crab almost a force of nature, so to see him overcome with such ease was fascinating – a triumph of intellect over brawn.

Qadan's shriek was echoed by her pet spirits, a stream of wind-carried flame arcing between the cursed paintings even as the tiles below rumbled with anger.

Irie pursed her lips, considering. In her way, the Unicorn was as bullish as Tetsuo. Her spirits were powerful, of that there was no doubt, but they were only three arrayed against a legion. Qadan could not match the monk strength for strength.

The name keeper's rage was like a jar of ink emptied into the sea. For a moment, it seemed the Unicorn might tear through the Bloodspeaker's spiritual defenses. Kansen scattered like startled crows, stung by the mix of earth, fire, and air. Even the monk took a startled step back, smile slipping as the raging inferno licked at the tips of his outstretched fingers.

His incantations blistered the air, such desperate blasphemies as Irie had never heard given voice. Called by the monk's horrid entreaties, kansen swarmed to the conflict, drawn like insects to a flickering candle. They would have overwhelmed Qadan's meager spiritual assault, had it not been for Naoki.

The Dragon magistrate was far more clever than Irie had

given her credit for. She stumbled to her feet, blood still dribbling from the corners of her lips. Naoki and Masahiro clung to each other, looking for all the world like a pair of drunks stumbling home after a long night at the sake den.

The monk watched them, bemused, but with the force of his rituals still bent toward blunting Qadan's spiritual assault, the Dragon and Crane must have seemed a laughable threat.

But Irie knew better. For she had seen this conflict play out in the Illustrated Archive, just as she had seen the next, and the next. It was all part of Iuchiban's plan, laid long before any of them had first drawn breath.

Although unable to match the monk in strength, Naoki had studied him better than anyone, perhaps. In the realm of spirits, knowledge could be more important than power.

Naoki hurled her jitte. The heavy, blunt dagger spun end over end, glittering like silver in the twisting firelight. It flickered by the monk's head, missing him by an arm's length.

His derisive chuckle was cut short by the sound of tearing paper. The monk turned just in time to see a particularly beautiful rendering of a large cedar rip down the middle.

The reaction was almost instantaneous. Bloody ink oozed from the tear, which yowled like a wounded tree cat. The screen's heavy frame seemed to shift in its setting, gnarled roots and vines writhing like wind-tangled hair. A mass of twisting tendrils exploded from the frame to wrap about the monk's arms and legs, dragging him back toward the widening tear – its ragged edges like the maw of some blood-streaked mountain wolf.

It must have been a guess on Naoki's part, if an educated one. There was no love lost between Bloodspeakers. Even in the fullness of his fury, the monk had been careful to spare the rows of carefully curated art; it was clever to assume Tsutomu's paintings would treat the monk as they would any other threat.

But alas, cleverness would not be enough.

Rather than struggle with the vines, the monk merely bowed his head, lips moving in terrible invocation. Blood oozed from constraining roots. It sheened the monk's body, dyeing skin and robe deep vermilion as he brushed aside the desiccated tendrils like so much dry grass.

His counterstroke set the Dragon magistrate reeling back, body quaking as Masahiro desperately tried to stem the flood of crimson with bits of wadded silk.

Tragic. It reminded Irie of the Crane romances Tomiko was always reading. Idly, she wondered how the Isawa was handling Heaven's Blaze. Poorly, no doubt. Tomiko had never possessed the fortitude for monastic life – a petty noble elevated on blood rather than talent. But such was the way of the world.

For now, at least.

"Irie!" Qadan's hoarse shout roused Irie from frowning contemplation.

She glanced around, blinking.

At last, it was time to intervene.

Tetsuo, Masahiro, and Naoki were down, Qadan spitting curses into the air as her pet spirits' power began to wane. A heartbeat, perhaps two, and the monk would stand triumphant – a demon in crimson robes elevated to the status of favored disciple.

He stood, head thrown back, eyes wide and gaze piercing, a hungry smile on his cracked lips. A calculated front, the posturing of a power-hungry courtier who has somehow achieved a position far out of his depth. For all the power, the ambition, the bloodthirsty regard, Irie could see what the monk could not.

He was afraid.

Her hands fluttered like moths, voice threading the crackle of flame, the shriek of wounded wind, the growl of aggrieved stone.

The monk turned, one hand raised as he gathered a fistful of kansen, ready to meet Irie's attack with an overwhelming flood.

But she did not strike. Rather than blast him with the uncompromising might of the Empty Flame, she drew upon its power to craft a more subtle snare. A dark mirror, a tomb within a tomb. It surrounded him, ephemeral as mist, invisible to all but the monk himself. He lashed out, a coruscating twist of underworld flames cutting the empty air. There was nothing for him to strike, only the yawning eternity of the Empty Flame, an endless cavern echoing with the agony of his own inadequacy.

It was a small enchantment, little more than a twist of fire, air, and void, but it cut to the heart of him. Just as Irie had known it would.

He stumbled, one hand raised as if to shield his eyes from a sudden light. And in that moment, his rituals faltered.

Silent as an avenging revenant, Tetsuo rose behind the monk, his massive arms wrapping around the old man like anchor chains. Desperately, the Bloodspeaker sought to regain control of his bound spirits, but Qadan was quicker.

Even in their weakened state, the name keeper's spirits could draw upon their bond. Qadan slipped to one knee, gripping her talismans like holy relics. Fire scoured the monk's face, tracing dark lines along his kicking legs. His scream was a thin, shrill thing, the wail of an old man helpless before the inevitable march of years.

Irie could not help but smile at the justice of it. He may have masqueraded as a monk, but the Bloodspeaker had not sought purity.

Blood flowed through his bared teeth. Expelled in a cloud of swirling mist and given terrible life by the monk's chants, it descended upon Tetsuo and Qadan, their flesh turning pallid and waxy. The Crab's grip began to weaken, just as the Unicorn slumped back, talismans slipping from palsied fingers.

Naoki was up, weaving unsteadily, Masahiro barely supporting her as they shambled toward the struggling monk. She had the Crane's blade, a lovely curve of polished steel, bright as a crescent moon amidst the swirling shadow.

With obvious effort, Naoki raised the sword in trembling hands. She did not press it to the monk's throat, but rather to the necklace of bone charms clutched in his white-knuckled grip. Like Masahiro himself, the blade was showy but serviceable, and it bit deep.

Bone charms scattered to the tile. The monk's chant became a choking gurgle, cut abruptly short as Tetsuo hammered his twitching body to the hard stone.

Qadan was true to her word. The inferno that consumed the monk's body was as bright as an imperial beacon, the white-hot blaze contained by a hedge of stone, its hungry flicker kept from the nearby screens by a small maelstrom of whirling air.

Gasping, Qadan slumped to her side, her spirits fading along with her strength. Soon the crackling of flames faded as well. Irie moved among her fallen companions. They seemed strange things, bits of flotsam scattered by uncaring fate, swept along by waves not of their making. Irie had wondered if it was destiny that had brought them all here.

Now, she was beginning to suspect it was design.

Through rolling cadences and calm, languid gestures, she coaxed water spirits into their wounds. But while they could knit bone and mend gashes, they could not return what was taken. Her companions might be healed, but they were far from whole.

It was some time before anyone spoke.

"You saw... Iuchiban?" Naoki asked as Irie ran a softly pulsing hand over a cut upon her brow. The magistrate looked on the verge of collapse, her eyes sunken, her fingers trembling like windblown branches.

"No." It was not a lie. "He did not speak, did not manifest, but I could feel his presence in the collected knowledge of the Illustrated Archive."

"Why did he reach out to you?" Qadan asked, always doubtful, always jealous.

"He did not 'reach out.' Any of you could have sensed him, had you the philosophical refinement." Irie straightened. "His power was present in all Tsutomu's paintings. I simply felt it more acutely. It was what the monk drew upon to ensnare you."

"But not you," Qadan said.

"I could see the illusions for what they were – ink upon a page, nothing more." Irie kept her voice calm, not rising to the Unicorn's bait. The ignorant often mistook wisdom for threat. Such was the challenge of those seeking to spread enlightenment.

"He was written into the scrolls, the books, the stacks themselves," Irie continued. "It was as if I walked through a part of his mind, his knowledge laid out in text, every word from his hand."

"Lies, most likely," Naoki said as she pushed upright, testing her legs. She would have fallen had not Tetsuo caught her arm.

"Undoubtedly." Irie could not possibly explain the nuances of the Illustrated Archive to Qadan, so she simply agreed with the Unicorn. "Iuchiban is arrogant. He believes us beaten."

"Aren't we?" Masahiro waved an anxious hand at the others.

The Crane had a point. Neither Naoki nor Masahiro looked capable of a brisk walk, let alone facing another one of Iuchiban's tests. Tetsuo's wounds may have sealed, but the Crab's injuries had been grievous. It was a testament to his uncanny fortitude that Tetsuo was even upright. Even so, he moved with a careful slowness, as if testing each muscle before choosing to put weight upon it.

"We have no choice but to proceed." Naoki took a few steps, unsteady until Masahiro stepped to her side. The two leaned on each other, looking as if a soft breeze might set them on their heels. Worthless against what was to come. If they had ever had a use. Qadan took the lead, Tetsuo behind, then Masahiro and Naoki, with Irie bringing up the rear. Without the monk's terrible enchantments, the screens seemed merely beautiful. A thousand doorways into other worlds.

Although Irie was no scholar of art, more than once she caught herself studying the paintings, especially those that dealt with Fortunes or rulers. They showed scenes of capricious deities, the Divine Siblings, their struggles and grievances inflicted upon the mortal world. Those scenes that featured nobles were often mundane – preparing for bed or the changing of clothes. Emperors, generals, and high nobility stood stripped to their undergarments, imperial flesh scandalously bare. They looked so small without armor and courtly robes. It was galling to think such folk purported to rule by divine right, just as the gods offered no justification for their divinity.

Names and blood. In the end, they were all that mattered.

A low hiss from Qadan brought everyone up short. Ahead, a large door was set into the wall. Carved of obsidian and cinnabar, it was circular in shape, a dark mirror of the Five-Dragon seal that had warded the outside of Iuchiban's tomb.

Next to it stood a blank canvas, an array of brushes and inkpots set upon a low table, as if the artist had been suddenly called away. Around the edges of the canvas coiled a small fresco. Made to resemble twining vines, it wound around the canvas, the curls and loops of the finely rendered tendrils forming distinct words.

You gazed upon my work, but yours remains unfinished.
Free of artifice, of lies. Give form to your desire and see it
made real.

Qadan shook her head. "Another trap."

"I am not so sure." Irie shook her head, memories of the bath house mosaics bringing unwelcome tears to her eyes. She knew now that Master Masatsuge had not possessed the monk's arrogance. He had known Iuchiban would never let him reach the center of the tomb, had spent his life preparing Irie for the task. She could not deny it, just as she could not deny he had sacrificed himself for her.

The Illustrated Archives had shown her as much.

"You have seen Tsutomu's paintings," she continued. "He sought truth in all things. To lie now would be to deny his art."

"Forgive our concerns," Masahiro said weakly. "We had quite different experiences with Tsutomu's work."

Irie made a face. "That was the monk. The screens were meant to transport us elsewhere, to challenge our perceptions and understandings. Instead, he twisted them into threats."

"All but yours." Qadan narrowed her eyes.

"I have more experience with such things." Irie kept her voice calm, reasonable. "My whole existence has been a quest for truth."

"And if Tsutomu does not lie?" Naoki asked. "If this canvas can conjure almost anything? What could we create that would aid us against an immortal sorcerer?"

"An imperial legion." Masahiro gave a weak smile. "Or perhaps the Seven Thunders?"

Irie ignored the Crane's prattle. "If Iuchiban's heart is beyond that door, it will not be undefended. We may be tossing aside our only chance to destroy him."

"The monk almost finished us," Masahiro replied. "Imagine what his master will do."

"I would rather die than take a chance on *that*." Qadan jerked her head at the canvas.

"Look at us." Irie spread her arms. "Naoki and Masahiro can barely walk. Would you have Tetsuo carry them into Iuchiban's lair?"

The Crab blew out a breath through his nose, but did not challenge Irie's assertion.

"If we pass through that door as we are," Irie continued, "we shall find nothing but death."

"I have heard enough." Naoki pushed free of Masahiro. Limping over to the brushes and paints, she picked one up.

"Beware–" Qadan began, but Naoki silenced the Unicorn with a chop of her hand.

"Irie spoke true. We would be a burden." She dipped her brush in the black paint, then sketched a tall rectangle upon the canvas.

Irie took a step toward the canvas, but Naoki was already drawing distant mountains, roughly rendered pine and larch spread along the curve of a low valley road. Naoki pressed her tongue to the corner of her mouth, adding vague clouds overhead, a round sun just peeking over the rise.

"What is that?" Qadan asked.

The magistrate turned. "A way out."

Even as she spoke, the scene took on new depth, color bleeding along the edges of the rectangle to paint the mountains and trees in hues of pink and burnished gold.

Irie could not help but admire Naoki's cleverness. "It's a door."

"But to where?" Masahiro asked.

"The foothills of the Great Northern Mountains, Dragon lands just east of the Unicorn Clan border." The magistrate took a step back, studying her work. "It is… was, my home. We would be safe there."

A soft breeze slipped through the painted door, carrying with it the smell of wet earth, hard stone, and the sharp tang of pine sap.

"If this is illusion, it is the best I have ever seen." Masahiro shook his head.

"I don't understand," Qadan said.

"We entered this tomb to prevent the monk from accessing Iuchiban's forbidden lore." Naoki turned, careful as if her legs were made of glass. "That is no longer a concern." She nodded at the cursed dragon gate. "This may lead to Iuchiban's sanctum, or it may lead to more chambers – either way Masahiro and I are unlikely to survive. We can still be of use, however. Although both his disciples have been destroyed, Iuchiban remains."

Irie nodded, following the magistrate's logic.

"Rokugan must be warned," Masahiro said. As usual, the Crane was quick to lend his support to anything that preserved his own worthless existence.

Qadan crossed her arms, scowling. "And if this *is* just an illusion."

Naoki met her eyes. "Then we are no more doomed than if we passed beyond that obsidian gate."

"There is sense in this." Tetsuo spoke as if passing judgment. "If those two face Iuchiban, they would only die, then live again."

Qadan threw up her hands, turning away. "Then let it be on your heads."

"Let us be about it, then." Masahiro hobbled up to stand beside Naoki. Gripping her hand, he sketched a wincing bow to Irie and the others. "I would like to say it has been a pleasure, but it most distinctly has not."

Naoki drew in a deep breath, as if she were about to dive into the sea. With the barest of glances back, she stepped through, Masahiro at her side.

The change was instantaneous. Naoki and Masahiro's outlines became little more than a rough sketch, the colors of their robes changing to match the muted dawn tones of the painting. They took two steps into the scene, their movements like woodblock prints laid in sequence. Then the image began to fade. Ink seeped into the page like rain upon parched earth. In a brief span of heartbeats, the canvas was blank once more.

The tiled vines surrounding the screen writhed and shifted, swallowing Tsutomu's message. There came a soft creak to Irie's left, and she turned to see the obsidian gate had come ajar. Like morning fog, its opening presaged a sudden chill, although heavy with the dust of ages.

There were no words exchanged between the three of them, only nods, jaws tight and backs straight.

Tetsuo led the way, fists raised, Qadan to his right, her talismans clutched in steady hands. Irie followed on Tetsuo's left, shoulders high in expectation of attack, a score of terrible rituals dancing on the tip of her tongue.

She had expected darkness and danger, cold stone and terrible peril, a thousand shrieking kansen bound to deadly purpose. Instead, Irie found light and warmth, familiar stone columns fronted by panels of richly stained cedar. The chamber smelled of wood and old parchment, of candles and curling plumes of incense.

It smelled of home.

Irie stopped, a shiver tickling up her neck even as she brought a hand to her mouth. She should have been surprised, shocked that Iuchiban had perfectly replicated Masatsuge's chambers, but all she could summon was a vague sense of relief.

The foundations of this chamber had been set centuries ago, long before Irie or even Masatsuge. Each supporting the others, the stones had been laid, rising in vaulted angles, a perfection of form, its stolid beauty unmarred by embellishment. Hardly the lair of an ancient, immortal sorcerer.

Irie had thought Iuchiban prideful and cruel, but he was neither. Finally, Irie understood.

"It was a test." Her words came as a breathy whisper. "It was *all* a test."

"What is it?" Concern edged Qadan's rough voice. "Do you know this place, Phoenix?"

Irie's tongue seemed to fill the whole of her mouth, her throat scratchy as old wool. There was nothing she could say, no way to put this truth into words. Neither Tetsuo nor Qadan had sat at Masatsuge's feet and explored the philosophical underpinnings of creation. They thought the world whole and just, could not see the lie for what it was.

A feeling of profound sadness spread through Irie's chest, twining agonized fingers through her ribs, up her spine. The true horror was not that her companions believed the illusion, it was that they would die to defend it. The path was clear, but Qadan and Tetsuo would not, *could* not follow.

Fingers crooked into claws, Irie summoned the Empty Flame.

"What are you doing?" Tetsuo took a step back, eyes shadowed by lowered brows.

"We are but dross." Irie's voice came hard and cold as river rocks. Her hands came up, invisible flames crackling. "Bound to a broken wheel."

CHAPTER THIRTY-THREE

Qadan had never trusted Irie, not really. The Phoenix elementalist possessed that distressing capacity for self-deception that often afflicted scholars who spent too much time in debate and too little in the world.

Even so, she had never thought Irie would betray them.

It was Kahenu who warned her, the subtle shift in the fire spirit's aura presaging the elemental upheaval of Irie's muttered ritual.

The Phoenix was bleeding. Crimson threads dissolved amidst colorless fire, Irie's summoning visible only by the waves of heat that twisted the air around her.

For all his apparent surprise, Tetsuo was quick to attack, not even the slightest hint of regret on his heavy-boned face as he drove his fist into Irie's midsection.

The blow should have folded the half-starved Phoenix like wet canvas. Instead, she merely hopped back, a remorseful scowl upon her skeletal face as her summoning blossomed into terrible immediacy.

Tetsuo stumbled to one knee, crimson stains spreading across his scorched and ragged robes. With surprised horror,

Qadan realized his wounds had reopened. It did not seem possible to undo that which the spirits had made whole, but it had been Irie's ritual that set Tetsuo's bones and stitched his cuts.

She had his blood.

Qadan circled the two, searching for an opening. Although her spirits were powerful, they were not subtle, and a burst of wind, fire, or razored stone would be just as likely to scourge Tetsuo as Irie.

The Crab samurai's breathing hitched as a gruesome panoply of gashes, gouges, punctures, bruises, and breaks rippled across his body. He threw out a hand to steady himself, the other snaking out to hook Irie's heel.

This time, she did fall.

Qadan was quick to seize the opportunity. Her voice became the aggrieved roar of burning grasslands, Kahenu's name spilling from her lips like white-hot steel. Irie's Empty Flame was a perversion, Bloodspeaker sorcery designed to disguise its vile foundations.

Qadan would see how it fared against *true* flame.

Irie's incantation became an agonized shriek as Kahenu's fiery lash scourged her upraised arms. But although the flames cut blackened streaks in her robes, they did not bite. Beneath the layers of scorched fabric, Qadan saw unblemished skin, pale and untouched. Irie's cries seemed mournful rather than pained, her eyes bright with tears as a wave of invisible fire swept from her outstretched arms.

Kahenu withered before the onslaught. It was as if Irie's ritual had sucked the air from the room, Kahenu's blaze lost amidst the greater conflagration, a burning brand tossed into a bonfire. Qadan could not breathe, could not think, the crushing weight of emptiness pressing in from all sides, seeking to entomb her in endless, invisible void.

With her last whisper of air, Qadan gasped out Eruar's name. The air spirit flowed about her, a small, yet powerful maelstrom, like the brief tornadoes that ripped across the trackless plains of Qadan's home.

She drew in grateful breaths, already drawing forth Gion's geode. Rather than add the earth spirit's power to Eruar's, Qadan bid them slip into the stone foundation of the chamber. There were other things below, dark and terrible spirits for whom even the memory of freedom had faded to mocking echoes. Fortunately, Irie had yet to draw upon their power, and Gion slipped among the kansen like a glittering vein of gold running through a seam of cold and ancient granite. Hidden from Irie's arcane perceptions, Qadan bid the earth spirit wait for the right moment to strike.

Brows furrowed, Irie gave an almost apologetic nod as she unleashed another crackling torrent of colorless flame. This time it was too much for even Eruar. The swirling cocoon of wind that shielded Qadan became both icy and stifling. Her breath misted in the air even as her arms went slick with sweat.

Irie redoubled her assault, voice taking on inhuman resonances as she filled the chamber with corrupt entreaties, her hands, face, even her hair bright with blood. She appeared a thing possessed, posture rigid, fingers hooked into claws as if to strangle life from the very air.

Qadan could not have withstood the spiritual onslaught, would have been sent tumbling like a poorly anchored tent had not Tetsuo staggered to his feet, lunging at Irie like a hungry ghost. Even with his full weight behind the charge, Tetsuo barely rocked the corrupt Phoenix. Whatever fell force underpinned her frenzied rituals seemed to have imbued Irie with hideous strength.

Rather than set the Crab samurai alight, she simply reached out with both hands, fingers sliding like knives between Tetsuo's ribs. Somehow, the Crab managed to hook an arm around her neck and draw her into a wrestler's toss.

At Qadan's call, Gion surged up through the stone. The spirit's strength filled Tetsuo's ravaged muscles, his body imbued with uncanny resilience. With a growl like tumbling rocks, Tetsuo thrust his hip into Irie. She clung to him like a hawk, talons sunk deep into its struggling prey. It was as if Irie weighed as much as a castle gate. Muscles trembling, Tetsuo lifted her from the ground. For a moment, Qadan dared believe the Crab might succeed in throwing her.

Then Irie ripped him in half.

Tetsuo's chest bloomed into a welter of carnage. Qadan's despairing cry was echoed by Irie. Soaked in the Crab's blood, she stumbled to her feet, her bearing one of supreme distress as she tossed Tetsuo's ruined body to the ground.

Qadan could have stomached the betrayal had Irie been heartless, even mocking, but the fact she could feel pain and loss, was still *aware* of the depths of her corruption – that was unbearable.

Anger filled Qadan, her ragged breath almost a snarl. She would have liked to fall upon the Phoenix like a pack of steppe wolves, snapping and tearing until Irie was nothing but a terrible memory. To come so far, face so much, only to fall to some weak-willed philosopher enamored by forbidden lore.

Teeth bared, Qadan gripped her talismans, but the spirits were spent. They would come if she called, now and forever, but to do so would be to doom them all. Iuchiban's tomb was a place of horrors, not only for the living, but spirits as well. Qadan would not see Eruar, Gion, and Kahenu bound and broken, their noble essences corrupted by blood rituals, their names stolen. To exploit such trust would make Qadan no better than the Bloodspeakers she faced.

She would never leave this tomb, but it need not claim her friends.

With a word, Qadan released her spirits from their talismans. They lingered, uncertain, but she bid them flee, turning entreaty to command with the power of their true names. It was a final, necessary cruelty, but one Qadan hoped would spare them not only from what was to come, but from what she must do.

Irie made no move to restrain the spirits as they slipped through cracks between the tomb's stones, too small for the eye to see, but large enough for beings made of pure elemental force. Whatever spark of gratitude Qadan felt at that tiny kindness quickly darkened as Irie took a slow step toward her, voice tentative.

"There was no other way. I'm sorry. I wish—"

"Don't." Qadan glared up at her. "Don't you *dare*."

Irie gave a tight-lipped nod. "I will make it quick."

Qadan spat at her feet.

Strange emotion twisted the Phoenix elementalist's face – anger, irritation, disgust – although at whom Qadan could not tell. Nor did she much care, for the gesture of contempt, however futile, had succeeded in capturing Irie's attention.

Qadan slipped a hand into her satchel, almost welcoming the sharp stab of pain as she clutched the bladed talisman. The name came as it had back in the crypt, before the door of Iuchiban's tomb, a whisper rising to a scream, imbued with every bit of hatred Qadan could muster.

Irie's surprise turned to anger as something shifted in the space between moments. She raised bloody hands, another dark invocation on her lips, but the name Qadan uttered rolled forth like a tempest, seeming to slip along the cracks in perception to tug at the warp and weft of reality itself.

No flame could touch it, no eye could see it, faster than a killing spear, sharper than an executioner's blade, it fell upon Irie, her stunned and stammering invocations snatched from nerveless tongue, fingers twitching as if to pluck at some invisible tapestry even now unweaving before her.

"But I... I was chosen. I was meant to–" Irie gave a soft grunt, her lips forming a small, almost petulant moue as she slumped to the tile. Whatever ancient and terrible force that had inhabited her bled away, leaving little more than the body of a frail woman, wrapped in frayed and bloodstained robes.

Hardly a sight to inspire anything more than pity.

Qadan pushed slowly to her feet, feeling as if someone had hollowed her out. She glanced around the chamber, such a small, unassuming place to carry such terrible weight. But Qadan had come for a purpose. If the heart was here, she would see it destroyed.

The room was a wide rectangle of cedar-paneled walls, the high ceiling supported by pillars of unadorned stone. If anything, the chamber appeared like nothing more than a lecture hall, tucked away in some remote dōjō, a master holding forth for some gaggle of disinterested students. There were no windows, no doors save the portal through which Qadan had entered. Apart from the benches, columns, and a low stone dais near the back, the chamber was completely empty.

Hardly the place an immortal sorcerer would secret his

heart, and still, Qadan could not help but try to find it. She owed the others that much, at least.

Carefully avoiding Tetsuo's broken body, she cast about for some hidden catch or loose stone. Unlike the other chambers of the tomb, this one bore no maker's mark.

A good sign, or a terrible one.

Qadan ran her fingers over the stone but could find no joint. The wooden planks fit together seamlessly, as if cut from a single, impossibly large tree. Ruefully, she found herself wishing Naoki were here. For all her irritating habits, the Dragon magistrate had proven adept at winnowing out solutions to Iuchiban's tortures. Even Masahiro might have been of use, if only to dispel the lingering desperation that made a painful hollow of Qadan's stomach.

Again and again, she found her gaze slipping to Irie's remains. Of all of them, the Phoenix had perhaps best understood Iuchiban's plans. Qadan sniffed at the thought. Better to remain in ignorance, then.

Still, Irie had been of use combating the traps, no… not traps. What had she called them? *Tests*.

That could not be true. The tomb had been constructed to defend Iuchiban's heart and knowledge, everything inside made to kill, and rend, and destroy those who would claim them. But if that was the case, why craft a solution at all? The Chamber of Statues, the Hell of Even Blades, the Painted Gallery, even the Shifting Labyrinth. All of it could be bypassed if one grasped each chamber's twisted lesson.

Like wind gusting through broken rocks, the answer came upon Qadan little by little. If Iuchiban was truly who she suspected, he had traveled far beyond the bounds of Rokugan, dedicated centuries to collecting all manner of arcane lore.

Despite his attempt to invade the Empire, despite his cults and bloody rituals, it was clear he did not see himself as a dark sorcerer, a conqueror, an undying fiend.

Iuchiban viewed himself as enlightened. As a teacher.

It was a wild supposition, born of equal parts desperation and exhaustion. And still, it made a strange sort of sense. Qadan had braved the tomb, seen her companions winnowed one by one. And here, at the end, there was no forbidden lore, no relics or treasures, no heart.

There was only a lecture hall.

"It was never here." The words slipped like mist from her mouth, unbidden, unwelcome. She drifted to the floor, legs folded beneath her, hands folded in her lap, head bowed beneath the weight of terrible realization. They had come all this way for nothing. They had fought, suffered, bled, *died* for nothing. The tale of Iuchiban's heart was just another web, spun by an ancient and terrible spider; one more lie to ensnare the greedy, the foolish, the brave. The only thing Qadan could not understand was *why* Iuchiban sought to lure others to his tomb. What lesson could such cruelties possibly impart?

There came a rustling from behind. Wood tapped on stone, the soft swish of sandals echoing each deliberate step.

Qadan turned, ready for whatever monstrosity shambled from the lambent shadows. Instead, she saw only a small man, hunched and precarious, his liver-spotted head framed in hair as fine as silk, the skin of his face so thin she could see the webwork of veins and capillaries pulsing beneath.

"Ah, Qadan." He spoke with the gentle pride of a grandfather acknowledging a child's first clumsy attempt at letters. "I hoped it would be you, but one can never be wholly sure, especially in matters such as this."

She stood, brandishing the razored talisman. "Who are you? What are you doing here?"

"You already know the answer to the first. And as for the second..." He laid a finger alongside his nose as if they shared some private joke. "You summoned me."

"Impossible."

"Hardly." He raised a hand, as if delivering some whispered benediction. "Thrice you called to me. First, in the mountain crypt when the monk ripped you from your spirits. The second, outside this tomb when the way would not open. The last, when ally became foe, when you had nowhere else to turn."

Qadan's gaze crawled to the bladed talisman, still wet with her blood. "You are no spirit."

"That much is true," he replied. "I am so much more."

"Iuchiban." Qadan regarded him through narrowed eyes, unsure if this was truly the sorcerer himself or another cruel trick. She needed to know more. "I did not speak your name."

"I have many names – Laughing Turtle, Tomebreaker, Truthseeker, He Who Walks Above, the Watcher Beyond, Wise Master, the Empty Flame, and many, many more." Smiling, Iuchiban turned away. A few careful steps brought him to the low dais, upon which he settled with a grateful sigh. "That is the beauty of mortals. Unlike spirits, a name need not circumscribe the whole of our being. It is a gift not even the gods steal from us."

"You are an abomination."

"I am a *solution*." Iuchiban held up one willowy finger, his unhurried tone that of a teacher teasing apart a thorny philosophical point.

"Lies." Qadan cast the useless talisman away, advancing

upon Iuchiban. She had little more than an eating knife, but it would cut throats as easily as joints of meat.

"Have a care, child." He regarded her, seemingly unconcerned by the blade in her hand. "That is no way to speak to a clan elder."

"You are no ancestor of mine."

"Am I not?" He pushed to his feet, suddenly looming despite being a head shorter than Qadan. "I studied philosophy at the feet of Isawa, rode the Path of Woe with Shinjo. I have seen sights that would bring you to your knees, faced foes without number, learned such secrets as would tear asunder the veil of your understanding and leave you a squalid, broken thing. I have fought, I have learned, I have *sacrificed*."

Flecks of spittle dotted his bloodless lips, his eyes like imperial jade. "All of it, *all* of it, to defend my home, my people. Eight centuries of torture and travail, and I return to *this*." He flicked his fingers as if casting away filth. "An Empire devouring itself, a preening, posturing collection of nobles and samurai lording over the common folk by dint of blade and blood and ignorant bluster. Nothing has changed. Not in a hundred years, not in a thousand."

He drew in a crackling breath, leaning upon his cane as he drifted back to the dais. "The people of Rokugan have not grown. They *cannot* grow, cannot learn. You are trapped, all of you, in a brutal cycle of suffering and rebirth." He studied her, voice almost wistful. "But I will set you free."

"Through blood sorcery?" Qadan could not keep the venom from her voice. "Through the binding of spirits, the stealing of names?"

"I do not expect you to understand." He shook his head. "Even I did not grasp the implications, not at first. I sought to take by force what can only be won by thought, by idea – a reshaping of mind and understanding, a rectification of names."

"The people of Rokugan would never walk such dark paths."

"You are right in that." He chuckled. "But I do not plan to rule over Rokugan."

Qadan leaned in, unable to turn away despite her mounting disgust. "If not the Empire, then where?"

"Oh, it will be here. It just will not be Rokugan." He winked. "Names have power, you know. The power to reshape minds, the power to change place, perception. One moment a bit of land belongs to the Lion Clan, the next the Scorpion, then it falls into imperial hands. The land is no different, but *everything* changes."

"Then why have your disciples raise an army of the dead?" Qadan asked. "Why the blood sacrifice of nobles?"

"The Shrike? The monk? They were not my disciples. They had potential, yes." He spread one hand, then the other. "To one I gifted the location of this place, to the other the means of entry. Had they but worked together instead of seeking to destroy the other..." Iuchiban tilted his head with a regretful sigh. "Much potential, yes. But I require more."

He pushed to his feet, seeming to unfold into something greater than a bent and withered man.

"I require *you*, Qadan."

She stabbed him, then. It was reflex, a blow without skill or finesse. The knife pierced his throat, ancient flesh parting like clouds before the sharpened edge.

There was no blood, no cry. Iuchiban did not fall so much as simply collapse, a ship's sail robbed of wind, silent but for the clatter of his polished walking cane.

Qadan took a step back, unable to tear her gaze from the crumpled body.

"Thank you." The words came from all around her, *inside* her. It was the old man's voice, stripped of age and infirmity. A feeling of terrible wrongness billowed within Qadan's breast. Cold as mountain snow, it spread through her, hopeless dread prickling her flesh and turning her bones to ice.

"You have passed my tests, proven yourself a vessel worthy of enlightenment." Iuchiban did not speak so much as inhabit Qadan, crowding out all other thoughts. The emptying void of her mind echoed with horrible reverberations.

"Prepare for your reward."

Qadan wanted to flee, to lash out, to curl up so small that she simply disappeared, but she could not move, could not speak, could barely think. It was as if her body were some child's shadow puppet, its strings bound to an unfamiliar armature.

Dimly, Qadan felt her hand raise, turn this way and that as a slow smile spread across her lips.

"Oh yes, this will serve." When Iuchiban spoke again, it was with Qadan's voice. In that moment, she could see the twisted snarl of his thoughts, his plans, his manipulations, a complex web of interconnected cruelties reaching across centuries to inflict his terrible will upon the present.

Qadan could feel herself slipping, thoughts, memories, beliefs drowning in the snarled vastness of Iuchiban's ancient intellect. Terror pricked the hairs on her arms, quickened her heart, the last vestiges of unconscious control left to her. Soon, even they would become his, bound within the weft and warp of his immortal arrogance.

She raged against the spreading shadow. Struggling to move, to breathe, to think, she hurled herself against the bars of Iuchiban's invisible cage. Only to discover there was no cage, no chains, no bars – only bleak emptiness, limitless and all-encompassing. It felt as if she were trapped deep beneath the sea, crushed by waters so cold and dark they swallowed all sense of direction.

Qadan could not fight back because there was nothing to fight against, no foe upon which her blows might find purchase. So she turned inward, drawing her thoughts, her memories, her regrets around her like a burial shroud. Unable to break free, she could yet preserve what remained of her.

"I could snuff you out, claim everything that you were, are, or could ever be," he whispered. "But do not fear, Qadan. I have not come to destroy, but to educate, to enlighten. You shall be more than a mere vessel; you shall be my first true disciple."

Straightening, he pressed a hand into the small of their back, then grinned. "Ah, to move without the patina of age."

Iuchiban brushed a stray bit of ash from Qadan's robes. She felt his touch, *her* touch, just as she saw through his eyes, heard through his ears, a prisoner in her own body.

"Come, Qadan, we have much to do." They spread their arms, faces lifted as if to feel the sun upon their cheeks. There came a shifting of stone, a grinding of steel and clacking of wood. Dust trickled from the shadowed eaves as the chamber unfolded, the light of day streaming in as the walls fell away to reveal a wide expanse of stone.

The sky was a vibrant blue, the clouds almost painfully bright in the afternoon sun. They stood upon a high plateau of striated granite, a sea of wooded hills spreading in every direction. The sharp kiss of wind tickled their hair as they moved to the edge of the plateau.

Qadan could not help but think of Eruar.

At least they remained free.

"I am glad it was you. The Phoenix had promise, but family is *always* best." Iuchiban drew in a deep breath, smiling as he stepped into the open air. His voice resonated through Qadan's trapped thoughts like the peal of a temple bell.

"Watch and learn."

ABOUT THE AUTHOR

By day, EVAN DICKEN studies old Japanese maps and crunches numbers for all manner of fascinating research at the Ohio State University. By night, he does neither of these things. His work has most recently appeared in *Analog, Beneath Ceaseless Skies,* and *Strange Horizons,* and he has stories forthcoming from Black Library and Rampant Loon Press.

evandicken.com // twitter.com/evandicken

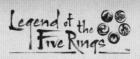

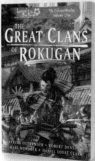